SUNY Series, Women Writers in Translation
Marilyn Gaddis Rose, Editor

Delirium and Destiny

Delirium and Destiny

A Spaniard in Her Twenties

María Zambrano

Translated by Carol Maier

With an essay about María Zambrano
and a glossary by Roberta Johnson
and a translator's afterword
by Carol Maier

State University of New York Press

Published by
State University of New York Press, Albany

Printed in the United States of America

Publication of this translation was assisted by grants from the Spanish Dirección
General del Libro, Archivos y Bibliotecas of the Ministerio de Cultura and from the
Program for Cultural Cooperation between Spain's Ministry of Culture and Education
and United States' Universities.

For information, address State University of New York
Press, State University Plaza, Albany, N.Y., 12246

Production by Diane Ganeles
Marketing by Dana Yanulavich

Library of Congress Cataloging-in-Publication Data

Zambrano, Maria
      [Delirio y destino. English]
      Delirium and destiny : a Spaniard in her twenties / María Zambrano;
      translated by Carol Maier ; commentary by Roberta Johnson.
          p.   cm. — (SUNY series, women writers in translation)
      ISBN 0-7914-4019-2 (hc : alk. paper). — ISBN 0-7914-4020-6 (pbk. : alk. paper)
      I. Maier, Carol. II. Johnson, Roberta.
      III. Title. IV. Series.
      PQ6647.A514D4513   1999   98-16222
      863'.62—DC21   CIP

10   9   8   7   6   5   4   3   2   1

Contents

Acknowledgments

One of the pleasures at the end of a long, difficult translation project is the opportunity to thank the many people who have contributed to the translator's work along the way. Our experience with *Delirium and Destiny* has proved to be no exception. Several institutions and numerous individuals have offered us assistance and encouragement, and we feel happy that the time has come to express our appreciation to them.

Each of us spent periods of time at the Fundación María Zambrano in Vélez-Málaga, Spain, where we were welcomed warmly by José Antonio Franco and Juan Fernando Ortega Muñoz. Similarly, both of us benefitted greatly from the translation fellowship that Carol also received from the National Endowment for the Humanities. The publication of this book was also made possible partly by the generous support from Spain's Ministerio de Cultura, the Program for Cultural Cooperation between Spain's Ministry of Education and Culture and United States' Universities. In addition, Carol received generous support from the Kent State University Research Council and expert guidance in grant management from Carol Toncar in Kent's Office of Sponsored Programs. Some of Roberta's work was made possible by the Department of Spanish and Portuguese at the University of Kansas.

To Octavio Armand, Brian Baer, Maryanne Bertram, Rogelio Blanco, William R. Blue, Andrew Debicki, Pedro López Gómez, Fred Maier, Rick Newton, Nelson Orringer, Geoffrey Ribbans, Fernando Segovia, Stephen Summerhill, Miguel Ugarte, and Juan Velasco, our heartfelt thanks for their generosity and collegiality. Their research, suggestions, and comments were crucial at many points, although we accept full responsibility for our interpretation and use of them.

Finally, although in many ways primarily, an extra word of indebtedness to Ronald Christ for his thoughtful, provocative reading of the entire manuscript; Rafael Tomero Alarcón for his cordiality and many consultations; and Teresa Fernández, for her help with the glossary.

Roberta Johnson
Carol Maier

September 1998

Note to the Reader

The reader who wants background information about María Zambrano and her work before beginning to read are encouraged to consult the essays by Roberta Johnson and Carol Maier. Explanations of Zambrano's references to Spanish history, politics, and figures will be found in the Glossary. Entries are not indicated in the text itself.

Introduction[*]

Writing this introduction seems impossible. Only a few sections of the book were ever published, and it was written over forty years ago; but for the book not to appear at this moment seems even more impossible and incredible. Why I am led to publish it, now, when I've had so much time and so many opportunities to do so before? Could I be moved by the desire to explain my life? Might there be some secret hidden here and I would like to bury it? No, I have not wanted to conceal anything. Publication is occurring on its own, inconceivably. Maybe the book is necessary so that people I don't know, people from different generations, will see themselves in a historic perspective and take the pulse of a life in which I am still present, present in my longing to revive this text and not abandon it to history's conjectures and possible researchers. I am here, still here now, to answer for what I have written.

But because the idea of publication does not meet with much resistance on my part, I feel somehow compelled to state why and how I wrote the book in Havana at the beginning of the 1950s. Someone told me about a newspaper announcement of a literary prize to be awarded by an institution based in Geneva (Institut Européen Universitaire de la Culture) for a novel or a biography concerned with European culture. There were only a few weeks left before the deadline, and without knowing why, I began to write immediately and did not stop until I finished. Maybe I was responding unconsciously to a mysterious summons

---

[*] Although I wrote this book at the beginning of the 1950s, I want to express my gratitude to the Fundación María Zambrano for the serenity and time that enabled me to publish it now, duly updated.

1

from the old continent. Now, in preparing the book for publication, I have made only a few minimal corrections in the verb tenses in order to bring the text up to date and therefore prevent confusions for the reader. The novel is a genre I have never cultivated, although I have written biographically from time to time, never about myself. This biography, however, had to be the one I truly lived, including my deliriums, which form a certain whole with the biography. Why wouldn't a genuine autobiography contain deliriums, which are not a fallacy of false daydreams? The same voice that asked me back then to emerge from myself and bear witness may be the one that now asks me to publish the book spontaneously and hurriedly before I die.

The announcement about the prize required the anonymous submission of manuscripts. After the jury, headed by Salvador de Madariaga, had awarded the prize to two other authors *ex aequo,* the Catholic writer Gabriel Marcel, who was a member of the jury, took the floor in order to express his disagreement with the decision, saying that *Delirio y destino* was the book that deserved the prize, not only because of its literary quality but also because it was the history of Europe and of the reasons why Spain's universality was so significant. The book was therefore awarded an honorable mention, and its publication was recommended to the Guilde du Livre.

María Zambrano
Madrid, 25 September 1988

Part One

A Dreamed Destiny

Good works cannot be lost, even in dreams.

Calderón de la Barca

Adsum

Because man's worst crime is having been born.

Calderón de la Barca

I

She had wanted to die, not the way a person wants to die when death is a long way off, but by going toward it. Death had not summoned her; she must have simply started out, chosen the path leading in that direction, or maybe she had made a mistake, maybe it was a trap or a mirage—an error. And the price of error is death. That's why dying is inexorable for everyone. Also because no one has ever been totally alive, and no one can be completely alive. When someone imprisoned but eager within us emerges into the light, whatever prompted that emergence can almost never be found. When we emerge, if no one appears, whatever we wanted has vanished, and we find only emptiness, negation. The meaning of NO, any no, is something we understand only after we have gone through this experience of negativity.

We learn that he, it, whatever we had hoped for, is not there, neither nearby nor distant. Then we realize that we live entirely alone. And to live alone is to live halfway, to be secluded, condemned, and also blinded; it means being held in reserve and kept on the defensive.

You can die while you are still alive. Death takes many forms: of certain illnesses; of another's death, perhaps even more, of the death of whatever one loves;

5

and of the solitude caused by a total lack of understanding, when there is absolutely no possibility of communication, when we cannot tell our story to anyone. That is death, death by judgment. The judgment of a person who should have heard readily and entered the depths of one's life is death. "Living is living with others," Ortega had said, and when living with others is impossible because one person interposes and pronounces judgment on another, on the thing born only when people share, that is death. One dies judged, sentenced to isolation by "the other."

And one calls then on the broad space of divine consciousness. And, as intermediary, on the thought, on the poetry of a few men who managed to open human consciousness so wide that all secrets could take refuge. Those men are the tragic authors: Sophocles, Cervantes. Tragic knowledge has discovered that "life is a dream," which Pindar says even better: "We are shadows of a dream." Shadows of a dream?

Shadows of God's dream. My life is not my dream, and if I dream it, I do so because I who dream am dreamed. God dreams us, therefore we must make His dream as transparent as possible, reduce the shadow to the minimum, attenuate it.

Is God dreaming me? Would it be possible to carry out His dream? Or, on the contrary, to become unborn? In the first instance, I face judgment, His judgment; the plan for my being is submitted to His justice and must withstand it, must stand before it. If all I want is unbirth I can betray Him, I can erase what He wanted me to be.

We are children of dreams, we are born from a dream, from the dream of our parents, from the dream of all nature, from God's dream. The tragedy of Oedipus, his "complex," is not the account of a real event but merely of one essential possibility of the human condition, of the initial tragedy of having been born. And of an initial conflict that always threatens to present itself, the conflict of not knowing the Father.

Being born is the only tragedy. Because to be born is to try to make the dream real. To be born is to carry out or try to carry out our parents' dream—initially God's dream. Maybe God dreamed a creature, his favorite creature, perhaps the Universe dreams us as its complement, and we are already dreamed, pre-dreamed in the flower and in the tree rising tall, in vast matter itself, which is also dreamed, which aspires to reality and can be used to achieve reality. Matter serves tirelessly, like that maid who is the Universe, that slave, the mother who serves until she sees, rising above her, crushing her, the grown man who forgets. Because the *boundless,* God's pure first daydream, a sketch of being, the shadow of being, must continuously become real. And everything that moves beyond the *boundless* shatters it.

To be born is to project oneself into a being that aspires to possess the universe. If there were not this initial taking possession, birth would not be the worst crime, and we would be innocent. The possession already present at the begin-

ning is the crime, the theft. Anaximander understood this clearly when he spoke
of the injustice inflicted by Being, a fleeting injustice, because all beings are
ephemeral. Except for the final harmony, the equivalent of the *boundless,* of original indeterminacy. And now, since she had not been able to die, she felt as if she
had to be born by herself. No one remembers anything about his first birth.
There is no consciousness that retains being's shudder as it is flung out, exposed
suddenly to the elements, without any handhold. Consciousness, the consciousness that now enveloped her solitude, must have started to form then, at the terrible instant when she had to open her eyes and breathe. How well she and
everyone else could measure the difference between the shelter of maternal
truth, where no effort was necessary or possible, and the thing that arrives suddenly: motionless, fixed images on a black void—the purely unrecognizable.

An impetus, an eagerness. Living is yearning, and beneath yearning, eagerness, appetite from the depths of one's self, original hunger. Hunger for everything, undifferentiated hunger. Perhaps there are tiny animals, or perhaps there
have been, that are born by devouring the body of the mother who harbors
them, by devouring their own clothing. Now, that clothing is consciousness,
something incorporeal, invisible, where everything that reaches it is reflected and
therefore seems to appear at a distance, to surround us. What would the world
be like seen from deeper within one's consciousness? But that's not where we
look from . . . In order to look, we must become somewhat invisible within, enclosed, and then emerge, toward the surface as far as it is possible to go. This is
looking's first impetus; later, we learn to draw back, in order to see better. We
discover the inexorable distance that must always separate us from everything,
even from ourselves. For the point where we stand—hungry for sight—is an
intermediate center between two realities: one's own reality and total reality.
Consequently, this center is unreal, a mathematical point that designates an abyss
and deepens it. Because looking makes everything grow more and more
distant, and "something" glowing within, which would like to emerge so as to be
seen, and also to breathe, gradually sinks deeper and deeper, retreating farther into
the darkness, perhaps even farther than where it was before it looked. The look
pushes back something that would like to become visible, but looking makes it
retreat first. When we look, we disregard the deepest part of ourselves, of that
nameless someone—of the victim, the one sacrificed to the light.

Is birth a sacrifice to light? That's why, when he realized he had returned to
his birth place, Oedipus tore out his eyes, rather than continue to be born and
accept the sacrifice of feeling himself sink farther and farther into darkness as he
saw more and more clearly.

And each time one is born or reborn, even in the ongoing birth of each
day, it is necessary to accept the wound in one's being, the split between the one
who looks and can identify with what he looks at—and consequently yearns for
it—and the other; the one who feels lost in darkness and silence, in the night of

the senses where none of the senses bears any message. And one must learn to endure this.

Night: she had always waited for it, from the time she was a little girl. She would wake up slowly, laboriously, always with the feeling that she could not cope with the coming day, and some of the efforts awaiting her would enter her brain violently, like knife wounds: she would have to eat, a bowl of soup at noon, and, worst of all, a piece of meat; she would have to tie her shoelaces a thousand times and walk by that hungry little girl she could not invite to her house, and during the afternoon she would have to play with "them," out in a cold wind that rushed, just as bored as she was, through the Plaza de Oriente or in the Plaza de Armería, overwhelmed by the gray stone of its impenetrable, arid palace, where from time to time a handsome coach would race by, bringing the king and queen back from some place or other, and she would almost feel sorry for them because they had to live there. The best thing was school, where she was not cold—it was near the palace, and there was a patio open to the sun where she went with her schoolmates; a small warmth would soften her soul too, and she would look at those girls with none of the hostility she felt for the others, the young ladies she was going to play with. She knew more than they did; they carried books and some of them could even write already, and all this was attractive, glowing. She too would enter that open secret of the alphabet and the mystery of numbers you had to chant. The teacher was pretty, dark-haired, and smiling; she had an encouraging voice. And when school let out, the young mother, who almost always wore a bouquet of violets on her sleeve and a small speckled veil fastened behind her hat, would take her hand, warming her with another hand she could feel despite her mother's smooth gloves. This was how she went walking over the hard asphalt, how she would promenade across the viaduct: the noise from Segovia Street rising from under it, a tree spreading branches she could almost touch, and she would gaze so longingly her eyes would sink into that bluish and, some afternoons, almost white distance bordered by the dark green of the Casa de Campo. The horizon, yes, the horizon, filled with light. She would want to stop, to stand still so she could drink in the light, as if it were the best food, her favorite, which she craved; and she would imbibe an instant. Then a pebble would dig into the sole of her foot through her shoe, something inopportune and wounding, or her shoelace would come untied, or someone would bump her shoulder . . . and she would feel weak again. But she was not alone. And if she did not have to play, in the winter a candy store was waiting with its lights already lit. And the house soon after, with a lighted fire, and outside, the night.

By then the shock of day had disappeared. Night was silence, the thrill of entering a secret place from which at some point we had been awakened abruptly, of escaping from the violence that forced her to be present, there, here, here, in front of everyone, being seen, feeling herself judged. Because everything, some things especially—certain buildings, the way people scrutinize us, and indifferent glances from the person we wish would look at us and caress us—make us feel the implacable judgment one feels first thing in the light of morning. Every day we awaken to be judged, to confront an unknown law that continues to be unknown no matter how much they spell it out, explain it, and even justify it for us. We know beforehand that at some time we have broken it . . . But there is no use trying to remember that; she could never remember it. Her memories would sink then, into her earliest childhood, where they would struggle to appear against a dark, fluid background. But then, and always, recollection, memory, appears as if it were arising from forgetfulness, from a dark background that offers impregnable resistance. And that is how we are, opaque to ourselves in the first, spontaneous form of knowledge, memory, in which we do not even try to know ourselves. Memory, the first, inescapable revelation of one's person . . . why this presentness of our past life, even though specific recollections disappear? Memory is always there, living; it never rests. And if it were possible that for an instant no recollection would enter our minds, the continual reference to the past would still be there, the impossibility of harboring any event, no matter how longed for, or any person, no matter how much love he might bring us from a clear soul devoid of inscriptions, devoid of footprints, of shadows.

To have lived already; to begin life from something . . . this had always meant sadness for her, grieved her, but now she understood the meaning—a fragment of the meaning—of that nocturnal rendezvous toward which she had run since she was a child and before; because night was pure and so long then. She wanted to undo whatever she had lived, seen, and accumulated during the day, whatever had fallen on her so inopportunely, like life itself, the fact of having been born, of being there, here.

She was here again, after having separated herself from everyone, from everything, until she saw herself. Alive, we see others seething with images and desires; we engage in constant commerce with reality or with its shadows.

And now, now she knew the desert, the unbounded whiteness. At first climbing up that hill was hard work, but then it was work no longer; there was only something called herownself, I, something that was not, because everything had gradually fallen away—what she thought she was, her "being" . . . now she knew she was not, that what had seemed so important was hardly anything. In the distance, a clarity devoid of any center and unlike any other, stretched before her, limitless; it was not the horizon or perhaps it was only horizon. She had not been able . . . an invisible resistance rejected her.

So now she was here; now and here, resentful, as when she was born. She did know that this was the first thing: resentment at finding oneself here; the mute nakedness of "being," in which nothing can protect us; a lack of protection, as if we were in life, here, only because we had been sent away and even shackled, rejected because "he," "it"— who? does not want us.

The horror of birth: Job asking his creator for an explanation. And those other tragic characters in search of their author so he can straighten out their tale, a horror . . . so then, no one is born innocent? To be born without a past, with nothing to refer back to, and then to be able to see it all, to feel it, the way leaves must feel dawn as dew settles; to open your eyes to the light, smiling; to bless the morning, your soul, the life one has received, how beautiful life is! Since we are nothing or almost nothing, why not smile at the universe, at the advancing day, accepting time as a glorious gift, a gift from a God who knows us, who knows our secret, our inanity, and overlooks it, who bears us no malice for not being . . .

And since I am free of that being, which I thought I had, I will live simply, I will let go of the image I had of myself, since it corresponds to nothing, let go of all images, of all the obligations that come from being me, or from wanting to.

I know now that the other, my fellow man, is alone deep down inside, as I am, and just as unable to protect himself. We are all alone; everyone is alone. So I will have no enemies, and I will not believe that anyone loves me in particular, nor will I wish someone did, as I wished before when I was consumed with a desire to be liked, loved. And wasn't that a barrier? Even a trap?

To approach the other with no gestures and no offerings; merely standing firm in the simple truth of being here, knowing yourself to be so insignificant, having seen yourself from your helplessness in the face of "that"—what to call it?— the maximum resistance that involves both life and death; whatever forced us to be born and keeps us here, forcing us to be born as often as necessary, whatever will one day let us die; this happens to everyone, to all of us, brothers in the truth of being here, in this primary reality. It would have been wrong to leave without knowing this, without having accepted it; beyond the joy of living she had sometimes felt, beyond the headiness of hope and pain, beyond all the innumerable feelings, states, and situations, without knowing she was here, without accepting it, simply, as a wisp of being, a speck of dust, eager to enter the light, to receive it in her poverty, to vibrate in harmony even if that meant a long effort of being born for countless days, from the order of everything. She had planned to get rid of her philosophy books, give them away, never see them again, and then she remembered something, then she was alive once more: "Ordo et conexio rerum idem esse ac ordo et conexio idearum." By beginning to live simply, without pretense or plan, that was how she could be—by taking truth as her point of departure, being little more than nothing . . .

Truth as her point of departure, in other words, being poor. Neither expecting anything to wrap us in splendor, nor appearing before anyone for any reason, assigning value only when necessary, without giving it much importance; going directly to the heart of things; addressing her fellow man without fear or pride, because she had seen it then, that's what he was—her fellow man, her brother. Poor and alone, all of them, without knowing it; although some of them probably knew, they probably knew it before she did. And some, many, of them, not only the ones who were poor in their lack of being, but the ones wounded by poverty, wounded . . . by so many things. Because we have enough being for wounds to open inside it, and until a short time ago wasn't she too nothing but that? A wound. She had cried so much because she wanted something they did not want to give her, because she loved someone who did not love her, because she felt like crying; she had cried since she was a child, reproaching life, implicating everything in her reproach, and she herself was the source of everything, because she was too rich and her parents and other people showered her with tenderness and love; because she had lived in those wonderful gardens but always feeling nostalgic for another, even more magical place, Andalusia perhaps, where she had been born and which she had left behind too soon; because she felt nostalgic for a lost happiness, even though she could only remember its loss, the constant experience of losing that happiness, because she so dreaded being judged. She only felt calm, whether alone in her room or in the garden or among people, when she sensed the presence she could not identify; she felt looked at, watched from on high, in other words, closest to truth, freest from interpretation. Philosophy had given her many things; but the principal thing, the one she could never repay was everything philosophy had taught her to reject, to hold in suspense as if it had no being—even to destroy—all the possibilities in her life. That was what some of the people who loved her the most lamented—she had been able, she would have been able to do any number of things, but why list them, if in the end they were illusory and they formed part of the image, which, like all images people form of themselves, is formed by the "could haves," the "would haves," the "if it weren't fors" . . . If it weren't for philosophy, for that foolish ambition—thought some of the people who loved her—she would have been or done this, that, or the other thing, she would at least be married, and that might have been true . . . Yes, that had not depended entirely on her, like doing or being. But . . . it was all right, everything had passed, and now the only thing left was this longing for truth and justice, for a way of life suitable to her inner poverty, for a way to keep from going too far . . . But such a way—truth was bursting in full force—such a way was not hers either, nor was it born now; that way . . . was there. Her father was entering the room, which seemed crystalline in the light of a winter day in a crystalline Madrid winter, a light that seems to come from the snow on the sierra, bringing the scent of pines, of the thyme that is always green, of the poor sierra, naked beneath the blue light . . .

And she sensed then the crime of having gone alone toward that shadowless brilliance, alone and without having been born yet. That's why she could not . . . Because she had not been completely born, that's why they had rejected her. She had seen what she believed to be her self become detached, like opaque veils with pale membranes, from the being that imbued her. And that being was left insignificant, crippled, and impotent in the presence of the light or, rather, in the presence of an unbounded brilliance, because there was neither an indication of its source nor any type of vibration, and the cold was unmitigated. She had no right, she had not been able. For once, justice, the thing that should happen, was occurring, and this was being accomplished, inexorably and simply, without even a sign that it was occurring; that's how simple it was. Pure simplicity, for those who have really been born, must be their being, but for her, who had escaped from time and patience—also from humility—it was simple negation, the No that is so definite it remains unspoken, because no words are there yet; only boundlessness, desert. She was alive, understood, now . . . she had to recover everything she had not known how to make hers, her nourishment. And she had to get inside, inside the dream that had engendered her. Her father watched her silently, because he knew, knew everything, as he always did. She saw him as he was when she was a child in those images her memory, pure mystery, had hoarded, and she remembered the time when she could not yet know what father is. And that "what" would call her and rouse her from reveries that must have been constant, because every instant she could remember was like this: she was looking at something in the sky, some kind of black signs—the swallows—and, "Look at the swallows!" he told her. In truth she was not looking at swallows, she was not even looking, since she was glued to them, neither close nor distant, it was only that the swallows were still, fixed as she was fixed, and her father's voice and his presence would make her stir within, make her abandon the stillness where she was glued to the image written in the sky. And there was another moment beneath the oblique, late afternoon light, on what must have been the patio in the house in Vélez-Málaga where she was born, as she looked at the branch curved high overhead, and there was a lemon hanging on it, which he cut for her and placed in her hand, although it rolled away from her . . . That was not a gaze, although they always caught her gazing; it was not a gaze but a being glued, caught, as if she were barely separate from what she saw. And her father would call her, peel her away from all that and make her feel separate, feel the strangeness of being something. And there was not only his voice and his words, which she did not always understand, but also him, his face gazing down at her from so high above, it was all terrible, would be about to make her tremble, but suddenly, before she could tremble, he would already be sending her the smile, the gaze that, even before his arms, would lift her from the ground.

The ground, which was her place, there just for her and for the cat, where she walked without quite standing, where she always fell back down again. And he would pick her up, lift her high in the air, and she would find herself beside his head, which she would dare to touch, and from being lifted up and held at the height of his forehead and daring to touch it, she must have gradually learned what that was: Father. And on those journeys from the ground to such a height, she must also have learned distance, and learned what it was like to be above, to see the ground from above—to look from on high at her father's head, at things, branches, walls that were moving, changing, and so forth—to be attentive to things that change, to see change and to see even while we ourselves are in motion, which is the first lesson in really knowing how to look, of the looking that is life.

And now she was the one lifting herself toward his forehead, laboriously lifting the weak shoulders, which pulled on the inner wound that opened as she breathed . . . Halfway through her journey she found the forehead that held the secret, the forehead whose dream had engendered her—her point of origin, from which she had fled—and also the law, truth, not only because it was in him, in the father, but because from the beginning he had taught her to love it, to lay everything before it, to look for it even though she knew it was invisible, because everything could be forgiven in those childhood years and overlooked in the adolescence she had just left, everything but lies, deceit: "Are you telling the truth?" And now, because she had found that truth, he was not asking her any questions; he was helping her to lie down, to sink, rather, to remain there, glued to the white bed, motionless, fixed. But she simply told him the truth, the truth she had just discovered: Yes; I am here. "I want to be your daughter, born from your dream!"

She was beginning to realize everything this involved: to enter life. And she entered from a situation in which any living with others was impossible; she was situated on the fringes of life and would be for a long time. The verdict was clear, more than a year of quiet, of "rest"; in regard to everything else, nothing or almost nothing; complete rest and nothing more. "You must choose between three years of rest and three months of life," she had been told sharply by the now brotherly voice that belonged to Carlos, a boy of her generation who had become part of the family and thus also became her doctor, the inflexible guardian she had met on the battlefront. He was entering the room then, his smile full of life, encouraging her teasingly. "Now you won't get away from us, they've caught you at the corner, you won't play hookey from 'school' again; look, it's a beautiful morning, you have your whole life." Yes, her whole life . . . ; but will I be able? And now, smile, your sister's coming. Something kept her from saying no, don't let her come, keep her away forever, she does have her whole life. So full of beauty.

Her whole life. The *boundless* reappeared, eventually she would have to cross it and it would be populated, but not now. Now she would have to slip into the silence of identical days. She had her whole life, but she could not begin to live it; she was here, but "here" was a bare white room, without any books, where visitors and even moving in bed were forbidden; she lay still, looking toward the ceiling or toward the window, tilting her head a little to one side. And what she saw were motionless white clouds, gigantic sky writing by the life that was projecting itself on its own, which everyone projected, and then, seeing it above their heads, bursting over them, they called "destiny" and also history. Madrid's blue sky was full of white, bluish, and gold-tinged clouds; suddenly they had turned into figures: horses, ancient kings, armies, monsters in combat, and there below, level with the horizon, a glorious wreath, a promise that seemed to frame everything, to bind heaven and earth, also began to form so as to join its elders and move with them high across the concave heaven. It was the history of Spain awakening at that very hour, set in motion from a heart and a hopeful enigmatic spirit, projecting itself on Madrid's implacably blue sky in 1929. Yes, all life and all history seemed to await her. It gave her time, it would give her time for everything: yes, I am here.

II

She lived toward the future or rather in the future since she had no present. She had been on the verge of falling into the past. But the same painful, fragmentary past rejected her. And she did not exactly have a past; she would have one only when she had already lived some of the future, since that lived future would be the recognizable past, her past. Because everything she had lived was appearing to her and it hurt, like a single wound; she was not disowning what she had lived, but she had no use for it; it would be useful to her later, beginning with this decision she had made now. She had decided to be born, but she would have to continue being born. Actually, she was living a prenatal state in which she inevitably found herself a prisoner of deliriums, and she would traverse dark corridors pushing on half-open doors, her small, motionless being unfurling. She had to hold herself high as she crossed the desert, fainting from time to time, falling into wells of silence, into negation. Living is a task that at some moments seems unperformable, the task of traversing the long procession of moments, of offering a resistance to time, which is the first action required by the state of being alive; then one must learn that "here" is very concrete, very precise, and one finds it unfamiliar. If I knew exactly where I am, I would know what I have to do. But "circumstances" can force one only after one has made a choice. In the prenatal-like state where she found herself, the circumstances resembled the semi-circle of clouds that arose from her bed; depending on how a person looked at them, they meant something or lacked any really definite meaning, as if they were malleable receivers. Only when she had entered deeply into the future and walked around in it would she be forced by circumstances. Now everything was suspended; *here* was very wide, everything she had done forced her to do nothing. No thread held her to the past, even though it was so close, to the life recently taken from her, except for a few companions, who could come to see her only on brief, widely-spaced visits, who brought her less and less news of what people were doing, of what they were doing. What was happening outside? She would know less and less, for what did *happen* have to do with her? The things reported in newspapers were not really happening; they were the peaceful surface that showed no sign of activity. The things that, like her, were moving in a prenatal state were not reported in the newspapers.

There was nothing left for her to do but go deeper, close herself up in her dream, as if in a cocoon, and allow herself to form. What dream would lead to the formation of her life, the entire life that lay before her? Having no plan, only her poverty, which she did not want to betray—she would build nothing on herself, she would expect nothing from herself, nothing for herself—the dream of Spain seeped into her and she began to live this dream alone. Also the world's dream, Europe's dream—for, like her, Europe seemed to be free of obligations, of commitments, of constrictive circumstances, free to choose—with a whole life . . . You could say that nothing constrained this peaceful Europe.

III

She had emptied herself of herself, and she no longer ached; she had lost her image, and that was a great relief. The image we form without realizing it can be pale, almost imperceptible; and then it's appealing and it produces what people call agility, aura, because it makes a person grow rather distant, which is necessary for getting to the heart of things. But there is also a dense, emotion-laden, almost corporeal self-image, and if its outline becomes at all fixed, the image has begun to develop into a *persona,* more real than and fed off the person himself . . . And as this *persona* grows and takes over of as much vital space as its fellow images will allow, the person sustaining it turns into something like a ghost.

This is how she had discovered it: she wanted to be faithful to the nakedness in which she found herself—her truth. She had begun to feel horror of her image, because the image is a curse, except for the imperceptible image, which makes a person agile and which probably only some very few people have managed to achieve. In spite of having been created at our expense, we find *it* agreeable. Any humiliation we experience so often stems from the image, since it is what confronts our fellowmen and is what we want them to recognize, although we also fear this. Then there is the image that other people cast upon us—their own shadows, and if they are not cast lovingly . . .

But is love, the image love creates, the real one? Maybe there is a real image, appropriate to the person? Isn't the person that intangible, indestructible thing? . . . whereas all images can be destroyed and are essentially transitory.

Nevertheless there is no love that does not create an image, that is not nourished by it, that does not at the same time offer itself in sacrifice. She knew that well. A schematic image, almost a cipher or a number, a highly abstract image, but an image. Love's nature is revealed in the abstraction love can form. Did the image of Dulcinea have anything at all to do with Dulcinea? This explains why

Cervantes, who must have loved deeply—and whose misfortune may have been so great that his love was reciprocated—made her nonexistent and replaced her with her contradiction or coarsest denial in Aldonza Lorenzo. That was not really necessary; things would have been the same and even more painful if there had been a reciprocal relationship between Dulcinea and don Quijote, as there is between the real being one loves and the image one abstracts from that being . . . And the fact that Cervantes, the master of subtle restraint, was carried away by this extremism, Cervantes himself, reveals a pain so intense that he allowed himself to take such a fierce revenge—the viciousness that prevented him from showing the more painful and hapless truth. All one has to do is forge the image, transporting it insofar as possible to the *heavenly tropes* of the incorruptible—disembodying it in order to achieve incorruptibility—and the person responsible for the birth of that image in one's soul will contradict it and seem like the most corruptible of people, more fettered by flesh and time than anyone else. All we have to do is love someone deeply, and we will know the extent of our own corruptibility.

Because love seeks identity, creates it . . . and that's why its image, the inevitable image, becomes abstract, like a hieroglyphic, like a sacred sign or an indecipherable cipher; something that now crosses over into the realm of the numerical. Is there anything better than a number for accommodating the two conditions—purity and enigma—the lover finds in the one he loves?

If love is going to be shared, lived, you must endure the life of whatever you love . . . If you don't, everything becomes much easier, as it was at the end for don Quijote, for Dante, for all the great strategists of love who made slaves of themselves although they were really free; in other words, they were able to attain will.

The image of one's self, though, is not usually characterized by purity; only if it came to us from a pure, distant, invisible place, only if it came to us from God, like a barely visible shadow that corrects our errors, our false moves, and serves as a guide, a model we come to see as it becomes actualized within us, and it does not offer one of those obsessive examples that corrects us the way pedagogues correct inept parents as if they were children, in the name of the "model child": God is the supreme educator. And so she rested from her image, which had been filling her with pain. Now she noticed the vague pain that is a sign of absence, a type of void that makes known its presence. It was not so much from her own image as from the other enigmatic image, a cipher of the inaccessible . . . Will everything one loves always have to be like this—a hieroglyphic, a sacred, incomprehensible cipher? Can there be a form of love that does not encounter resistance from the beloved thing, a love in which understanding or a desire to understand increases with love itself until understanding and loving, loving and understanding, become the same thing? Or a love in which the heart does not have to surrender, blind and hungry, hungry for reasons too, because it needs them . . . But when one has wanted to understand the other, the others, the others think they are being asked for reasons, for *reason,* and if those reasons are not enough, if they do not even get to the bottom of things at all, what occurs is an accusation of irrationality; when what is being suggested and has been hoped for, what the heart always hopes for without daring to say it, is a light that will illumine it even at the price of being consumed, for what does the heart care if it's consumed? The heart would give anything to see, for an instant, since it awakened from hunger, just like everything else that's born . . .

But everything you love grows enigmatic, becomes incomprehensible. And you only have to pay attention to something too intently for a kind of mixing to occur, a kind of confusion, as if we were trying to enter things too directly, as if even natural creatures defended themselves from this human interest . . . In nature itself, when you expect to see a landscape and look at it, the landscape turns into something that seems painted, opaque; excessive attention breaks the spontaneous communication, the nonanalytic understanding that flourishes where there is affection. And the landscape seen on waking, and an unfamiliar person when we don't yet know what he brings us, and even we ourselves, our souls when we let them emerge—everything, when we have been freed—takes on a clear spring light and seems weightless, even approaches transparency.

And is the shadow that envelopes everything our own then, is the opaqueness into which things and people withdraw, as if in self-defense, part of us? Is there nothing left but the path of action or the "aprioristic" thought that reveals nothing but itself, its own structure, as Immanuel Kant did in an historic fit of honesty, but also no doubt from a longing to break his chrysalidness. And he discovered will, the good will, which is not to have will . . . what Spinoza already knew.

Laboriously she had attended Ortega's lectures about metaphysics, scarcely missing a single one; their clarity was dazzling . . . he was absolutely clear, but even so she had hardly understood anything. This was particularly true in one course on the *Critique of Pure Reason.* With even greater anguish, she had attended a course about Aristotle's metaphysics given by the young professor Xavier Zubiri. And only now, by having understood those things, understood what had happened to her—and she still didn't quite know how to place this in relation to everything else, to "systematize it"—was she finding that intelligence destroys, by wanting to see from within, within itself. Could this be the Unmoved Mover? The total internal vision of reality, the being that is as it thinks itself, or by thinking its self, and in whose presence nothing could cast a shadow. And if I were to place myself in its light, without having any aspirations for myself, if I "reduced myself" as an individual, faithful to the things I have lived, then perhaps I would turn those things into an *experience,* one of those real experiences that give rise to knowledge, one of those clean experiences Kant prescribed without really describing . . . Because isn't there already something of the Categorical Imperative in the *Critique of Pure Reason?* To obey experience and only experience, to live according to something definite, would be to legitimize life, the fact of having been born, of accepting it . . . For she believed she had also extracted this from her philosophical labyrinth: the only legitimate knowledge is knowledge that has been assumed, that can account for its origins; in other words, only transparent knowledge, and transparent with a double meaning because it belongs to someone, is knowledge; the rest must be destroyed. She realized that this destruction had occurred for her, it had happened to her, and to the extent that she had contributed to this destruction by burning herself out in a bustle of agitated activities, eager to gulp life greedily, she felt proud . . . Careful! Careful! Because what she would have dared to want if it had been possible for her, what she was trying to do, was base her life on an adaptation to her lack of being, of entity: a way to be small and transparent.

And "loving" was now something she would not do again, not in the sense most often associated with that word. It's not necessary. Since philosophy—which had been her obstinate love—passed her by almost completely, since she barely understood anything . . . So many hours in class had passed before her, gifts of clarity and precision. But what did she know about the Pythagoreans? About the transcendental deduction of categories? The "schemata of being," but this was from Aristotle, and that whole parade of precisions and clarities had left her head filled with so much darkness and confusion. She was small, and she was incapable; when she could finally read, she would not read those books nor her inadequate notes anymore. So he would not suffer, she did not tell her father, since it was not yet the right moment; but it was definite: she would not study philosophy again; well perhaps Spinoza's *Ethics,* a diamond of pure light . . . She loved all that, yes, she did love that destructive clarity.

Remembering the Future

Certain *personas* unknown to her and other *personas* known just partially, as if she had left them forgotten in a corner while she sat, night after night, her head bent over her notes--*personas,* to identify them in some way, that had accompanied her since her childhood: maybe it was one of them calling her when, ever since she was a little girl, she would suddenly hear the sound of her own name in her ear, although at other times it seemed to come from very far away. Nothing but her name spoken clearly and never hatefully; at times it seemed to be a warning, or something less, simply a call, which never frightened her. But it left her suspended and somehow detached from the things around her, which seemed unfamiliar, and sometimes it even made her smile, because once they had asked her: "Why are you smiling?" She had no idea. And she felt happy when she was like that, not knowing, prowling among the plants in the garden, watching for red ladybugs with black-speckled wings, or looking for the little stones washed so clean by the water running playfully, but with great seriousness, in the irrigation ditch, sometimes on its way somewhere and sometimes in flight; but it was the same water, and there were nooks and crannies visible at the bottom, since the water did not run in a straight line but by circling around, like a sea shell, because water is round, as its drops prove, and, like the sky, it tends toward roundness. For the earth is round: it had taken her a long time to believe that, since she always saw the earth unfolding plane after plane or rising into a mountain, in search of the vertical, which was its work; earth was the place of work, whereas water and light were something different—recreation, pleasure, joy. And we are creatures of the earth, or so she thought she understood from everything the grown-ups told her; so are the plants and plants don't work; some animals do, and those that don't are raised for sacrifice . . . or they give the impression that they're having to pay because they don't work, and they can't be used for sacrifice. And men, grown-ups, work, although some of them are obviously afraid, always fearful they might die, as if their lives were a gradual approach to death, and they were death's animals, raised for death, which was waiting for them; and the voices that came from nowhere, since she never saw anyone who could have been calling her that way—those floating voices made her happy . . . they were not exactly in any bodies . . . Now it seemed that those barely out-lined, impalpable *personas* were about to emerge. Without exerting herself, she tried to find their faces, which they did not yet have. Nor could she give them faces because they were not eager to have them. They had barely any more pres-ence than the feeling she experienced during adolescence when she studied at night, in her room, late: a feeling of not being alone.

She had almost never even been alone, except at the moment when she could not die. Among certain human beings she was left feeling isolated, more than alone, and so she found their company unbearable. And she would remain silent. She was never alone as she prowled around the garden, nor in her room as a little girl, nor when she studied and worked on her physics problems; they had left her alone only that once and two or three times before, when she had really been wrong about something, at the times she could call decisive. It was as if she had emerged, as if she had run away from home . . . And now, here they were; to draw them, to capture their lives would be to write literature. A novel; she could do that, be doing that in the empty time given to her, while life ar-rived, the life she had before her.

But she realized in time; to follow their history, the history, of those *personas,* would be to continue her own story or to invent it. To invent herself, project her-self in the possible. And she was not interested in projecting. Only life; she wanted to reconcile herself to life totally. And to reconcile ourselves to some-thing that goes beyond us is to put our trust entirely in those projections—in their reason, their truth.

Life in the truth; to live in the truth—in a living truth that invades us and is found within us. She had left it aside, fascinated by things that were inacces-sible, or perhaps she had never accepted it unreservedly, and now she knew that all we have to do is disbelieve ourselves, disinvent ourselves, and life will invade us without causing any commotion. The doctor scolded her severely with his brotherly voice for having spurned her body, because a person can't do that: "You've given everything to your intellect and to who knows what else." But this was not entirely accurate: it's true that she had not thought much about the body, her body, and that she had made limitless demands on it, the way we make demands on everything that sustains us, but she felt no animosity toward her body; she felt no urge to protest when, in the railroad station very late at night, the colleague who was then her doctor and was now almost her brother had told her sharply, with the authority of one who sees the truth of things, that she was almost a skeleton and that her body barely obeyed her. In the "talk" at the provincial city's Ateneo, where she had been sent to represent the Madrid group, she had spoken in a dull voice and had not been able to eat the whole day . . . like almost every other day. But she had not attached much importance to this, preventing her parents from knowing that she was constantly weak, wanting only to give herself completely, not knowing what she was doing, exhausting herself in a passion for knowledge and action focused on one point: Spain. In this she was not alone either.

At the end of the last semester, one morning outside the Residencia de Estudiantes, as she was walking to the Instituto Escuela, she had run into a student from another department who had been in her philosophy classes. They had only spoken in passing, only snippets of conversation; a founding member of the Federación Universitaria Escolar (FUE), he was always in a hurry, and she had barely come in contact with that group, isolated as she was in the "philosophers' " corner. The "philosophers" hardly took part in student life; there were very few of them and they neither formed any groups among themselves nor allied themselves with anyone; they were each distinct, each had a small and sometimes grotesque individuality that caught the attention of students in nearby departments, who would often gather to watch them leave one of their aesthetics classes, which at that time was held in a kind of crypt from which they would all march out in a line up the narrow stairway. They were strange, and since she was so thin and never opened her mouth, for a long time they thought she was British.

A few words exchanged quickly, like signals, were enough for something new to spring up between them, an understanding between brother and sister. He was waiting for her when she walked out, and he read her a few pages from a manuscript as they sat on the porch wall at the Residencia de Estudiantes, under the air moving through the tall black poplars; the concave sky dipped down to embrace the city, and in that air it was possible to sense the breath of the city, a human breath, full of life. The two of them had hopped onto the brick wall, and they were two birds that understood each other through the music of words, the music of sense . . . and he quickly alluded to some colleagues in different departments who had all recently finished their studies and all belonged to the FUE which, as she already knew, was "apolitical." Yes, they would continue to be apolitical. They did not want to get involved in politics but to facilitate an opening up of Spanish life, which was covered with an official falseness, a nonexistent continuity because there had been an uneventful break in the fading, "pulseless" continuity of Restoration Spain. "We young people have been drawn to the generations of men who are now 'mature,' and they've taught us a great deal, but we expect still more from them, and it's up to us to approach them and ask for it; we have to awaken them to the common task they don't seem to notice; we have to summon them, it's that simple; in every university in every province there are already groups, our people, who think the way we do, and beyond the university and the cities there is rural Spain, which needs us for provisions and presence. This is not the moment to scatter and bury ourselves individually in our professions, but to make ourselves present; It's a moral question, one of reviving communality, of social renovation; this is the time to build Spanish life, which is flagging now, after centuries of inertia. They, today's 'mature' thinkers," have taken up the disconformity and faith long concealed in the criticism of nineteenth-century writers such as Larra and Ganivet and in such 'movements' as the Institución Libre de Enseñanza, to which we owe this space of lucid student life, simultaneously European and ancestrally Spanish; we need to unite the two definitively, reconcile the split between Spain and Europe that has characterized Spanish life for such a long time. When Spain existed, wasn't it universal?" It was the moment for her to enter "Our Time" totally . . . Yes, we would go to speak with those older people, all of whom had been youth's teachers, outside class and even beyond the realm of the university. They were . . . simply the people we were reaching out to spontaneously because we sensed them in Spain's future, in our future, for weren't all of us together something like the visible face of Spain? And it was necessary to prevent this face, these heads from continuing to remain unattached, separated from the trunk, paradoxically invisible even in Spain; for Spain was still not visible, we felt Spain more than we saw her, and we were yearning to see her, and it was necessary, absolutely necessary, that she become visible to the world once more, healed, whole, and self-possessed; she must be young and awake after her centuries-long sleep, whole despite her history, beyond her history, real, present . . .

And the words continued to fall in the morning air, like bright glass beads, like water, and she heard the sound of Spanish, which resembled the rivers in the nearby mountains—water, water splashing against stone, the most liquid water against the staunchest stone on the planet, and that's how all Spain was, ancient and cleansed of history.

When they had come down from their perch, another boy appeared; she recognized him from having seen him in Ortega y Gasset's classes, and he was one of the "group." She had never exchanged a word with him, but it turned out everything they had heard at the same time began to speak naturally within them; for them both, a crystal-clear lesson that was life detached itself from Ortega's words and his books—for her who worked so hard to study philosophy and for the others who had never studied it formally. And something like a fountain, like one of the streams gushing down from the sierras at that very moment, after the thaw, burst uncontrollably into their words, a stream, barely a trickle of water, born between the oldest rocks on earth, from the untouched snow of a crystalline thought—ice fused with the sun of their youthful souls. And all they wanted was for it to keep flowing, for newly inaugurated life to keep flowing throughout the entire body of Spain . . . They alluded to their teacher's books that had impressed them most deeply— *El tema de nuestro tiempo* [The Theme of Our Time], *Ni vitalismo ni racionalismo* [Neither Vitalism or Rationalism]—and to his entire style, even to the voice itself, extremely young and pure, of the man who seemed to have emerged from the very center of the Guadarrama Mountains, a sign awaited for centuries to awaken sleeping Spain . . . He, Ortega, was on his way to Argentina at the time, so they could not speak to him, but they would speak to the others, to everyone, and they would do everything possible to make their elders understand them; they needed to meet the next day so they could look over those manuscript pages, rewrite them if necessary.

They did this. She met the other members of the group, complete strangers to her but ones quickly identified; there were two girls. That's more or less how a meeting should occur, in the way a flock of birds gathers because from their different points they have faithfully followed the same commands of the light and temperature of the "season." They were children of the season, of the same generation, who had been rather solitary until that moment, as she had been herself, but she guessed that all their spirits were open to their surroundings, even though they had been shut up in their books, in their student rooms, perches from which they had descended as if summoned to a magic convocation. And magically a flock, a group, a brotherly band had formed . . . Gazing at the blue mountain range from the room in the Residencia de Estudiantes where they were meeting, listening to the singing of the birds entangled in the black poplars, she had a vague feeling that perhaps they had belonged to some tribe, some original group of remote Iberians, of the indigenous people from the Meseta who formed Spain, those first inhabitants nobody knew anything about, but who had never given in to anything.

They divided into groups of two or three, to go and see each of the elders individually. A few of the young people had some connection with one or another of the older generation's members, but most of them did not: even so, they were received generously and listened to openly and nobly, with a restrained courtesy appropriate to the age difference and commensurate with the comradeship that prevailed instantly, magically among the young people. And they all attended the meeting the young people had organized in an outdoor cafe on the outskirts of Madrid, since the owner had some connection to one of the young men and loaned his place on the condition of complete secrecy, although in fact there was no question of a conspiracy. Instinctively, however, they had arranged everything covertly, the way one arranges the first date of an honest affair that in due time will be entirely legitimate. No one had any thoughts of something clandestine, but rather of something secret, of something whose birth had just begun, like a silent spring under the stones. They all attended, as a distinguished full professor pointed out; he was one of the youngest and most serious—so serious he did not speak a word throughout the whole meeting—and when they pressed him to say something, he answered: "Do you think it's a small thing that I've come, that we've all come?"

Not all of them were professors; there were politicians and writers, including one person they had frankly not even considered . . . their meeting with him turned out to be somewhat acrimonious, and it had fallen to her to go and see him, along with two other members of the group. Don Ramón del Valle-Inclán had insistently told them they should go:"Go to see Manuel Azaña, he has a very good head for politics." They went . . . and he himself opened the door of a rather modest apartment on Hermosilla Street. The room where he received them was filled with books and had almost no chairs; it smelled rather like a cell in a convent. "Yes, I know why you've come to see me; don Ramón persists in thinking that I have a head for politics, but the truth is, politics don't interest me, nor do I think I have the least ability for politics or that I'll ever devote myself to politics, but go ahead . . . "

"We didn't really come to talk about politics exactly, but about something broader, something that precedes politics . . . " But he wanted to be specific, or to make them be specific, and they could not, nor did they want to be specific at that moment: what they wanted to form was not a political party. "Then join one of the parties that already exist, one of the Republican parties, because I assume that the Republic is what you want." They looked at each other in some embarrassment, which he took to be hesitation: "But what do you want then?" "Well, that's for Spain to say, we only want Spain to wake up, because Spain's awake now, but we want Spain to become involved in life, because Spain is not dead anymore, we want . . . a morality, a life for everyone." He jumped in impatiently: "But all this has to be defined, made concrete; and it will occur through an Institution, through a change in government." "Yes, but first . . . that change of government must have the support of a human base, of an integration, of an understanding, and of a will, which must be uncovered, because it will not become apparent on its own, although it's there." And they left the meeting with the impression of having come up against a logical, scholastic, and very thorny mind, someone rather like a definitor or a secretary to Philip II. A feeling of uneasiness kept them from speaking as they walked downstairs to the street. The truth was, they had not thought about those highly specific issues. Of course they wanted the Republic, there was no doubt about that, but first . . . it had to be created, before it created itself. They understood each other without specifics. And they tended to resist the pressure will puts on thought to end up in definitions; they wanted to breathe easily, deeply, in unison--not only the pulse but also the rhythm, the rhythm of a common breathing. But would they be able to say this the next day, would all the others agree, think like this--if they were forced to define themselves, in other words, to turn into something already there?

Perhaps the most brilliant figure of all, a doctor, was expecting them at the only time he had free, after his office hours. "But I work relentlessly. I'm a lone sniper." "Well you'll have to come down from your tree, so we can march together on the ground, we have to be together," the young man who knew him dared to say. "But how? How? Yes, we ask ourselves that too, and we're going to find out." "You're just children, though, and you want to inaugurate the history of Spain." "Why not, don G.?" and in fact one of them spoke up passionately in defense of what they were doing, a young boy who is still alive and who was almost a member of the group, since he had justified himself before those anonymous twenty-year-olds.

Among the elders, however, there was an intermediary: young and impassioned, he was even more enthusiastic than the other young people, because the enthusiasm that survives early youth is even more intense than the enthusiasm of youth, which seeks awareness instead. In a person nearing forty, enthusiasm is now greater than awareness, like a fire that breaks out again after having been squelched; for people who have been able to keep the flame alive across deserts and through gales, this is the age at which enthusiasm breaks out again even brighter, as well as warmer. They had been immensely fortunate, as the one who started the group told them that morning outside the Residencia de Estudiantes, in that they had been able to count on him from the beginning. A professor of law, his specialty was criminal law, that "subject matter" into which jurists, touched by poetry, in other words, by life, pour their uncontrollable longing for justice and even for fantasies of redemption. He was one of those jurists who are drawn to crime in search of the criminal and his possible redemption, of the "man," the "person" who exists in spite of everything, or exists because we probably find it necessary to believe he exists. She did not know this young professor; she met him in person, as she met all those rather "mythological" men at the meeting. But in his case they already knew it would be necessary to follow him and have proof later; they counted on him, even though his collaboration with them would leave no visible mark on his life, because a melody forms only when the notes are heard as they truly are. Of them all, he was the one who had already gotten underway, the one who had set himself in motion by setting the others in motion.

And there was a young writer too, made even younger by making himself "accessible," by not having been carried away by rhetoric, and at the time he may not have finished one of those books that places an author at a distance and sets him apart from everyone else. His novels and essays had always revealed a restless consciousness, a non-literary consciousness; he was very concerned with an "examination of conscience," both his own and that of Spain's national reality, and at the moment he was the one who most closely followed the thinking of Spain's Generation of '98. The way they established contact with him was opposite the way they approached the professor of criminal law—through the restlessness that had prevented him from finding any peace in his work, even though he had successfully completed several books, a restlessness that would also prevent the young people from worrying about the success of their individual futures. He felt no enthusiasm and in time his conscience would grow calmer, but this was not evident at the moment.

They would also continue to see the brilliant doctor-writer with some frequency; he seemed to unite conscience and enthusiasm, as well as a hesitation that at times they found disconcerting. This meeting with him had been polemical, direct, almost a hand-to-hand combat. And they were pleased by the way it had gone.

The large meeting took place, and the elders listened to young people were heard, although only a handful truly understood what they heard; the decisive thing about this meeting was that "they," who formed a kind of constellation in the life and on the horizon of Spain, had not been together for a long time, at least not some of them, and perhaps they had never been together. Those young people were able to understand a situation that never occurs in one's youth: separation from the people with whom one shares a sense of purpose. When people are young, there is always life, living expression; in community even the solitary task of studying and reflecting is often performed with others, or one thinks it is. Of course that group was composed of young men and three young women who until then had all been alone, but that was simply because they had not found each other and because what they had been doing had no particular significance. And this is what marks the difference. When you are young, any significant task is lived communally; when you get older, the significance of the group, of destiny, is not necessarily lived communally; the people who seem to be signifying the same thing with a single sign written in the sky of history are in fact isolated among themselves, and they hardly exchange a word with each other. That night, thanks to the young people, the elders who made up this constellation of Spanish life exchanged several significant words, albeit not a great number of them; an agreement was born, and an undefined commitment, a kind of half-formed vow, but one sworn before the youth of their country.

And each one of them had been himself. The "noted writer and outlandish citizen"— don Ramón María del Valle-Inclán—had referred to an episode from the time of Isabel II as if he were referring to something absolutely current. The socialist politician with a liberal background made a short but verbose parliamentary speech, a kind of generic, abbreviated rehearsal, as if he were practicing his delivery to see if it was in working order, and no doubt they all had the same impression: that he was in fine form, although the matter at hand was not addressed directly. Other elders mostly observed, humbly and contentedly, almost like young people. Sullen and reserved, the person "who had no talent for politics" remained silent, almost as if he were absent, as if he were enclosed in a space apart from the others.

She felt herself living in a different space now, ever since her adhesion to this group of people her own age, because it meant contact with members of her generation, something she had not had before, although she had certainly had companions, friends beside her, but they had not been linked by any common purpose, and if they were engaged in some new way of facing life, they were not aware of being together. And the most wonderful thing about this embryonic—not unique—generational group was that (after how long?) they had banded together because they felt rebellious, rebellious against the elders; they had not set out to "overthrow old values" in order to establish their own, in search of "new routes." Of course the word "new" cropped up often in their conversation. But this "new" must have meant something different, not the new for which so many generations before theirs had argued with the "older people" . . . In any case they had gone to their elders, who at some other moment would probably have been called "old," because "old" has been used by several generations to refer to the generation immediately preceding their own, to men who have barely entered maturity. These young people, on the other hand, regarded their elders as the end result of an impetus whose origins lay in the far depths of Spanish life; and they experienced even this impetus, this tradition of criticism and disagreement, not as dissidence but as the persistence of an ancient, universal, and broadminded Spain, where life had been possible in all its dimensions—a Spain where your soul and your will did not feel stifled, as they did in this present Spain, which they wanted to transform rather than overthrow, for "revolutionary energy" was something they did not feel at all strongly, if they felt it at all. An impetus to live, yes, to live with their elders, with their equals, with the illiterate, with the peasants, with the workers . . . "Living is living with others."

And this was what was new, what must have been new, this longing for a deeply shared life, a life of integration, of order, and this facing up to the "circumstances": Spain, "our time," our duty to know this time fully, to fulfill our commitment. They had not been at all drawn to the warmth of a utopia—justice, perfect happiness, single-minded greatness—so they did not feel the need for violence. Or perhaps in Spain utopia was just such a determination to live together?

That's why they found it so difficult to define their position. They were not working from any revolutionary, political, moral, or aesthetic program, although this did not seem to worry them very much. One of the most intelligent members in the group was an art student, and they all went regularly to concerts and to the Prado museum; but they were not a generation of aesthetes, even though they felt art passionately. There *was* a style, though, a desire for style, but they did not even refer to it as style. One of the young women had written that "We prefer the drawing to the color," and another, "We're going to be serious in the liveliest way possible." This was not a code, but it *was* a key for anyone who wanted to understand them: they were moving toward a simple way of life, one characterized by a sincerity so absolute there was no need to formulate it, renouncing and even feeling an aversion to the "literary" and the "artistic," loving simplicity—something related no doubt to the sportive spirit of the young people who had graduated recently from the Instituto Escuela and belonged to the FUE. And something fundamental was the way the two sexes related to each other; they had a kind of initial creed, or rather an unformulated promise, since they formulated very few things: there was a horror of and an aversion to both coquetry and conquest. The boys made fun of "donjuanism" and the girls of prissy women, of the hostility and separation between the sexes that gave rise to so many distortions. And it was understood that if the art student were to fall in love, for better or for worse, he would not betray the first loyalty, loyalty itself, the first commandment. So it was unlikely that "affairs" would occur in such an objective, essentially chaste atmosphere.

Nor was this "ethics" exclusive to their small group. It was the way of life found in the university, one that had arisen immediately, since women had begun to attend the university "naturally" only a short time before, and without any struggle or hesitation, a spirit of living with others had acquired a clear, sharp outline among students of both sexes, even though it lacked definition. And everything that united them was like this: the spirit of the university, the moral ambience of a university that uninterruptedly and without sensationalism had been renewed and assured. And their group was simply an expression of what the university could offer Spanish life, which explains why they not only had no program but also avoided one. This was an attitude, a change in attitude that was taking shape as it acquired awareness. They wanted to be the vehicle of this attitude, which was very simple, very direct, a sort of asceticism of the imagination; without realizing it they were rejecting the delirium that had devoured Spanish life in the nineteenth century. They were escaping from delirium and the resultant suffocation; they wanted to find the happy medium, the ratio that would make it possible to live with others effectively and vitally, that would permit Spain to become a habitable country for all Spaniards. And since they took it for granted that such a change of government was inevitable, they did not insist on it; their vocation was to transmit the new attitude, the melt-water born at last in the rocky heights of the Guadarrama, from the thaw that became cascades, streams, and rivers running down from the mountains to revitalize all of Spain. The vocation to be a pulse, a deep breath that teaches how to breathe freely and confidently. Flowing water, and pulse, in other words, blood . . . New blood, purified by the free air that had just freed the Spaniards from their obsessions, their laziness, and their pride, blood that could move hearts and minds toward reality. No, they were not aware of everything, but the words they used with increasing frequency, all the words they emphasized, outlined one metaphor—the metaphor of clean blood that before long would be spilt.

Thought apparently tends to become blood. That's why thinking is so serious, or perhaps it's a question of blood having to answer for thought. Throughout entire eras, for several generations, thought continues along its silent path. But when a thought is formulated, when it crystallizes, blood fast finds that it must answer for thought's transparency, as if the "matter" everyone prizes, the essence of life, life itself, flowing and hidden, must pay for, or at least authorize, the "purest," freest, and disinterested thing man does. When a secret is revealed, when part of our "hidden being," part of the reality we experience through resistance but not presence, is made accessible, blood inexorably plays some role, and one of its roles, its chief role, is to be the means by which everyone receives nourishment—the oxygen blood receives through breathing—the primary role of life, of all life. And breathing requires the right environment. Breathable air.

Thought that reveals reality creates vital, breathable space. One of thought's vital roles is to make the atmosphere breathable, to free human beings from suffocation, which is caused by a lack of inner space, when consciousness fills with shadows and uncertainty, when the shadows of others and one's own shadow have made the inner space, the primary space in which we move and breathe, far too dark. Under such conditions, when we want to relate to our fellow man who finds himself in a similar situation, it is simply impossible to live with others and, consequently, to live at all.

And so thought becomes blood; it enters blood and insists on bloodshed, because it is impossible to deny thought simply. It is impossible to deny the thinking that makes us live, that creates a space where we can breathe, a horizon where our lives, even our most personal lives, come to form part of reality, encounter the lives of others, and take shape by interacting with those lives. We cannot deny this, even if we want to.

And Spain at that moment in 1929 could no longer deny the thought that had been spilling over her continually. There has always been too much blood, an excess of blood in Spain. The thought that was enabling Spain to breathe again had itself been gathering strength in both words and deeds. In few places on this planet does thought become life as quickly as in Spain, because it springs from life, and we Spaniards are barely permitted the luxury of any abstraction. One could say that among Spaniards an unspoken but fundamental attitude keeps thought from taking flight. Our thought has always been restrained. Perhaps our proverbial "sobriety," our asceticism, has meant that thought for thought's sake is frowned upon in Spain. So that when Ortega y Gasset wrested his Vital Reason from Aristotle's critique of the idea of "disinterested knowledge," he introduced this Spanish attitude into philosophical thought.

It's an attitude that leads one to see the most vital action in thought, in the thought we were living to the extreme, insofar as the inseparability of thought and life is humanly possible, as in Aristotle's "the act of thinking is life." This also explains the terror, and the hatred of intelligence, the desire to kill intelligence because it is life. The crime a person continually commits against the real reveals what is real for him and to what extent. Crime is the most irrefutable proof of the reality something has for someone. But at the actual moment a person commits a crime, he never knows what he is doing, because as he commits it he has forgotten his own reality. A person who thinks as he commits an act of faith does not know completely what he is doing either, nor does a person who desires something resolutely; nor does anyone know completely what he's doing, whether for good or for evil. And honest or heroic action differs from criminal action because its desire for something to become reality is united with love—is joyful desire for something to exist. And this is how their group of young people, without having read Spinoza, felt desire for Spain, joyfully; they wanted Spain to exist, to finish with existing. Was this criminal, was this a crime? . . . They would have to pay for it as such, with their blood, with their deaths, with their lives.

At the time they could foresee none of this. Their words were free of any bitter taste, of the slightest tinge of bitterness or resentment; the least outbreak of violence would have clouded the transparency in which they breathed, and this is why it was so difficult for them to formulate any kind of a program, and if a person did not understand them immediately, if their desire was not obvious, there was no possible explanation. In truth, they did not create any propaganda; perhaps they would realize that when occasional spontaneous propaganda let loose its thunder throughout Spanish soil.

Instantly a network was formed with the universities in the provinces; they planned to make some trips, not to strengthen their convictions but to strengthen their ties with each other, to . . . But why be more specific? When she met them, they had already been publishing two small weekly sections in two Madrid newspapers for some time.

❧

They appointed her to one of those sections, which were signed, because it was unavoidable, the newspaper insisted on it. "You will have to sign," they had told her. They had all tried to find some way around the question of the signature, appending only their initials, but this was not possible either. At the same time, though, there was nothing subversive in the lines they wrote during those days of censorship, and the red pencil crossed out very little of it; in truth there was no reason to. They disliked signing, not because they desired secrecy but because they wanted impersonality, because their "writing" had nothing to do with the desire to create literature, to enter the world of Spanish letters at a moment when it was flourishing so intensely. They watched Spain's young literature with ardent interest; its most brilliant expression was found in *La Gazeta Literaria,* a nucleus of renewal, not only in literature but also in film, in painting, in all the arts, and in an entire style that they would have called "anti-Galdosian"—if they had been reading Galdós then—with respect to the Spain of Galdós. They felt a familiar affinity with this writing, a certain shared attitude, but they also felt a difference and, above all, literary writing was not what they felt called upon to do. It was fine that others did. So much movement in literature and the arts made them feel somewhat apprehensive that it might all die out before, before reaching the goal they desired for it, apprehensive that this was a stage and that because it had found, was finding, an appropriate, successful expression, it would die out like a bonfire lit too quickly. And although some members of the group, like she herself, had always written from an inner necessity and deep down inside considered themselves potential writers, they had never thought even for a moment about sending something to one of the *La Gazeta*'s contributors with whom they were in contact. It never occurred to them to do that. "Personal" writing was an activity they had postponed for now, and even though some of them were allegedly writers, they made every effort not to seem like writers. No; they wanted to write impersonally, because they felt that they were the vehicle, the instrument of a thought that was not "personally" theirs, one that came from somewhere far away and was now finding expression, had become visible not only in books but in activities, in reforms, in the changes occurring in moral views, in groups of writers such as the so-called "Generation of '98," in attempts to reform Spanish pedagogy and the national modus vivendi, such as the Institución Libre de Enseñanza—in sum, a plan for life. A clear will that finally had needed to seek expression in a philosophy that not only summarized and surpassed all those efforts but added something entirely new for Spain. Philosophy, pure, authentic, but Spanish philosophy: an unequivocal sign that by following the surest course—with a method, with a system—Spain had recovered her universality.

Not one of them wanted, and in fact they avoided, what is commonly thought of as "personality;" sometimes they made fun of it, and of the personality people thought possible, of their quest for it, of the people themselves who had spent their whole lives pursuing it. Personality was what made them shun "literature," and what made her so happy about her attempts at philosophical activity; in philosophy she would never have personality.

They wanted to serve, to serve in the way consciousness serves life, by gathering it up, unifying it. This was why they decided to go to the labor meetings. They would speak to the Socialists respectfully and in solidarity and to the Anarchists with a longing to understand. They would "convert" the ones they wanted to convert, draw them away from the romantic mentality found in people who read outdated historical novels, draw them away from the cult of violence and rescue their true ancestry; because they suspected there was a hoard of strength, health, simplicity, and precious faith hidden in those people. As for the Communists, there weren't any in Spain. In 1929 there was not, strictly speaking a "Communist party." There were a few enthusiasts who acted in good faith—romantics and residents of a very exasperating dictatorship's benevolent jail.

In the fall when the time came to prepare their talks, the insoluble problem arose: should they announce their names on some posters one of the boldest artists had designed for them? And what should they do if they didn't sign their names? Wouldn't that mean going out only to speak from behind a curtain, the way people blamed the ancient Pythagoreans for doing?

The hall where they addressed the cigar workers was full. She was last on the program; two male colleagues had spoken before her. Almost all the leaders from the earlier meeting were there. This gathering was not really a political "meeting." But what was it? There may never be another one just like it. They spoke almost without a topic, as they spoke among themselves, in their own way, and the women—all of the cigar workers were women—understood perfectly. They were serious, their eyes sparkling as they listened. The young people were not sure why they had picked this union, the heart of working-class Madrid traditionalism, fearsome because of its gibes and wisecracks, and of all the swaggering typically associated with it . . . Maybe this was why: "to take the bull by the horns." And there was no struggle, no imposition, no "pedagogy": it was a moment of "pre-established harmony," as in music. The tone was set from the beginning; it was just there. Between the venerable presence of the men—the most illustrious men of the sciences, the Spanish university, Spanish letters—the cigar workers, and them, the young people, there was perfect harmony. Words had merely provided the cadence in a concert improvised by a Mozart-like musician.

They felt happy as they left the headquarters of the cigar workers' union. Her own happiness was similar to the feeling that had filled her soul the few times she had understood something in philosophy. But when she could understand, her happiness was like a beam of light flooding her mind, and her entire soul would be stirred, although this could not last. Afterwards, "what" she had understood would slowly become diffused, even become apparent, because she needed a long time to see its implications and consequences, the "order and connection" established by thought—an idea, a single idea, between thoughts that until then were antithetical, confused impressions, disparate sensations and even "facts," which acquired significance as they assumed an order. This happiness, though, about the "concert," with the cigar workers, about the unplanned harmony, came from her heart, from the darkest depth of her life; the important thing was not that she had spoken to these women but that she had spoken with them, with the heart of Madrid as if there were no social classes. The pulse of Spain, its throbbing, had created that harmony, that living silence where words fell like music; meaning was expanding, the horizon was opening, breathing. Filled with this same contentment, the elders shook their hands; no one had given in and deep down they felt equal, because they had obeyed without giving in.

And it was this pulse, the serene, impassioned throbbing of a life that transcended hers, took her, seized her, and led her toward the threshold of her own life. Because she had never even dreamed of abandoning philosophy, or the classes at the Instituto Escuela, where she was just starting out as an instructor, beginning the harsh, difficult training of teaching boys and girls about to enter adolescence, who were still almost children. Everything about her new activity was difficult: the time of her classes, the group of young people; the material itself, which could not have been further from the concerns of her own philosophical group. But this account has to do with a different history . . . a different story, to which she gave herself feverishly, flushed with the same fever that would begin at precisely the time she was to enter the classroom in the duskiness of late afternoon, just at the moment her impatient students were anxious to leave. And she could barely speak, something that would continue to happen and to grieve her as she threw herself madly into life. No; "she had not spurned her body," as they had told her, she had not felt horrified by it; it was because she had loved too much, she had fallen in love and gone head over heels; she had fallen, but she had been driven by love, swept along by a rapid, increasingly frenetic pulse she could not control.

Suddenly she now found herself "here," without disciples or teachers, without a group of colleagues, without anything, aware of her pulse, only her own pulse, like a bird that wants to rip the heavy bars off its cage, at a point of suffocation after breathing so widely and deeply, in the pure oxygen of her new life as she rushed to get those ideas into her blood immediately, into everyone's blood. She was falling, though from trying to glimpse something new.

She understood fearfully, trembling and alone, that the plunge she had made—tried to make—into life, into the life shared by everyone, had perhaps been only a substitute. Something lively, in place of . . .

She was not trembling because she was afraid that the truth of what she had lived would be censured; what she wanted was to find the legitimacy of her life. This is why she wanted to empty herself completely, to see herself as she had seen herself at "that moment," but this time with the eyes of understanding, "from here."

And she began to see that her eagerness, the determination to pour herself into life, the hurried efforts to exhaust herself, the "enthusiasm" that so easily could be confused with faith, had all sprung from "the impossibility" she had experienced, from that rejection. But perhaps faith springs from a different root? Couldn't it also be born from a NO, from something impossible? Something impossible, but something that rejects us inexorably? Because it seemed to her that she had always been rejected by everything she wanted, by everything and by something nameless, or if this were not the case, she was the one who was saying NO, when people were not saying it to her. She had always lived under a NO that took the most diverse and most banal forms—the color of a dress that had mattered to her, an outing or a party when she had wanted to go. The first concrete NO was the lilac tree she could not see bloom one bitter spring, not far from Madrid, when she was little, very little. She had never seen a lilac tree, nor lilacs themselves, and day after day she watched the tree in her garden they had told her would soon bloom with lilacs. But she got sick with some kind of fever, and she could remember pursuing that lilac tree in her dreams, the tree that was going to be covered with strange, wonderfully fragrant flowers. When she was awake and able to speak again, it seemed odd to her that her mother would shy away from answering her questions about the tree, that she did not bring a branch of the flowers to her in bed; and when they were dressing her so she could go out into the garden, her mother said: "There weren't any flowers on the tree; it's still very small; next year it will have flowers." This was what her mother told her; later, though, one of the servants, who did not realize how cruel her remark was, told her there had been flowers but now they had withered.

She saw the tree, however, and she always considered it something precious and separate from the other plants in the garden because of the flowers that for her had been invisible. She always believed the tree had bloomed; she preferred the flowers' cruel bloom— those very flowers—to the tree's not blooming. She would not let herself be consoled; she preferred the existence of the flowers to consolation.

It would always be this way. At every "it's not time," or "it's already over," or simply "it's not for you," she felt a rebirth of the love for whatever she was denied, a love now stripped of any possessory illusion, a simple love of the object's existence; so let it be that way, so it existed, even if I never find consolation for not having had it. This proved to be more than consolation: certitude, affirmation . . . And by remaining half-dead like this, she later began to bud with life. Life . . . In the void of unfulfilled love, of the unseen tree, something was springing up, something: the tree, more real every day, which had formed in her mind when she was a child and would never leave her—the cipher of an invulnerable existence. Everything she had not been able to offer of herself arose in greater proportions, undiminished by the collision with "reality": the tree in bloom, but not as much; the cipher, but not entirely. And this is how she saw it now, thinking, wondering if everything in life one really does, and not for lack of something else. . . . Yes, in all lives, except perhaps in the case of saints, or rather people who simply obey without ever having been chosen, who were born to obey from the beginning, people who need no consciousness and therefore have none: saints—some of them—workers, or merely mothers. Where does vocation come from, then? Vocation or love; vocation and love. Why had she studied philosophy, which she DID NOT love? To fill an initial void, or an early void, experienced when she was still a very young woman? Hadn't philosophy been born, not only in her affection, but also in the world, "for lack of something else"? What has one lost when one searches relentlessly for knowledge, an unconsoled knowledge, which accepts the object's refusal but at the same time discovers that the object is necessary, discovers an "aporia"? Because of this cruelty, this renunciation of consolation, the tree exists, but it is impossible to see the tree itself; so let's renounce even that. Let's just say this is how it appears to us— "that the idea exists, but we don't know where or in what form"; and in the end, perhaps it does not exist either, but we have to keep thinking about it. Parmenides discovered "that being exists," or rather, what he would not discover is that being is, even though it may not exist, or that being is not and . . . so let's think about it. And he saw later, that when he thought about it, it existed.

And if one thinks that being does not exist, that there is no being, isn't one doing the same thing for the benefit of a radical reality? Hasn't all knowledge started from an acceptance of refusal with no consolation? This is why we Westerners will not be able to follow Buddha, since we accept refusal without moving from "here," without adding another refusal of our own, even in the case of love. What love—a love one does not have even in dreams—is the source of one's love for a specific being? Isn't it an invention? And, because it is an invention, it moves one to action. Don Quijote set forth into the world in order to fill the world with his exploits because he had no Dulcinea; but if he had not lacked a Dulcinea, would he not have done the same thing in the instances where she had failed him? And Dante, who did not approach Beatriz, because he was afraid she would accept him, no doubt wrote his poem for want of the Paradise he had not been able to enjoy. But he would have found it impossible to enjoy that paradise if he had not done something to deserve it—for example, descend into the inferno. Human life is in itself ironic, and where humanness begins, irony begins: the greater the humanization, the greater the play of reflections between being and nonbeing. Humanness is the actualization of nonbeing.

She was trying to prove this—the NO that hounded her, the suspicion that her impassioned activity had arisen only "for want of something else," from the impossibility of living with a cipher, a human being who for her was something like a mathematical object, a cipher. And how could she know for certain when her unbidden affection for philosophy had begun? She was pouring herself into life now, trying to mirror what had happened to her "there," on the threshold. Now this was her only task: to reduce herself, empty herself completely, to take her life back to its foundation. The foundation of her life had been summoned, asked what it had to show for itself, to show itself. From that moment, she was free, she had time. This was the YES: abundance, arbitrariness, and imposition.

Time, still, as at high tide, would buoy her hour after hour lacking beginning or end, blank hours that no thought dared enter, much less any emotion or image. She been raised above herself, above "the river of her consciousness" and beyond its reach except for the most fleeting of thoughts, if that word can be used to describe minor outbursts of disruption in this type of equilibrium. She disregarded, and detached herself from, herself and her circumstances, which were reduced to the watchful presence of the inseparable beings at whom she would glance only to be sure she had not died. She was not dead, but neither was she alive, since living is insecurity, fright— "living is yearning." And this indifference was becoming a prenatal state once again. Because everything surrounding her, her immediate environment, was an intimacy without pores or oppression. She breathed within the affection of those close to her.

And the "outside" was not present; the world had come to seem so full it felt inaccessible to her. She sensed, she imagined, and even her senses were growing sharper, as if they wanted to break loose from their center and go off in search of information. Subtle sensations, previously lumped together, began to appear; she barely saw objects now, seeing instead shadows, lights, reflections, which floated at first in a void that made them unreal, as if what we understand by reality, by "world," were a hollow. Slowly, though, the hollow was filling, very slowly. She found it hard to endure this double nonbeing—the nonbeing of oneself in the void of the "outside."

She had rejected the shadows of her *personas,* rejected her shadows, minor outbursts of being that brought to light what she was herself: a minor outburst that had not been able to resolve itself and now had to live its life as a larva in search of being, as a hunger of being. This is what living must mean—pursuing this passion that permits no rest, suffering this eagerness, accepting your own being and, at the same time, continuing to be, continuing toward being, facing the risk of being erroneously, of being something other than what you had glimpsed and prefigured, of being both "the other," one of the multiple others possibility offers in its mirrors, and the one, oneself.

But how to achieve not being either "self" or "other"? It would be necessary to know yourself first, as a point of departure. How can you clarify authenticity if every action creates or deforms us, if everything we have experienced in our lives casts its shadow? Who measures our authenticity? Only someone whose eyes must be able to bore through us to the depth of our souls and reach us from that depth as if his sight originated there spontaneously, precisely, and clearly as if it were a gift to us. Only if we were natural forms of an intelligence that must conceive by engendering, that will find itself, whole, intact in each of its different images—only if we were "united," even while being many.

Living is errancy, but in the archaic sense of straying or wandering about, adrift after a "uniqueness" that pursues us relentlessly, in the cradling cavity of reality that never goes away, although it does not let us fall in either—a maximum resistance that forces us to emerge, to support ourselves. The cipher of this resistance, love, or vocation forces us to be Him because it reveals nonbeing to us.

And this void of the world, this hollow, was gradually filling with poetry, the first unitive action. Poetic and indistinct, reality soaks into us. Are words, our words, born from nonbeing, a resounding in the hollow of what we call person? Human words are initially echoes, just as our light is reflected. To speak spontaneously is to "lie," to overflow in some way and to let "things" overflow, let words go mad. In order to do philosophy one must be oneself, one would have to be oneself; poetry does not make such an extreme demand. And she could not even claim poetry's words, mad and empty though they were. The poems hoarded in her memory echoed in an empty time; from the nearly eternal books by the poets of her present, from those poets, she was gleaning an echo and an ancient resonance—the memory of Spain's being and nonbeing.

***

Poetry had burst forth radiantly. Juan Ramón Jiménez had been its harbinger, but even Juan Ramón's own poetry was read more insightfully when the young poets appeared. Federico García Lorca came first and Rafael Alberti immediately after him, like a twin star. The publication of Alberti's *Marinero en tierra* (Sailor on Shore), which shared the National Prize for Literature with a book by Gerardo Diego, was pure happiness, like daybreak. And there was also Jorge Guillén and Pedro Salinas, whose *Entrada en Sevilla* (Entry into Seville), such clear, sharp, precise prose, was published in the first issues of *Revista de Occidente*. The Spanish language was paring down, turning into crystal, and exposing its pure core. It was proving to be a language of fine lineage! And it was experiencing a new daybreak, prompted by the fragile little songs in Alberti's *La amante* (The Beloved), by the mysteriousness found in the work of Emilio Prados, a poet of insomnia and memory; by Luis Cernuda's poems, which she knew only because she had read something about Cernuda in an article by some famous writer in Madrid's *El Sol;* and Vicente Aleixandre's transparently brilliant poems, which were like a cave of fantastic stalactites.

Lively poetry journals had sprung up here and there in the provinces and even in the villages. There were many different voices but just one harmonious music: *Litoral, Mediodía, Alfar, Parábola, Meseta*—carrier pigeons from an old pigeon loft that had been partially walled up for a long time. And loved by everyone, García Lorca had brought the *romance,* the ballad. Not long before, Alberti had published his latest book, *Sobre los ángeles (Concerning Angels),* in which he had angelically consumed stage after stage of his poetry, in a rather Mozart-like way, without calling any attention to what he had accomplished.

There were also the magazines *Carmen* and *Lola,* preceded by *El Gallo Crisis* (The Rooster "Crisis"), which García Lorca had founded in Granada—"The cocks quicken their song and dawn is breaking," some words from the *Poem of the Cid* that seemed so accurate.

And this poetry of "cocks" breaking dawns had the ability and the grace to make familiar voices newly visible; instead of silencing the voices that had been present for some time, they made them reverberate. One of those voices belonged to Miguel de Unamuno and another to Antonio Machado, whose *Soledades (Solitudes)* and *Galerías* (Galleries) named the landscapes of the soul clearly and deeply—the landscapes of Castile's countrysides, holm oaks, black poplars, and mountain thyme, and the moon-drenched landscape of pure Soria. Machado and Unamuno were poets of the ancestral purity hoarded in Spain and in the Castilian tongue, preservers of fearsome Spain's everlasting virginity.

Poetry was a word bursting whole in all its purity from the cave of Spain—where life began, the first heartbeat, memory and forgetfulness—a knowledge formed of forgetfulness and divination, a nonjudgmental consciousness, an ingenuous justice, as unwilled poetry always is, poetry that arises in response to the historic moment rather than to "personal" estrangement, a luxury cultivated by a few.

And the poetry that, like dawn, brings innocent justice, because the consciousness that does not set out to be a conscience is the one that denounces most forcefully; devoid of any judgmental intent, it exposes and sings reality, which should be set forth without defining. For reality includes everything, everything that has never been quelled, that has moaned voicelessly, everything condemned to silence, to a death that is half life, latent life: the suit that is too short or too long for the "poor child," and his embarrassment; the happiness and the sadness of the penniless fisherman; the mute laborer; the field frozen stiff; and the rights, all the rights of this minute reality in which no one can be separate, this one single reality. And also the gods: the Iberian god, the unknown god, and the nonexistent god. All this is communion. Where, if not poetry? Miguel de Unamuno, essayist and rector of Salamanca, who was prompting the national consciousness and stirring the souls shriveled by Spain's long winter, had been in exile for many years and many years before had produced *The Christ of Velázquez,* a poem of communion through the white form of a bloodless Christ, a Christ who was light and word, the one who could save us from the wrath of our unknown god. Because the only god that can save us from the anger of those first gods with their demands for blood, the blood of human sacrifice, is the god who, being light, brings love, words, bread.

⟨ ═══ ⟩

And in those hours when it was so hard to tell sleep from wakefulness, in the emptiness of her room, from a memory empty of images, came the words that name, that conjure the most ancient god of all, Cronos the devourer, the god of time, oblivion, and memory. Reading *Concerning Angels,* perhaps in her dreams, she stopped at a poem she could not find again later: "The angel of Forgetting," of the eternal forgetting where the dawn is born: "oblivion, source of the dawn," "a desert preexistent and inviolate," "where everything finally comes, nothing comes to pass" "imperturbable oblivion, source of the soul . . ." And she learned to wake up at the first sign of day, her balcony window open so, if only for an instant, she could see the dawn, the light without memory that blesses our sleep.

To wake up is to be re-born each day. And the light is already waiting for us, whatever history or story that we must continue is already underway. To wake up is to enter a dream already in progress, to come from the pure desert of oblivion and, first thing, to enter our bodies, to remember them without rancor, to begin to inhabit them and reclaim our souls, with their memories, and our lives, with their tasks. Waking up is like entering a cocoon spun by countless industrious worms; we pick up our threads again and return to work on the cocoon, where the worm-man labors tirelessly, producing the dreams that become objectified, making history.

Spain Dreams Itself Awake

History is dream, man's dream. If human life is dream, someone's dream, we resemble that person in one way or another, because we are dreaming too, dreaming our unfinished being in many ways, especially in poetry, in all art, and in action—even in technique there is dreaming. And if there is dreaming in everything, this is because there is dreaming in the action common to everyone, in man's generic action *qua action,* which is history. Philosophy undoubtedly arose from the call to awaken. This explains why philosophy developed as history's adversary; it aspired to a different history, one of awakened men, and it could not avoid creating utopias—the utopia of reason creating history. The Historical Reason that philosophy is currently about to announce will constitute an awakening from the utopian dream, from the dream of reason. But when we stand before reason, reason insists on history, as Heraclitus commanded when his now-ancient voice tried to awaken the men of his day. Now philosophy is demanding that we awaken while seeing ourselves in our dreams—to awaken without abandoning our dream of ourselves.

To awaken without abandoning our dream of ourselves would be to dream lucidly. This is the intense yearning for something about to happen that is experienced at certain moments in history—both individual and collective history—when a people awakens while dreaming itself, when it awakens because its dream, its project, demands this and requires a people to know itself, to dissolve the bitterness stored in its memory, to bring hidden wounds out into the open, and to carry out an action that is simultaneously a confession: *self-purification* by doing. At the historic moment when the Republic of April 14 was about to be born, Spaniards were about to do just that; they were about to recover from their wounds.

41

Because all Spaniards, especially those who had attended primary schools, high schools, and universities—the educated Spaniards—had grown up with the bitter taste of Spanish decadence mixed with an ancient pride in Spain's grandeur and with an inkling that the grandeur had been squandered. Several explanations had been proposed for this. Spain is an enigma, a kind of sphinx in the desert that attracts and bewitches hundreds of travelers, but very few of them draw closer in order to carry on a conversation. For who would dare to talk with the sphinx? And the sphinx is doomed to be a sphinx until someone truly talks with her. This position of being doomed to isolation had led Spaniards to feel that they were the victims of an injustice wrought by history, that they were the doomed of Europe—the victim who always figures in one scenario, locked in a dungeon while the party glitters way above, the one doomed to obscurity and denied a hearing, while everyone else lavishes each other with words and attention. The victim, the doomed, hungers for someone to listen to him; and even if he had everything, he would still suffer the most terrible humiliation men can experience: having no one listen to them. This explains why Spaniards speak so fast, don't much listen to each other, and assume they know what their opponents, in other words, their interlocutors, are going to say. It also explains why Spaniards shout when they speak, something that must date from a particular period, because people have trouble finding words when they have been removed from common conversation for a long time and feel afraid they won't even use the same categories, the same sets of values that the others, the people in the world, use . . . Even the problems themselves seem unintelligible because they have already been posed by others. And can there be any greater defeat than not having a chance to pose the problems for oneself, of first having to learn "how the problem has been posed"—before speaking, before thinking, and even before feeling? This must always have happened to the defeated.

Spain was not exactly defeated, though. Spaniards in general were not aware of any defeat, and they did not feel defeated; what they felt was something more subtle and more complicated. On the one hand, and this was when they considered it in intellectualized terms, they suddenly felt afraid they had either committed some "sin" of negligence or excessive generosity or naïvete. On the other hand, they felt victimized by other peoples' incomprehension. Nothing made Spaniards happier then or makes them happier now than a sign of comprehension on the part of someone from another country; you could even say that the loss of political power and wealth, or the absence of prosperity, has never tormented us as much as the fact that we are not understood. This was the most painful and most important thing: What people will say! What people are saying!

"Oh, they've begun to understand us; there's an English writer who says . . . "
And this made us happy.

But what had really happened in Spain? Since the nineteenth century, people's awareness of Spain, of the conflict involved in being Spanish, had been growing stronger and broader. At first this was a question of isolated individuals, writers, of a solitary soul such as Mariano José de Larra, who committed suicide when he was 29; they say it was because he was lovesick, but in fact it was Spain that made him sick. Angel Ganivet also committed suicide, far away in Finland, half a century later, at the historic moment of 1898; they say he was ill, and he was ill—Spain made him ill. To be Spanish was so painful, such an open wound, that some could not bear it.

Then after the second half of the nineteenth century, although they did not intend that their words occasion it, two immensely creative men locked gazes from opposing perspectives. Marcelino Menéndez Pelayo—historian, Catholic to the extreme—chronicled Spanish science and philosophy in a sort of "sacred" book that was like a rejoinder to the accusation, hurled at Spain from the four cardinal points of civilization, that the country was resistant or opposed to the "enlightenment" of thought and was given only to passion. A fervent, objective historian of heterodoxy, of all the heterodoxies that existed in Spain, from Priscillian, until the very day of his own death in 1912, Menéndez Pelayo was nevertheless unable to chronicle the Church of Swedenborg, founded in Valencia the following year with a dubious amount of conformity. Opposite Menéndez Pelayo, sharing his passion for Spain and surpassing him in living knowledge, was the novelist Benito Pérez Galdós, chronicler of the underside of Spanish history, of the deep emotions that lie beneath historical life, everyday life, and even of history itself, reflected in the daily life of his gigantic work, the *Episodios nacionales* (National Episodes).

The two men were in conflict because they had opposing diagnoses of Spain's "illness": Menéndez Pelayo did not even admit the illness. Instead he blamed the modern world for its insulting incomprehension of Spain, which was intact and invulnerable to all heterodoxies: Catholic, humanist, and eclectic in its thinking, Spain's fundamentally harmonious spirit had fled from the extremisms of the great philosophical systems, spurred by love for a moderate, human wisdom and sheltered by revealed truth. Menéndez Pelayo's history is a poetic vision of a Spain assisted naturally by science. Dilthey might not have scorned it entirely. Galdós, whose examination of Spanish life was more inspired and more profound than his formulation of the problem and its solution, auscultated, looking with the impassivity of a great writer into the most secret nooks and crannies of the heart and its labyrinths. His "thesis" was that of the "leftists": Spain would have to learn to be tolerant, to practice a moderate freedom enriched by social reforms. England offered the natural example. The point of departure of it all was Galdós's "hypothesis" that Spain must relinquish its supposed greatness, its novelistic notions. Cervantine in some ways and also Flaubertian—the Flaubert of *Madame Bovary*—he novelized the novelistic qualities of Spanish life, its delirious self-invention, the unreality found in the higher social classes, in the middle class, seat of all novelistic notions. In Galdós, the common people are as they are in reality—true, like the word of God.

Among his countless characters two ingenious figures stand out, marked by the stamp of poetic, tragic creation: two women from the *pueblo.* The first is Fortunata, daughter of Madrid's *pueblo,* of Madrid itself, who dies "bleeding away": an innocent, primitive, "Magna Mater" who in some ways is an embodiment of Cybele, who presides over the Villa from her triumphal chariot at the Plaza de Cibeles. The other woman is the protagonist of *Misericordia (Compassion),* the best novel written in Spain since *Don Quijote.* She is a maidservant who leaves the village of Alcarria and comes to the Villa, to the central meseta that, along with La Mancha, seems to be the sacred land of Spain; her life is anonymous, she is a soul from the same family as Felicité, in Flaubert's *A Simple Heart.* On this woman rest and subsist both the fragile world of this "exemplary" novel's novel characters as well as the woman's mistress, a lady whose fortune has fallen and for whom the servant must beg "incognito" in church doorways. This servant has her truth, as Fortunata has her inner "idea"; she has her gospel, which turns out to be . . . the Gospel. When her mistress speaks in an argument about pride and dignity, about "things a person cannot put up with," the servant tries to draw her away from both reality and her own novelistic ideas, steering her toward the poetic truth of "vital reason." "Truth," she tells her, "truths were once big fat lies." And she ends by telling her mistress about the ultimate reason that makes it possible to put up with any instance of unreason.

"Hunger and Hope"

"Hunger and hope." Her thoughts were filled with both as she wandered in her solitude. Finally, her doctor-brother had given her permission to read a few pages a day and thanks to a mysterious coincidence, which turned out to form part of the "preestablished harmony," she found herself reading Galdós, whom she hardly knew. Some writers from the Generation of '98 had dismissed Galdós because he lacked style; and the young literary generation of the time, the prevailing literary taste of the moment, repudiated him as the symbol of the Spain he had portrayed so relentlessly, the middle class suffocating in its "novelistic character"—confusing the mirror with the image it reflected. This rejection was nothing more than one of the fluctuations that occur as a matter of course in the appraisal of a writer's work over time: glorified when he dies, he is later inexorably condemned and then, implacably, enjoys an enthusiastic "revival." It happened that she was reading Galdós for the first time, and she realized that she was reading Spain from within, that this was the way to enter Spanish reality from her isolation, that she was standing in the presence of the forlorn Spain forgotten by the young people, who had been born in the new Spain. She realized that she was also returning to the Spain that had always existed, to the Spain of substance, to the fresh, pure wellspring from which history's waking dream arises, the waking dream carried out by the minority, when they carry it out. This is the wellspring of history, of every history, and its innermost substance; the primary reason for history: hunger and hope.

Spain, its *pueblo*, had bottled up hunger and hope for centuries, the centuries of Spain's famous "decadence." Hunger . . . in literature has clearly been the obsessive theme of the picaresque novel since the sixteenth century—a hunger that gnaws at the gut and leaves the blood ridden with worms, but one that also sharpens the intelligence. It's true that whether Spaniards are from Madrid, Andalusia, or Castile, hunger has led to the kind of honed profile found on medallions. This may have resulted, at least in part, from hunger caused by not having and from abstaining once one does have, from not being able to get used to or accept that it's possible to live without feeling hungry.

She was remembering, she remembered, the girl who came from the rugged mountains near Segovia to work as a servant in her house and how she had discovered the girl sitting in front of a piece of meat, in tears, because she could not eat it, she who had dreamed of meat and wished for it so much. The girl confessed that as a child she had lived on onions. Her mother would go out to the fields and leave them about six pounds for the whole day, and she and her little brothers and sisters would eat them with a bit of bread as they got hungry. Some nights, but not always, they had stewed potatoes, in the summer there were tomatoes and watermelons, but meat . . . she knew people ate meat, but she had never eaten it, and its redness was revolting to her. The only red things she had eaten were tomatoes and watermelons; the whiteness of fish was also revolting to her, because it's different from the white of onions. It took them a long time to teach her to eat. And this extreme case led her to think about Spanish sobriety, which is a form of pride, pride that one can subsist on nothing or almost nothing; and in truth there are clearly other causes far beyond the simple fact that one had to do without. She wondered who might have coined the expression "to kill hunger." It said a great deal about this hostile attitude toward hunger, about the belief that hunger is an enemy to be killed, rather than a signal from nature to which we should respond with pleasure. All of this was valid for the central meseta, Andalusia, and Extremadura. The Basques are very different, and they resemble the French or Belgians, no doubt because they eat, and they enjoy eating; the need to eat doesn't trouble them at all. In Andalusia this need almost makes people feel ashamed, especially the women who live on mere nothings—little cups of coffee, small salads, tiny sweets. The sight of a woman eating meat hardly creates a proper impression of femininity, and it implies a certain threat to the man; he's the one who should eat meat, if anyone should, because that's how things are.

And she would watch them, her Andalusian men, slender as needles, always seeing them in profile, their profiles striking, their waists slender. "I've got my eyes on a boy; slender-waisted, dark, and tall," so went the distant song that came to her from her childhood in Málaga and her Andalusian grandfather who raised grapes, the magnificent grapes of Almería, a delicacy on exquisite tables way off in England, a country she knew only through commercial contacts—the sterling pounds that had sustained her mother's childhood, although everything had slipped from her hand since then in a mining venture involving some fantastic mines that must also have gone to the British.

❦

There they stood with such schematic presence, emblems of Spain and its living sum and substance: the Andalusian worker knocking olives from a tree with his long pole, the one hunched over day after day, keeping the field so sparkling you could eat off it, caring daily and tenderly for the vines rising above the spongy, dark, cherished earth. This was the worker without work, sneaking by shamefully like a shadow, slithering around street corners, running from even his own shadow, "stung" by shame at having to lean on his brothers, at not bringing his wife what she deserves—"I would even give her my blood, and I can't bring her nothin' "—walking beside the fence around the land owned by the *señorito,* who has lived up there in Madrid for centuries, land devoted to raising bulls, or to "nothing, and a person here just rotting."

Hunger and shame. No, not everyone was free like Beninga, the protagonist of *Compassion,* to take to the streets and beg for a bit of bread. A man is different and young. And a man who is on his way home after working all day also feels ashamed—finds it "tiresome," as they say there—ashamed to let it show. Because both not working and working too much are embarrassing; and if a man meets up with someone on the road as he returns, he says, "Yes, I've just been out for a little stroll," or "walking on the land, since it shouldn't be left alone too long." Any excess in a person's dependencies is embarrassing, in man's dependence on the body. The body should not weigh heavily or become conspicuous, either in its presence or its needs. "I'm the boss of this 'unger," that man out of work answered when he was offered a job that did not appeal to him.

"I'm the boss in my 'unger" . . . The thought had undoubtedly helped make it easier for him to endure hunger, made it possible to keep from doing something crazy and totally unexpected—the feeling that in the end none of this is what matters, that a man can endure and conquer anything, that this is the only way he's a man, which is what really counts. "Man is the measure of all things," especially the things that most affect him, that must never get the upper hand over him, over his intangible solitude, the poet's "unrelenting solitude." "I travel as if a prisoner; my shadow walks behind, my thoughts ahead."

Andalusians verbalize their metaphysics of solitude, anguish, and freedom in their couplets. People from Extremadura are like this too, but they are more secretive, less given to expressing themselves, except in actions—the actions of a virginal man, an Adam ready to discover the world and then settle it far across the seas in a land he never saw, wherever that world might be, a man who traversed the ocean because he was drawn toward round, virgin land. Extremadura is silent country, where Spain's entire silence has been gathered, whole, and transferred to paint by one painter, Zurbarán, the greatest mystery of the mystery of Spanish painting, with his still, quiet white, his silent white. This land of quietism and action was something Zurbarán carried in his blood. No doubt it had been passed down to him from the ancestors on his father's side, who had always been Extremadurans, because he understood "quietism" from within, and he also understood how a person could be willing to leave and "burn all his bridges." Couldn't those two things be essentially the same thing, the same attitude? Either burning your bridges vis-a-vis the reality of the world, of all reality, in order to look for God in nothingness or uprooting yourself from everything you know and from the "been," because of a longing to be born or reborn in a virgin land—dismantling your life in order to set out, to face daybreak.

Andalusians, Extremadurans, Valencians—but also Levantines, from Spain's eastern coast—many of whom now lived in Barcelona, made up Spanish anarchism. It was really very strange, because they could not be understood "ideologically"; you had to consider their sum and substance. For many years, as far back as the end of the century, they had comprised the poetic, tragic chaos of Spain's political and social life. Their chaos could remain dormant for years, even decades, then one day it errupted in a bloody week of untimely, misguided assaults that cost Spain irrecoverable victims, among them, in subsequent assaults, such politicians as Canalejas and Dato. Casualties of societal conditions, they ended up as canon fodder, providing a frightening shock for the rich and powerful. But the anarchists were really interested in laws relating to societal conditions; and maybe the first thing, before giving them the minimum wage and an eight-hour day, should have been consulting with them and getting them to talk. Now, at the present moment, such consultation was necessary—it was necessary in order to make them emerge from their isolation as the condemned, because not all "victims" endure their situation without going crazy and becoming violent, without turning into executioners themselves. Isn't this what a person expects from people if he has truly condemned them? If only all these heterodox souls could be saved. Maybe anarchism has something to do with quietism and illuminism, the heresies the Catholic historian had examined with such a deep passion for understanding, such profound sympathy, despite everything else. Now she understood, and she sensed that perhaps the orthodox historian had studied heterodoxies in order to study them—the anarchists—from every century of Spain's history, because to reach an understanding of them would be to get to the heart of Spanish life. And if understanding them were active—action and not merely theoretical study—what would happen then? Is it possible to understand the heart of something, get to the heart of it, without getting one's own heart involved at the same time? This would mean, then, converting them and becoming converted oneself; it would mean everyone becoming converted together, something like experiencing revelation as a group. And doesn't a country, in order to be a country, need to have this experience and to renew it? Didn't France really become France only after Joan of Arc, blazing all alone in her fire, revealed to the French people their ancient soul and destiny, which they had to experience together, generation by generation, until eventually they understood it, understood each other?

Spain had Isabel of Castile, whose image evokes the people of her native land as well as those from lands farther north, who have something of her thick blood—blue-eyed people with the vocation of taking command. Such people are leaders, and northerners—they come from the north. That's why the Castilians' hunger was leaner, more impenetrable than the hunger of southern Spaniards. When Castilian expression did burst out, though, from hunger or from some other need, it was the sign of something very serious; because people who give orders do not express themselves, and they never confess. Only very rarely in a people, or in a culture, have the expressive ones been in agreement with the ones who give the orders; and if this has occurred, it has been at a different moment, when the leaders are no longer in command. As long as they are giving the orders, leaders neither express themselves nor feel happy about others doing it for them. This explains the state's tendency to be inhibitive at all times as long as its grandeur lasts, and why the poet is viewed with distrust, and why in every well-constituted republic poets are considered, felt, to be something of an enemy, since they openly state things that must be concealed and at times contained. Power tends to be taciturn.

And when the people who are born to issue commands and to have a share in governance, even though it may be by obeying orders—which is a type of participation—finally do begin to express themselves, what usually bursts forth is a wave of cynicism. This is what happened in the case of the Spanish picaresque— a cynicism that followed contention among the powerful—, Castilian cynicism. Cynicism also looks at reality from the vantage of power, without having power. This accounts for its insolence, an insolence greater than someone in power, contained by taste and caution, can display. Cynicism is a typical example of an attitude that reveals a historical crisis, but one that only affects the protagonists of history, at least in any important way. All the rest of the people go on with their lives, their poetic lives within expression; the Andalusians, for example, live in

continuous poetry, which they create just by speaking. And the same thing occurs in romantic Extremadura, which produced almost all of Spain's few romantics, and where the silence is even more profoundly poetic. Certainly Spain's best poets have not come from Extremadura, but perhaps Extremadura, more than any other region, is poetry.

At that moment, the people who mattered were the Catalans and the Basques, united only by the similarity in their protests against the law, the old Castilian law, which they said felt oppressive. They are closer to Europe, which means they experience their romanticism differently from the Extremadurans. Theirs is a political romanticism, poured into a nationalist yearning, into the longing, perhaps, to perform nationalism's great feat. They had more vitality than was permissible to channel into "decadent" Spain, as if they had been less affected by that decadence than the rest of the country, and they had remained more whole, or they felt less adherence to the tragedy, if there was a tragedy; they were not at all willing to consider themselves "defeated" or the victims of injustice. So in order to escape from this position as Europe's "modern-day victims," they had to turn against Spain and against Castile, the perpetrator responsible for Spain. Castile had been in command then; let Castile shoulder the blame for the consequences that followed from the historical mistakes. They themselves were "up-to-date," with their modern ethic, one born of work. Had they really worked more than the rest of the Spaniards? Or had they worked better and with new methods, the result of their wealth and a different attitude toward work? They had accepted industry and commerce, in contrast to rural Spain, Spain of the peasants from the arid meseta and sunny Andalusia.

It was undeniable though, that the Catalans were more close-knit—not so much because they all had a common political sentiment or purpose, because that's how Catalan society is—there is less separation between the classes. Catalonia's bourgeoisie listened to its group of intellectuals, poets, painters, professors, and musicians and heeded them more than occurred in the rest of Spain with respect to similar groups. And in turn those intellectuals and artists reconstructed a bond they sensed between both themselves and the Catalan bourgeoise and Catalonia's historically peasant *pueblo*. Because even though Catalonia was the most industrialized region of Spain, it had also preserved the wealth and spirit of its peasantry, of a countryside filled with songs and poetry. The music in Catalonian life demonstrated this unity in Catalonian society. There were choral societies in each town, and *coblas,* the bands that played *sardanas.* There was also the *sardana* itself, the ancient circle dance in which one relives the original unity a people experienced as they held hands and gazed together at the same sky, defining themselves for the first time as a people now in their land.

And the Basques too had a pride in their race, which had existed since time immemorial, for they did not "date" back to a specific beginning. Mute more than silent, many of them spoke Castilian as a learned language or boasted of having learned it. They were healthy and hardworking, and they practiced a morality of efficacy, approaching its spirit and mentality to the extent that any enigmatic Spaniard is capable of a collective effort. Although Saint Ignatius of Loyola, that enigmatic genius, discovered a highly efficacious "modern" method for directing the will and was able to reduce, schematize it and the primary desires—along with Don Quijote, who was another genius of will and love, according to the parallel Miguel de Unamuno drew between the two figures. What could the Spain of hunger and hope have expected from the Basques? They had neither suffered from hunger nor been waiting for hope. They were farther along hope's path; their hope had already become a demand.

And before Spain could make demands as a people, it had to dare to hope, and hope was now breaking free.

Hope was being freed, thanks primarily to the dissidents, those who disagreed with official Spain, who were seeking the cure and the remedy for the feeling that Spain had been a "victim of history," of its own mistakes and of the injustice of others. They were the ones seeking an understanding with the world. The way to heal the wound was by emerging into the world so that Spain could try to understand, to emerge from its provincial resentment. This must have been the sincere feeling that prompted someone like Sanz del Río to set out for Germany in the year 1849 in search of philosophy. He returned with Krausism, a philosophy of secondary importance expressed in such difficult terms that it proved unintelligible in Castilian translation, and this occasioned not a few jokes, including jokes by Menéndez Pelayo, the guardian of tradition. Krausism turned out to be something of a summary or precipitate of German idealism, one of those "doctrines" born as an imitation of the implicitly luxurious great systems that arose against Plato and Aristotle. Because Stoicism, Epicureanism, even Cynicism itself, for example, were simplifications and reductions that occurred in an effort to place the most basic and necessary ideas—in other words, a morality—within the reach of the ordinary consciousness, an effort to make that morality "viable," as Ortega would say. And Krausism was nothing if not moral, although what the Spaniards who decided to follow its labyrinthine path deduced from Krausism was even more moral. Above all, Krausism lacked the style that "Stoicism" achieved so magnificently, and style is what makes it possible for a person's thought to be assimilated; this is one of two necessary conditions if thought is to become truly viable. Although Krausism's basically ethical "system" harmonized with the "Spanish character," its total lack of style clashed sharply with that character, and that style is the second of the two qualities characteristic of things a Spaniard most craves and therefore comprehends most readily. It was truly unfortunate!

Sanz del Río's gesture, however, did have far-reaching consequences because his reason for going to Germany was deeper than the one mentioned above; he had gone in search of ideas, it was true, but also, and above all, he had gone in search of particular ways of life appropriate for a social class that had always been very small in Spanish life—the intellectual bourgeoisie, the upper bourgeoisie. Spain, arrested in the seventeenth century, has had a bourgeoisie; a "middle class" is another matter. This explains why we have lacked creative energy for science and industry, for ways of life that reached their peak in Europe during the nineteenth century, especially in France, in England, and even in Germany, although there they took on a slightly different cast. We did know about all this, because the men who attempted to raise the level of Spanish life by using Krausism as a moral tool learned about it—the men who wanted to create this new, or almost new, class of professors, scientists, intellectuals, and artists who formed part of a living society, and who drew their incentive from that society and their sustenance from the State. These men also wanted to stimulate in Spain's tiny bourgeoisie love and concern for things of the intellect. But there was still something else in their effort. There was a religious basis, something that could be likened to a rebound of the religious reform that failed in the sixteenth century, something of a rebirth, beneath this new doctrine, of a once-glorious day or a Spanish "Erasmism."

The Institución Libre de Enseñanza was born, then, in the second half of the nineteenth century from this climate of Krausism and from an awareness that Spanish life was anachronistic. This awareness stressed emphatically the errors attributable to Spain, because the Institución was determined to become reconciled with the world by forcing Spanish life to catch up with modern times. The Instiución's founder, Francisco Giner de los Ríos, was one of the most singular Spanish men of all time; as in the case of almost all the exceptional Spaniards of this period, it's hard not to wonder what Giner de los Ríos would have been in a different age. The question seems to answer itself: he would have been the founder of a religious order. He is just as mysterious, efficacious, and impossible to grasp as those founders, who are always a little hidden by their deeds, even though one suspects that they, their personas are much more interesting. Spain's debt to Giner was incalculable. A series of cultural institutions was created directly under his influence or under the influence of his disciples. The most direct of those disciples was Manuel B. Cossío, discoverer of El Greco, a professor of pedagogy at the university, and the director of the Pedagogical Museum. Enigmatic, and elegant of spirit and bearing above all else, "Señor Cossío" held onto a last, secret bit of his wisdom, which he never revealed. And it was hard to find any university without some chaired professors who had passed through the Institución in some way, either directly or indirectly, and who formed a whole constellation that included the largest segment of the faculty. Some of them participated specifically in politics and within their respective parties, they succeeded in creating a particular atmosphere, something that was more a matter of style than an ideological content.

And Spanishness had always prevailed within the Institución itself as well. Krause's "philosophy" had faded gradually until it disappeared, and what appeared in its place was a style, which Krausism never had. This could be seen in the Institución's two most outstanding figures: "Señor Cossío" and Fernando de los Ríos, both of them symbols of the most genuine Spanish style. Cossío's hands made the same gestures in the air as hands painted by El Greco, and don Fernando's smile was the same one my father had—that smile of the Marqúes de Spínola in Velázquez's *Lances.*

A style and a few rituals, such as the excursions to the Sierra del Guadar-rama, which took on special significance of a sacred place, a source of energy, and health, whose dark air, snow, pines, and bare rock described the image of a par-ticular life—poor, diaphanous, and happy. There were also excursions to little-known places in Spain that were not touted by conventional tourism, and here Castile triumphed! It was the Castilian landscape that inspired the Andalusian Giner with his ideal and with the Franciscan way of life as it were. And then came the revival of popular songs: singing those songs in a group came to form part of the rituals shared by the young people. Not only contact with the foreign, with "the world" was needed, but also contact with oneself—burrowing.

But in spite of everything made possible by the will of this man, in spite of everything, one would like to have known him, him himself; because he did not write very much, preserving a characteristic of persons who have walked the paths of history without writing, influencing others with their words and with actions that are almost invisible even as they're performed. He must have been an Andalusian in the Stoic tradition, and a rather Pithagorean one; he had also left a line of often-quoted successors: "Some Institucionalistas say . . . " "The people from the Institución Libre have resolved it like this . . . " There must have been a very deep-seated mysticism at the center of his activity, because he poured every bit of that activity into a world from which he always remained apart.

The movement associated with Giner was born not so much from hope as from something that preceded it: need. Need allows no hope until someone very needy is actually in the process of being satisfied, just as a people who are hun-gry do not know what is wrong with them; they must be offered enough to eat in order for them to start suffering from what they lack. And even then, it will be some time before they feel the force of their hunger, the transcendent hunger that is hope, the hope that is total hunger—the non-being that becomes appar-ent to itself in a positive way because it is located in the future. In situations of extreme poverty, however, the future has been obliterated, because people who are totally poor have no future. An action, whatever action is most necessary at the moment, is what we must offer to living human beings if we want to raise them from where they lie prostrate, if we want to make them feel what we our-selves feel; at such a time, impersonal gestures will not be enough to bolster an inner sense of the future in that other person.

And of all the institutional realities created because of the inspiration of this enigmatic Andalusian, perhaps the most efficacious was an ability to make

Spaniards of a particular class feel they had a future and to awaken that future within them.

This is what the Partido Socialista Obrero Español (Spanish Socialist Workers Party) achieved, and it was a very decisive factor in Spain's dialectics of hope. The party's founder, a worker named Pablo Iglesias, had been an austere man who lived in the same, or even greater, poverty in which he had been born. He had been able to imprint a certain character, if not a style, on those who followed him. And at the moment the same thing was happening to him that had happened to Galdós; he was referred to rather ironically, as a symbol of something that had to be surpassed, or had already been surpassed by his own party. There were some very good examples in that party of nationally prominent politicians who had fled the workers' fold. Julián Besteiro was one who remained faithful to the tradition of Pablo Iglesias. He was a professor of logic from the University of Madrid, an "institucionalista," who radiated a profound goodness. After speaking with him for only a minute it was clear that one was in the living presence of the Kantian "good will" Besteiro had examined so thoroughly; he had begun his career with some brief studies of Kant's philosophy. Besteiro was elegant, with the reasoned excellence of a man who comes from a long line of gentlemen and who have thought about things a great deal; he stood for continuity with the tradition of Pablo Iglesias the worker, and in all his long years of struggle, Iglesias could never have dreamed of finding such a follower. The Socialist Party was not a bit "Marxist." It had fought, and tenaciously, for social laws without confronting the monarchy directly, except for one moment in 1917, which appeared at the time to be decisive, but it passed.

The Socialist Party, however, had become a national force. Above all, though, it had been and still was a form of Spain, and it branded the workers with its seal, both demanding from them and giving them a morality. The sum and substance of the party was moral as well, and it also came to acquire a style—the spare, proper style of the "native" Madridian, the "honorable typesetter who earns four pesetas and don't owe none," found in Julián from the *Virgen de la Paloma,* who sings "common people have their hearts too" and belts out a virile cry from deep in his breast: "my face reflects the spirit raging inside me." This is a man with a temper, one ready to do anything, ready to die any at any moment, if anyone threatens his self-respect; a gravely happy man who does not miss a thing, not one thing that passes before his eyes, a man with a quick understanding and a definite opinion about some public person, an incident in foreign policy, a girl crossing the street; and a man always a little on his guard for fear someone might put something over on him, and just the suspicion of it was what drove him crazy, made him ready to do anything, to kill perhaps, to kill himself, although he was no lover of violence, which is for beasts not men, but they should not have provoked him or tread on his manliness. And that is why death is there as a door always open and a solution when a man finds it impossible to maintain his self-respect by employing his Velázquez-like profile so identical in angle and outline to that of the good Philips IV and III, now kings from Madrid and the first Madridians with an awareness of the place that had assumed its role as center and capital of the Spains; when it was impossible to maintain his self-respect by employing the same restrained, natural elegance that Velázquez had captured, that Madridian something—a certain way with the line that let one see only whatever was most essential, just as Madrid's sky shed clarity and grace, but without surfeit. And native Madridians were like this in everything—when they flirted with women, for instance. Those dreadful bricklayers spying on everything from their scaffolding! Their tongues were so quick their comments had her skin burning a little, but not quite; sometimes she had seen them smile with a mixture of sarcasm and respect.

Did they hope, did they believe in something? That would have been difficult. They were like kings without thrones, people of the old school who carry their own laws inside, so deep inside they do not even realize this is the case. Some of them had been fierce dissidents, and they would stand apart from the group, rolling their cigarettes by themselves; they would look aslant at people and would not move back from the sidewalk so a person could pass; while others would say: "Move over, man; don't you see the queen of Spain's about to pass?" Or, with a touch of irony: "The señorita might trip." And they would step to one side to keep her from tripping. This is what they had done until now in public life—they had stepped to one side, letting everything pass, but they started to take things seriously now, more and more seriously. And there were no longer parades on the First of May; her father used to march in one of those parades in Segovia, wearing a dark suit and tie, surrounded by men in their Sunday shirts and corduroy jackets, but he soon gave that up.

He gave it up, her father gave up being a socialist, and he never again joined any political party. His experience was something she too would carry inside, bound up with Segovia, because . . . because of course he had not been born for politics, but this is what happened: there had been a crime, a foolish crime. Late one night, the eldest son of a conservative, fatherly political boss, one of those young men people call *señoritos,* who did nothing but party—work was out of the question—and who played at everything, made a bet with his friends that he would go into the street and shoot at the first person who walked by. And it turned out that the first people to walk by were a pair of newlyweds who had just returned from a village where they had spent their honeymoon. He shot, killing the woman. Things were rather agitated at that moment, because of the signing of the armistice or peace treaty, and everyone became radicalized, especially people from the *pueblo.* The workers among the socialists wanted to go to the funeral, and they presented their request to her father, who was the group's president. He agreed to go with them on the condition that absolute order would be maintained. But then, once things were underway and the cortege was assembled behind the body, the "idea" arose of changing the route so they would pass by the killer's house—the house of the political boss. The president was opposed and, since he could not get them to obey him, he left the procession, followed by a group that went directly to the cemetery. He resigned irrevocably and would not change his mind; he never became involved in politics again. "First," he said, "people must be educated," and that is what he did.

Yes. People must be educated, "the underdogs and the elite . . . together," she had always heard her father say, and they must be educated until they reach a profound understanding, equivalent to what existed in the Middle Ages, because modern tolerance is not enough: to tolerate is to put up with, and although that's a start, it is neither creative nor charitable. Living more with others means that our basic passions and longings operate harmoniously. It means having more bread and more hope—with others.

And active hope requires and seeks knowledge—profound knowledge: poetry, philosophy. Prior meditation more than science. Pure philosophy needs that meditation too; without it, philosophy withers like some imported plant.

Meditation, which is a getting inside. To think is not merely to capture the objects, the realities facing "the subject" as well as those at some distance. Thinking entails a movement that finds internal verification, so to speak, within the subject himself. If thinking does not sweep the house clean inside, it is probably not thinking but merely a logical clarification in which things already thought outside are repeated. The thinking person clarifies himself, explains himself to himself, comes into himself as he looks at himself, seeking his unity; in his search he is always guided by, depends on unity as he looks, looks at himself. When a person looks at himself, even though he objectivizes himself, he himself does this, and therefore he enters into himself. And once a person is no longer in touch with reality, or is in touch through delirium—when we have become *alienated*— then meditation is the cure. The alienated person has no hope, and cannot have any, since he is imprisoned simultaneously by and outside himself. In order for a person to see hope as it arises, alienation must break down, because sometimes hope emerges invisibly. The alienated individual suffers from delusions of persecution because he wanders about, and he cannot, does not know how to situate himself, so he has no real base.

Thinking creates a fixed base for the one who thinks—it takes one inside both oneself and what one thinks about. And the separation between subject and object occurs, in fact, on the basis of an understanding achieved, the solution to a conflict that could have led to extreme alienation. This separation involves positioning oneself so that there are no distances, so that nothing either alienates us or carries us away, so that neither will we be deprived of reality. And then as one enters into reason and reality equally, one recovers the ability to sense similarity. Historically, even in the history of philosophy, being has been seen this way— when the reality of objects was lost, one's fellow man was left hanging.

And we Spaniards had skirted alienation in the nineteenth century, heading toward the "delusions of persecution" into which we have seen certain peoples fall since; and although there was some objective basis for our alienation, as there always is, the tendency had to be curbed. Thought's role is always medicinal. The medicine is bitter sometimes, but poetry sweetens it, if only by mixing it with a bit of delirium. Poetry is one order of delirium.

As doctors, first and foremost, is how one would have to define the writers of the Generation of '98, the year in which Spain lost Cuba and Puerto Rico, the "last jewels" of its colonies. The fact that the *pueblo* was indifferent to Spain's loss and flocked enthusiastically to the bullfights the very day it occurred, has always been cited as an example of the lack of popular awareness at the time; but a hidden wealth of wisdom can usually be found in the lack of popular awareness. Indifference was a sanction against Canovas's impulsive politics of "the last man and the last peseta," to "save the honor of the crown," a sanction against the "feats" of some general or other and the poor administration of recent times—at least we had gotten rid of an embarrassment!

Spain found itself alone. It had never been alone, because the same year it achieved national unity it discovered its first lands overseas. Now, then, for the first time, Spain found itself alone with itself, like a mother after all of her daughters have been married. Was this not the right moment to meditate? Alone, and misunderstood, alone and feeling sick inside, like a poor, half-crazed mother.

And the men of '98 were meditators, not so much because of the content of their work as because of a shared attitude. In all of them there was a withdrawal, a sort of *epoché* applied to history, and to everything, since they had wound up, as and with, whatever was least consequential. They meditated meticulously on the most minimal reality, with a strong desire to know things inside and out; and they had a specific purpose, which Galdós may have lacked, one that was more epic, more grandiose than his—an awareness without bitterness, a settling of accounts, but one prompted more by sensibility than by reason, which would have been useless at that moment. To meditate is also to recapture the way things—the landscape, the people, the men, and the nation—felt at the beginning, to feel immediate reality, which makes us more open to the reality of the world.

There is something in all of them that one rarely finds in writers; they were shy, and they had the delicacy of literary timidity. They said everything half-way, always suggesting more. This was true of Azorín, Baroja . . . In order to show that Unamuno did not really belong to this generation—he was personally and literarily about ten years its senior—the following would be enough: Unamuno always said that everything entered the reader's mind head on, not slithering, but battling its way in.

Ramón del Valle-Inclán did not belong to the Generation of '98 either. He was younger than Unamuno and older than this group; his style was different, and he had thrown himself into a world of tales and expression. Nevertheless, the same timidity also weighed on him; because he did say everything, when it came to saying things outright, but at a different time he would have written more directly as well. Toward the end of his life, with his brilliant *Esperpentos,* his tongue was loosened. He was a great man, and when you saw him out for a walk, you sensed that Spain's entire history walked with him.

The most meditative member of the group was Ramiro de Maeztu. He was Basque and, a wanderer in his youth, he had traveled in England and the United States. Maeztu wanted to bring Spaniards comprehension and understanding through the Protestant mentality, the Catholic *in crescendo,* found in traditionalism. His book *La crisis del humanismo* (The Crisis of Humanism) responded entirely to European concerns, and it anticipated them as well—decades later he addressed this same topic with undiminished energy.

The act of meditating on Spain—the members of the Generation '98 did this mostly in Spain—started with Unamuno who began his series of essays back in the 1880s. Ganivet followed; he belonged to the same generation as Unamuno and was his complement in so many ways, the other side of the same coin—that of suicide. Unamuno was yearning, a yearning in every way imaginable to affirm himself in the life beyond.

Meditation on Spain arose and intensified because Spain is either conflict, or it faces the world by encapsulating itself in a proposition, a proposal, a metaphysical thesis. Angel Ganivet approached Spain as the first possibility; Unamuno as the second.

Ganivet's *Idearium español* (*Spain, an Interpretation*) presents Spain as conflict, without specifying the conflict; without transforming it into a problem. He depicts Spain's paradoxical "being" using the image of the Immaculate Conception, of a woman who reaches old age as an absolute virgin, having married against her will and given birth to many children . . . This was Spain's situation at the moment Ganivet wrote, just after Spain had relinquished its history as an empire. Spain was absolutely virginal, as if it had never entered history, as if it had never drawn action from within itself; it was still, indifferent . . . prenatal.

But history continued then, as it always continues, and it does not forgive; one must return from any limbo, whether hell or paradise.

Unamuno had proposed, however (and before Ganivet's meditation appeared), a "metarritmisis," a conversion of Spanish society in which an altered situation—or rhythm—would prompt the existing elements of that society to form a new body.

She had begun to read Unamuno when she was very young. One afternoon, nosing around in her father's library, she found a lecture titled "¡*Adentro!*" (Get inside things!) It had been delivered in Málaga about the time she was born. She read it avidly without getting up from the floor: she felt she was devouring it. The copy was dedicated to her father, which aroused her interest even further because it meant the lecture was part of the mystery that her father's youth represented for her, the time when he was alive but she was not there, a mystery that would later extend to the Spain of a period she now felt must have been like the dark, still, mysterious hours before dawn, hours that seem to hold the secret of the new day, hours she knew well from the insomnia she had suffered since she was a child, a persistent insomnia that medicines could not cure. She thought she knew why. As the night wore on, a sort of yearning would build up, a sort of hope in some secret soon to be revealed, in some mystery whose face she would miss if she fell asleep. It was also because she experienced the same sort of gestation the deepest hours of the night undergo at dawn—as if the new day were already there, hidden and latent—and she had to hold on until night gave birth to day. The first ray of sun was the sign that now she could fall asleep. And then sameness, the fact that everything had occurred in the same way she had seen happen before, would plunge her into sleep, and she would feel happy because she had watched over the night. So even though she was very little, she understood when they explained to her that the Church of the Knights Templar in Segovia was different from all other churches because in the center there was a sort of crypt where the knights used to spend the night keeping watch over their arms. If no one keeps watch when everyone else is asleep, this means there is no one who loves, no one who really hopes. Unamuno had been one of those Templars who kept watch, in the deepest, darkest hours of the night, over the arms, the faint pulse of the promise that day would be born.

At that point in the "Restoration," Unamuno's voice had been growing louder, becoming more and more the voice of outcry. And although he was speaking to men, before that, and more than to men, he was speaking to the unknown God he wanted to awaken. No one had ever cried out like this in Spain before, and perhaps no one since Quevedo had spoken like this, without any inhibition, almost without modesty. There was something European about it, as in so many aspects of Unamuno's personality. A professor of theology at a university in a small German city, he struggled with all his might to know God. And every day he was more of a Job, asking God for His reasons, or a Jacob wrestling with his angel. Unamuno would have liked to be the father of all Spaniards, of the "each one" of them all, or of all of them as if they were one. And he never tired of inventing creatures, characters, whose independence he felt and discovered before or at the same as Pirandello—some of his characters cried out before him just as he cried out before his God. And because he was so hungry for authorship, he seized on Don Quijote, wanting to rescue him from the Cervantine novel, from the irony and impassivity of Cervante's gaze; he wanted to make Don Quijote his own by turning him into a tragic character, into a tragic protagonist, one of faith. "Lord, I believe, help Thou my disbelief!" he exclaimed tirelessly throughout his poetry and prose; and he must have uttered this short, fervent prayer continuously and insistently.

He had clashed not so much with the regime as with the person of General Primo de Rivera as the highest shepherd of Spain, its patriarch, the one who communicates directly and alone with God and has received the charge of leading Spain toward the new day. Unamuno found this interference unbearable. So he left Spain; they banished him to a small island in the Canaries, and after that he went into exile. He lived in Paris for a time, but the land drew him back, and he planted himself in Hendaya; people used to tell how every afternoon he would go right up to the line that marked the border and call out loud insults to the dictator. His books reached us and so did his messages, the "pages of freedom" he wrote in collaboration with his companion in exile, the politician and writer Eduardo Ortega y Gasset. Unamuno's absence was more active than his presence would have been. And he must have known that.

José Ortega y Gasset, on the other hand, had remained in his position, and up to that moment he had given no indication that the phenomenon of the dictatorship made him feel uneasy; he gave the impression of a person engrossed in his work. Ortega's thought was reaching maturity, and in 1927 he had published *La rebelíon de las masas (The Revolt of the Masses),* first in supplements to *El Sol,* which he had founded and to which he contributed assiduously. It was a joy, a gift to find that one of his supplements had been published or to see his signature beneath a column. Reading him made you want to live.

Ortega's thought was an exercise in hope, intellectual charity. And everyone, each of his readers felt that Ortega had thought for him the things he himself had worried about—what the reader would have liked to think, what was forming in the reader's soul without taking form. He was one of those rare writers who allows a reader to believe he himself has written what he's reading. I believe this is what many Spaniards felt as they read him; they believed they were the authors. "Vitality, soul, spirit": didn't I write that myself, wasn't it perhaps mine? Hadn't I also written *El tema de nuestro tiempo (The Modern Theme)?* And I wasn't the only one; I believe that each of us had written it, each of us young people.

Yes, reading Ortega made you want to live. You saw that life is something good, intelligent in itself, that life is as intelligent—or more so—qua "intelligence," as what you had thought was intelligence, reason; you saw that life is reason and sticks to reason, its own reason deep within life itself. And this enabled you to love life, to want to live it with faith, hope, and joy.

And even though Ortega's words were painful sometimes and brought grave warnings that held glimpses of a none-too-pleasing future; even though his voice sounded like a reprimand and called on us to wake up, as Heraclitus did in his day, as philosophers do when they speak to everyone; even so, this did not undermine happiness or confidence. Ortega's reason was maternal; it made possible the birth of a new soul, of whatever was best in our souls, which was forcing its way toward the light. And this was not only true for Ortega's students at the university—I had been lucky enough to be one of those students "officially" the year before—but for everyone, for any Spaniard. It was not necessary to study philosophy to be one of Ortega's students, to owe him something very deep and indelible. People felt that way, they knew this; and no one in Spain had ever propounded a thought that touched the hearts of so many people so directly—so many people with different backgrounds, from different classes, professions, and positions—that is, everyone.

And for this "everyone," *El Sol* brought together, first and foremost, the names of almost all the best writers, as well as the names of specialists who had something to say—Ramón Pérez de Ayala, Gómez de la Serna (simply Ramón), Madariaga, who published *Englishmen, Frenchmen, and Spaniards,* Machado, Gabriel Miró . . . And it provided reputable, lucid, international information, a view of the world that came from an ability to look at things clearly and perceive them discerningly. Reading this newspaper, you could feel the future and time on the march.

The air was transparent in Spain; there was visibility and there were people to take notice. This is why a certain anguish intruded suddenly into Spanish spirits, one coming more from without than within. But Europe was no longer "without" for Spain, and one did not even have to be there to be in it. Unamuno's polemic against European "progressivism" had been left behind, and even he himself didn't remember it now. Thought had cured the wound of incomprehension. There were, there continued to be wounds, both our own and Europe's; because Europe's wounds, and above all Europe's preoccupation, were ours as well.

Return to the Land

That spring "things" had happened; the rhythm of Spanish life was picking up. The students had made their disagreement with the general's dictatorship quite clear. In truth, though, there was not a real dictatorship, and it was not the general's; it was simply the same anachronistic regime, anachronistic now with respect to the living reality of Spain. The parenthesis of the Restoration had to close in order for Spain to open fully to the fresh air of a renewed history. The time was approaching when history would be infused with deep renewal, or rather rebirth. A flexible, living monarchy that truly synthesized national reality, would have been able to continue . . . It was less a question of revolution than of "natural" need, one as close to natural as something in history can be. History does have a sort of "naturalness" . . . in certain changes that correspond to the idea of history we've had for centuries: "nature" is spontaneous order, the opposite of anything violent; the thing most opposed to "natural"—to the idea of the natural—is revolution. And what's most "natural" is for nature's vital force to break through the form containing it. Form collapses of its own, a worn out entelechy, in order to make way for the entelechy that has been forming slowly with the invisible patience of life, even the life of history. Because living demands a great patience, a becoming in the time, experience, and birth pangs of history.

And suddenly one day history's protagonist is someone different although still the same. A nation's image in history or the image of a person in his individual life makes someone who looks at the image from without, or who loves it "conditionally," think that it's nothing more than an image, or less, for one does not experience it as an image, because one does not have a feeling or does not actually feel that reality is much more. Something is truly loved, though, only when one knows—because one feels—that reality breaks through the image apparent to us, in the way that Spinoza conceives of his *Deus sive Natura,* of whom space and causality, which constitute our world, are the two attributes we know, only two, although the world—and reality—are infinitely more.

This is why, when one loves something of human make-up, whether a living person, a nation, or a "culture", one cannot help feeling a "nature" subsisting beneath its history, and one accepts the history achieved by whatever one loves as the surface of its real history. And this history is only the fragmentary appearance of its deepest, inexhaustible bed. So one expects changes and mutations, not with resignation but with amazement, the same way we await the dawn, always hoping that it will be different, that it will be sunny, but also that there will be something new—a different sun or something no one has ever seen before, something we would hail as soon as we caught the first glimpse of it.

Life . . . Now she accepted and loved life, seeing in it everything that *Deus sive Natura* had gathered, not only from thought but also from longing, the original hope of the human soul; because philosophy, metaphysics, and poetic philosophy may not have been thinking what longing demands.

And she realized that philosophic thought allows us to dare to feel what we would feel in any case, but without daring, which means that the things we feel would end up half-born, the way our feelings almost always end up. This is why the lives of so many people never amount to anything but an attempt, an attempt at life. And this is serious, because in some way life should be full in this attempt at being, which is us—in this non-being that can neither give up being nor remain, continue as it is.

Living humanly must mean gradually bringing feeling into the light, leading it toward understanding from its dark, confused beginning. If intelligence does not "rescue," does it really comprehend? If comprehension is necessary, if—as Aristotle claims—"all men have a natural desire for knowledge," it is because what they feel weighs on them so heavily and because they can neither stop feeling nor trust only their feelings. The trusting person is in for the bitter experience of Oedipus, who knowingly let himself be guided by his feeling of trust. If it were possible to make feeling and thinking the same "thing," the same action, then, yes, Aristotle was right: "the act of thought is life." And, no, Aristotle was not wrong; this life is life, the act of thought, except that our thought is narrow, dark, and scattered. Our thought is not truly thought.

She believed that in truth she had learned just one thing from Ortega's lessons. He had been so kind in her metaphysics "exam." He had shown such sensitivity—she had seen it—to all the passion she had felt, to the suffering she had endured in order to understand. That's how true teachers are; they see you better than you see yourself, and they understand you because they think you're better than you are. And she remembered what Hamlet says, something her father repeated time after time, always in regard to some inter-personal conflict, when Horacio tells him: "My Lord, the actors have been announced; you must receive them as they deserve." Then Hamlet, the Prince, the true Prince, answers: "No, much better than they deserve." This was the obligatory action, which her father had required her to perform like Hamlet ever since she was a little girl: treat everyone, anyone, better than he deserves. And, he would add, "sometimes this is the only way to treat a person as he truly does deserve. Could Hamlet know for sure that Shakespeare was not one of those actors?" And he would conclude: "in all forms of domination—and teaching is one of them—this is how you must proceed."

And "this" is how Ortega had treated her when she was his student. It was not that he made her feel she was worth her weight in gold, because for a young person there is something more important than worth, and that is being. When we're young, or perhaps always, we feel that we're being when we feel that we're looked at and listened to—when someone we look to, identifying that person with intelligence and truth, looks at us; because it's impossible to stop believing that in some way whatever is looked at confers reality on the gaze that discovers it. Evening after evening she had watched as bits of reality that had been wandering about in her mind, totally unconnected, like ghosts, had appeared and taken on reality and life. It felt as though her thoughts, which were like obsessions, were turning to liquid, were beginning to form part of her circulatory system, which is a system of thought, and system is, must be, whatever our minds are made up of, even though it never becomes objectivized in a "system" or in the outline of a philosophical system. Simply in order to live, in order to travel through life in whatever profession and class, in order to . . . anything, in order to be able to stand on one's own and accept the fact of having been born, there has to be a certain order in one's mind . . . an order not at all like a mosaic, a motionless geometry, but like the order that emanates from a unitary action. Because unity, our unity, is created, and this is order—the action of the single something unifying the thoughts, deciphering the feelings she had felt while she was so enslaved. Yes, understanding what one feels, without abolishing it, without ceasing to feel it; yes, an intelligence that redeems whatever is most distant from itself. And even people who cannot begin to attempt this with the entire reality surrounding us need to attempt it in their own lives. She would have liked to explain it to him this way, to offer him that testimony, instead of the "outline" of the course he had asked them to make, which was also a testimony; maybe there had been both in her outline; maybe he had understood.

Because of this "unity" she felt growing in her mind, she had felt free, free . . . even to stop studying philosophy, free to face life, the task that within her would prove to be hers, if she had one. Being a student of that teacher was not contingent on one's studying philosophy, which is why so many people in Spain felt they were his students and why Spanish life had undoubtedly changed as it gradually became impregnated with his thought. This is the type of communication that can transform a people, influence history at a given moment, make history without proposing to do so, the history that grants us freedom to be what we must be, so we can obey necessity freely.

And she saw that the freedom won in this way had played an important role in the "natural" way she continually allowed herself to be guided by the impassioned feeling that bound her to those young people—her colleagues—in an almost formless movement; and she watched her completely formless decision continue to bud—the decision not to continue studying philosophy, not to make philosophy her profession as she had intended. Instead, when she returned to life, she would simply begin to live with others, with people who work, with them, who are to society what the obscure feelings we have inside are to us: whatever is passive, whatever suffers, and also the place where the secret of the future is gestating; where the future suffers before it is born; where you find a mixed truth—the truth that comes from living face to face with necessity—and the truth of hope, which is the birthplace of the unexpected gesture that one day affronts everything—something of a weak spot that must be cared for, the fragility of the common man who can just as easily deny his destiny in an instant.

Because there is nothing so delicate as the hope of the humble, this is the hope Sancho had, and Peter—the rock that only became unbreakable after it had cracked three times. No comparison was necessary with our Lord Don Quijote, and even less with Christ. Wouldn't a few people have needed to accompany them, literally be at their sides—people they believed to have the continuity that comes from thought, so they would acquire a bit of experience dealing with doubt, vacillation, and even anguish? But when she saw it this way, she did not think she was strong enough, and she felt that once again she had let her ambition go too far, maybe even further than when she wanted to study philosophy. And she felt anguish was beginning to brand, overcome her. Yes, to keep studying philosophy was to accept, to acknowledge that the unity she'd inferred was just that, inferred; and it was something no more than outlined, a weakness to be cared for within herself, within her own life, a life that had yet to become, was not ready to engage in extreme combat, to give other people as much as she received from them. To keep studying philosophy was to know that she was still becoming, still being born, because the action she had dreamed about was more characteristic of a whole being, of a being "true to itself" in the form of a living truth. The struggle between wanting to be and wanting to offer herself wholly, as if she wholly were.

She could not solve that. And she understood that life, her life, would have to be both. She would have to move between one and the other, to jump from one to the other, to continue her own becoming at the same time she was approaching the becoming of everyone else, of something that for her was not and could never be "everything else"—the "circumstance" on the verge of transformation that she could never renounce: Spain.

And in the midst of her anguish, she felt that she was awakening, that she was going to wake up again . . . by dreaming herself. What she had to do then was prepare herself to watch over her sleep, her own sleep, all by herself, because she was the only one who could take responsibility for it. But was this possible? One's sleep does not flow into the common sleep, when there is such a sleep, and we are surrounded by it, when we live among . . . How can you be sure of not being a sleepwalker, a sleepwalker of history? And how can you be sure you have not "denied" yourself? Because you either are one of the people who watch over sleep or one of the people who simply sleep, one of the dreamed—you are "rock." And rock cannot "split" any more than absolutely necessary . . .

She wanted to serve; this much was certain.

Her anguish was giving way to awakening, surrounded by the awakening of that gentle Madrid spring. The air was light, the sun was clear and energizing, and the leaves were budding as if there were a particular communication moving among all things; the insects had appeared, and you could hear the birds again. The elements and their creatures also formed a "system," there was a unity moving throughout all of them, a living understanding that is found in everything, beyond the limits that seem to keep beings separated at other times, a common rhythm that even includes the stars in their journeys and the grass sprouting in the cracks between the rocks, one that makes the distant constellations of diamonds rotate within the same circle and along with the golden hedge mustard that had blossomed in the eaves on her neighbor's roof. "Walking as the planet's axis turns toward the summer solstice/ the almond tree green, the violet faded," wrote Antonio Machado, bard of the Castilian countryside's humble spring. Spring, which is more authentic in poverty, the goddess of awakening, can be seen more readily in lusterless creatures, in nearly arid lands, in the dry elm, where new, green life bursts forth in three leaves, in things that barely breathe—to awaken is to breathe, to begin to breathe within the common rhythm of everything that breathes.

And now she could receive an occasional visitor. She got up a few hours each day and during those hours some of her friends would stop by, with their wide smiles and their weightless words, the few words that, like birds, convey enormous meaning with small bodies. Isn't this the way birds converse? All that's needed are a few swiftly spoken words. Isn't this what's called understanding each other?

They almost always came to see her together, the budding art historian and the official writer for the FUE. A clandestine literature had sprung up, because in that short time the students' activity had become partly clandestine. They told her about some of the things they'd been doing, laughing, although those things were very serious.

And although she had done nothing to deserve this—perhaps it happened because of these two young men who came to see her—one day her house in Madrid was searched by the police. A pair of "secret" police arrived at two in the afternoon and asked to see her father. They told him that "with his permission" they would return in three hours to conduct a search on account of his daughter, "a serious young woman, but a rather restless one." They were very respectful, and they examined her books with growing amazement; not only were the books mixed with all the others in the family library, they found their number and "subject matter" overwhelming. "What things you read, señorita!" And the book they chose from them all as a suspicious title was one called *La cuestión social* (The Social Question), which belonged to her father. It contained the papal encyclicals about that topic, and it was a shame because she never saw the book again. That was all. The police said goodbye politely, giving her a piece of friendly advice: "Don't get involved in these things, señorita; be careful!" They were good people, and so was the man who dictated. History was following a "natural" course; the buds of spring were beginning to appear on the trees. At such a moment no one is bad. Pursued and pursuers alike were smiling.

Since fall, a few more young men and two singular young women had been increasingly involved with the group, attracted more by what it stood for than by its activities. The women had come to her house together in the early fall, shortly after her talk at the cigar workers' local. One of them was very young, in the bloom of a youth that seemed to lack for nothing. She was Cuban, but she had been raised in Spain, the daughter of a writer who was the consul of his country and a friend of many of the "elders." Without participating actively in the group, just by being present, she contributed all the generousness of her youth—the type of vibration that creates an atmosphere, an understanding echo, something very necessary and valuable to a person who is alone, as she knew so well.

The other young woman was a very singular Andalusian with a history. There in her land of window grates and carnations, she had suffered an unhappy love affair when she was an adolescent—a fiancé, one of those fiancés who disappears one day to marry "someone else," and the young woman dies soon afterwards from a mysterious, uncontrollable disease, or wilts away alone behind her window grates, or becomes a nun. Becoming a nun is what this young woman had done in her own way. She ran away from home and went to Madrid, where she learned a manual trade, one hard for female hands, living like a worker and putting in eight-hour shifts, her beauty erased but not destroyed, her elegance indestructible in a mannish turtle neck sweater and a timeless tailored suit—her perfectly drawn head had the same expression and gaze as some of Zurbarán's or Murillo's saints. She was also a student at the university. She went to classes in the morning, and in the afternoon she worked at her trade; and she studied (but when?). Fatigue was clearly taking its toll on her magnificent eyes and her entire face; she barely spoke, and when anyone talked to her alone she would break into a kind of monologue. She seemed to be walking along an inaccessible, steep path, the way people walk when they've made a vow to renounce everything. She never joined the group completely because she didn't have time and because of the solitude she could not break through. One day she tried, but she could not find the words . . . it was not a question of words.

There was also a young man who had allied himself with them; he was something of a writer and something of everything, and his life was difficult. He had gone through various trades and occupations, as if he were on a pilgrimage through different levels of society and even different countries, and when he reached their group he felt he had entered a safe port, as if he had found his home, and the crease of bitterness you could see beside his mouth began to disappear. Because not all of the young people lacked a history; and others, even though they did have not a history of their own, had a suffering caused by some indefinable thing—the subtle, constant suffering that comes from an excess of sensitivity, from having a delicate soul that's incapable of expression, from modesty, or from not yet having experienced the final rent that provokes expression. For only when innocence has suffered to the limit is it capable of expression—rent innocence, goodness that has passed a thousand and one nights in pain, when one is good. Because you wait, you are waiting for the friend, the beloved, something certain and living at last, and you would not dare to speak, for fear that a word, a single word, might reveal your torment and drive off whatever it is forever or that it might somehow decrease your virginity, which you want to give intact. This happens frequently to girls. It's different for men, although some of them are like this too, some of the men who have had to endure the thousand and one torments; one of them, for example, is the man who let loose completely to write the *Quijote*. Others did not wait so long as he did because they had less patience; patience retards expression.

Fe, the young Andalusian woman who remained in the group with her was not at all expressive; there was something good and fresh about her entire moral and physical person, and she must have suffered, always suffered, the way certain sensitive plants suffer. She never complained, nor was there any reason to complain. In short, she came from a good family and had been educated at the Instituto-Escuela, which meant she had been blessed with games, laughter, and colleagues in the best environment, and that, as an innocent, she herself may not have known that she had always suffered, that she had been suffering her whole life. Now she was smiling happily. She was so tiny, and she had such melancholy eyes!

And now, after her illness, she found that the meaning of the group had changed, or else something that had always been there had become more pronounced as the group also moved away from the official "form" that had lasted

only the short time they were an ambience, atmosphere, an understanding that
was circulating. None of them could brag about having any special understanding, because it was something far more wonderful—there was an understanding
moving among them, in every gesture, in every action, in the community that
joined them, a community made of intimacy and distance, the distance one needs
to be a person, even when one is.

This is why it was so hard for them to express themselves, as it was for Fe,
the girl who spoke the least but whose presence was felt the strongest; because
that's what they all were, a presence, something that would not have been possible without all the thinking there had been in Spain. They could neither express
themselves nor act on their own, because they were the sons and daughters of a
beautiful Spain from whom they demanded nothing but obedience. And this is
why they were more innocent than their age and background would suggest.
When human beings obey or require obedience, they tend to fall mute, like creatures in nature. All rules and disciplines that require obedience also demand silence. To speak, above all to speak in one's own name is already to rebel. Obedient
people need either to command, even to speak, or to have received command,
to have been commanded with a charge. How much effort it cost Saint Teresa,
who spoke so easily and expressed herself so clearly, . . . to speak about herself!
Only if you think death is near, bringing the loss of something that was your
soul, a soul that contained you and within which you had your own soul,
breathed, moved, and was; only if it becomes necessary to give an account of that
soul, and time is running out, or if the soul's time has come; only for this reason,
and no other, are certain books written. During that period, all we did was write,
as did even "the writers," for the Sunday supplements that ceased publication,
because . . . it was no longer necessary. Who decided this? Maybe no one . . . but
it was understood.

Summer separated her from her friends once again. They scattered to go on
their vacations, and she went with her family to a house not far from Madrid
that had trees and a kind of circular pool with one red fish swimming in it.

Madrid has everything, although it may not appear to. There's the northern
landscape that is always green, with shady spots along the Manzanares River, and
the highway to Irún and the Casa de Campo. It also has a desert to the south and
the east, from the Madrid side of the capital of La Mancha and New Castile, especially La Mancha because it's flat, although there are neither vineyards nor
wheat fields. This land is arid and desert-like, as befits what was once the capital
city of an empire so ancient and so modern along an unknown, secret historic
route, which received something of both the Asian and the Egyptian empires;
since it predates Rome, it's like children who turn out to resemble their grand-
parents. And that's how we were. Children of Rome, we most resembled those
who came before us and for whom Rome was "modernity." Spain, daughter of
Rome, is older than Rome.

Except for its light and its paintings, Madrid had the down-at-heel appearance probably found in certain Oriental cities that preserve an inner splendor even when it's no longer visible. The same is true of a people who offer all the characteristics of first-class urban population but are nevertheless naive and capable of great angers, history-making angers, a people capable of historical spontaneity.

She had gone to spend the summer on the side of Spain that faces the desert, in "Ciudad Lineal," an effort that dates from the beginning of the century. The trees there had never gotten very leafy because of the scorching summer heat and very cold winters. No doubt the purpose had been to construct a comfortable, pleasant bourgeois neighborhood, but it wound up more like a small city in the wake of some disaster, some revolution. Its 1890s-style *quintas,* with their untended gardens, its neglected streets, its spaciousness reminiscent of another century, and its current lack of sparkle suggested some Russian city close to Moscow. She did not know why, but it gave one the sense of a revolution that had left people either as the proprietors of that whole place in ruins or faced with the need to earn a living, which meant that only a few rooms in their two-story *quintas* were inhabited and in their gardens they had planted cabbage and potatoes—a real contrast to the raspberries, the pond, the vines, the spacious carriage house, and the stables for horses. One sensed that the style of the turn-of-the-century upper bourgeoisie was providing a framework for a different, somewhat "proletarian" life, something that must have occurred in Russia in so many once-"pleasant" places.

The landscape there is almost exclusively horizon. There is nothing but horizon; the earth is flat and colorless, the sky high and pure, and the skyline immense. This was what she loved most about Madrid: this steppe, this desert more than its northern side as the capital of the mountains, with their river and vegetation, and of the city's present-day life. Why did Philip II not build the Escorial here? It would have been even more majestic, its theocratic significance more visible, because deserts are places that give rise to theocratic history, which, like all earthly histories, is born in sight of the horizon—"Lord of the Horizon." Isn't that one of the names given to Amon-Re? And it was in a desert that Moses gave to his people the Law God had placed in his hands. In the desert both polytheism and even a belief in a particular God above all others are impossible; the only acceptable faith is that in the one and only God. And it's unlikely that this faith, felt and received in the implacable light, the only light, which roams over the shadowless land, will lead to anything other than theocracy; it's unlikely that the history men make as they live beneath this light, facing this pure, abiding horizon, will find any other path.

The Church must have found it very difficult in the early days to devise some form of organization that would not be theocratic with respect to history! Since the dividing line between spiritual and temporal power is so fine as to be barely visible at times, both the Emperor and the Holy Roman Empire followed the narrowest of paths, but it was next-to-impossible to formulate theocracy from the standpoint of Christianity. The march of European history, however, has followed the opposite course, leaving religion free from the responsibilities of power, although not free from those of history. Philip II was perhaps the only seriously theocratic monarch, the only theocrat whose power was temporal. For him, the Pope must have been "the other," to whom he nevertheless owed obedience and submission. There must have been such great struggle in his soul, a hidden struggle he did not dare to articulate to himself! He must have suffered from such insomnia in his distant monastery! Because there he was, on the other side of Madrid, or behind its back, pacing with his secrets along endless corridors, talking to himself, like Hamlet, thinking about incoherent motives he could not allow even his own lips to divulge. Philip II took the history of Spain to the limit of what is humanly possible, where history meets dream in a metaphysical thesis that would bring immobility if it were to be realized: one monarch, one sword, and one cross. But was he the single representative of that cross? The vicar of his Christ . . . A monarch and an empire in His name. He had received the kingdom from God's hands, of this he was sure, and he would have to surrender it intact to God. This is why the El Escorial would have been better here; in this desert to the east of Madrid, it would have been even more visible than El Escorial is—"the rock" that, together with the book, is the symbol of Spain, a sacrificial stone, an altar where a self-ordained priest offered Spain, the whole of Spain, once and for all. Maybe the sacrifice was accepted?

Maybe it was, maybe Spain, its history as a nation, had been devoured by universal history, and this explains why the Spaniards had wound up as they had; like Greece, like Egypt, like the Sumerians, they had wound up as part of a history that, according to Hegel, is completely sacred. But if history, all history is sacred, as Hegel says, it's probably because only universal history is history . . . and the rest is anecdote or spoils.

And Spain, the spoils of universal history, real Spain of flesh and blood, *pueblo,* a *pueblo* suffering hunger and hope was beginning to show signs of awakening, of forgetting previous history, universal history. Would Spain have an hour just for itself? Would universal history grant Spain a truce so it could rise up, so it could forget and wake up? Because all awakening is forgetting, and someone who is waking up forgets, in order to pick up the thread again in the coming hours. And there must be an hour granted as one's sacred right, an hour of forgetfulness so one can begin to breathe, like the hour they give a newborn baby.

At times she was afraid that hour would not be granted. Since she could speak now and even go out a little, in the afternoons she would walk in the garden with the doctor who was going to be her brother and with her father. It was Europe that troubled them. There were no houses on that high moor, and they were on the edge of Crudad Lineal's small "city", where they felt the vibrations from Europe almost physically, since deserts are fine places for eliminating distances. Of course, for deserts there is no such thing as near or far, only being or not being, being present or not present. And at times Europe felt entirely more present than neighboring Madrid—now next to empty because of summer vacations—than Spanish life itself, which was still churning in some "underground" way. This agitation was like an increasingly intense beating of a heart full of life, one asking to take possession of the body that belonged to it. And if Spain was that body, the air where Spain was going to breathe, the place where it was going to maneuver was Europe.

"It would have been much better, incomparably better," her father was saying, "if what is now going to happen in Spain had happened before: perhaps 1917 was the last of the good moments, because Europe was different then, and in that Europe there was still a 'liberal' framework, with more room and fewer conflicts than we find surrounding us now. The same thing always happens to us," he continued with an almost desperate passion, "we arrive early or late, but never on time! Spain is anachronistic with respect to the world, and in the First World War that just ended we lost the opportunity to synchronize. It would have been sad, because it's sad to participate in a war, but if we had become involved, our current situation would be different; maybe we really would have begun to participate as part of the world, of Europe, to participate—live—in a common rhythm."

"But now," she was pointing out, "isn't it the time anymore—now?"

"We'll make it be the time," Carlos, the doctor who was almost her brother, said impetuously. "Europe needs us. That's why, because we've lagged behind, we might be able to lead; we have a vitality, a youth to offer them. Maybe we can offset Germany; we'll see, when Germany makes up its mind, because the future of Europe depends on Germany, and that's a fact. So does the future of Russia. Maybe it will be possible to create a social revolution, or rather a change? Right now, Europe needs to find itself, and we can, must, help Europe find the beginning of a solution."

And her father, rapt in thought, gave a glimmer of a smile. He knew how to listen as few people can, and he had taught her this since she was a little girl— "you must know how to listen; Spaniards never listen." And he listened so much and so intently that you had a better idea of what you were talking about when you felt your words being gathered up that way; you experienced their full weight and your own responsibility, and this same experience allowed you to discover whatever deceit, exaggeration, or haste there was in them. Talking to someone who listens reveals to us, without the listener saying anything, the degree of truth, and above all, the degree of conviction there is in what we are saying. The person who knows how to listen serves as the other person's conscience, and this means that sometimes a silence can occur suddenly—the silence of a speaker as he addresses his conscience or stands before it.

Because later, when the two young people talked by themselves, on their own, they let their fears and their anguish emerge. They both felt absolutely certain that a military conflict would reach Europe; this was not a calculation on their part but something they felt, which made it hard to communicate to older people or people who did not feel it. And perhaps their colleagues and friends also felt it. Things like this, though, are hard to say anything about, since one feels them with respect to one's own life, which is the way things are felt. What led them to have these fears was not an examination of the social and political situation in Europe but the certainty born of, imposed by, a feeling coming from knowing "this time" they would be involved. How? This *was* impossible to know. And one day he said to her: "I've always had a sense that there was a dead man on my back, one who traveled with me, someone who died in the First World War when he was my age, leaving his life unlived and his words unspoken, and I've sensed that each one of us carries such a man; they've left us their lives to live as an inheritance. Now, in the next war, we'll be the ones to go, and we'll be the dead. I know that I'm going to die young, and that's why I feel such a great sense of urgency; this is what frightens your sister so much and what no one understands, this urgent need to do my work. From now on I won't have any more time to be with you and your family. I have the hospital, my books, medicine, and I must fulfill my obligation to them; I was born a doctor, and I must be one, even if I'm not anything else, because I'm well aware that I won't be able to be more. As for the rest of it . . . they won't let me, they won't let us; we're a sacrificed generation." He continued to speak, his voice almost threatening: "You must watch what you do, so you don't get yourself thrown into the bonfire before you have to; you're a woman, and you might be able to escape."

I answered: "No, being a woman won't save anyone in this instance; our destiny is for all of us, and that's how I feel it. I too sense that presence, someone's company. Or rather, the company of all the young people who died in France; I don't know why it's the ones from France especially, maybe because of Peguy, but I do sense there are Germans with me too, and all the young people who died—their words on the tips of their tongues, some of them with their words unformed—the void of a sacrificed generation . . . One void calls to another; I know that we're marching toward the same sacrifice too, that they won't let us speak. And what we want to achieve might be lost. Because we, the members of our generation, do have something. You know what I mean? I don't see us—or the young people in Europe either—as 'revolutionaries'; we aren't looking for revolution, and we might be the way out of, the solution to all the aborted revolutions, the way to 'move beyond' the rebellion within all of them. Our elders were more rebellious than we are, because they ran less risk and had more freedom. We're closer to danger, to the edge of the abyss. That's how I see us, all of us, of them too, especially the Germans. They won't let us alone though, and they'll even force us to do many things; what I'm most afraid of, even more than death, is that no one will understand us." And this was where they felt the great-est solidarity, in their "lived experience." They argued and argued about every-thing else, although there was another feeling that drew them together, one that can only be described as "religious."

The young people in their group, like those who made up the real student vanguard, did not share the anticlercial sentiment so characteristic of "leftist" ideology, especially one segment of it. This was one of the reasons they had remained detached from anticlericalism, this and because they believed that the social question was the most important of all, the one that truly stirred them and led them to look favorably at the Socialist Party. They did not have anticlerical sentiments, which in their eyes bore the stamp of something very nineteenth-century, something people had moved beyond, and they made fun of those sentiments sometimes. Most of them were not Catholics, and many of them had received secular educations, although that was not true for her. The question of the Church was not one they debated, from either a religious or a political standpoint; no one planned to attack it if the chance arose, but they were definitely not going to back down about certain things. Education free of confession was a dogma for them; it was something they expected from both the university and the spirit of the university, and the separation of Church and State was not even a topic for discussion. They thought this separation was in the interest of the Church itself, especially those who were somewhat familiar with Spanish history; it would allow the Church to become more independent and to find its true countenance.

They were not really preoccupied with religion. In their minds religion and absolutism were identified as something that concealed life and were entangled with a call to stop feeling that one is "here," on this earth where we live. They did not have the head for this or they— the majority of them—would have writ-ten a kind of *Discourse on Method,* in which the fact of being alive, life, would emerge as the only proof: life here and now and the duty to live it, and not just wholly, for life was also to be lived lucidly, lived as a lucid life appropriate to our current condition, to "this." And although they were not all involved in sports, they worshipped sports, worshipped the elements and wanted to be in contact with them: being in the sun, being outside, playing fair, "looking at nothing ex-cept what's right in front of me," "what I have to do." And she felt older because of her religious upbringing and because she had been trained to think philo-sophically in a more complex way; she felt that their attitude was a sort of *epoché,* a state of being in suspense, an abstraction, and she felt that when they said "life," they did not accept all of life but only this life, the one I'm living now, an instant. Maybe they wanted to live the instant? Or maybe they weren't strong enough for more, maybe the instant was so solemn now, so crammed with future, that to accept it with integrity, with full responsibility, was already "religious" but they were not aware of it?

Carlos, her doctor, did know, however. He was older than the rest because he was a passionate person, and he had lived everything fervently, because he had lived in one of Spain's older provinces, and maybe because there was a contradiction buried within him, and he suffered from it, even though he could not define it for himself. He not only suffered from the contradiction, he had gotten to know it in an even deeper way, because he was a man given to soliloquies. Of that circle of friends—"the group" as such had disappeared by then—he was undoubtedly the most religious, because he was the most tormented. He did not consider himself a Catholic; he had thought about the problem and no, he knew he was not. But he thought about all problems with a religious feeling, from the standpoint of religion and his own acceptance of the "here and now," of "his here and his now"; his nature was one of total surrender, of sacrifice, and the day he could not act accordingly he would shoot himself, although this was not going to be necessary, since they were going to shoot him. He was not reflecting on death but running, rushing toward it. This meant he was in direct confrontation with his problems, all of them, with respect to whether or not they were ultimate, absolute. Every decision had to be made as if it were his last. He could not live provisionally, and he was always saying goodbye to something; living for him was a wrenching, a constant wrenching himself from everything, from whatever moment was passing, from what he had done and achieved, from the patient cured, from the book studied, from his happiness, from himself. He was wrenching himself from everything, and it seemed that every conversation one had with him would be the last. He was going through some difficult, very difficult moments because he had wrenched himself from his city, from his mentor, from his position as an adjunct professor at the university, from . . . In order to come to Madrid, to embark on a different course as a doctor, he had wrenched himself from his plans to take the examinations for a full professorship, which were already underway and in which he was sure to be successful, and in Madrid he would embark on a specialization in tuberculosis so he could marry her sister. And now he was also going to wrench himself from his coexistence with them so he could devote more time to himself, all alone, to his studies, his science, as if he had taken a vow to enter a religious order. But in the meantime, the two of them talked and talked, while her beautiful sister, sick now despite her beautiful youth, followed his treatment of rest and silence.

The topic of their conversations always wound up being essentially the same: Germany's vacillation, Russia's "theocracy." And of course they were not the only ones who looked at the Russian phenomenon in that religious context; on the contrary, this is how it was usually dealt with among certain groups of people, at least the intellectuals. Because the "Russian phenomenon" reached Europeans after the days when the great Russian authors had been so enormously influential, when Tolstoy and Dostoyevsky, especially, were translated into all languages and read hungrily, like medicine and like bread. These writers had already been read by the generation before theirs, the generation of their parents in fact and read quite differently from French literature, for example, or English literature, or any literature including their own. They had been read "religiously," in all senses of the word. And they were like two paths within the same religion: Tolstoy and Dostoyevsky. "Which one do you prefer?" They, the young people, had read Andreyev, Gorky—some of them passionately, the same ones who had a passion for Baroja and those little novels that had just appeared, and for writers already working within a revolutionary framework, journalistic novels, like the famous *Ten Days That Shook the World,* books consumed all over the country, all over Europe, and not only by young people. Editions multiplied in all languages. Gladkov's *Cement* was the most recent; like *Cities and Years,* it was much discussed.

Reading this literature was not in itself any indication that one believed in Communism, since this would have meant that all Europe was Communist. Trotsky's *My Life* was a best-seller in Europe somewhat later. Like Chaplin's films, Honneger's music, Picasso's painting, they formed part of the moment. There was an aesthetic interest, a vital interest as well; it was . . . living the moment.

But the moment could not be lived because—although they did not realize this—at that moment history was liquid, fluid. And history was like that because Europe was living the moment of its flowering, and when something, a culture, is fully mature, everything has become liquid, and it can be assimilated; people live in a fluid time, one common to everyone. The "river of history" flows without stagnating behind impassible rocks; the current pushes beyond everything. We can only live wide open to the moment if we live within the flowering of whatever historical zone surrounds us, because time is fluid then, as open space is fluid. This is how European life was at this time. And the same thing must have happened at some period during the Roman Empire; people must have felt that the horizon before them was wide and clear, and there must have been an eagerness to know everything, to understand everything, to be interested in everything, an eagerness that welled up not only in the same people who are always afflicted with this passion, but also in other, more reluctant souls, because this is exactly the response prompted by such wideness in a person's vital horizon. In an open, populated space, one looks in several directions and feels his attention span and his visibility give; and in Europe there was visibility at that moment.

But that wide European space was populated. It was not like this Spanish desert where revelations, total communion, occur at sacred moments. Europe was populated and, what's more, it was "full"; the world was wide, but it was "full," in the way Ortega had used that word, as "symptom" in his diagnostic *Revolt of the Masses.*

A mature Europe, but such a full one. Would it prove capable of really being one Europe? And this was the moment, the exact moment of European unity.

That was something she did feel, felt more as a phenomenon than a project, since the same feeling was not in her consciousness alone but also in those of the others; although the differences did worry them, increasingly . . .

Summer is the season of storms. Some days, entire weeks, especially in the deserts, are the long, anguished brewing of a single low-breaking storm. The clouds move in from a distance, black clouds that advance slowly; they stop, recede, and it's possible to watch them cross the clear sky like heavy ships, because the sky they have yet to reach is still clear. They drop their shadows over the earth; empty and uncluttered by vegetation, it can accept the patterning of those shadows, which is like the sign-writing of a still unknown, universal language whose interpretation humans have not been able to agree about, so they all read it in their own ways as the language of their "natural" history, their universal and sacred history.

And that's how the plain was—filled with signs and imprinted with shadows—the first day she could go out and walk once more on the Earth.

Multiplicity of Times

As she reentered life, in the garden of their country house, fallen from the limbo of the Guadarrama snows, from the silence of solitude, several "times" seemed tangled together in a confusing way, like a net of different meshes she had to walk into. She was approaching life again, and this meant discovering, rediscovering the different times that had enveloped her from childhood to the "age of reason," as a cocoon envelopes a larva. Having almost become unborn, as she was reborn she felt aware of each temporal garment. She was "here," in this time, in how many times? And because this confused her, she vacillated; at some moments she did not know which time to enter or which time she was in already. Some mornings, as she awakened to face the new day, she felt like a dove that's returning to the dovecote and has to enter its hole, but which one? Through which chapter in her life? She had to remember what was happening now, and this was not easy because . . . nothing was really happening; she had merely come back to life. Since she came back with neither project nor personality, refusing the image that becomes mask, and since she wanted to keep on this way, exactly as she saw she was not, she felt keenly aware of those temporal garments, the layers of being thrown over us, by the diverse times and by successive, compartmentalizing time. "I'll start here, set out on the page," as if she were beginning to read the textbook for a required course. And for a fleeting instant she was about to enter one of the holes from the past, from the time when she was a little girl or an adolescent, and in that briefest of instants she even reached a better understanding of something that had stuck in her memory like a lump, a clot—a flash of understanding that she would unravel later or find it would appear to her already unraveled and clear. And at times, such an instant would end before it was over, made even more fleeting by the terror she felt when it seemed she was about to enter the hole of the future, and sight failed her. Something of those instants remained, though, and she was not able to prevent them from giving rise to images, which would appear to her in a dream or slip out in some phrase when she was talking with her family, a phrase she would not be able to explain. That's why her father would just stare at her sometimes, without saying anything, whereas her mother, who must have had the same thing happen to her throughout her entire life, but in a far more intense—more pure—way, would tell her: "So, daughter, you know it too! Because this is what I see." And simply, clearly, her mother would utter forecasts to which her father would listen in silence, because he could neither refute them nor agree with them, and he did not want them to be true. Her mother did not want them to be true either; on the contrary, they grieved her, but she had not been able to stop them. Once her father had said: "And why is it that you, a woman, know these things?" "I don't know, they just occur to me; but look, look carefully, don't you see that?" And there would be some tiny detail the newspaper had published in one of the last sections, a word picked up in passing from a speech delivered by some statesman, and even a faint gesture noticed in a photograph. Then her gentlemanly father would respond: "Well, yes, you're right, you do see more clearly." "Right, no, because it's not a question of being right, of reason; that's how things are going to be." And her "that's how" was rather somber, a disaster that was hovering over Europe and would first hover over Spain, in spite of how well everything was going. And as she said "that's how," her enormous blue eyes would turn green, almost phosphorescent; there were many colors in those eyes—blues, grays, and greens—when her mother allowed herself to speak from her inspirations—as she had observed when she was a little girl, obsessed by their changes. Her mother's black hair would accentuate her rather sunken temples, and her white skin would look pale, as if it were made from something other than flesh; all of her, and she always tended toward a certain incorporeality and seemed very small, although she was rather plump. She would become somehow unreal, but more present than ever, so that she was there as if she had come from another place, from another time, as if her body had not completely materialized or become flesh—it was impenetrable, smooth, and unreal, like a camellia, or like a piece of ancient, unworked marble. And she would fall silent, feeling self-conscious, look at her small, perfectly drawn hands, and raise them like two dove wings: "Oh, if the powerful people in this world would listen every now and then to what no one dares tell them." Her father would smile ironically with a hint of admiration: "Obviously, dear, there are no more sibyls."

The confusion of times. If we lived in just one time, maybe there would be no confusion; if the only time, as she now realized, were the one she had worked so hard to establish for herself: successive time as before, after, now, in a linear way—time, the invention of consciousness. When she read Bergson she was enraptured by his critique of time as an image and likeness of space, by the discovery of *la durée* and intuition, and she felt certain that there is no difference between philosophy and music, that they both do something analogous with time—maybe gather time like a chain, perpetual enchainment, from the surface of consciousness and propose a numeric or verbal system that can make the time-as-succession through which we're dragging ourselves seem like a single instant.

Because we experience the instant, a particular instant, as the end of our striving for an irrepressible aspiration, and this might be explained by the fact that happiness occurs for an instant. But maybe it doesn't; maybe happiness is just forced to take the form of the instant, which is unity in scattered time, transparency in time.

And what we see, when we see, is seen in an instant, and an instant later it's gone. As she rediscovered life, in the garden of the Madrid country house, she experienced the same "discoveries" she had made there in the magic garden of her childhood, although now she was fully conscious, and amazed by what was happening. Now her consciousness was limiting the "magic," and this is why she wanted, would have liked to seize that garden. Because in this garden the "constructions" from the first garden would replace an incipient, quickly demolished construction of thought. She needed to form her own idea of what happens with time, of our adventure in time, now that she had felt and "seen" time arrive as a wrapping even more decisive than the one provided by her body, by being alive, being here. And without a body, which they had reproached her for not taking care of properly, not even taking into account, without a body one would also be "here," if one were wrapped in time. If it were possible to perform an *epoché* of time, at least of successive time, of the numerable instants that follow one after the other, each inscribing, as it passes, the same figure, the same law—before, now, after—if it were possible to be free from this, then you could continue to have your body and still not be here, completely "here." Your intelligence would be free from limitation, since it would not need to foresee, and it would not need to remember or to rely on memory's data. Your spirit would be free from fear and hope, as the Stoics wanted—*Nec spes nec metus,* which means possessing time or being free from its passing, not feeling it.

"Impassivity"—a virtue the Stoics emphasized, although to her it seemed to sum up the entire ancient "philosophic life"—cannot be achieved with respect to passion until it's achieved with respect to time, until the passing of time is not felt. And then even love and hate would be impassive—something, it seemed to her, the mystics achieved in love and certain souls among the defeated in hate—hate that lasts for centuries without showing any sign of life until one day it explodes. Wouldn't such hate be unbearable if it had been felt!

Why did the mystics succeed in abstracting time almost entirely and live in two times or in three, as in the case of Teresa of Avila, whom she had not thought about for a long time, although she had begun to think about her recently?

Maybe it was because Teresa of Avila lived the "instant" in ecstasy, lived historic time through her actions in the world—among worldly things—and also lived the time of meditation. And through Teresa's life one could see clearly the decadence possible in meditation, its "for lack of anything else." And with respect to wanting to achieve or find, in action, the equivalent of the moment of ecstasy, she was now discovering what it is about action that draws people and how action is a form of "ecstasy"—true action, not agitation. This explains the passion revolutionaries felt, or at least some revolutionaries, who were men of thought, of meditation at first, but who abandoned thought and meditation for action, because in action they would no longer feel this "for lack of anything else." Because only ecstasy, in whichever of its forms, seems to exhaust the longing, the expectancy in human life, the waiting that each instant of successive time brings us, the promise that remains unfulfilled as we watch the same law carried out again and again. And this was how she discovered that law means hope disappointed, that what we awaited with respect to time and everything else is larger than the law and goes beyond it—that justice is not enough.

All those things formed the confusion in her mind, particularly at noon in the garden, when she followed the same "rite" she had performed in her childhood; because in this garden there was also a large avenue edged with raspberry and red currant bushes that seemed to collect all by themselves every bit of the sun's warmth, every bit of the noon's slowness. Because "nature" gives us multiple times, various rhythms, slow hours when plants live the life of sleep; plants never wake up completely, and they sink into sleep and abandon the most minimal of struggles, which is vegetal life in its "struggle for life." Botflies, like bumblebees, flies, and ants capitalize on the opportunity this offers; since they're animals, they can mount their night watch at any hour. Only animals fed by their masters can allow themselves the luxury of returning to nature while they sleep, like Watteau's marchionesses; because animals, human animal included, that enjoy the luxury of a highly advanced civilization can return to this time of natural sleep, which follows solar rhythm and air temperature. An animal like the ant, the bumblebee, or the fragile ladybug, which must earn its living, must be awake and "capitalize." This is the animal's primary rebellion, its dissent from Paradise, something of which remains almost intact in plants. And she was emerging at that hour, following the principles of her childhood, following the first law of her soul, in search of a way to go deeper and deeper into a universe of defeated, sleeping plants. She pursued them, but not like an animal out hunting, an animal in pursuit, because only rarely did she hurriedly break a raspberry apart and put one of its tiny sections in her mouth, and if she did, it was to feel the earth purified in that flavor—the earth permeated and transfused with sun—and dreamily enter its world, its time.

And this gave her a way to enter the time flowing beneath consciousness, where being forms without agitation—the time of the vegetable world where there is not even a hint of consciousness, because no consciousness is needed.

Vegetable things do not have to be attentive, because they do not move; their growth occurs inside. Since man does move and man is alone, because he is outside, because he has been born, because he is "here," man must be attentive, because he still has to move inside himself among his multiple times. And if he is born slowly, he can feel and see how he emerges gradually into this "here." Would the plant notice this if it were born even more slowly? Maybe the plant has been born? Isn't it "inside," completely inside, without ever having experienced the agitation of emerging into the outside? Yes, this must be what Max Scheler means when he says that man is the only living thing not adapted perfectly to any environment. Ortega had stressed this emphatically, using Max Scheler's long commentary as an introduction to an idea of his own. Yes, in Scheler she was sure to find the secret of the confusion of times and the anguish, the feeling of frustration, that would invade her after the momentary ecstasy among the plants; it was as if she had reached the garden and the gates had opened slightly for her, but then only an instant later she was out, outside, aware now that she had been rejected.

She was fleeing human time. It seemed to her that it was all she had ever done in her whole life: flee the human, retreat from successive time with its obligations and attention to other people, and even more, retreat from time as a pact, or the result of a pact, made after one has tasted solitude. Love must be the search for a way to go deeper and deeper beyond consciousness, in the world of dreaming, to approach hand in hand the gates of the inexorably walled, only half-open garden: an instant when one brims with certainty, feeling that doubt has been abolished forever, and tunneling into being itself—into the intact secret. Nothing occurs there, which is why it seems eternal, as the clichés proclaim, because a person believes he has reached the opening at the end of the center of the "being" that never emerged outside the unborn. But then he must return to the world of the born, and he is different now; and then there will be living together, which means adapting to and in circumstances, collaborating now with the time of "outside," and after that . . . after that comes judgment, doubt, uncertainty, and even *Non serviam*.

Friendship corresponds to meditation, to the life of consciousness; it is walking together, being awake together, or at the same time. At the same time, but not in the same time, as in love, which, were it to be realized, would be living an identical time. And how can a time be identical, how can identity occur in time, no longer inside time, but in time itself? To fuse both times or descend to one time, that of dreaming, where being forms, as in plants—this must be what people expect of love, what they pursue, and what a person can never be sure he's attained, since the only expressions of love we know are the "classics," which are hard to understand. And besides, love flows into poetry, and poetry has its history, albeit an "internal one." This means that love has already been objectified; and which part of this objectified expression corresponds to the history of style and which part to the truth of the event? The loves most expressed are the ones least lived, the ones not realized. What does anyone know about the happy loves? Love would have been achieved from within, in the silence of being, and being neither needs nor permits expression, just as the plant does not express itself because its being coincides with its dreaming, is a dream realized, and this is how fulfilled love should be—free of history.

Because there are no histories of love, even though they have consumed so many pages of printed literature; love is really outside history. What emerges into history is nothing but the suffering caused by the absence of love, its frustration, or its trace; and love itself is invisible, like the "beloved" of Saint John's *Cántico;* we know it through the glow in the eyes of some lovers, through a particular distance we feel separating us from the pairs of lovers that are always protected by a *Noli me tangere,* even among friends, and in this they resemble fruits and flowers, because they are not in step with us, even though they live in our midst, because their thoughts are always elsewhere, or rather, because they aren't thinking about anything, or about something we consider nothing.

And if love were this—living in an identical time—it would lead to death or would already include death, it would be having died already or not having to die, to have passed or to be passing through death and life at the same time. One identical time would hold life and death. And the entire universe as well. How could words have spurted through, through what fissure? At most they are nouns, like St. John's "My beloved, the mountains."

And now she was feeling that in this "live the instant," which was engrossing so many of the best people, and was the watchword of the moment, there was the longing to free oneself from successions, to shed the past, and to be left innocent—the exasperating search for innocence in "this culture," after three centuries of exasperation from living according to one's "conscience." And there was the longing to emerge from oneself, to live outside oneself, a running to embrace something that will fill the void to overflowing, that will put an end to longing and the torment caused by a hope that cannot find a scenario, or by a scenario people have placed impossibly far away. "Here and now" seemed to be the young people's motto, and through it they understood each other in spite of any political creed—when there was one—and across borders. They were out to conquer lost time, the instant, a form of the alchemists' philosopher's stone, the "blue flower" of the German Romantics, and, in a "secular" and therefore more modest form, to conquer the Holy Grail. Won't Europe, won't we Westerners, always have to be looking for a lost treasure, a drop of divine blood, a drop of original time?

And so she ended up with just a few notes, only an outline, for the novel she would have written as a way of trying to explain to her father the "confusion" of times, the multiple times in which she had been submerging herself. Without a scenario, a plot, she meant; without passions, because this would be the passion—the passion in multiple times, the one that makes it impossible for us to be understood by either plants or animals or . . . friends, or truly to be understood by anyone. In order for this to happen, you must be "outside yourself" or very much within, but not in this to and fro, this shuffling, this coming and going from the greatest depth of your soul where almost nothing penetrates, from the lake of calm and quietude to the shock that lets us know we are among "other" beings who also live in a time—theirs. This explains why nothing draws people together like belonging to a single generation, which is a form of time, a time that's external, circumstantial in a particular way, that's in a kind of temporal wrapping. The same can be said of something almost the opposite: domestic, intimate, familial time in the continuity of shared shelter, of life in the same burrow, where the memory of the dead, even the dead not yet known, of the ancestors, is as real as the presence of the living—immemorial time that hovers around atemporality, the memory of feeling the presence of a common ancestor who was and is, who will not let us break away totally, be born totally to the solitude of the individual. The ancestor who promises we will not die alone.

Yes, the novel about the multiplicity of times, a sort of journey of the soul accompanied by consciousness, remained unwritten. How lucid it would have needed to be, and how humble, so as not to cast her shadow! It would have been something like a descent to hell, to "the deep caverns of feeling," where one begins to feel time, which is a sort of hell; and any bit of purity we retain, the poor larva of something better, an original seed, so eager that its eagerness opens it to the hell of temporality, hurls itself into those depths. And when that hell calms down and community, the time of the soul lets one feel more settled . . . because the most horrible thing about time is feeling it by oneself, being alone with the rush of time . . . hell. Could this be it, just this? And through the soul, in the soul, we feel community, communication in any case; which is why the person who goes to hell has lost his soul, has been stripped of the milieu in which he found himself with everyone else, not only with people like himself but with all zones of reality, with the whole universe. That "milieu" which man lacks, according to Max Scheler and Ortega, might well be what people have called soul—a milieu conducive to demonstrations, a place where humans and creatures gather together and their order becomes clear, because "milieu" comprises order as well as things. And nothing that presents itself to man seems real unless it occurs in an order, a relationship; she had wept with happiness when she found this, suddenly like that, in the first pages of a book she had "stolen" from her father's library and read just as she was on the threshold of adolescence: Ortega's *Meditations on Quijote.*

To lose one's soul is to lose time, shared time, and then the heart will be left alone with its beating, the larva throbbing alone in its temporal hell.

That's why we feel ourselves drawn to the time where everyone else lives and moves, because we're afraid of hell, of time by ourselves. And there are

certain marches that mark shared time and rhythm. Each age and each generation has its own march, and we feel so drawn to that march that we'll go anywhere, because the important thing is to march together, to march *with,* until
death.

   She could not write the novel that would unravel the confusion of those
times. She did not have a clear enough perspective on things, and she did not
have the time either—now that the luxury afforded by her illness had run out.
She was almost completely well; she could emerge, and during the summer she
had spoken in public without suffering any ill effects. She could begin to march.

Return to the City

I

Finally she could emerge, go out and walk along the streets, march to the rhythm of the crowds. But she walked slowly, as if she were under water, as if she were floating, not in the air but among the people. She seemed to be a foreigner and someone offered her the *Guía de Madrid*. "The Guide to Madrid" . . . How curious! Spain is very labyrinthine, but it's always offering guides. Maybe for lack of something else? Maimonides's *Guía de los perplejos* (Guide for the Perplexed), Father Granada's guide for sinners are like so many classics—nothing but guides—even if their titles suggest something else: Ganivet's *Spain, an Invitation* for walking the rugged terrain of Spain's subhistory, its everlasting prehistory; Unamuno's *Vida de Don Quijote y Sancho (Life of Don Quijote and Sancho);* Ortega's *Meditations on Quijote;* and the other guide, the most Spanish of them all, Saint Teresa's *Las moradas (Interior Castle),* all the "dwellings" through which men and Our Lord had made her pass. There is so much charity in every dwelling and in her gesture, as she holds out to her fellow man the ladder of experience to be climbed laboriously! But will it help us; do these dwellings really help us? Won't we either have to inhabit each of our own "dwellings"—so that one day, near death, even if we're young, we ourselves will be able to hold out that ladder lucidly and assuredly—or be forced to sink without leaving the double trace of the ladder's passion and understanding?

She did not know why she shivered as she was offered the guide, because suddenly she did feel foreign, standing there in front of the "native" offering it to her so generously, albeit not without a touch of irony. But of course! Maybe he could tell she was Spanish and had gotten lost.

Not lost, though, since she remembered and even if she had not remembered . . . even among "our own" we have the right to get lost, without being lost; getting lost among our own people means, can mean, clearing a new path or retrieving a forgotten tradition, because one can never know for sure that the national "heretic" is not faithful to the first man, maybe to the first man of all, who is fighting to recover his voice and place in history. Maybe Spanish history, because of its sheer magnitude, has not been entirely faithful to that native, the indigenous man, the first and last, and the essential man, who is also the protagonist of history? Is it not possible for a glorious, apocryphal, or partly apocryphal, history to exist within the realm of human possibility—even human possibility, where everything is possible? And what about everywhere else, in Europe, for example? And in the world to come and the world that was? Doesn't man, this falsified man, have to appear time and time again before his apocryphal "evangelists" to demand what is said and understood to be "human" and in truth justly belongs to men?

Walking along amid such thoughts, time after time she would run into people walking past her, the people who owned the streets and the city, whether they were natives or not, because they were not returning from another time, as she was, because they had not been alone and were not suffering from a hunger for community. It was hard for her to approach any one of them, *one,* and say: "Tell me, how are you? You've been alive all this time, you've been living all this time without any interruption; tell me, how's life?"

She never did this, of course, but from time to time, as if led by something uncontrollable, an occasional man and even an occasional woman would speak to her, just to talk, "for no reason," or if they had one, it soon escaped them. And she couldn't help answering them. One day in the subway a man started to talk to her; he turned out to be close to one of the leaders she knew, and he ended by telling her: "Señorita, I don't know who you are, but here in Spain everything is going to change, everything, and more than 'they' think. If on that day you need someone, call me; I'm here at your service, I'll be there for whatever you want, because I know you deserve it." And he added something else: "For anything that might come up for you, because we're going to go 'beyond,' I mean things will go 'beyond.'"

What was this "beyond"? Maybe the same one as always, the one Spaniards sense when they wake up, feeling they've been hurled toward some "beyond." For is it worth moving, initiating any action at all, "unless you intend to go beyond?" This is the mark of Spanish affairs—either they don't move or they go beyond whatever is known, visible, prudent, run the whole risk. What did that man know, what could he know? What was already happening down there in the subhistory that had been still for so long? More than ancient hunger, it was hope stirring, hope launched in search of a scenario.

The "group" had scattered and the young people's life had taken on a different configuration. Active groups had sprung up within the Federación Universitaria, organized only to the extent action required; and this action was poetic, totally invented. That's why it was constant. No political actions were planned. This was something more serious; an ambience was being created, an atmosphere that was gradually enveloping the life of the city and of other Spanish cities. There was a magazine and an underground literature whose tone was always humorous, sports were very popular, and there was a great upsurge in the life of the city, in the movie houses, and in the cafés; and almost daily something would happen, something that would be effective because people found it amusing.

And this happy time was a sort of community; everyone felt they were floating in a sort of slight intoxication. No one was thinking; "they" no more thought of defending themselves than "we" thought about attacking. It was not a revolution but an evolution of natural "time," like the rhythm of the seasons; you only had to do what you do when you hear the strains of a music that turns out to be your own: follow it, follow the music in the air of life.

Because signs, voices were arriving from all over. Without any propaganda, with barely a few small clandestine leaflets passed from hand to hand: the "Pages of Freedom" that Unamuno, a feudal lord in exile, tossed toward his country from Hendaye; the leaflets distributed by the FUE; and above all, words, gestures, even the way people walked—something was changing.

"And if those in command had known about this," they would have paid attention to the rhythm people assumed as they walked along the street, the rhythm of human steps resounding on the pavement.

Because the rhythm was changing; this was neither the illusion produced in someone like herself, whose rhythm was slower, nor the rebirth of life in the city as people returned from their summer vacations. The change was coming from farther away. She remembered the Madrid of her childhood, the terrible Sunday afternoons and the even more terrible afternoons of holidays. She could still hear the feet dragging along the sidewalks, and they evoked fallen arms, empty faces, as if life were terribly heavy, and not life but the weight of a void that hindered one's movements and made them seem useless—the worst kind of tiredness. She remembered that lack of rhythm, the way people dragged themselves along, and that void with its shrill stifled sounds, a motionless air ripped by piercing, dissonant trumpets.

Spain, Spaniards have accomplished two types of historical actions and on a scale that was surely gigantic: one, resistance; the other, discovery and incorporation. Resistance to Rome, to the point of suicide. Conquest, reconquest of the Arabs. Until that moment, in other words, until January 2, 1492, the history made by Spain was of a kind that produces no remorse. Resisting and recovering are two fundamental actions of life, the life of someone who exists, who stands tall.

They're part of the "naturalness" found in history, of the actions people perform inexorably, also virginally. Up to this point no nation has "sinned," and the "crime of having been born" does not appear. This is how things must have been for faith to be born, fused with a clear idea in Isabel's case and blindly for men who had never seen the sea until they embarked on the conquest of an enigma: faith is a display of confidence, of life affirming itself because it feels free, unburdened by the weight of the past.

Unlimited confidence was not the only thing found in that "adventurous" undertaking to discover the New World. There was also a belief, with its corresponding image, in the universality of the universe, a belief that provides both the supposition and the horizon toward which a person innocently directs his will. At that moment, when Spanish unity was forged and the great myth of the discovery of the New World turned out to be true, the state was "built," born in view of and for the purpose of universality and constituted with universality in mind, a state whose first step broadened the Law received from Rome in order to include a world Rome had not foreseen.

Would it not have been enough to go forward, in keeping with a birth certificate as pure as history permits? Apparently history does not permit this. "National Unity" had to be consolidated with the expulsion of the Jews and with the establishment of the Holy Office of the Inquisition—in other words, with violence. And doesn't the use of violence inevitably lead to some loss of freedom?

Must any unity involving humanity always be accomplished through violence rather than spontaneity? Apparently it is not possible, it was not possible then, to attain a "natural" human history, a spontaneously occurring order, the maturity of a nation, in the same way a fruit ripens in nature, where fulfillment is attained because the heavens intervene at a preplanned, protective moment.

The man who lives at rare moments, such as the moment of the almost immaculate birth of the Spanish state, should allow himself to enjoy his ability to perceive, rather, enjoy his inability not to perceive, the difference between times—between his personal time and historical time—and an even more subtle difference between the time of the history he has created and history's time. Every history must be lived in its entirety as a unity in whatever feat is being accomplished or event is taking place—instants in which man must live within history as a plant lives within the cycle of the seasons; any agitation must be barely perceptible, because nothing resembles quietude more than action completely carried out when its own time, its own precise moment has come, and in a world that offers it almost no resistance.

This is history's high tide: no matter how great an effort some people are forced to make, they will probably not have the feeling that they're sustaining history but that history is sustaining them; although this may not provide an explanation either, because it would mean that people were fully aware of what they were doing, and such awareness only comes with disillusionment.

Innocence, spontaneity, time when it's become almost undivided, when it's close to a unity that pulls the past into the present and erases the future as something one can count on: to experience this is to approach paradise, the figure of life that paradise represents for man's eyes, at least Western eyes. When Western man becomes aware of his nostalgia, he creates poetry or music, and sometimes he even thinks. People have also searched for paradise in history, yes, even in history, and even in history they have apparently found themselves for brief, fleeting moments—paradise, which is life in unity, in a single time, ecstasy, or action, lasts for one moment.

And afterward? Right at that moment? What was causing her sense of irreality, of history turned nightmare? She knew it was not a question of being deceived because she knew "the immediate data of her experiences" were not deceiving her: the parades she had watched as a child, when Spain's African Army marched past the palace—the little soldiers with sunken, sparkling eyes and yellow skin stuck to their bones, trying not to drag their feet as they walked in front of the palace—where a tiny figure waved from an inside balcony; it was Princess Isabel, "the Chata" or "Snub-nose," as people called her with a familiarity that showed how much they loved her, and she was alone because "the rest of them" had not appeared. No one would appear to receive that sad parade, nor would any rider, mounted on a white horse with a wreath of laurels around its neck advance alone to the front of the parade—this was the horse of general Pinto, who had died at Barranco del Lobo, in the slaughter inflicted by the Moors. No one would appear, not even the people. A few groups of women had come with small bouquets of live-forevers and branches of laurel, which they gave to the soldiers. One of the soldiers offered the maid who had taken her to the palace the branch he was holding in the only hand he had left: "Here, sweetheart, for you!" as if at that moment, as he entered his country, sick and mistreated, he understood for the first time the symbol of glory his country had held out to him—as if he were returning from the victory of Lepanto, as if he had been Miguel de Cervantes, as if Cervantes had been so fortunate. And did someone appear after Lepanto, as someone is supposed to? They have always told us that someone did, and so, yes, someone certainly must have appeared—Philip II. He was "someone," and someone who always appeared when he was supposed to to make an appearance; but then what happened, Lord, what happened to us that we returned so soon and so defeated and from so faraway?

And now, now the man who had struck up a conversation with her very naturally in the subway so he could talk with her about "historical" things, had given her a warning: "Señorita, we're going beyond." "Plus Ultra" once more?

II

She was talking one sun-gilded September afternoon, one of the last afternoons she spent in Ciudad Lineal, with a colleague from the old group who had
been very friendly toward her. He was neither a university student nor a worker;
but he spoke about the workers, and increasingly on their behalf, because he
worked in the offices of an important railroad company where he was surrounded by workers. In her group he had worked passionately, intelligently, and
effectively, his Marxism—he said—temporarily set aside; he was a communist
who had not joined the party, since there was not exactly one to join, and he said
it wasn't the right moment either. And the truth is, it seemed he had been able
to set "Marxism" aside without much difficulty. He had read a little bit of Marx
but more of Engels, whom he said he preferred. Now he felt the time had come
for him to separate from her group, and this was painful for him, especially to
separate from her, and he had expected her to take a different position, because
she was a university student but not an intellectual. "You, who are so involved in
life." "Me, involved in life? It must be because I've been close to death," she said
to herself, because to speak of death would have been incomprehensible:
death . . . like love, does not exist—neither does pain, only work, marching together, and serving the total unity that embraces us and frees us from being me
alone, from private life, from the false intimacy of the bourgeois family . . . no;
the individual must become integrated into society through a different kind of
relationship. "Don't you understand?" Well, yes, she did understand, in other
words she understood as poorly as he did, since what had drawn them together
when they were working within the group were things that involved feeling,
things they agreed about; the difficulty arose in the interpretation of feeling.
Those were the two reasons they had spent so much time together before she
got sick, talking incessantly and agreeing infallibly, when there was no "theory"
to come between them. They agreed about the joy of serving others, serving
everyone, anonymously, and above all those "others" meant everyone who was
hungry and thirsty for justice and bread, for bread, Lord! They also agreed about
not spending their youth acquiring a "personality" or even securing a position:
professorships, jobs, promotions were petty things. Not a job but a destiny and
not an individual destiny but one inseparable from the common destiny they had
to build with their sheer hard work. "Don't you see," she would sometimes say
to him, this is all something religious; you can't deny that you have a religious
soul; at another time . . . " "Don't say any more," he would cut her off, "what
does that have to do with it? I'm living now, in my time, in 'our time'; established
religion is useless to me, and I don't want to get lost searching for another one.
Besides, religion's not something you invent." "I agree about that, religion can't
be invented, but it's something you can have without being aware of it; because
the soul exists, you know, and we're given our souls with our traditions and cul-

tures stamped on them, and besides, the soul has a configuration, the soul is not inert . . . and within the soul a movement of the soul's very own carries it out of itself, prompts it to emerge from itself, and if it doesn't, why . . . ?" "Stop, I tell you, you have to get over being metaphysical, for when there's no longer a class struggle and we're already . . . "Then she would be the one to interrupt him: "In Paradise." "No, here on earth, but really here, when the best of us have stopped looking up at the sky and thus letting them take advantage, control, and exploit." "Yes, 'here' on earth, yes, I agree that we're earth's inhabitants, but you believe that some day we'll see the abolishment of . . . well, hope, which is what can surpass everything, and to say hope is to say yes to freedom, dissatisfaction, and more—unappeasable longing, hunger that always returns.' And sometime she would dare: "You don't believe, don't see, that the revolution has been nourished by Christian souls, the souls of Christians exasperated because here and now we are not in the kingdom of charity, where everything is shared . . . sharing bread and soul, you know? not being alone, not even to die." "But back up," he would say, "don't go off so far." And she remembered now, although it was impossible to tell him, that he would reproach her for wanting to go beyond, because that's how their arguments had always ended, with him taking her to task in an effort to make her "come back" from so far away, where she had landed in one jump.

Now, that afternoon, it was clearly the last time they would talk this way. There was something inaccessible about him, a reproach of her that had built up, as if everything that had separated them before but not caused a rift had now solidified, a reproach that materialized in a repeated accusation: "You, who aren't like them, the intellectuals—you, who, a person with so much life, refuse to come to the place where real life is."

Real life; no doubt this was what had gotten them into so many heated discussions—their different understandings of it, their ability to agree only about the present—the moment—but not about the past or about the future; and real life encompasses everything . . . They had not talked much about history, but now she remembered a fragmented argument, how he had looked sullen, grim, and it was already impossible for her to understand him. He had never been like that; on the contrary, sometimes he had told her with a smile: "No, at bottom you can't bear to see religion attacked. You know I'm not obsessed by this like those republicans who are holdovers from the last century and like people God has made 'atheists,' but sometimes I'm about to say something and I stop myself. I'm telling you, because I don't want to hurt you." And one day when she acquiesced to his words, he attacked her directly: "But why won't you let us talk about that too? We can discuss it." She could not discuss it, though; silence clutched her throat. Discuss it! Do people discuss something that hurts so much it pierces their souls? And now that he'd become so distant, discussion seemed even more impossible, because she knew that playing games with and against reason doesn't reveal but hides certain parts of life, the thing they call "spirit," a word she did not like to use, but what else could she call it, especially with a layman? She also remembered one day that he noticed how she shrank back as he referred contemptuously to "feudalism." She had let herself go that time, maybe as a kind of compensation, thinking there was no reason not to . . . But she had felt something tense up in his soul: "But talk about it, tell me, what do *you* think of feudalism? Why does it bother you if I attack feudalism? You know very well that the large landowners . . . " "But *you* know very well that the large landowners represent the decadence and perhaps the betrayal of feudalism; of course I'm not going to say feudalism should return, although to some extent it should, maybe we should even rescue its meaning, but I don't know, I really don't know." "Keep on, keep talking to me." "No, I can't, the reasons don't come to me, and maybe there are no reasons for everything I feel; maybe it's a question of something in one's blood."

And now maybe this was what separated them, the unspoken reasons behind the "things of the spirit" and the "things that were in one's blood" that had solidified, as reasons tend to do when they're not expressed clearly. In this case it was her fault, because she had not known how or not been able to reason things out all the way. And reasons are not inert matter that becomes attenuated as it crystallizes. No, crystals formed from unspoken reasons are indissoluble poison. She watched him as he walked away from her, and she felt it would be forever; with his back hunched slightly, his black hair sticking up like a crest, and his chin sunk down, he looked like a large eaglet returning with a wound, instead of the prey it had expected, to its nest, its high tower where it watched over the horizons of the future. And he left her with an accusation: "You have so much life, but you refuse to participate in real life."

Vitality . . . real life. What difference was there between them?

Real life, yes, real life was what she wanted, although she did not dare to call it that, and it was the only thing she was looking for. She had even given up philosophy for it, had given up all her projects; she had accepted being "here" completely. The rest would come in addition. "Here is here—one's circumstances." "I am myself and my circumstances," she had read some time ago in Ortega's *Meditations on Quijote,* which had been published about 1914. Now she felt she had understood it: making a decision to be here, accepting the circumstances—the multiple, confused times—meant accepting "the confusion of times," too and the will to clarify them; the confusion would gradually clear up, if one was loyal. Isn't accepting the circumstances also a question of loyalty? The loyalty Ortega himself had called "authenticity," life lived in truth, a modest truth, a moral truth for which we can answer. This is what she wanted to adhere to, something for which she could answer; and she would face up to her life, her own life, as it was happening to her here and now. She would accept it, yes, but she would not limit it beforehand by describing a circle; no, she would not create the circumstances, and she would not moderate them by cutting off one of the multiple times that had arisen for her, cutting herself off inside the things she had lived "authentically." Is a person guilty if instants of the time that belongs to death, or rather, the time that belongs to dying, slip into the time that belongs to life? "Death" means something has already been completed; not "dying," though, for dying can very well be here and now in life. Because it seemed to her that she was filled with dawn, with life—life, provided life was open to its horizon uncharted by any human geometer—, mysterious, clear life, daughter of the cipher that represents a mathematics, which, like reality, was something she could not love if it was not inexhaustible.

She had not been able to tell this to the brotherly colleague walking away inexorably; it was useless, because he would have said that he already had authenticity, loyalty, loyalty . . . It was useless. She continued to think about it a little more, remembering the atmosphere when they talked sometimes but forgot about "theories." And she saw the two of them as they had been, and it was a bit as if in truth they were looking for just one thing, which was difficult to name, but its name had come to her spontaneously: sacrifice, they were victims in search of sacrifice. And the insurmountable abyss arising for her must have existed because they wanted to sacrifice themselves before different gods: in his case, the future made eternal present; in hers, a present that would open into an eternal future and save the past. Please, God, don't let anything of what has truly been be lost! It would have been entirely useless, though, if she had called out to tell him that; he might have begun by rejecting the idea of "sacrifice," and, if he accepted it, he would have delivered an even more relentless accusation against her, saying something like: "Yes, that's it, you're going to sacrifice yourself to the past, whereas I . . . " No; it was useless.

Some friends and colleagues were back now from their summer vacations, and some of them weren't as close to the group now, because they had joined or simply become associated with one of the incipient political parties, or they were looking for self-renewal and now felt the weight of specific tasks. The imminence of what was coming forced a person to take sides, to act with a greater sense of commitment; you could say that some part of their youth was coming to an end. She could not think, though, she did not want to think—to project—but to obey. And so in one respect she returned to the classes she had barely just begun to teach at the Instituto Escuela. This was her only responsibility, and one she found so fascinating that fulfilling it left no trace of effort; it was not a job, and since it didn't feel like work, she worked, truly worked. Her friends took her to a tea room, a sort of crypt, where the students of the Federación Universitaria met one day a week. There she met up with some of her colleagues from before and got to know some new ones; and she noticed that the tone had changed—it was more vital, passionate, truly passionate because of a large strike that had broken out in the university and spread uncontrollably to several universities in the provinces, and they responded more spiritedly than one would have expected, some of them on their own initiative, although in connection with the universities in Madrid. Now, with the school year starting, university life was resuming; but there were no classes at all for her to attend because her professors were still away. She did have the university atmosphere, along with the "vital" comradeship of her colleagues and a task that had been entrusted to her—that of writing something . . . here too the rhythm of things had changed.

Everything had changed in a year. One of the first fall afternoons, she went to visit her Cuban friend at her home. The young woman lived with her parents, way at the end of Serrano Street, in a bourgeois neighborhood very far from her own neighborhood, which was both seignorial and popular and was right in the heart of Madrid—the Madrid of Calderón's *autos,* of Quevedo, of the old palaces, the kings, and the popular festivals. The rhythm of the Salamanca district, where her friend lived, had changed too, although not as much, with its tea rooms and few stores, its mansions inhabited by the modern aristocracy and the "upper bourgeoisie." When she got there, she was still feeling a little numb after the long seclusion that had become a part of her, as is common after the concentration that comes from solitude, which is a type of condemnation: "a vitality greater than life." And all the extremely intense preoccupations of her own life, the conversations with her future brother-in-law and her father, her mother's prophetic-sounding visions, everything in that garden on the margin of real was amassing in her mind, isolating her from the life everyone else would have led "together." When one lives an intensely separate life, one is clothed in a kind of cold air that isolates a person from others, and one feels eager, even rushes to enter a vibrant atmosphere, to feel the vibration of people who have not been alone. And the warm, welcoming world of that Cuban-Spanish home was good for her—the girl's hospitality, the life overflowing from her heart and even from her young body. They had just returned from a beach in the French Basque country, and she seemed to have brought back some of the happiness of French life "in which everything was possible," as she said; "every way of being" is possible, and no one gets lost there, since they save anything at all because of whatever value it has—everything; and "if you lived there, what you would become and what you would be already would be saved too." "But I don't want to be anything, you know." "Yes, I realize that I'm back in Spain. Here even people who are something do not want to be anything; of course this means that one day, suddenly, and without anyone who isn't in on the secret suspecting it, something magnificent happens, and then, without having wanted to be anything, they find themselves being everything." She had been born in France and raised in Spain; her mother was the perfect example of a Creole woman, full of calm and maternal tenderness. When she went back to her own house carrying a toy animal made of rags, her mother said: You've obviously been with some people from down there, from the South; they don't plague a person with 'problems' but offer true hospitality." She'd arranged to go with them, planned for them to take her—that's how she felt, that she had to be taken everywhere—to see a marvelous new invention: the talkies.

She went without feeling much enthusiasm, afraid of the change that was making the shadows talk, because film was her art. "Respect me, I was born with the cinema," Rafael Alberti had written at about that time. She had come to film when she was an adult; it was the art of our time, and she loved it passionately because film was abstract, even if in a concrete way, since it made you see, gave your eye another pupil, brought freedom from the gaze and even from dreams. In the wake of that world of dreams bestowed, film must have roused dreams never defined, perusing passions and landscapes and gestures, the very gestures of the earth, that's how it all seemed to her—something like the great earthly documentary. The face of the planet. And now it was necessary to see film immediately, to see it anew. But she was afraid that once the silence of those shadows was broken the spell would be broken too.

Fortunately the shadows did not talk; they were "white shadows in the southern seas," and the new development amounted to nothing more than the synchronization of music and gestures, which is exactly what life should be: a fiesta.

If that's the way it were, if life emanated from its own music . . . But, isn't that how life is? Doesn't life have its own music, and more, in this age of the machine? Machines had always intrigued her because they "have" music and because they're precise; one goes with the other. Only precision can produce music—music or silence. So when something achieves perfection, whatever perfection means with respect to that thing, it has music. She had been surprised so often to find herself hearing a song from way in the past when she rode the subway, just as she was drifting into its void, its dash between blank walls, as if the noise from the engine and the cars were uncovering that song as they slid into the void, as if they were making it spring up inside her, as if a gap that was usually closed were half-opening, a crevice in the cave where her insides worked incessantly, like machines, and you could hear their secret, silent music, a mixture of moaning and joyful singing, an indecipherable, sweet secret that erases our fear of the dark, which is apparently the first homeland we have. We are made up of many parts, but consciousness is the only part of it with no music, since consciousness concentrates on the flow of time, as if all we needed to do was surrender to time, to any of the multiple times we inhabit, and we would hear the music of that time. Consciousness is the only part of our makeup that does not sing, as if, on the contrary, one of its tasks were to silence the moaning, clamoring, traitorous voices—to silence the signs sent from the half-open hell, the echo of a remote paradise. But even here in "historic time," an uncontrollable music always breaks out—from people's footsteps in the street, from the tone of their voices, from what they say and how they say it, from their movements and even from their gestures. Consciousness would need nothing more than a keen ear—what makes the ear keen is a well-hidden center of silent harmony—and it could size up the changes that have occurred and the ones now brewing in history, consciousness could hear the future as it forms.

In Madrid people were listening to a different music now. There had always been music in Madrid life, as there is in the lives of all great cities. This was a Mozart-like music, which a few "masters" of the popular theater called *género chico*, transcribed faithfully at the end of the nineteenth century and the beginning of the twentieth. At that atonal moment when Spain was collapsing, Madrid's heart, and to some extent the heart of the entire country, continued to beat thanks to generous doses of the bracing *género chico*. Now the music heard in the street was the music heard everywhere: American rhythms, the expression of a discontinuous vitality broken by constant syncopation, and in the future, perhaps people will find the sign of our times in the obsessive syncopation of that highly abstract American music. And you could also hear cloying Argentine tangos and a few Spanish songs playing discreetly, almost timidly.

The life of the city, however, exhaled its own music, a sound that was getting louder and continually growing sharper—a certain melody, a rhythm that was moving toward *presto,* a sort of *allegro alla marcia* that was just barely suggested . . .

Maybe she was imagining this. But that's how it felt to her as she walked home after leaving the theater. She had not wanted them to walk with her, she wanted to listen to the music of the city, because she lived from her ears, from the things that enter through our ears—words and music, those she trusted. Of course always and before there was light, her magnet. And light goes through changes too.

Maybe she imagined this as well, but that's how she pictured it: Madrid's diaphanous, defining, almost miraculous light had become more vibrant, less distant from human life, and it shared in something of that heightened musical pitch; maybe there was simply more life, more vitality, and the light scattered in a different way. When a whole crowd of people crawl along lacking any vitality, the light seems to lap at their silhouettes the way it laps at a beggar, or mistreated animals, or a sad man, sliding over them without splintering into reflections, without starting to sparkle a bit, making us see that they're all opaque.

Today's crowds are opaque—neutral, devoid of both glitter and rags. As Spain's glory faded, tatters, the glory associated with ruins, disappeared. There are no ruins in Madrid either, and there were none then. Madrid had been busy bringing itself up to date by modernizing its construction technique and hygiene. And of course it's true that Madrid had not experienced the most glorious days of Spain's history, which had left their mark on other, now provincial cities, with their rundown mansions, their wretched narrow streets between walls guarding magnificent gardens, as in Castile, where no one expects gardens. Glory, historic splendor, always leaves its traces in ruins, in irregular spaces, in jaggedness and even abysses of squalor and splendor. There was no glory in Madrid, which Philip II made the capital of Spain, something that apparently had to do with Madrid's proximity to the monastery of the Escorial in San Lorenzo. You could say that whenever Philip II, lord par excellence, needed to speak with his God in secret, he went to San Lorenzo, as if from the secular city to the sacred city adjoining, and finally he stayed there, abandoning Madrid to the palatines and bureaucrats. And the Villa had taken its rise to Court in stride easily, as if it knew that Madrid deserved this in spite of everything, and that one day it would be proved. Madrid had proved it quite some while later on May 2, 1808, when it rose like a sea against Napoleon. Because Madrid's movements are oceanic, even though the city is set on the meseta, on the plateau; it roils like waves, overflows, and then shrinks like the sea, which seems uncontainable but retreats, shrugging its shoulders, withdrawing into itself . . . until another wave comes.

And these ocean-like movements appear in Velázquez's horses. For instance, in the horse placed in front of the royal palace—which should have served as a warning to the lord who lived inside; its four hooves are suspended in the air against a backdrop of clouds, and its flowing tail bears the animal's full weight, supposedly thanks to Galileo's calculations. And you saw them in Madrid's women, especially the ones who still wore shawls, the ones quivering with cold, curling and coiling themselves up but then disappearing with curvilinear, water-like movements. And you see similar movements in the men, the erect, steady Madrid natives who veer around sharply when something offends them, turning disdainfully in profile the way the sea pulls back its waves when it reaches an unappealing shore. You also saw them in the noise of Madrid crowds at the bull fights, at the theater, in the cafes—like a piece of the sea pent up in a cave, or roaring in the bull ring, echoing against the walls the way the sea echoes in the hollows of the cliffs. These sea-like sensations must have been even greater in the eighteenth century, in the days of the "manolas" and the "chisperos," a sort of ocean fauna—Neptune's children who flocked together beneath his fountain.

That's why in Madrid people search the horizon for the sea, around Rosales, and also from the Ronda de Atocha and the Paseo de Trajineros, which seem so much like ports, docks. They search for it. One of Galdós's characters would walk off his hangovers near the Prado, hallucinating the sea, lost in a delirious "interior monologue." People search Madrid for the sea, and they look for the sea because they sense it.

It's Madrid's soul, the soul of the city, a mouth to the sea opening in the center of the peninsula; it has its tides, and high tide was starting to come in. But peoples, like oceans, have their extraordinary tides, the ones they don't expect. This was the tide you could feel growing now.

And she made an effort to cover Madrid every day, walking endlessly, although not unenthusiastically, because she was afraid her pleasure might soon come to an end—the pleasure of feeling immersed in that atmosphere of sea-like vitality, being splashed from time to time by some wave in the crowd, receiving a jab from some elbow and then a curved gesture of rectification, a kind of bow: "Excuse me, señorita, I hadn't noticed you." She liked to watch the gas lamps begin to glimmer along one of the wide avenues because it brought to her soul a moment in Málaga, a moment when she was very young and that glimmer had taken her by surprise; perhaps it was the first time she had seen this, and at the same instant she felt a salty drop from the dark of the sea—a sort of sonorous baptism from the Mediterranean, one that had never rubbed off. The sea's baptisms are indelible. And if it was spring as she walked in one of Madrid's particularly sea-like places, and she saw the gas lamps start to glimmer, even the smell of acacias and tuberoses would become the smell of white magnolias, which must have been shining mysteriously at that moment in the salty city, beneath a low sky facing a blazing incandescent sky.

And now every Sunday that swarm of sea-like movements—which previously had only the bullfights and the theater—because the movies don't draw people together, was drawn to the hall of a huge movie house to listen to the city's symphonic orchestra play classical music Madrid-style. The program never varied very much—the same works were repeated, and the public loved this repetition, especially the emphasis on the beloved in Beethoven, among others. People listened to the Fifth Symphony as if it were a Mass, an *auto sacramental*. Sometimes it was devoured more than heard, like a sacrament. She enjoyed going to partake of that communion as much as to hear Beethoven. The vital current would flow first among the musicians in the orchestra and the conductor, until the orchestra sounded like a single instrument, like a single instrument with many voices. And there was a drawing power in that unity, or maybe it would achieve its definitive form as the current from the audience found its way toward the orchestra, fused in a single ear, a single open intimacy. Because in order to see, we must emerge, and in order to hear we must sink deeper, all the way down to whatever the mystics call the "depths of the soul," that's where we take in music; from there we begin to experience the profound communication, the time, "the self" that verges on identity, and it is from those "depths" that instants of true life spurt.

As she walked, after leaving the first of those concerts she had been able to attend, she was musing about this, about how true life seems to consume vitality, to require a great deal of vitality as fuel. It's a still flame that shines alone, in a person's inner darkness, or that appears like a miracle in the midst of the crowd, first as one thing, then turning into another—into the rare moment when you realize that you and others are breathing together, and to breathe together, to heed the same rhythm, is almost to become a single soul. The reverse is also true; when people heed their differences instead, they breathe with different rhythms; what's felt is the hurried or labored breathing of the other, the outsider. Maybe some day somebody will invent a device for proving love and dissent, some gadget that will tick out the rhythm of each person's breathing in a group of people who claim to love each other.

That day in the immense hall of the Monumental Theater there was the rhythm of a single breathing, especially when the audience was listening to Beethoven and his Fifth Symphony. The crowd was unaware, though, or probably unaware that Beethoven had dedicated it to them in his own hand because of their uprising against Napoleon on the 3rd of May. The humble populace of Madrid was unaware that Beethoven had paid them this tribute, but the tribute was fitting, for people fit well together, even if they do not know each other, when they vibrate at the same diapason; and there are instants when they achieve the same pitch of real life.

"Could a moment of real life be achieved within history?" She was talking to herself as she walked home along upper Atocha Street after leaving the concert that morning. A bright October sun was gilding the gray stones, the modest houses, the crowd. None of these things was opaque. Neither was her soul, but a seed of anguish was stirring deep inside it, something that usually occurs after happiness has led one to externalize, to open oneself totally to the outside, to lose oneself in unity. And losing oneself always leads to a letdown, to perplexity. Could this be, is this possibly what has just happened? And then what will happen? Is it or isn't it, will it continue to be? When you're happy, you feel as though you're emerging from yourself, but actually you're attaining a state where you feel neither inside nor outside yourself but inside something that's swallowed us up, that overflows us, and carries us along but then subsides, and you must regain the balance of your habitual consciousness. And since consciousness was abolished at the instant of happiness, consciousness can provide no evidence, can do nothing but wonder: Is it or isn't it? And if it is, in what form? Where can this participation be proved? And if such participation can be proved, does this mean that some substance is engendered within it?

When she got home her mother asked her a little uneasily, "What's happened? You look so upset." "Nothing, nothing; everything was fine." Because she did not dare to say: "It's because I've felt happy, mother . . . we all seemed about to enter Paradise together; we were all one soul, and I'm afraid, I'm afraid."

III

Autumn has a summer too, the instant when its gold ignites and turns to flame: the air gets denser and the light softens, becoming corporeal, more visible than in the summer. The sun allows, even invites us to look at it; before setting, the sun grows pale and seems to be a ghost of itself, a pure image of solar light, a heavenly body that has yielded to the demands of the human gaze without fading at all. Autumn, more than spring, is the moment when the sun and earthly life celebrate their marriage. Peace and a secret tenderness permeate everything, including human life. This is the moment of friendship, when people feel they have friends, even if they don't, a moment when people feel the intimacy friends experience, and when they cement their friendships if they have them.

That fall friendship was finding her, the friendship of those colleagues who had become friends and the friendship of other young people who had been turning up unnoticed. They used to visit her house on Sunday afternoons, and that afternoon one of them would be new . . . to a certain extent, because "newness" is not something one experiences at times like those. In an atmosphere of true friendship, as there is in the autumn air, everything seems to come from far away, perhaps from forever.

And those friends made their way to her house from different neighborhoods, from different occupations. "The new one," Ulysses, arrived last because he was coming from a soccer match; he was an athlete and something of a myth among the students, although he didn't really belong to any department. No, absolutely not; he was studying to be a sailor and preparing now for the theory exams, waiting impatiently for the practice that would take him out to sea. There had been an aura of myth around him for the last year because of an incident during the big strikes. And he'd been forced to pay for his triumph during the strikes by spending forty blessed days in the Modelo prison. This put the finishing touch on his legend as a man of action who was something like a "natural force." A lively pilgrimage would arrive at the jail daily, a procession of young men and women whose mocking faces defied authority, because Ulysses was not the only "force of nature" that had sprung up among the students.

She had met him recently, at a meeting in the crypt-like room of the cafe where those students went once a week. She had been sitting with a small group, and he had approached them in a way that seemed rather British, asking to be introduced to her and expressing surprise because he had never seen her there before. And as he walked her home he told her with the pure candor they breathed: "I never would have imagined that a being like you might turn up here." "What do you mean, here?" "Well, here with us." "You think I'm that strange?" she said, feeling a twinge of anguish. "No, but you'll see, it's not that; I mean, yes, I do, strange the way a bird seems strange when it has stopped in passing, just for a moment and maybe to deliver a message; You were sitting there almost without speaking, and I was watching you, wanting to know what you were saying, sensing it was probably something worth hearing." "Well, the truth is, I was listening; maybe that's the odd thing." "But you're from far away; you seem like a little bird from the mountains, a quail." "Yes, I was in the mountains, although not this past summer—before; but I didn't feel comfortable there because the air was so thin, it was bad for me, it burned me a little inside." "Yes," he understood, "yes, of course, that's why I didn't know you, but that doesn't explain why you seem to have come from so far away, it must be something else." Then his tone changed and he asked her almost sharply: "But what do *you* study?" "Me! I studied philosophy; I've finished at the university, but I keep studying." "Ah, of course, that is, that's what I was saying," and he felt comfortable, or less uncomfortable, convinced he'd come up with the key to her strangeness; and he immediately began to speak again. "No, that doesn't explain what you are either, it must still be something else." "Something else, but look, I've already told you about two things: why I came, what it was that pulled me out of the mountains; and . . . philosophy; isn't that enough?" "Maybe, because after all I don't know anything about either of them, but people want to know you, to be your friends."

And he had come that afternoon, making it evident that he was different from them. He was not an intellectual, he had to make this obvious, because his family was, and one of his relatives eminently so; this was why he had to make them notice the distance between himself and the others. He was a dissident . . . from what? From that life of professors and intellectuals; he would not have wanted to be one of them for anything in the world.

He was there emphasizing his dissidence and hoping they would put it to use. His rebellion took the form of a desire to serve, quickly, efficiently, and with deeds, not with words. They knew how to talk; after all, he enjoyed listening to them, and he was a good listener.

There was not much for him to listen to, much in the way of specifics, because they wanted to formulate some project that would involve action, and a few of them spoke and then a few others, but there was no discussion, no analysis, and they would let their words trail off so other people could speak, until one of them concluded: "But why worry about planning what we're going to do, when so far everything has been turning out really well without our planning it."

This was true; everything was turning out really well—there was a favorable wind filling the sails of their boat, and the oarsmen had not even needed to know each other for the boat to move forward without a foreman, because the "elders" never gave them orders or suggestions, not even the professor, the youngest elder and the one closest to their age, had ever given them any suggestions. The elders laughed with heartfelt glee when the young people recounted their "exploits," as if they were sorry they could not have been there too, but suggestions, orders . . . , never, not from any of them, not even from one of the members of their own group, although there was a "leader," the founder of the FUE, who was imprisoned far from Madrid, after being in many jails, and maybe he would arrive soon. They had true respect for him. He was also the eldest of them, because he had been a student some time ago; but he had a lot of experience, he was prudent, and he had always possessed a sense of unity. Someone should have written a biography of him to have copied and distributed among both the students and the adults. They were not trying to construct an "idol," since nothing among them was premeditated.

What were they talking about? What do people talk about when they're filled with enthusiasm? Although the weather had not turned cold yet, there were some logs crackling in the fireplace, just for the fun of watching the flames, and they didn't turn on the lights until very late, after they'd had tea. Like the fire, their hearts were playful; it was as if they were in the mountains, looking at the city from above, waiting for the chance to enter it on the day of joy. And suddenly they found they had moved from serious words to jokes, to small totally improvised dialogues in which they dramatized the ways of life they wanted to eliminate: sentimentality and patriotism, fastidiousness, professorial pedantry, the pomposity of the false "artist," stupidity, and even evil in all its many forms. And this spontaneous theater, this farce, must have served to exorcise the ghostly realities they sensed lying in wait in the darkness surrounding the sheltering fire and the protection it afforded. Life lived in history retains much of the magical structure within the forest, especially for the innocent hearts that enter it—for those innocent of history, society is filled with spells and fabulous monsters. They have a premonition of this and they light their fires by uniting their hearts; and they reinvent conjuring, the exorcism that purifies the air and the soul itself. Society is still magic.

Reassured now by their theater, they returned to serious things, to their passionate enthusiasm for saving a soul that had been lost and hidden for a long time, for "opening the Cid's tomb" and all the tombs of Spain's history, and for descending to the infernos of history so that all the innocent souls would be free to leave and live the life that was rightfully theirs. Because Spain's dead had all been forgotten for a long time, and the false traditionalists spoke their names in vain, because they felt that history had to become *liquid,* living. What troubled them more than anything, the center they returned to again and again, was the moment Spain separated from Europe, when the struggle of the Counter-Reformation—and therefore of Philip II—had come to an end. This was consistently the theory most widespread among the "leftists," which presented the Counter-Reformation, Spain's obstinate involvement in the struggle for the Low Countries, as an immense historic error. In fact, Fernández de los Ríos, creator of "the humanistic meaning of Socialism," had been just as obstinate about the importance of the universalist, European, nature of the policy held by Charles V, who did as much for the Holy Roman Empire as he did for Spain and who made an immense effort to keep the Protestant schism from succeeding. The Counter-Reformation hid Charles V's efforts to achieve a united Europe, and his design became the obsession—now a last hope—of his son, Philip II. "And we no longer feel that Europe is one . . . , that Europe must be one, and soon, very soon." And Spain is here, inert, powerless to do anything, powerless to revive the great theory, one now free of religious rankling—pure political theory.

And then a pit would open in their stomachs, turning their enthusiasm to despair as they contemplated Spain's withdrawal from international life. They felt a sense of urgency, they wanted the moment that was approaching to come quickly, so they could participate; because they had something to offer the world, and it was not right that they would be forgotten this way. None of them believed in the decline of the West. They had found the book "amusing"; it contained a wealth of historical information because of the diagrams and bold juxtapositions of styles and periods from very different cultures. But they believed the opposite: Europe was at a moment when it could start to grow, providing it found the appropriate, original solution to the conflict between liberalism and socialization, by pulling that solution from the deepest part of its essence, and providing it transcended the nationalities without destroying them. The nationalities would all have to relinquish the essences they were grasping individually, as an individual must do when he creates, when he submerges himself in something—they would have to pour themselves into a supranational unity. Europe would also have to make the journey to its infernos; no one could be denied words or a voice if history was to flow freely, if it was to be a channel for everyone.

Young Ulysses was the last to leave:"I want to tell you something." And she felt a bit startled as a fear, clenched tightly inside her, sprang up readily. "Don't you agree?" he continued, "Look, all of you give me the impression that you're hoping for too much, and you more than anyone, or maybe it's because I hurt more for you than for the others; I already told you what I think about you." "But tell me, are you afraid of something? Of what? Of the police maybe, afraid they'll arrest us, because you know, in reality . . . ""No, none of that will happen to you, because it's not in your karma"—he laughed and muttered something between his teeth:"Now you see how well educated I am. No, it's that your souls, and yours in particular are too open to this business of 'the others' . . . Yes, of everyone, of history, as if you did not exist yet; you're willing to give yourself completely, and that's not good.""But you, my friend, what have you done yourself? Maybe you wish you hadn't done it? Weren't you about to get mixed up in something serious, and then weren't you in jail?" "Yes, and I will be again if necessary!" "Then you mean you would give your life." "Of course I would, but without hoping for so much, without hoping for everything, like all of you." And seeing her silent amazement, he added:"That would not be 'ethical,' as my uncle Fernando would say: you have to risk what it takes for what you believe is right and necessary, risk everything without hoping for everything." He finished with a clear, sharp laugh; she laughed too, in spite of herself, at his affectionate teasing, which did not prevent her from respecting him, and she promised to think about what he had said, because she had not been aware of it, at least not in that form. She did not believe that her hoping, or her giving, had gone so far; she had not felt she was going "beyond" the intoxication enthusiasm entails. On the contrary, she had just been reproached for not wanting to go "further." Now she was being reproached for the opposite. She felt a bit anguished, a little dizzy.

"You would have to follow my example and live a very basic life," he continued very seriously. "You see, I only feel right when I'm among the elements, especially when I'm paddling my canoe, which I've built myself, or when I'm touching the ground, kicking a ball." "But my condition would hardly allow me to devote myself to sports, and besides I don't see that it's necessary." "Well, maybe it's not necessary for you. The thing is, nature, the elements, isolate men from each other, they preserve man's solitude, the intangible something we carry inside; I don't know what to call it, you probably know, but I want to protect it. I'll give my life, but I won't give 'that.'" "Well, what about ethics?" "Ah, ethics." "Don't you see that it's also elemental, as elemental for man as holding his own in the canoe, as having built it well?" And they decided to keep talking about this. Since it was hard for her to go to the country, they would go to the Prado; she had not yet paid her "elemental" courtesy visit, and besides, just in case . . . "What, are you afraid the paintings might not be there some time? That place is like the Guadarrama." Yes, like the Guadarrama, as "natural" for the Villa as for the Court, so much a part of her, of her eyes and her heart: an element. Could it ever not be there for her?" And she thought to herself: Why does enthusiasm collapse so readily into anguish? Why is beauty, certainty, so frightening?

There was something reminiscent of a temple about the Prado Museum; set in a very plain location at the center of Madrid, it was bathed in the same light found inside, in the Velázquez rooms—the same luminous element that made its way from the blue mountains to perch on those canvases where Spain's history was displayed so simply. Paradoxically, the most enigmatic history of all the countries in the West appeared there with such simplicity that an eminent woman and her stately personages could present themselves without dressing up a bit, looking almost naked in spite of their clothes, almost like the classic gods. Was this perhaps an "innocent" history? One created because there was no other choice and created by "showing one's face"? How strange! Maybe when the Spanish were at their zenith they "showed their faces," something Spaniards usually don't do, and that's why history is the way it is, and the Spanish had been forced to retreat? At times clarity presents the greatest enigma. There in the Prado they saw the Philips of the House of Austria—simple, even when seated on a rearing horse, wearing a silk sash and a feathered hat, because that's how they dressed, and the rider looked elegant because he was the king, but in the background, there were bare mountains and pristine light, not a room and a throne. They saw Philip II also; a ghost now, he was looking straight ahead as if to say: "Look at me; see what's left of me, of that lovesick boy, after all my struggles." And in the Titian room they saw Charles V, the one most rapt in thought, withdrawing increasingly into himself. And the poor Bourbons that Goya painted were puppets of history. Who was ruling over their children? They realized that it was not painting as such they were looking at but what was within painting, what painting revealed through its invisible magic. Not that painting was real. Velázquez a realist? Not even Goya was. What about the sculptors who left us naked images of the gods, so that when we look at the gods in photographs we see gods and not the work of a sculptor? When a work has reached completion, its center, even the sculptor's style disappears. Who is Velázquez? No one. Where is he? Even though he painted a self-portrait so complex that the viewer is forced to think "Velázquez and his circumstances," Velázquez at work, just as he was? That's why his painting forms part of the elements.

What is the elemental, though? They both continued to wonder about this. Isn't it a thing that has become totally complete, a thing in agreement with itself, true? And is there really true art? Isn't art entirely a lie? But art you see as art is different from art that makes you see. "I come here because I don't see; I realize that I don't know how to see, that in truth there have been only a few times when I have seen something. Of course there aren't many visible things either," she was saying. "You mean worth being seen, don't you?" "Of course; does everything that's here in reality 'show its face?' No, only a few of all the many things that are real truly let us see their faces, appear." "You mean the rest are monsters." "No, I mean they're half-born fetuses, larvas, or some sort of remains. Life and history constantly consume all living things, persons, and cultures, which means that not all of them are always in a position of visibility, because they are not whole. Cubism and the Cubists seem to know this: they've disregarded everything, revealing only the pure forms trapped inside things." "Then today's man has no face?" "Maybe that's true, maybe everything gets carried off by the crowd, and you can't see the individual, and this is what interests me the most." "The work by 'your teacher' that I know best is *The Revolt of the Masses,* and that's why I want to be a sailor; at sea the individual still counts." "You're exiling yourself then. That's not good, that's running away, you have to stay and face up." "To the masses?" "Yes, to the masses, because that's the task we've been given. Or don't you think that if what they see in front of them are unhidden faces—whole persons—they will no longer be masses and become a people? What's more, you know very well there is a people, you know there is." "Yes, that's why it will be tragic."

She did not dare ask him to explain his prediction, because the same fear gripped her again; but luckily another one of their colleagues arrived, the art historian who was now definitely "hurtling" in the direction of their group. "After it was over" he planned to go abroad, not only to study but to look at Spanish painting from a distance, from the perspective of everyone else, especially the Italians. She had figured out what he wanted: he was hoping that, seen from a distance, something very immediate and familiar, but also mysterious, would assume a form, a writing one could decipher. Some people need to hold the book at a distance so they can read it.

They began to walk toward the exit, but before they left, without saying a word, she made him stop before the Zurbáráns in the Gran Galería, in front of the *Still Life,* with its white tablecloth—whiter than anything—and the bread! Both had been painted or transubstantiated into matter that was imperishable. And the white of the habit on the contemplative saint! Where did that white come from? It emerged out of itself: it was not received, reflected light. The light in Zurbarán arises from matter itself, which contains its own optimum light, as in Cubist paintings. There is a great deal of Zurbarán in Juan Gris, the Madrid bricklayer.

Zurbarán believed in things, in their substance, not in their appearance, so he did
not need to strip them down to mathematical forms. Juan Gris, however, painted
the mathematics of disembodied things. Does this mean that the world had become substance for the sake of man? In Zurbarán, matter is sacred, because God
exists and He is nearby. In Juan Gris, space is empty and things are mathematical
copies, equations; but the same precision is found in them both, the only difference is that now God is distant. Do flesh and soul disappear when God has left?
Oh, mystery of painting, mystery of the incarnation! Could we be entering a
Pythagorean universe? But here in Spain . . . yes, blood and soul exist. That's why
it will be tragic!

   She said nothing to her two companions as they talked to each other while
she stood lost in her Zurbaranesque trance. She had her secrets, and this was one
of them—this painter she never dared talk about. Because she sensed that Zurbarán had captured an ultimate secret, a purity even more difficult, more mysterious than the secret of light that comes from on high and is reflected, the purity
of each thing, each thing here below—the earth in sanctity. And she could not
talk about that. Sanctity, saintliness is what frees us from tragedy.

   Hadn't there perhaps been enough saints in Spain? She could not even voice
this thought either, she could almost not even voice it to herself. It had appeared
like a strange light—one of those thoughts that blaze for an instant like flaming
lamps in the darkness of our anguish. Because ideas, visions, the feeling that allows us to make sense of an enigmatic incident can appear in anguish. Sometimes a luminous abyss opens, making us afraid that both the reality we inhabit
and what we think about it may be nothing but the mask of another terrible reality that's withheld from us because we would find the knowledge of it unbearable. There are moments when someone brings us this reality in something
humble and simple, in something almost invisible, like Zurbarán's white—the
whiteness of that bread, of those linens. But we can't bear it and we need to return to the "human," the flow of our pallid thoughts.

   Why did what was coming have to be tragic, and how did that companion
know it so well? She was walking up Alcalá Street by herself, and it was the time
when the sidewalks and outdoor cafes were crammed with clusters of *señoritos*
talking happily and feeling so sure of themselves. Would they be tragic too?
Would they be the tragic ones and not the *pueblo?* The *pueblo*'s lot has always been
epic events, not tragedy. The *pueblo,* and only the *pueblo,* refuses to move, or if it
moves, it gets carried away, which is what happened at the storming of the
Bastille or on Madrid's 2nd of May, and its action takes the grand impersonal
form of the Author with a capital letter—of history. "Who killed the comen-
dador?" "Fuenteovejuna did, señor," Lope de Vega said, recounting the action
taken upon itself by an entire village after just a few of its inhabitants had participated in it—an avenging action on the part of the *pueblo* that kings must obey,
at least some kings . . . the really royal ones.

No; the *pueblo* never turns toward tragedy on its own. Tragedy resides in a specific person—an Oedipus, a Segismundo, a Hamlet—but without coming to an end in him. Such men are not the *pueblo* but man as an individual, in his utmost solitude as he confronts being and nonbeing: a man invented only half-way, who must carry out an action that is not his, one he did not choose, and a man who does not totally exist because he is not entirely alone and because he is not entirely aware of what is happening. Hamlet is aware, and for this reason he already belongs to the novel almost as much as to tragedy. There has not really been a Christian tragedy, a tragedy after Christianity, except perhaps *El condenado por desconfiado* (The Man Condemned for Doubting), who is partially the quarry of divine grace, partially the believer.

Is this how those *señoritos* in Madrid were? She knew that deep down all the *señoritos* throughout the whole country were the same. Would they be condemned for doubting? That's not really the nature of a *señorito*. *Señoritos* don't doubt, as many idioms show: "That guy doesn't fool me"; "Don't get taken for a ride, boy"; "No, I know what's coming" . . . Of course you also heard this from men in the *pueblo*, the cocky ones who inhabit the confused sphere that exists in every large city between the true *pueblo* and the *señoritos* or the urban European bourgeois, the ones who live by never letting themselves be deceived totally, the ones who live by deceiving and by deceiving themselves: deceiving time, killing it, as they say: killing time.

"Killing time"—what the *señorito* almost always says when someone asks him what he's doing. Isn't this the crime committed by a few Spaniards, one they, of all people, should not have committed? And since when? Wasn't their shared symbol Don Juan, the great killer of time who also killed love and death, death itself?

The same pen that created the figure of the "Doubter" also constructed a poetic refuge for the character that prowled around Seville: "the Trickster." In both of them there was the same fundamental disbelief—absolute in Don Juan, and agonized in the "Doubter." And it does not matter what form the donjuanism or the agonizing doubt takes. The "plot" doesn't much matter, because the outcome will always be tragic—tragic in the form of nonexistence, the form of Christian tragedy that within Christianity is the only tragedy, the "worst crime," perpetrated by the most "unfortunate of men." Isn't this the tragedy of sinking into the denial of existence itself, denying oneself, denying oneself in God, denying God within oneself, killing time, His gift? Saying that our being is . . . for nothing; reducing oneself to nothing.

With what pretext? For what reason? It makes no difference, because explanations can always be found. When she reached this point in her thoughts, the cause of her fears returned, along with the hesitation Ulysses's words had awakened in her. And she said to herself: no, she had accepted life, birth, the need to continue being born; she could not "doubt" her enthusiasm, enthusiasm . . .

But she knew very well this was not what Ulysses had suggested to her; a hint of something else was emerging in him, another traditional mode of denial: the retreat to the elements. And this sounded familiar to her. She had promised to think about it, but she had not been able to very much, since thinking was always difficult for her, and maybe she had said something rather pedantic when she told him that "she would think about it." But it *had* sounded familiar, like "Stoicism." Wasn't it the Stoics who countered Platonic "enthusiasm" and Aristotelian rigor by discovering that kind of retreat to the elemental, to a life lived in harmony with the "elements"? The Stoics also based everything on "the ethical." Man is a rendezvous of elements, and life is a loan to be returned willingly when the time comes, as Seneca said so elegantly, "cutting one's customary figure," because he died almost like a bullfighter who goes into the ring certain he's about to meet up with a bad bull chosen by death as its emissary, and he fights exactly as always, with the same elegance, executing the most difficult passes, as if he will hear the final ovation when the crowd in the plaza has stood up, and he has stood up taller, straightened, as he stands in profile at the center of the ring feeling immortal. But he knows he is not, knows that any moment the bull will seize him treacherously and illegally, because this is an unknowing bull, and that's why they gave it to him, because he could have managed with the knowing ones; he knows that he will not leave the sand on his own two feet, that he will die "with his shoes on" and that only an image, an idol will accept the final ovation and the silence. Seneca left us his forever-unchanging profile and his blood falling drop by drop, forced to leave his veins rhythmically, restrainedly, like the fire deep within the universe that ignites temperately and goes out temperately . . . Because the essential thing, since being is not possible, is to be in a way appropriate to this fire, like one of its sparks, but temperate.

And she felt certain that when it came time to die, not only the "Stoic," a descendent of Seneca, although he was unaware of it, but also many of those "doubters" and "tricksters" knew how to die this way—standing sideways, outlining the most precise of ciphers in the style of their ancestors, and she felt certain that others would die blazing in fires they had kept hidden their whole lives and that the *pueblo,* when its turn came, would die innocently like the man in the white shirt who figures at the center of Goya's painting *The Third of May, 1808.* They had just seen that painting and walked passed it without saying a word: the man opening his arms in a cross, instead of pressing them to his defenseless chest, responding to the rifles with an unnatural gesture, beyond the instinctive fear felt by all animals as they face death; giving up his soul, which leaves his body before the bullets reach it; holding his entire soul—which cries out to heaven—in his arms, embracing the world, cursing, blessing; and in his eyes, which also leave his body before the bullets reach them, and in that scream . . . What is that Celtiberian in the immaculate white shirt forever screaming to us, as he gives up his soul? The scream, my Spain, of your animal, of its soul pouring out over death, a soul that will not stop at death's banks but empty into life? The scream is one of life!

And that life, that scream of life must now be taken up and that soul must be given to the body deserving of it, the history worthy of it—that soul must be enabled to live and to produce life. Dying, dying, yes, everyone is aware that Spaniards know how to die well, even with precision, with moderation, the quality most lacking in their lives. The important thing, though, at the present historical conjuncture was, is, to find the possibility of a life equal to this dying, which might be the opposite of what's occurring in other places, to find the moderation and the way of living that our death deserves. Europe had found its life and learned how to live it, but we clung to our dying.

The next time she spoke with "prudent" Ulysses, she would tell him about the "discovery" she had just made. It happened because she took Alcalá Street, where she found herself walking in the middle of Madrid's *señoritos,* although there were some people from the *pueblo* too—the fauna that gives a city character: the waiters, newspaper vendors, and shoeshiners who were all inhabitants of that moment, and it happened because she saw them and listened to the timbre of their voices, because of the writing their hands made in the air, in contrast to the kings and personages from the past, from the Spain now "canonized" in the history found in the Prado. Maybe all discoveries—even discoveries of something like the Mediterranean—occur when a person sees two different images of the same thing simultaneously. Because the images are simultaneous: the real image falls over the image that is still throbbing, although in this case it was the image of an image, which is so much the better, because the image of the image captured the "essence" of the real thing more completely. This is the virtue of imaginative art and its justification. When one perceives the essence, what Ortega would call the "consistency" of the real thing, one can grab hold of that thing and pin it down; then the thing, the person, and even the landscape have been elevated to the category of icon, of a sacred form that holds a secret but diaphanously, and the thing has been removed from the flow of time so that people who live in the future will be able to find it and incorporate it into their own times. The existence of an image in art enriches the "complexity of times" that preoccupied her so much; and because it enriches complexity, it can be confusing, as something enriching always is. This explains why a purified frame of mind is necessary if one is to look at an image clearly. There is nothing more dangerous, absolutely nothing, than looking at an image when one feels upset or disheartened, when one's gaze is cloudy. Looking at images or icons is dangerous; how dangerous depends on the importance of the "essence" they hold. People have always known that looking at an image can bewitch the beholder; it can be fatal.

So now she had made two "discoveries" that morning. Oh, she was well aware that they weren't "discoveries," phenomenologically speaking, because people had surely known about them for a long time. But since she had made them, she wanted to talk with Ulysses again and with her other friends. In truth she would have liked to tell not just her friends but all those *señoritos* sipping their drinks so delightedly about her discoveries as she saw the two images simultaneously: the temple of tradition—the Prado Museum—and an image of the national life bursting forth at that moment. Her discoveries were a warning, a simple warning: "Be careful with your images, with your icons of the past, because they can bewitch us or kill us; we must transfigure the tangible essence of any image or icon, bring it back to life, not the reverse." All icons ask for their freedom, every form is a jail, but icons are the only earthly way we have to preserve an image without spillage. Words are also forms that capture and oppress. And to know how to look at an icon is to free its essence and bring it into our lives, but without destroying the form that contains it, and leaving the form as it was; this is difficult and it takes training. To know how to contemplate: wasn't that what she had been asking of philosophy? And philosophy had answered by presenting her with a demand. Doesn't everything that truly has something to offer start out by making a demand? The demand for an implacable training. Knowing how to contemplate must be knowing how to look with your entire soul, your entire intelligence, and even your entire body; this is "participating," participating in the essence contemplated in the image, turning it into life. And then you're beyond remembering and forgetting, because once we achieve something like this we cannot forget it; it has transformed us, made different people of what we were. In the same way, although she could not recite them point by point, not even if she skipped many points, neither could she forget what her teachers had taught her in those lessons she always felt so certain she had not understood. And now, as time passed and she began to enter life again, she saw that something indelible had remained of her implacable training; and the happiness she felt about this blended with the happiness of her "discoveries." Isn't that the only way to understand the process of discovery?

She kept going over and over the question of images and the *señoritos* who were stoic tricksters, doubters, or . . . bewitched *señoritos*. Sitting on a fur rug in the corner of her room. Sitting on the floor, she would write in a notebook on her knees, because writing was something she had done spontaneously since childhood; it was her method for untangling the threads, of working her way out of certain confusions or into others—other confusions that, as now, would be fluttering about behind the obvious confusions.

All images belong to the past, not only the already-formed images we're offered but also the one that has just formed in my mind. What's more, the formation of an image is one way that the past is revealed to human consciousness, because so long as I face something, before an image has formed, I am not truly "facing" but "in" something, and I am not fully conscious of being different—I'm engrossed, and we have no sense of time at such moments, or if we do, time takes the form of the present, of the fullness we sense in the "present." When we are enveloped by a circumstance, as we always are, no image forms—this is the fullness of the present that allows us to participate fully in the things around us. But when an image has worked loose, and it appears as an image in human consciousness even though our situation has not changed, and we still face the same surroundings, something has gone on—both meanings of this expression are valid here, because something has happened and something is now gone—in fact there is no past unless something has "gone on." And this something that literally goes on when everything continues unchanged is the image that has formed in my mind, and this is how the image sends the past something I grasped of what I was seeing or feeling. The same thing happens, and happens even more forcefully, in the case of a concept rather than an image, because the concept is less vulnerable than the image; it holds the abstracted, separated "what."

Every essence, every "what" belongs to the past. Whatever lacks an essence or has not yet displayed its essence—there's no difference—becomes, comes toward consciousness, which simply lets it pass unless it discovers the "what" of that essence; if the "what" is discovered, consciousness isolates it and pins it down, and at that very moment the "what" belongs to the past because *it is*. Is Being always static? And what can happen then? What can happen to us?

When we encounter an image, we can turn back toward the past with it, even the past that has just gone on. When we encounter a concept, we can feel ourselves fill with certainty, with freedom, because now instead of looking at reality we can leave reality behind, because we've grasped its essence; we know what's important about it—we know it. We feel free, feel we have control, and if we keep on this way, substituting concepts for realities, we can take charge of everything, although that everything will lack . . . reality, if reality is understood as the things that resist us, which is how Ortega defined it and what she had discovered in his course. "Is it possible for us to know real objects?" And also to know the inexhaustible, the multiple—whatever it is that, regardless of how much we conceptualize it, will always have a background from which becoming reaches us.

If we turn toward the image still imaging us, it will change into an idol for us. Like the image of any beloved thing, it will end up becoming hermetic, on account of its fixedness. Nourishing at first, it will later alienate.

Because we must partake of the essence contained "carnally," perceptibly in the image and captured intellectually in the concept—the image must serve as nourishment for us. And this is how it pours back into life again, and life acquires a new dimension that allows consciousness and soul to communicate, and then consciousness is not alone in its task of conceptualizing and dispatching toward the past. Because it is consciousness that brings the past to reality, which is a way of sending it to hell, of freeing itself of reality. Whereas the soul—essentially memory—stores reality. When too many images have been stored in the soul and when consciousness neglects them, because it is so pridefully aware of having created them, a split occurs in a person, a double-entry life. This is sterility, an inability to create, not only works of art or any "work" at all, but an inability to create the most "elementary" thing needed by human life—the space for living with others. Because memory in this instance does not become history; memory is history only if it comes back to a person's consciousness, if consciousness takes memory upon itself once again. In order for history to remain present in each life, in individual lives, a double movement must occur. The consciousness that rejects the things going on for us, and sends them back toward the past, must take up those things again, rescue them . . . redeem them. History is a sort of assumption of things condemned to the past—which is everything that goes on—into the light of the present.

But when images have not been formed by us, when they are images from a historical past that appear to us spontaneously, which is how the historical past occurs, tradition is what results. Because tradition is the residue of history, which flows in persons who are not aware that they have history. For them historical time takes the form of the present, as in one's individual life one is located in the present when neither image nor concept has been formed yet. A people who lives in tradition lives history in this form of the present. Of the present and of myth . . . the past has gone on to inhabit a remote time, the root and beginning of everything, where everything that has happened since originated. And this is why peoples who live in tradition do not live the past in the usual way, but live instead in a present whose roots are sunk in a remote time separated by a qualitative abyss. They do not experience any confusion about possible times, which explains why their spontaneity has been preserved intact: their "idols" are too distant, placed in a way that makes them more apt to adopt than enslave. Such peoples live in a single time, which is creative and poetic. Consciousness is not tensed in order to form images and concepts continuously, so a people lives from a few already-formed images and concepts kept faraway in a sacred place. When the need arises, there is communication through inspiration, that is, communication with something on a qualitatively different plane, such as a principle, a root, or a guide—gods, the dead, legendary figures . . . And when something in the present makes a strong impression on them, they mythologize it, elevate it immediately to the plane of the qualitatively different and superior. This explains why respect, the spontaneity and intensity of respect, is the sign of a people who lives in tradition. And if the sign is negative, it relates to a different category of myth—the monstrous, the "never seen," which reappears periodically; it must be taken on and killed—this is the dragon that emerges from time to time. If one suffers defeat and the dragon remains, there is nothing to do but withdraw resignedly, although spitefully, and hope for "better times." For the *pueblo,* time has its own structure, and time is cyclical—what is happening now and what can happen correspond to something that already happened once, and everything that happens once will reappear again. This is how people bear the unbearable.

For a person who lives from his consciousness, tradition is the past, and it appears to him as such; he *faces* tradition but he is not *in* it. And this is where conflict arises: one's first response is a move to reject tradition, to abolish it, having sensed its evil spell. Consequently a person's conception of history is both arbitrarily rational and utopian, because it will always lack substance. The substance in the things of our lives corresponds to the past, because substance already is. And every life needs some substance, some support for consciousness, which inevitably must be the consciousness of someone and be from somewhere, be in relation to some starting point. Consciousness never starts out from a state of total originality, since it has arisen from a conflict or, at least from a difference between planes of life, between separate times; although it's true that modern philosophy, to an extreme in the case of idealism, has become pretty much worn out in its effort to discover an originary consciousness, a consciousness with no beginning. Descartes was the first; but once he had discovered the original consciousness with no base, he quickly accepted "the given," "the circumstance." Not all men are philosophers, however, and even if they were, they would not be Cartesians or idealists, whose method is antithetical to the "spontaneous philosophy" of the ordinary man. This ordinary man is continuously confronting a tradition; either he attacks it or falls, gazing in fascination, before its image, its ready-made images, icons from which his untrained eye cannot draw the necessary participation. This is the traditionalism in essences that deny any possibility of participation. And when one of those icons does not admit participation, it's because in some way, inside that icon, there is still a man from the *pueblo.* That man, now fully incorporated into city life, which is the life of consciousness, of the time of consciousness, comes up against the images of tradition. Since there are many images, and since the essence each contains is not always pure and devoid of internal contradiction, how can he partake of it? How can he be open to such participation without "examining" his consciousness—his conscience—before both and through those images? This is something that all historical figures would have to undergo if they returned to earth. Or maybe they do undergo it in whatever space they inhabit: an examination of consciousness, an examination that renders them fully conscious of their role in history, but conscious of their mistakes, not their "sins." They must account for their mistakes before men.

And the historical past, the past that most closely controls the time we are living, must be redeemed by consciousness through such an examination. Unless this occurs, the personages and monarchs of the past—men of state, royal favorites and generals, bureaucrats, and all those who determined the present through their errors—will be left in the hell of history.

There is a hell for each time, since there are many times. The soul has its hell of images, loves that die before they can be born, unrealized poetry; the heart has its depths, which are why it beats. And consciousness . . . consciousness holds all hells, since it creates them. It is consciousness that sends loves and images to hell, consciousness that creates the past, and consciousness that stratifies—consciousness whose watchfulness keeps the things and the dead that go on from truly going on, from becoming poetry. It is only right that consciousness would have to work, have to exhaust all its tension and watchfulness, in order to rescue the past: bring the past into the present and subject it to the implacable clarity of consciousness, bring to the plane of here and now the examination of conscience that the past cannot carry out there in its hell, where it is ignorant of the consequences its errors have brought us. Bringing images into the light and looking at them, looking at them until their essence seems diaphanous, until their presence is transformed into an essence that admits participation: "Yes, this is the price of having discovered the 'essences,' of bringing them into the present from their infernal pits, because this is the only way they will be free to fly to their 'celestial spheres.' The 'things that happen to us' and the things that 'have happened to everyone,' can become protective ideas, principles, only when they have been examined to the ultimate degree. In the meantime, Dulcinea will remain enchanted."

Because at that historical conjuncture Spaniards were preparing to disenchant Dulcinea—the lost essence—by offering her an appropriate form. Did this not require some implacable training, what's called "ascesis" where it was discovered? What about don Quijote's penitences, the penitences of an *hidalgo* who preferred to go mad rather than become a doubter, who preferred to treat even women whose social position was far from ladylike as ladies, rather than ever be thought of as the "Trickster"? She felt, although it was something unspeakable, that those *señoritos* needed a cure in the form of that unmentionable virtue called purity, purity of heart and mind. But she was not the one who discovered it. Miguel de Unamuno had actually shouted it to us in his sonorous, prophetic voice. And wasn't it maybe found as well in the outlook and work of an Azorín, a Baroja, or an Antonio Machado—the poet of pure water? Wasn't it in Ortega's thought too, albeit implicitly, as such things in philosophy are? Wasn't the chaste way of living together, established among the young people of the "new generation" by their spontaneous determination to free themselves from the hells of "sex," a form of that (unspeakable word!) purity? This determination made possible the existence of their gracious, happy friendship and brotherhood, and it allowed them to circle hand in hand, the way people do in ritual dances in order to revive some ritual ancestral dance of disenchantment, some of those first dances in which the men and women of a tribe would circle rhythmically in a set pattern in order to disenchant themselves from the spell of their dead, in order to disenchant their dead by making them dance, calling to them to dance together, to dance with them, far from their moonlit landscapes, at the stroke of fierce noon.

Because only this ritual dancing, when the living and the dead, the present and tradition, join hands and dance together, can break the spell that imprisons Dulcinea.

The young people were not alone in feeling this way. Everywhere, the un-affiliated, the ones who usually kept to themselves, began to reach out their hands to each other; even some traditional enemies—separate social groups and different ideologies—joined hands. The first steps of the ritual dance to combat the evil spell had already been taken. There was talk of various "pacts," which was the word of the day, the order of the day that clear autumn.

Historical Conjuncture

I

The new school year began in October 1930. The last months of the previous semester, the University of Madrid and many of the universities in the provinces had barely been able to function, because student strikes followed one after the other with increasing intensity. The most prestigious professors, the representatives of the new university, unequivocally declared themselves in profound agreement with the students; professors and students came to be two sides of the same coin. It began to look as though some of the professors would have to resign from their positions, and in fact some of them did. The Academy of Jurisprudence, which determined juridical meaning, had sponsored a series of lectures delivered by the men best able to interpret the sense of the law and the lawfulness of city life. In addition, in their lectures the speakers had thoroughly examined the situation of the state and society, outlining at the same time the roles the new regime would need to play. The new constitution of the Republic was roughed out, and you could see the Republic, the way you sense the presence of an awaited guest who's approaching your door. The Republic was visible now, just as the only solution to a problem is visible once full information about it has been presented with the utmost precision and clarity. The Republic was inevitable.

Inevitable, because history reaches these moments of mathematical precision and natural spontaneity that occur simultaneously. At such moments more history is made and, paradoxically, those who are alive most actively do not feel either the effort or the danger—the weight of history. On the contrary, life is lived within a mathematical rhythm, in which events begin to occur, with the exact precision of sequential equations—events that take place in separate places or in different environments within the same city, in different social groups or even in analogous groups that have different "ideologies." One could say that reason, as presented in Ortega's "Tesis metafísica sobre la razón histórica" (Metaphysical Thesis on Historical Reason), becomes explicit, although not at all fatalistically. A reason achieves freedom itself: "We are free by necessity," implying that freedom can be declined or ceded, but it is there. Life and history crawl along and everything is a question of "killing time." But when freedom is lived, because a choice has been made in a single instant of lucid decision, then freedom is reason—vital, Historical Reason.

To what extent does "fate" form part of history? When history is surrendered to fate, as individual lives are, doesn't it disintegrate into a negation of itself, although one that cannot be carried out, which is what (perhaps!) happened to Spain from the time it withdrew from the world, from "this world"—the modern one—until it began to wake up? Because Historical Reason will have to become more specific; the same reason, the same kind of reason cannot be valid for everything that has happened in history. Hegel's "absolute spirit" is also achieved through a negation of the self, because one denies one's own existence in order to . . . and then crime, historical crime does not exist. Won't "historical reason" have to account for those crimes, while leaving them as crimes of negation, as negation, as denial, even though negation has been "surpassed"? For in history, in history's reason, man's ultimate resistance is born very perceptibly— the "No" that must be overcome violently, with the violence of thought, of thinking, the most violent action of all.

No doubt they're brief, these "historical moments" when there is agreement among all forms of reason which can be expressed explicitly; and no doubt such moments necessarily involve the worst dangers, because those reasons can become detached, and some can become obliterated, fall into the seemingly ever-present void that threatens even the most lucid human actions—the dark depths lying in wait for the most lucid thought precisely as it is embodied. Maybe there is an individual "passion" that corresponds inexorably to each form of reason?

No one would have thought so at that hour when the course of events was upon them with a seemingly mathematical spontaneousness. It's curious that man apparently follows the same law in everything he does. When one of his works reaches its perfection, that work does not immediately manifest its characteristic features but those of something exactly opposite: perfect architecture seems to sing; we seem to experience painting within time; the history man makes with his passions and his mistakes seems to share the precision and the objectivity of mathematics and the inevitability of natural phenomena.

Inevitable and expected history may be, but despite man's certainty that history will occur, he awaits it with increasing impatience. More than impatience, man experiences a softening of the soul, a thirst for presence similar to a thirst for the truths of faith, which can transform true belief into something almost identical to exasperation.

Inevitable. What were they doing, those who felt obliged to do something, to avoid that exasperation?

But could they actually do anything that would really be *doing,* doing in a positive way, and not see happen what happened to every task they performed as either action or assignment—all of which turned into collaboration with "their enemies," almost as if they were simply playing a part envisioned by the author of the work, making the outcome more inevitable?

This is what always occurs when human activities give rise to a new and qualitatively different action, to one that is creation. This is what was happening at that moment; they were living one of those rare moments of historical creation. Because one sign of creation is the fact that such a thing occurs—an activity or its result attains the characteristics of whatever could not be more distant from whatever occasioned it. Maybe only then is there true creation.

No doubt history, which is always being made, because the making of history never stops for a single instant, nor does its unmaking, which is a form of making it; and even saying "*No*" to history is a way of making it, even that . . .

Just as it's a sign that creation is occurring in history when the opponent can do nothing in the face of "the inevitable"—"do," in the strict sense, not that of avoiding defeat, which is something different. For in the rare moments when man creates, no one is defeated and no one wins, in the strict sense, which does not mean there is no enemy. Something is hidden in the shadows, something that is not the defeated one, the opponent with clearly defined attributes, but rather the one that always loses: the dark resistance that can emerge tall and which can also *embody*—embody the void in the world of men.

An instant exists, though, in which the creative process absorbs everything. As in music, there is a key change that raises everything, even the voids of the soul, the inexpressible negations that appear in certain lives, even in personal misfortunes. One of the most reliable signs that such a process was underway was the inability of personal life to attend to its own conflicts, since it was not free to become wrapped up in the things that were happening to it alone; and no one could be totally "unfortunate," because personal life was raised, jolted out of itself in the creative process transcending it. In such an instance, this transcendence includes every occurrence, no matter how important, even the words and the men who themselves are players in the process: everything is enveloped in a "more" that transports events and persons and carries them away to a higher plane—"something that seizes every `science and every consciousness' transcendently."

No doubt this is what the "totalitarianism" of recent times has tried to imitate. Because all creation, even human creation, is threatened by mimicry's diabolic game. "Creative evolution" has carried this mimesis ever since life began—plant life, animal life, and even . . . Can we say for sure that in geology and even in the heavenly constellations there is not some mimesis?

The "history" of European totalitarianism marks the most diabolic moment of mimesis with respect to historical creation: the need to face the void of this "something" that's transcending everything provokes the annihilation of the individual, a mechanical discipline, and immediate terror. The paroxysm of the masses imitates enthusiasm, and the masses themselves imitate the *pueblo,* which is alive and organic, in the way empty expanse imitates eternity. And innocence imitates itself with the total, absolute indifference of the man annihilated in the face of his fate. So instead of spontaneous mathematics, the mechanical motions of a forced march.

In truth, so far as we know, this mimesis of historical creation had never before been attempted on such a grand scale, had never been realized so profoundly as in the time just passed in our Europe. And the terrible fear has arisen that its "passing" may have been somewhat mimetic too—that the time may have passed without completely passing, that it may be able to feign even man's ultimate truth, which is defeat.

This might explain the rites of collective purification found in the great religions of the wise Orient. It might explain the waves of relentless terror, the "extermination" some statesmen ordered coldly at certain hours. Unleashed terror can also be mimetic. Maybe it would have been enough if that Europe, still enveloped in its own falsification, had experienced a long hour of peace, of the peace closest to the absence of history: creative forgetfulness.

Creative forgetfulness. Spanish life had such a forgetfulness at that historical juncture. Many things had been forgotten; because creation so closely resembles the impossibility of totally inventing oneself. True creation would mean creating, creating oneself, from the origin, and whenever man creates he goes back to his origins—he becomes un-born and he is innocent once again.

Evidence of this could be seen in the figure of the dictator, Primo de Rivera. He was the one who "stood up," who faced up to the fight in which he did not seem to believe seriously for an instant. He could not have. If he had seen how serious matters were, he would not for an instant have continued to play that role of deceitful mask. In the first place, he was the one most deceived, perhaps the only one who was deceived.

He was not acting from bad faith. He damned himself simply by serving, by stepping in to cover a void. What would have made a man agree to do this? What weak spot in the human condition would have allowed an assent like that to slip out? Ignorance first of all; he did not know . . . "He had learned to govern in the political club in Jerez," as he said himself. Of course it later became clear that one can serve this apprenticeship in far worse places. And it's difficult to accuse Primo de Rivera today, because he was honest—he did not feather his own nest, although he permitted others to feather theirs, and he was cruel on only two or three occasions; he was a man with a good heart, and there was much of the "gentleman" in him. But he was doing something he should not have; that was all. Generous and jovial by nature, surely he sometimes felt the anguish of his wretched position?

When he seized power, Primo de Rivera justified himself in the name of a particular "racism" that was nothing new in Spain—the "racism" of the military caste, the only "pure element" and, by the look of things at that moment, the natural lords of a nation whose civilian government, in his opinion, was showing signs of "incompetence." This birth certificate was the most serious thing about his rise to power.

He got into polemics with the students and the intellectuals. To their arguments, he gave a "personal" rejoinder, an obvious sign that he had no understanding of the situation, that he was not a statesman at all; that he represented the Spain that reduces everything to domestic terms; and turned the entire "objective" issue into an internal, family affair, or one to be kept within the family. For him, what should exist was the family, the military caste, etc. "The other" comprised those unruly students and those outlandish citizens—writers and intellectuals.

The presence of Primo de Rivera's dictatorship signified a continuance of the disintegration that characterized the nineteenth century, of the sad moment in Spanish society when, for every class, "the rest" were "the other." There are both historical and individual situations like this: ways of responding to reality that define whatever one is not or one cannot assimilate as "the other." This is an infrahistoric way of life, in which people who must share a territory, a language, a past, and, what is most serious of all, a future, feel nothing but the differences they express so crudely as "the other," the others . . . the incomprehensible, which nevertheless continues to be there. It's a kind of slipping back into a wondrous realm where reality appears discontinuously and seems to be composed of homogeneous units separated by insurmountable abysses. Spain slipped back that way when it touched the hell of its infrahistory formed of tribes marked by pure in-breeding; and now there were some people who reacted with a fervent "out-breeding": they wanted to break out, emerge into anywhere, so long as it meant blending with something different and foreign.

Now was the right moment to reconstruct the nation, recreate it, which was precisely the creative process taking place. The Republic was the vehicle, the new system. Reality was the nation: reality was being recreated.

Because all the elements were there now and because the spirit was in the air, all the efforts to revitalize Spain made by the renewed generations of thinking individuals had finally gotten "the whole of Spain" breathing. The thinking that is born from a single individual and creative effort, which is always individual, had spread, creating a collective thinking and a collective key in people's living—a moral key, which was life. The nation was being recreated now in the style of the modern age, in the world of consciousness, and not through warlike ventures, or through victory over secular enemies, or against any surroundings, but because of an internal need . . . This is why it seemed so much like a birth, a self-invention, the creation of a work of art or of thinking.

It was the historic event of a nation actually raising itself up, taking upon itself, its consciousness, the body constituted centuries before—in reality Europe's first modern state, so as to form itself again. And this is rare . . .

Because revolution is something different. The French Revolution was an intellectual movement, or one based on faith in a universal principle, and a profound upheaval of French society that made possible the emergence of a new class, which was not really so new. Doesn't the "bourgeoisie" come from the medieval burgher? And this class, which was new insofar as its aspiration to seize power, proved to be the creator of the nation at that stage, but within a continuity. The French Revolution effected only a very short break with the past, and a new continuity was soon established, not the one embodied in the monarchs but one embodied in society itself, in all its dimensions.

And the Russian Revolution, which was also carried out in the name of a universal principle, tried to achieve a utopia. Within a few years, a continuity was established with the Russian history of a somewhat distant moment, that of Peter and Catherine.

In Spain, though, historical continuity had been broken for three centuries, and this action, this demand for a change of system did not occur in the name of any originally revolutionary principles—it did not occur in order to make a revolution but to make Spain itself, simply to make Spain itself.

And this making itself a nation was occurring by necessity, in light of universal principles, since something can only be created in light of universal things. This was doubly true in the case of Spain, because the Spaniard, when he decides to assimilate his history can only do it authentically by looking at universal things. At that time this was even more true than ever, since there was no war against anyone, no conquest to pursue—no Moors to expel, or New World to discover. It was Spain's Dulcinea, Spanish life, that wanted to free itself from the spell of its interrupted history, to realize its pure image, to recapture its soul. This was not only a question of politics, of art. It was a question of being born, of becoming flesh in the body of history, of a true history. Yes, it was something rare that had happened very seldom, something that perhaps, perhaps had never happened quite this way, quite so radically.

No one was angry with anyone, not even with the dictator, who seemed to have been taken most seriously by Miguel de Unamuno. This may have been because Unamuno was the eldest of all the "creators" and the one most consumed by a vocation of fatherhood, and he might have felt that he had been supplanted "personally." He had returned from his exile in the spring of 1930, having downed the last drops of his exile in Hendaye, right on the border between Spain and France. His literary work from those years was certainly not the best of his multiform production, because he also suffered from a hunger for fathering words. This manifested itself in wrathful shots, poems that were in fact curses, short bursts of prayer, and even conjurings—he believed that strongly in the power of the word! Since he had written *La agonía del cristianismo* (The Agony of Christianity) in Paris, this small, great, frustrated book had been published in French before it came out in Spanish; in it he obsessively expressed his hunger for fatherhood, for fathering in the flesh and in the spirit equally. As often happens, his characters and their situations are the "negative" or complement of their author; the longing that "Father Jacinto" suffers to father flesh and blood children was in reality the reflection of Unamuno's own hunger for children of the spirit, and on two planes—the plane of history that survives through the ages in what Unamuno called metahistory, and the plane of eternity, in which he would have believed totally if he could have known he had children there. His way of believing in reality was being able to engender it; truth was found wherever one of his children was born.

We all went to meet him the day he arrived in Madrid at the Estación del Norte. It was the first time a crowd had gathered in tribute to an intellectual, because of a "poet," and this was a crowd formed of "each one," as Unamuno wished, of individuals who were not dissolved in an amorphous mass. He went straight to the Ateneo, where the words seemed to tumble out as he spoke. We would have loved to see him more serene and priestly, but . . . since we loved him, we loved him the way he was. It was him, and he was there, among us, after a long absence, and we could feel that the size of our souls had increased because of his presence. That day was a day of certainty, perhaps because we saw ourselves, saw ourselves all together for the first time.

Another return took place a while before, that of Antonio María Sbert, the student who had founded a broad student movement, the Federación Universitaria Escolar, and for this he had endured so many jails, confinements, and absences. That time there was not a welcome but a triumphant cortege, a joyful procession, that wound through the streets of Madrid. It was formed by young people, who felt an increased sense of authority in the presence of their older brother, even though none of them, except for a few of his own contemporaries, had ever been very close to him; he was on a different plane, at a certain distance. And this was good for those young people. It impressed on them something they themselves possessed spontaneously: discipline, because these were spontaneously disciplined young people.

Jail stays had become frequent occurrences for the students throughout that whole period because of small incidents of violence and the strikes that followed one after the other, as implacably as a natural phenomenon.

The configuration of political parties was different now, although in appearance nothing had changed. The old, almost extinguished republican parties had re-emerged and some intellectuals who came for the most part from the so-called "reformism" were in the process of forming a new party. Since the beginning of the century, the reformists' goal had been to reform Spanish life from within the monarchy, but they now saw that such reform was impossible. This party corresponded fully to a liberal ideology open to social reforms.

The Socialist Party was the hub of the situation, however. What was happening in that party? Not much, by the look of things—which nevertheless were important things. Associated with the Unión General de Trabajadores and affiliated with the Second International, the Socialist Party had been strictly faithful to the interests of the working class; politically, it too had been "reformist." The Socialists had also experienced upheaval, back in the years 1917 and 1918, when the movement for regeneration and reform in Spain died out and the First European War had imprinted European society with upheaval, with a space of openness to new possibilities that made it seem as though everything could be changed, and the "old traditional customs" fell. There was an instant of rebellion; large workers' strikes were unleashed and the most "conservative" of the Socialist leaders went to jail. A period of agitation and strikes followed, but it was sealed hermetically when the dictator appeared, and in the eyes of those who wanted "law and order," that period justified his appearance. Since then the U.G.T.'s masses of workers had not stirred. Neither had the Socialist Party, and it even seemed obvious that for awhile there had been something of an agreement with the general's dictatorship. The general tried to show that he understood current social issues by employing rather spectacular methods, such as creating the Ministry of Labor and the *comités paritarios* composed of workers and employers. A certain influence of Italian fascism could be detected in these methods, and in some of the young ministers in the dictator's cabinet. What were the Socialists doing now? This was the question repeated with a bit of rather anguished impatience by those who believed in the Republic; it wasn't possible to wait for the others any longer. And prompted by the political intelligence of one of their "elders," in fact the one who had attended the meeting of the two generations, the Socialist Party was changing its position. It did this the way a huge ship makes a turn—slowly; the ship was heavy and it carried a cargo for which its captains felt responsible, one they could not lose. Their movements had to be absolutely precise: this was a difficult journey that could be presented in nautical, almost mathematical terms: it was a question of making the Socialist Party aware of the enormous strength of the U.G.T., the strongest and most disciplined union in Spain, and thereby getting the Socialist Party positioned alongside the Republican forces fighting for the freedom the Republic offered, but without provoking the working force as such to rush into the arena. This may not exactly have been the thinking, but this is what happened, and such delicate maneuvers could never have been carried out effectively without strategies to guide them.

Such was the case. Indalecio Prieto, the one with the most political mind, began to move toward the Republican line of thought. As did Francisco Largo

Caballero, the tireless worker from the U.G.T., who had devoted the years of his not short life to the organization, with the same daily patience, the same impersonal energy that other practitioners of his trade also put into their daily tasks. He looked Nordic because of his blue eyes, and he both brandished a lackluster oratory and lacked luster as a person, for he was a man of few ideas, a stubborn man, one of those men who seem impassive because they have a single passion.

As for the other large union, the C.N.T. of the anarchists and its corresponding "political" association, the F.A.I., it acted quite moderately with some exceptions.

All of which meant that the change was occurring with the least possible violence. Neither industries nor transportation systems were paralyzed, bread was not unavailable for even one day, and there were no shootings on street corners; or rather, there were the occasional shootings at the students involved in the riots at the entrance of the old university on San Bernardo. The most intense incident was the one that occurred one morning at the School of Medicine—a brief, hard fight that produced a wide echo.

It seemed natural to believe that the Republic would be established in a legitimate way. Wasn't this perhaps something that had never happened before in history? Did it not involve, if this was how things happened, an extraordinary feat? Because no one was aware that there was anything extraordinary about the occurrence; people knew it was happening and that was all.

With this certainty the inhabitants of Madrid returned to the city from their summer vacations with such deep conviction they did not even realize the "miraculous" nature of the event to come.

II

The autumn air was weightless, and it vibrated with an incitement to live. Do the light and air of a city maybe change in accordance with the historical moment? It is man who measures these things, so the answer is probably yes. The light knows what is happening among men, and even more, it knows what is going to happen—the light prophesies. Do prophets maybe read in that light a plot summary of the future? Or the sign even more than the plot—the quality of whatever is brewing? Because the light seems to gather this and show it to anyone who knows how to read its transparent body; light has a body, a fleshiness. Light is only abstract at some latitudes and on some days, at some moments in history when it seems to withdraw, to be there without any vibrations for the sole purpose of performing its function and illuminating indifferently, as if it were only doing its job. This is the worst moment for men, even worse than a moment of darkness, because it's the signal that a tragedy is being enacted, that a sacrifice is occurring. The most inhuman of moments, it occurs when the light refuses to be present, even though it continues to make objects visible in the necessary way. This is the light of need, light reduced to a necessary function, light that illuminates without either participating or permitting any participation at all; it's the sky that withdraws and leaves man in the most desolating state of abandonment, where he must depend on only the things he needs and nothing else. When grace has been refused, and a crime has been committed, human life holes up in the walls of need; nothing is actually lacking, but the soul dies and a person withdraws in order not to die—life is simply a series of necessary functions.

At that historic moment the light of Madrid was more vibrant than ever. Weightless and fleshy, light was making its presence felt; it was a luminous body. Madrid is a city of few trees, but the trees there were, now gilded with autumn, turned the city's atmosphere into a golden ember, and a golden rain seemed to be falling over this gold sprung from earth like an offering to the light, as if their love for that light, a love in search of its likeness, had prompted the trees to gild themselves. And maybe because of the strong summer sun at the beaches, her friends looked the same way to her; they were not sunburned, but they had retained a bit of the sun's light which they reflected. Because the human face can take on the sun's color without taking on its light, the way sunflowers do and certain lotus blossoms, whose nevertheless pallid faces offer obvious examples of solar "mimicry." And only when color reflects solar light, light and not color, does the soul smile, expand. When the light of the sun appears in the light that radiates from the human face, it's because that light arises from within.

This might be one of the secrets about the way light changes—it is absorbed, neutralized by totally opaque bodies and environments, but when things have a bit of light of their own, the two lights combine, sparking a golden fire, a luminous body.

She had noticed this immediately when she arrived from the light of the Mediterranean, from a metahistorical light so full of ancient history and the eternal youth of its myths, which almost prevent one from assuming another, human world. The man of today does not feel alone enough in the Mediterranean, alone as man, because he is fascinated by its dance, and the forms playing in the air, which present-day history always fails to see or reduces.

The light of the Mediterranean has its own permanent history, a very maternal one for those of us wounded by our contemporary history. Such a wound had not yet occurred, so when she returned to Madrid she found Madrid's special light, which allowed her to feel the inevitable hope.

Since she did not belong to any political party, and student life was changing so rapidly, she really had nothing to do. She was planning to return to the university, but in a new role, as an assistant who would teach one class, the History of Philosophy. She was not formally a student anymore, although this did not mean she was exactly a professor either.

In fact, she had regained some distance with respect to public things, and she had begun to form part of the "atmosphere" of that diffuse body. She had no set role, no function to carry out; like so many others, she formed part of the soul and the conscience of the history occurring at that moment.

This "change" had not come about only in her case. As the struggle became organic, many of the participants who until then would have been considered active began to form part of the atmosphere that any living thing, whether a being or a living, vital reason requires during the process of development.

Because of this atmosphere, her persona began to relax and, like the atmosphere, her life seemed to have several layers, with the same vibration passing through all of them. But she had to concentrate on the "work" she was developing, if "work" is the best name for it; because, isn't working on something, developing some project, also developing something a bit extraneous to the concern that is most immediate? And as she taught her class, she taught the material to herself, forcing herself to think aloud, afraid of having her thoughts heard there in the same classroom where she had listened so intensely to lessons that were marvels of philosophical precision and rigor, to the implacable teacher to whom she owed her understanding of the fundamental difficulty, of philosophical thought, the experience of "the aporias," the training in passing through stretches of desert—training in the anguish one suffers in the face of knowledge that holds back but at the same instant appears, affirming itself, being. What is affirmed by its own no.

And now, having passed through precisely the anguish caused by the inaccessibility of philosophical knowledge, she found her passion for philosophy somehow legitimized, as if it had been necessary for her to endure this, the refusal that must have been such an important factor in the decision she made while she was sick to abandon forever something rooted so deeply in her memory, in her personal life, something that bore no date.

She had always felt hard-pressed to answer when someone, some professor, had asked her "Why are you studying philosophy?" Because unlike other sciences, philosophy arouses this demand for an explanation, as if there were a reason embedded in the very decisions to devote oneself to all the other forms of human knowledge, but to study philosophy was something strange and ambiguous even for seasoned philosophers, as if there were many reasons for those other studies, although there may not have been a reason for them either. The hard thing about coming up with a response was that she would have had to answer when she was at the end of philosophy, when she had already scoured it, drained its last drop, when she no longer needed it. Philosophy was like a stage of her life that had ended, as if she had already lived all she was going to live, as if she were already dead. And she would answer: "Because I have to die, and I will not be able to do that without having seen and without having seen myself, because I will not be able to die without having lived the truth; and since ecstasy, complete love, or the infinite charity found in saints will never come my way; since I will only live humanly, since I am `here' . . . ; since I am suffocated by memory, the implacable gift I have apparently received, which leaves me without a horizon or a future; since I know I will not be able to live all life—all the life there is— in a single instant, which would mean experiencing the presence of the Universe, from heresince I must learn to live in time, since I must be a `person,' must live the human condition; and since . . . "Yes, since as far back as she could remember, she had seen and sensed her father bending over his books, whose indecipherable titles promised her that she would learn, earn a life like his, and have access to his world, the origin of his words, his silence, his `person,' and the grandeur that separated him from everything and put him in touch with everything—the solitude from which one understood everything. And there were also her grandfather's books, which she had held so many times when she was alone, running her eyes over the tiny comments written in his precise hand; this grandfather she had never seen, with blue eyes and impeccable manners, was a withdrawn man, serenely insane from a passion for truth and justice, who died in poverty far from his century-old oaks. Something had burned out in him, she knew, she always felt it; an earthly story of land had come to an end. Her parents had been "exiled" by then in Castile where no one from her family had lived, because no one had been "landless." She had grown up that way, feeling exile and the fact that she had lost her tie with the land and her small family history, which had turned into something remote, something myth-like, from "long ago"— when the "myth" has been lost, what can one turn to but thought? Yes, from the very beginning of her life, philosophy had been for "lack of something else," had been the only solution, the only way to live without those things, without betraying them, the only way to obey in this freedom that lets one be nobody anywhere at all, lets one be just "one more."

But there was still something else that authenticated her as a philosopher, and it was more obvious to her every day: a sacrifice she had been forced to make on the threshold, the moment fixed for sacrifices. On the threshold. On the threshold of her "serious" studies she was forced to renounce music: "You have to take something seriously, if you make the decision to do it," her father demanded. So she was forced to choose. Maybe it was because music has a more generous nature than philosophy, since it reaches people who neither create it nor have an "inside" understanding of it, maybe for some other reason she chose philosophy and said goodbye forever to creating music.

She had resigned herself. When she read Bergson two years later, she felt enormously happy, happy that it was possible to rescue her lost music, since Bergson created music at the same time he did philosophy, he created music with this thought . . . because he was precise. He had made precision the essential virtue of his thought, substituting it for Cartesian *clarté*—she thought now—and everything precise contains music, is music. Then this must be the secret, she felt—

only felt—at that moment, of Plato's requirement about geometry, which she could not understand very well either. At its most precise, philosophical thought must also be music and mathematics: the Pythagoreans probably had the key.

Even so, she still had that hole, something like a wound, because she lacked any talent for mathematics. And this explains why she felt even more destitute when she learned about Aristotle's condemnation of the Pythagoreans, from a teacher who knew mathematics thoroughly, who even "explained philosophy in mathematical terms," as she realized the first time she heard him. Because she had identified unknowingly with those Pythagoreans Aristotle "condemned," in the way adolescents often expose and simultaneously hide themselves by identifying with something or someone very different from them, although they have only the faintest image of it—there is some obscure feeling involved, or something they've latched onto and assumed was common knowledge, but later the opposite turns out to be true. What could there have been deep down in her soul that had something in common with the Pythagoreans plunged into the shadows by Aristotelian clarity? She had no way of knowing, but the rebellion inspired in her Aristotle's condemnation of the Pythagoreans made her recall at that moment, as the intensity of the present erased the memory of the incident with her teacher, how long ago, long before she finished her undergraduate degree, and long ago, from the very beginning, she had identified philosophy with the Alexandrian School, which she undoubtedly knew about from hearing her father talk about it, and from a history book by a student of Victor Cousin, which she had read avidly, devoured with more passion than if it had been a novel, and which, to tell the truth, had not aroused her avid interest as an adolescent. For her, as she encountered philosophy, she sensed for the first time, in her naive way, that the Alexandrian School *was* philosophy. Could there have been any other? And she must have learned about it from the Platonic saying she had once heard her father recite to a student: "No one enters here without knowing geometry." She had taken his remark so seriously that she began to study geometry, crying because she did not understand it, because she did want to, she wanted to "enter here." She wanted to. But she had never been able to study mathematics; the few mathematics courses she had been forced to take in high school, and her "uncommonly brilliant" performance, had cost her many bitter tears and sleepless nights, and even the memory of it was unbearable. How could she forgive Aristotle for his implacable disdain! "Those so-called Pythagoreans"! She recognized that insult: people from the Mediterranean used it, and it was what her grandfather, the one with the vineyards, would say when he looked down on someone: "Him . . . I can't remember, oh yes, they referred to him as So-and-So." And he would repeat the first and last names precisely, which added to the insult. How could there be first and last names for a person because that was "how they referred to him" or "what he was called"? Whereas the name came out with no hesitation when he was talking about someone he respected, and then it was not how they referred to that person or what he was called; the person had a name of his own.

And now here they were, the Pythagoreans. It was incredible that she would be the one who had to talk about them, seeing how little she knew! But in fact she did know them, she knew who they were, and on the basis of knowing who they were she tried to understand the thought attributed to them. This is what one must always do with the defeated: sense or have some presentiment of who they are before setting out to decipher their fragmented thought, and she read the notes from her classes over and over.

She traversed the labyrinth of Aristotle's metaphysics with great difficulty, following the thread of his polemic with Pythagoreanism, which turned out to be everything she needed: his theory of ideas, of course, the serendipity of "substance," the make-up of "nature," the reality of man, the existence of philosophy itself. And she began to understand the reason for her sacrifice, for sacrificing music specifically, because the knowledge discovered by the Pythagoreans could not, by itself alone, provide the reason for "being here"; their knowledge did not justify "incarnation," being here in a body, or rather, they justified these things for religious reasons, as an expiation, but it was a question of something more, of accepting life in this situation, of finding vital reason. And Ortega was already beginning gradually to announce this vital reason through his commentaries on Fichte. Music and mathematics do not lead to a full acceptance of the world, because they leave man's being in constant travel without anything fixed; they imply no "obligation," no "commitment," although Pythagoras and his followers themselves did make commitments, because in the end they were philosophers. But Aristotle had seen clearly; philosophy could not be founded on Pythagoreanism.

Because Aristotle had looked from "here," making man the protagonist, even though he dwells entirely in nature since there was no other place. The decisive thing was that man *was,* that he had finally acquired being, which could be summed up in the strong sentence that concludes one of Aristotle's discussions about ideas as genera: "A man is the son of a man . . . "

"A man is the son of a man," but man engenders history as well as sons. And in so doing, in making his history, he looks beyond himself. History is not born from a single man, it must have a tradition, or he must be drawn to something; history is something born with a particular determination, in a circumstance. This "participation" was what she had felt at the symphony, this unity of time and soul, this "ecstasy." Is there nothing born from such an ecstasy?

And history does have ecstatic moments. Isn't history, every history, made by participating in an idea that is governed by and attracts reverie? Yes, "in the way objects of will move and desire . . . without being moved by those objects." Then do ideas, "principles," engender too? Wasn't this the stubborn "idealistic" longing of all Western culture, which is practical and idealistic, consubstantially?

What measures will be necessary to ensure that something engendered in such exceptional "ecstatic" processes will be permanent? Won't anything born this way be most threatened when ecstasy is most pure and participation most intense? Max Scheler had separated "spiritual values" from "vitalistic values," showing that the realm most easily assimilated to the Platonic ideas is weak and fragile, and showing at the same time that it's impossible to renounce ideas without renouncing the human condition. On that love, a type of *amor intelectualis,* the person is based. And what about history? What about the direction discovered unexpectedly in history, in Western history through all its ups and downs, its terrible falls, and which seems to be consistent, into developing into a person . . . into "personal" history, the way a person develops. Man lifting the veil of his own history in order to rescue that history from the well of terror, free it from injustice in order to detach it from the animal residue that from time to time reappears, and lift it out of the void of amoral inertia, from the swamp into which man falls himself, from the trap of active non-being that is tedium, inertia . . . which leaves things open for trouble of the worst kind. Because life cannot stop; it keeps living, making history in the void, which eventually fills with the most extreme instincts and with something worse, with the limitless cruelty of the human being as he wreaks vengeance for finding himself lost in the void. Such viciousness is unknown to nature, which apparently follows only the path of need.

And in every creative process there is an instant of the void or a test of the void. This was the test approaching at that moment, as she watched anxiously with her being and her non-being, as she sat among her "pupils," with her book open; and the other book was now completely open in the street, in the atmosphere of Spanish life. Classes were interrupted often by strikes and various incidents, since the battle was being waged in the university. No blood flowed there, but blood soon flowed a little way off, within the nation's geographical boundaries and within the boundaries of the struggle you could now feel entering its last chapter. No one asked, "What's going to happen?" but "How will it happen?"

"Participation" was now a reality. How would this become apparent? Where, in what form, and when?

A Moment of Silence

People did not recognize the silence spreading over their city on one of the few days when winter's darkness descends over everything. And when there is life, this darkness throws the lights and the vibrations of a city into relief, recreating the city as a more intimate place—a house, or rather a refuge—in the center of a forest; then Madrid fulfills the final requirement and proves that it's a real city. Because winter's dismal days indicate whether a city is able to shelter its inhabitants by rescuing them from despair, whether it can irradiate vital warmth and function as a heart. In the open spaces of southern cities one is hardly aware that the city and its citizenry are working as a heart, because one feels the cosmos itself throbbing in a single rhythm common to earth and sky. In the southern provinces, life is open to the cosmos, and there people's virtue is hospitality: the offer of shade, a roof, a cool spot where one can take cover from the merciless rays of the universe, from the cosmic fire and dust into which the earth disintegrates—the burning dust winding in whirlpools around the face that's come straight from the fiery center. But in northern countries, when the frosty air lacks any vibration and everything, even the light affirms its absence, the human virtue is warmth: the offer of a fire and human companionship that will let a messenger feel the beat of a heart encouraging him to keep going even though nature has broken down all around him. Cities in the north, more than those in the south, must serve as the beat of a human heart and a living inner world; their life blossoms in the winter, which is the moment for coming together, for a common vibration in music, thought, and friendly words.

Madrid, a city of central Spain's vast exposed tableland during the summer, has always turned into a northern city during the winter. Slashed by frosty air, it becomes the capital of an area around the Guadarrama mountain range. Even on clear days, which means most days, the city becomes hollow, concave, so that everyone will fit. And Madrid is friendly; a true, great European city, it irradiates, throbs like a heart, even though it was poorer in those days and had less sparkle. It's not a question of more or less, though, but of being a real city.

That's why she did not recognize the silence, the hollowness of that winter day. The cavity created by the city was there, but it was a void—you could not feel any heartbeat. Maybe that's how it was a century before on the day Larra committed suicide after preparing a written statement of his vision, of Madrid as a cemetery where you can read on a common grave: "Here lies hope." Maybe it had been like this throughout the entire nineteenth century; the heart of the city must not have been beating, and this accounts for the occurrence of those frightful nightmarish episodes in which the gallows played an important role— the gallows and arriving there in a large basket dragged by mobs shouting "Long live chains!" And it also accounts for so many similarly sinister episodes that sank into the void formed by all of Spain, beginning with the return of the "the Desired One" after Napoleon was defeated, as if the country had been forced to pay for that too, for the gesture of supreme, desperate resistance on the part of a people that does consider things carefully because there is something more important, more vital than the system someone wants to impose on them, even though it may mean an improvement, a much better system than the one now governing undeservedly. "Objectively" it was a mistake to oppose Napoleon, but it was a question of being or not being. The Spanish people were made to pay for that "being" with the fate they "desired," which sank them and even drove them to the most abject depths.

The series of Spain's civil wars began with the death of that lord, as if Spain's fate were prolonged beyond his mortal life in the equivocal inheritance that divided the Spaniards. Did it divide them or were they already divided? And why didn't the ones who were "absolutists" and those who were "liberals" end up fighting together against the invader? Why did such fierce discord follow the Spaniards' sacred unity in defense of the inalienable being of their country? Something must have happened within the heart of Spain. And Madrid, the capital, was left paralyzed. It ceased to be a city and became something sinister, a decaying city whose pulse is so weak it cannot be a true capital and repair the national life. At such times the city does not become a village but the rubble of a city found in "lower" class neighborhoods—the low morality characteristic of a skepticism that lacks tenderness, the tenderness that flourishes in large cities, which involves sensitivity and understanding with respect to the smallness of everyday living. During that period Madrid fell into a bitter, merciless life given to crime and to the spectacle of capital punishment, which is the luxury large cities allow themselves when rancor gets the better of them. A province rarely enjoys this spectacle and usually watches it with terror, as something greater than its own forces—a distinction made thanks to destiny's indulgence, although it's a distinction experienced as disgrace. The large city, however, when its heart collapses or rancorous rage gets the better of it, indulges in the spectacle of the guillotine, of the gallows, of the dull murmur of shots from the firing squads; this is the crime characteristic of the large city. The country has a different crime, rural crime, committed when one family takes revenge on another or when a family destroys itself in a rage; rural crime is linked to the family, to ancestral rancor; it's the crime of an ancestor, of a gene. There is also the man-to-man crime, one more characteristic of the small Mediterranean city, which is small but still a city, a "polis" in miniature, where the individual allows himself the luxury of his private crime, his alone; this might often be the reason people kill each other—their argument is nothing more than a pretext for feeling more like an individual, for having one's own nonexchangeable crime.

Because apparently a different type of crime corresponds to each form of existence man has reached in his march through history: "Crime can be expressed in many ways."

And the capital has its crime, defined by law, for which it is the seat. The city is where the legal crime of execution is formulated and carried out, and served up as a spectacle to everyone, to the city that, like an idol, needs victims. Because it seems that every idol will inexorably have its victim. And idols characteristically lack hearts. It doesn't take much: a person becomes someone, grows heartless, and begins to act like an idol; his heart stops for just a moment—a moment of silence—and crime is lodged there.

Crime can also lodge in the life of all men: one's heart is inhibited for just one moment, and one no longer hears its voice or feels its communicating warmth, its irradiation. One feels then the cavity, the hollowness within oneself, the idol that needs to be nourished with a victim; and one feels a desire to kill, the need to kill—a love, a friendship, an hour of possible happiness, even to commit the greatest of all crimes: to murder hope. Both people trained in some form of asceticism, whether faith or anguish, and simple people who have faith in their hearts, know that when such a moment, that moment of silence, arrives, they must retreat—withdraw into the moment or make the moment withdraw into itself, use the hollowness within to collect the silence without and wait, even if not hopefully: endure this pause in breathing, ready for anything, even the very end! When there is no "inspiration," one must prepare to expire if necessary . . . and it usually is not necessary—inspiration returns.

Inspiration always returns, but when inspiration returns, it must not discover that we've committed a crime in the moment of silence. Spain's moment had lasted a long time; it had been a moment as endless as the nineteenth-century winter midnight after the return of the country's desired fate. Inspiration had been coming . . . slowly; now inspiration was present and at its peak, and it had discovered that we had committed many crimes—accumulated during three civil wars, and committed during all the persecution that went on in the "Ominous Decade," and after, which were so shameful . . .

And you could feel all this on that terrible Sunday in the very dark of winter. The execution had occurred far away, at the edge of the nation's territory, in Jaca, a small city almost on the border, where the garrison had revolted against the . . . state of things; it may have acted before it was supposed to. And the leaders were given a very quick trial and shot the following Sunday in the morning; they were two young captains who said they had been "responsible," who did not turn back. The capital had not been present at the spectacle. There was no spectacle; it was a moment of silence that Spain observed when the country learned what had happened.

She was walking through the paralyzed heart of the "lower class neighborhoods" the afternoon of that breakdown, with her father and "brother," both of them overcome by the memories of many crimes, reliving in barely spoken words, in choked sentences, the sinister events that had stained those same stones a century ago; because time doesn't matter, when you're afraid that a situation belongs to the same series. The same thing could not happen this time: on the stone pavement where they walked a man's body had shattered and agonized, but he had inspired an anthem of hope that was now being sung again by the Republic. And that time the "legal" crime decreed by the fatal "Desired One" had been perpetrated by the *pueblo,* which had become degraded, converted into a lower class rabble, a mob enraged at man that made the gates of hell fling open, something that happens at certain moments when the heart hushes in the bowels of a large city. Because viscera are hellish, hell itself, when they are not governed by the heart, the mediator and noblest organ of all, which distributes its "logos" among the other organs. This is something Empedocles had expressed in the form of an ancient prescription, the earliest medicine of all—tragedy and early philosophy: "Divide the logos carefully, distributing it carefully among the viscera." When the heart abandons them, the viscera are pure hell.

History passes through such hours, which can last for a long time, as happens in some lives. And maybe all crimes could be avoided if people came up with some way for a supplementary heart to replace the one that's stopped working because of the void; if a warm, rhythmic wave would arrive from another, larger and more powerful heart when a heart stops and leaves the living viscera abandoned and moaning; if one person could loan his own suffering heart to another person who's about to commit a crime.

They were walking in the anguish of the absolute silence that will receive, as they flow into it, the silence of each individual—the silence of each individual who remains silent. Not a single voice could be heard and there was no sign of a single living soul. The streets and large plazas were hollows where the viscera throbbed dully. They had shut themselves up, which was a good sign in the middle of so much hermeticism, a good sign seen from the long collapse they were recalling as they walked. And when dusk fell that sinister afternoon, a different hellish viscera, the machines, the murder machines, appeared instantly. On each deserted corner, a group of soldiers was assembling a machine gun—the image of viscera mechanized, moving with neither inspiration nor breath. The soldiers seemed mechanical too, the way soldiers in the firing squad must seem to the eyes of the one about to fall, wrapped in his own warm blood. Viscera grown cold . . . which always turn up somehow at dictated deaths.

Cold viscera. Could that be how they feel to a person condemned to death, from the time he knows his end and has been told the hour, the moment? Does life continue to be life when you can count the beats of your heart one by one, knowing they belong to a defined series—I have so many left—when you already know the number of hours, minutes you have to live? If life is governed by numbers, to know those numbers is to be dead already. This might explain why one's knowledge of oneself must be limited, because as long as life continues its course, it must retain a bed of unconsciousness, which is how the inexhaustible nature of life, the life enveloping us, is reflected in the human life of each man. We know that life has a limit—ours—but as long as life is life it must function by participating, in some way, in the inexhaustible nature of total life. To know the number of instants we have left to live is to be posthumous now, to be forced to breathe, to have our hearts kept beating after we're dead, to be forced to speak and to stand up but remain silent: to be forced to walk the last steps, until we find ourselves facing the unreality of those de-brothered men who lack any bond of community at all, who are mechanisms, men who are also condemned—to be machines, to be turned into men possessed by a trigger.

She felt nauseated, and she felt a profound pity from deep down in her stomach for the soldiers, who looked as though they were made of cardboard; they were cold, and they had their hands resting on their machines, ready to shoot at a moment's notice. Yes, pity and disgust; and a scream caught in her throat, the scream that arises irrepressibly from the bottom of one's heart in the presence of any dictated death—execution, or war scenes, or the image of men ordered to kill, with their machines on their shoulders—a scream that has yet to be heard universally, rhythmically, crossing every border and every abyss: "Don't shoot, don't shoot!"

Had a condemned man facing a firing squad ever let out that scream? No; what you hear are opposite screams: "Shoot, aim right for my heart!" This is understandable. It's what the victim screams as he rushes for dear life toward death, as he allows himself the final luxury of dying voluntarily, of dying alive. The one who will give the order to shoot would scream it too if he had not grown cold in that instant, condemned to participate as well. And so would the onlookers if they were not also growing cold, assimilated by terror, fascinated or spellbound by the act in which a life stops according to an assigned number . . .

Who could scream that scream? Someone entirely alive at such a moment, free from the usury of death.

The scream growing cold in her throat was choking her. It was the scream we choke back our whole lives when, under the spell cast by evil, by dictated death, we participate through our silence in the crime committed by others, because our hearts do not leap forward to awaken theirs. Will the heart ever be strong enough to break through a conscience spellbound by the evil it sees being carried out? And this evil does not have to be death. The slander spoken in our presence, the dispossession committed before our eyes, and the infinite cruelty of a gesture or a silence in response to one's brother all require strength, the strength to shatter the moment of silence that suspends life when God is killed in some way within one of our fellow men. No; she did not do it. Nausea rose in her throat. She felt bewitched.

The soldiers did not shoot. The city refused to face them: people plunged into silence, participated in the moment of silence occurring that morning in the Jaca countryside. Breaking through the labyrinth of machine guns, the small family group returned home and, without saying a word, started to stoke the fire in the fireplace, sitting beside it until after midnight.

Inspiration

I

The rhythm resumed quickly, but now it was different. Like a surge of blood it coursed through the body of the nation. You could feel the acceleration inspired by surrender, the rushing of blood ready to be spilled. There were no further executions. The army did not continue its raid and had begun to behave itself . . . The arms were silent and it was words, attitudes, and people that rushed like an uncontrollable river within the Modelo jail. Modelo was full—some students, a few workers, intellectuals, politicians, and the group of men who had formed the "Provisional Government of the Republic." Now there was even a government, but how would the Republic itself arrive?

Outside the door, every afternoon at visiting hours, there was a throng of people many times larger than the permitted number of visitors. Not a few of the people got inside, but they got in to stay. The life of the city flowed toward that jail just at the edge of the border of Campo de la Moncloa, and Modelo became a kind of center where everyone felt impelled to go, whether or not they had any personal friends among the prisoners, so they could tell themselves: "I went."

And a net started to form around that center. All of them, especially the students and the workers, had to be sent the vital goods necessary for winter, which, although rather mild that year, was winter nevertheless; above all, they had to be sent encouragement, the beat of the supplementary heart, even if they didn't need it . . . At such moments of participation, does anyone think about what's needed? Although the heart may be the most necessary organ, one never has to alert it to need, because the heart is also the organ of participation. And there are

139

no limits to participation, or the heart gradually describes them around itself, according to its own reasons; participation has its private limits, but they are not formulated and it may not be possible to formulate them. When the "logos" scatters among the viscera it renounces the word as a total form of expression and becomes action, gesture, stance . . . inspiration that in every moment finds the unforeseeable solution, the human miracle.

Almost miraculously she was finding the time and the energy, remaining faithful to a kind of vow she had made to herself that she would not belong to any political party. She was working, traveling here and there, and knotting threads in the net that kept all of them in touch with the prisoners and with each other. She did not follow a particular program, nor could she, and she never even considered getting involved in any particular action, any subversive project. Were there such projects? She did not know, and there were no signs of any. The outcome was certain; it would take something inspired, something unforeseen. It would take almost a miracle.

The net she was involved in did not entail much of a conspiracy; it was the net formed by handshakes and by glances as they met, the net that required the least organization to capture life as it overflows, life at the moments when it has a more liquid quality than ever—water that's spilling beyond the limits of its own body, that has surpassed itself at every instant. It can't be pinned down. Wanting to is a crime, one that not even reason has been able to commit since it realized that reason itself imposes life's laws, life's shadows. Ortega often used the metaphor of the net in class to talk about reason as it attempts to capture multiple reality— the net that imposes its very slight but indispensable structure, since reason is indispensable to human life. The net, a living structure, forms tissues; there's a net in the blood. And the net is a metaphor of transmission; it transmits participation, knots threads of friendship and feeling. Instead of orders, it transmits impulses, subtle vibrations, and inspiration; that's why it captures the channels water makes in order to acquire form. Because anything human must have some form, and because our dream of a liquid life flowing undammed is still far from coming true, far from a life free of nets as well because there would not be any differences, only the abysmal, transparent depth of the waters where the fish, spirits of the waters, could live just by breathing. This would mean pure abandon in the waters of life, the chance to breathe once again in the waters of the first day of creation, waters unsullied by combat. Utopia, only utopia. The net is the thing least foreign to the spirit of the waters, of the life that requires no organization.

The net was spreading through Spain, carrying so many communications that it seemed as though all Spain were present. Presence, society in its complete form, occurs in struggle against absence and insurmountable distance. Life will be this way as long as each of us and each of the others—everyone—cannot all be present every moment. Such life would no longer be human life, the life of the being that can and must hide, that needs to discover itself all through history.

In the sinister hours no one appears, everyone is hidden, even from themselves. Terror conceals us, turns us into jungle animals. And these shameful hours leave us faceless—"we lose face." In inertia one is present in a kind of void, of minimal presence; and this occurs among people who see and deal with each other. In the distance, hollows, chasms of absence open in the living, vital horizon. People only live with other people if they are connected to them in some way, only if there's a reason. During periods when history is expanding, when something is being born, when hope, shared hope appears, we have a greater presence, and the size of our persons, of our souls seems larger to our fellow men; we emerge with them, together. Distance is abolished, and there is a presence that links people who do not know each other and probably never will. If they do meet, "they think they've known each other forever" although they've never seen each other. It's the hour when hope enlarges the area of contact among the members of a people, a community. But from there it radiates to everyone, to all men, and it is present to them all; anyone could call us, call at our door. The ancient religions teach us that the door must be left open for the unknown guest who arrives unexpectedly. Not to welcome him can mean not welcoming God Himself. Awakened hope confidently opens the door wide to the brother who's just arrived, because that's what everyone is: "He's our brother."

That's how it was. Strangers had known each other forever; there were no strangers, because no one resists presence at such moments. The moment of the kiss on the cheek, of the counterfeit presence, was still far off.

II

One morning they learned from the newspapers that the dictator had gone; in his place there was another general who had been associated with him when the dictatorship was first established. Although the government had been seized by a member of the military, it had been formed under the sign of civilian rule, and it was seeking to enlist the liberal-minded European-style intellectuals who had never been involved in politics. This was merely a last, late inspiration that the king seemed to accept as a way of saving the monarchy: call for participation from the intellectual men who would eventually make up the Reformist party and from others who had never belonged to any party and had remained incorruptible, avoiding any dealings with power. It should have been enough to awaken the sleeping king, to make him awaken to the beat you could feel in Spain. Throughout his reign, not a few people had pointed out to His Majesty that the intellectuals had become very present in national life—not to warn him against the intellectuals, but to make him realize how valuable they were and what they meant as a figure of renewed Spain. Some aristocrats, among them some women, had taken the initiative to have the king meet a few of those men personally, the ones who were most important intellectually but took no part in specific political action. And the liberal mentality of the intellectuals created a particular atmosphere, a sense of living with others, between a small group of courtiers and a particular zone of intellectual life. But His Majesty had not profited at all from such inspirations, and the only thing achieved was something that lent to Madrid life the scale of life in a European city, in a Spanish city from another era, when the nobles and the "intelligentsia" were not unaware of each other and even enjoyed a degree of familiarity, which the nineteenth century completely destroyed for us. But this clever, narrow bridge over the channel surrounding Madrid had not been enough to span the ever deeper and more multiple chasms between national life and a nineteenth-century monarchy.

Now it was too late, no matter how much certain well-intentioned souls— some of them feminine and from high society—traveled back and forth knotting the threads of a tapestry impossible to reconstruct. She and her group also wove their net, which proved powerless to catch any "spirit of the waters": even in official life there were no internal contradictions. It would have been necessary to eliminate military interference completely. This was no doubt the inspiration that came to one skillful old liberal politician, a cultured man whose spirit was receptive to every vibration, one of the few people who had wanted Spain to abandon its neutrality in the First European War in favor of the Allies, with the aim of participating in the historical rhythm of European synchronization, through the support we would lend to our "natural allies." But the general who replaced Primo de Rivera had a different "inspiration" of his own, one even more daring with respect to eliminations, one so daring that he himself had to step down. He was replaced by a cabinet presided over by an admiral, a liberal-minded man whose thinking reflected the spirit of Spanish naval tradition. To avoid the impending shipwreck, they needed a great sailor, and His Majesty must have finally realized how precarious things were. The alternative was clear: either accept the inspiration offered to him or continue to follow the course he had chosen some time before at the direction of his own inspiration, the course of hurrying the dictatorship along.

But that form of dictatorship could not be hurried. They would have needed to construct something different, to build a structure that some of General Primo de Rivera's collaborators had attempted unsuccessfully. This would have required nothing less than the construction of a Spanish fascism whose purpose, unlike that of Italian fascism, would have been to defend and shore up the current system, nothing more. Obviously, it would have taken years to devise the capitalist system necessary to shore up, to remove the structure of the nation, in short, to create a complete revolution. And the king had no revolutionary calling, nor did any of his advisors. On the contrary, he had arrived at this precarious situation through inertia. There was perhaps a third option open to him, which was to force "the impasse": a military dictatorship, but one more violent, one ready to shed blood, to persecute, to create a revolution carried out by the police—terrorism from the seat of power. But was the army prepared to do so at that time? There was no sign of it, nor was there any reason to believe that the monarch himself had decided on this course, since he gave no visible signals of having decided to go "beyond," to go so far as terror in order to keep his throne. And it's unlikely that he had serious intentions of leading the country to absolute subjugation, to a terrorist tyranny, much less of provoking a civil war; in any event, the accusation against historical masks probably cannot be formulated in those terms. He did not do it, nor did he give any indication of trying.

He had given up hope when he accepted the inspiration of the sibylline voice. What would have happened if he had paid attention instead to the temptation, slipped into his ear by such a voice one day now long ago, to wrench Spain from the paradise of neutrality during the time of the European War? Can any politician with a true calling love neutrality? Isn't the political mentality the most serpentine of them all, the one that every day faithfully follows the serpent's promising whisper, which hope resembles so closely? Would there be any politics if once and for all everyone complied with the whisper that awakens hope, or rather, exploits it in order to realize ambition? Would politics exist without the ambiguity between hope and ambition? Without the essential possibility for human hope to become fascinated, to get sidetracked; without the things that occur tragically or gloriously—ambiguously—in one's personal life? "I was hoping, and then it was offered to me" or "I was hoping, but it was offered to me." The day when no one can say this, and only on that day, political passion will have ended; man will have exhausted this aspect of his passion.

And there are people who do not go when it's offered to them and only go when they're allowed to offer—which does not avoid passion, as in this instance. Yes, she was waiting and it was offered to her, it must have been offered to her more than once, but she accepted, and without further ado, only when the offer consisted in allowing her to offer, to offer herself. And passion seems to come to a specific end that way; it's limited, and it's consonant with the warning and the "ethics" of prudent young Ulysses. But passion ends when triumph arrives and later, later, if the hour of defeat arrives and one is there too, it turns out that one is there so that he will now pursue passion forever—pure passion, but now pursue it in the void, now without hope. What history will this be? The history of a hope not fascinated by ambition but scornful of it, the history of a hope that refuses "temptation." But won't there be several temptations, so that we'll even have to commit our souls in the march of history, so that we enter historical times without any possibility of escape? That young generation shouldered those times with happy, impassioned spirits, with sportive, ascetic spirits. They almost all said "no," as she did, to the hour of ambition, although it was certainly not unlawful, and this meant that later they would be early for the hour of definitive passion, of certain death, or of life in agony, as certain as death it-self—the agony of surviving.

The hour was approaching, the hour of certain hope, still free of the temp-tation that could bewitch it—the hour of pure, absolute hope, the hour when the thing one hopes for must be brought to reality. No ambition is possible at that instant. The ambiguous serpent from the "other side" was asleep, not yet whispering in the ear of those already condemned: "If you do this, if you're smart, you'll have power." Whom did the serpent serve, whom did it want to serve?" Ambiguous, more diplomatic than ever, it served hope. But there are innocent serpents that feign temptation, because without temptation there would appar-ently be no history.

The inspiration that there could be a history with no serpent! If we had built a theory on that inspiration, if we had even tried to rough out a plan for the construction of a system, ours would have been just one more example of the utopias that have arisen in the Western world, although this one was more modest, because we had no talent for systematizing. But we did not even go so far as to become conscious that this was our fantasy—our delirium imprisoned in the destiny that resulted. So if we served inspiration in all innocence, our in-spiration was even more utopian because "utopia" was absent.

Utopia is the place where inspiration about history comes to Westerners, confined at times, as if in a jail where some persistent individuals go to rescue it—the ideologues accompanied by their wardens and jealous definitors with their measuring, determined to make sure that their inspiration does not flow into history, that they will continue to carry its water, to utilize it for a single windmill. An inspiration without a utopia has a different, rare history. So few people can relate it now, the history of our inspiration, of our delirium, a delir-ium of purity so quickly condemned by destiny. And fatal destiny is nothing but history itself refusing inspiration!

At that moment no one thought he would have to relate this history, be-cause hope not fascinated by ambition believes it's free, without history. Even so, deep down in that hope, the other utopian hope that dares not speak its name was burning, the hope that the curse, the serpent's spell has been broken once and for all, that the inspired history will spring up now that people had learned to obey—the history free of ambiguity that man creates in obedience to his inspiration, a transparent history that does not sweep men along to passion's fatal end.

They never articulated this among themselves. It was no doubt implicit, however, in the "No" the majority of those young people, my friends, answered to the suggestion that we act, that we occupy seats in our glorious Constituent Courts, especially since we were the first to have a premonition of them, an in-spiration implicit in the "No" that returned us to our private lives exactly as we had left them three years before. With eyes now bewildered and empty, totally empty hands there was no need to wash, we resumed the tasks we had interrupted; still young, we were not yet quite mature enough for the places we had forfeited, because others came along who had not needed to offer a thing, not one bit of their lives in order to enjoy the comfortable life offered to them.

That No, at a different time was Yes, to the definitive hour when we met again briefly. The first days of the "Madrid front" consumed many of those lives, and you were sown forever in the places we had walked during weightless hours on the last of our ritual excursions, along the banks of the Manzanares in the Sierra, where both the boy who had attended my "classes"—the one who seemed to be the youth offered up in sacrifice in each generation, as if in the name of everyone—and the sculptor of Guadarrama granite, greater in achievements and in years, would later remain. Between them they mark the boundaries of the generation that served hope without ambiguity; they never spoke the word "sacrifice," and they would not have accepted it as a definition of their actions, because it was something so natural! As it was for the ones shot in distant provinces and at crossroads, like the beautiful girl, so full of life, who had collaborated in Pamplona; like her husband, governor for only two weeks, which was nevertheless long enough to make him keep fighting until he fell, riddled with bullets, in the courtyard of the governor's palace. And like Fe, cut in two by bombs right at the border, holding her little girl by the hand. And years later, in exile, the suicides, the one who had stopped her at the very threshold of death, her doctor brother who, far away, had wrenched, separated himself from the person he loved most, and when he returned, when he wanted to reintegrate himself into the Western world and the normal life of exile, he could not; and he wrenched himself from life once more, this time forever. And the one she saw day after day, bent over the galley proofs, over the books he had to translate, hanged in a hotel room in a Mexican city; and the other writer flung from the window of a spotless university in the United States, and the other one, yes, and still others—almost all the suicides of exile belonged to this generation that participated just to offer, to offer itself; and the torture without any imaginable end that was in store for the defeated who remained inside. Yes, I understand you, I understand you.

The suicide, the historic suicide we thought we had exorcised forever was something we carried in our destiny. Obedience to their inspiration to say no had now made them say no to life, as the result of having followed their inspiration of hope and closing their ears effortlessly to the ambition that makes hope ambiguous: suicide through training in the unpremeditated pursuit of one's inspiration. Inspiration returns and within an hour its irresistible downright no drowns any possibility of resistance, because life has been surrendered many times, because no one has drawn an image or made a mask, the historical mask that allows one to hope, armed with patient ambition.

All these deaths were already occurring in our lives when the hour arrived, the hour of hope's fullness, when everyone's life was a pure presence that seemed not to contain the possibility of death; because death comes from one's being hidden, and the person who becomes present, is completely present, will be completely, will be nothing but now, free from any finish. And we can experience that in this life once we have given everything for the common hope, without holding back a hidden part for ourselves. But now I cannot relive that hour, enter it through the corridor of my memory without naming all of you. A person does not weep when she's writing. That's a rhetorical figure, and besides, I don't want to weep for you, I'm just calling to you, because that way I call to myself, so I can feel your voices mixed with mine and answer that I am still here, and so you can call to me from the silence into which you have fallen, from the life of what we could have been, from the other silence that was growing alongside us, so different from the silence that survives now and faces the deformation imposed by the deformed image responsible for this way of living with our roots in the air. Life has split for us; we, the survivors, have our roots exposed; you, the dead, are the roots, nothing but roots sunk in earth and oblivion.

Everything was now in that hour—our entire fate. We disappeared in the wide sea of a life that belonged to everyone, so we were already lost, a generation without personality, with nothing but a silhouette in spite of ourselves; we drowned in the triumph of the hope we had raised with our bare hands. Then the tragic hour raised us up again; hope raised its victims, but as hope sank into defeat it hurled us once more toward our stark lives as survivors—a generation of half-beings, because only together could we make a being, a being with its complete history. "Utopia," our utopia, has scattered us carefully: you, the dead, were left with no time; we, the survivors, were left with no place. This makes us seem to have been sacrificed to hope, with no masks, without the protection of a definite name, of a personality—simple victims, as if we had come naked to history, to its costume ball. Carried by others, possessed by others, by men who wanted and managed to possess, we entered that cavalcade dispossessed, and we had dispossessed ourselves, which made it impossible for us to march with the victims or the slaves, and no group would welcome us under the banner of its struggle . . . except perhaps the vanguard of an unmasked history, a history of man free of all ambition to possess anything and uncompromising about nothing possessing him. Its vanguard, the witnesses, the testimony that once someone wanted this type of history, rather, that someone refused all histories, that someone simply obeyed the inspiration of unadulterated hope, are perhaps the seeds of another way to be man, of the nakedness and renunciation in history itself, of a responsible innocence, a way to follow one's inspiration through conscience. A way of fighting with the serpent.

The dead have no voices; their voices is the first thing they lose. We can hear them within ourselves, in the music that erupts when we're most oblivious, as if we could never be alone. Faltering words come to us, syllables from the land of the dead. A voice, choking as it tries to speak, wants to tell us its history, its story.

Anyone who has died prematurely, who has died violently, needs to have his story told, because a person can sink into silence only after everything has been said, when he has drained his life as if it were a single sentence, brimming with meaning. We can surrender our souls only before a life whose reason gathers our own reasons in its flow—the reasons behind what we lived, what we were called to live. But when that bit of destiny sank like an Atlantis into the hole of a bottomless history, when you sense an ancient god at work once again, the ancient god that devours its children, who have even been stripped of time, then you cannot accept silence. Because there is a silence of reason fulfilled, and it will join with all reasons to widen harmony's course. There is also a dissonant silence that leaves a faltering word in the air, reason turned to scream, and even the condemned man's skeleton dispossessed of its truth: the silence enveloping inspiration that has been murdered.

The Hour

It seemed like a long time since the dictator had relinquished his power and left Spain. In pictures he looked sad, old, and grief-stricken; maybe the hour made him realize how sad a countenance there was on the deception he had been put up to. When he arrived in Paris he must have been like a creature worse than wounded, one humiliated by the affront that weighs on a person who has put his heart quixotically into a deception devised by others. He also arrived there poor.

Elections were called, not for Parliament but only for municipal councils. An attempt to rescue the country that way was a good inspiration, and one consistent with Spain's "feudal" history; they would start with an institution that represented Spanish law throughout the country at the local level. Although they would have been afraid if they had remembered what mayors and councils had been capable of in Spain's history. Wasn't it the mayor of a village very close to the capital who declared the Napoleonic war *urbi et orbe?* "I, the mayor of Móstoles." What about that incident? They did not remember it, or maybe they did; the serpent whose memory goes back so far, the inspired serpent, may have remembered it and remained silent. The announcement of elections was published and with it twenty days, twenty, of complete freedom of written and oral expression for campaigning.

That freedom came the way people's ability to use their bodies must come after years of crashing against courtyard walls when they took a walk, the way extensive dialogue comes after long periods of soliloquies or only speaking with other initiates.

There was a lack of political training, which is one of the most serious forms of damage such a situation can produce in a country. A generation had been denied access to seats in Parliament, had been given no opportunity to measure its strengths and ideas against "reality." Except for the mature politicians, everyone was emerging from shared soliloquies, from monologues spoken aloud; the hour had come for them to appear before all the others and account for the solitude in which they had lived for so long.

People must always account for solitude; be it paradise or hell, solitude must be subjected to judgment, to purgatory. There is not just one solitude; there are solitudes. After emerging from any of them, people must appear before others and present their solitudes to the community and have them undergo the definitive test of whether or not something useful to everyone can be extracted from them—some thought or effective action, a purer way of being with others. And if there is no such thought or action expressed when that solitude is pressed for its juice, it will be sentenced to eternal sterility, to capital punishment as payment for having squandered a great treasure.

For they had been together as discrete souls, but as Spanish solos; Spain had been increasingly present for them, open like a horizon in the process of unfolding. A person who is alone feels the presence of the reality he is missing. In that instance Spain had definitely been growing more and more present, but the confrontation with presence was missing; and now they were heading right toward it.

There was no choice but to go. All Spain was waiting in each nook and corner. The bullrings were opened for crowds that filled them to overflowing—they were like cups that cannot hold another drop of wine from a jug still full to the brim. Spain was waiting at the doors of those bullrings, and at that particular ring crowds from outside the town made way for her group seriously, with silent expectation, with restrained eagerness.

She found herself entering a city in La Mancha with a small group of men from different political parties. They had come by car across don Quijote's fields after passing quite close to the Cave of Montesinos, one of the secrets of the Spanish labyrinth, of Spain's charm. After crossing the central plain, whose sacred places had been mapped by Cervantes, the prototype of secular ingenuity, they had reached a border city at the edge of the Manchegan region.

The crowd awaiting them, already assembled in the bullring that harsh Sunday in early spring, was not agitated. Nor was it filled with the enthusiasm that means prior surrender to whatever might be spoken; people were simply standing in wait. And that's what was so impressive, because the crowd as a whole was marked by the solemnity usually associated with a single individual. All of them had been alone too, so that two solitudes were approaching each other. And experiencing it in those terms somewhat lessened her panic, which had been growing increasingly acute during the trip—the terror people experience when they emerge from their solitudes to appear before the crowd. But now she saw the crowd as something made up of solitudes, which as a whole formed a single solitude. And there was the silence and the distance that must exist between two

people who finally meet after knowing for a long time that they are engaged—
an old fashioned marriage.

In the dining room of the shabby hotel she watched the serving plates pass
in front of her eyes as if they were something intangible; she was fasting, looking forward to a different food. She admired those men she had come with—for
their chatter, their laughter, their composure. One of them was silent and restrained; he was a socialist more accustomed to working on behalf of that crowd
than meeting it face to face; he didn't say anything, just took notes. After several
cups of coffee—the only thing that would go down her rather constricted
throat—they left for the bullring. It was full and silent, with none of the usual
refreshment vendors shouting in the stands. There was neither sun or shade; the
day was neutral and the crowd was neutral too, or seemed to be. There was no
way to sense what the crowd was feeling; it was a crowd wrapped in thought that
had withdrawn into itself so as to listen better, to understand better, to watch.
She would not have had the courage to speak first, but fortunately ritual etiquette
had placed her last, and she had time.

She noticed that while the speakers talked and responded to the applause,
as if in an ancient ritual game, time had been transformed for her. Once again,
she was being saved by the multiplicity of times, because she no longer felt "in
front of" but "in," as in the children's circle game she would always start to play
in fear because she knew that she would have to walk into the center of the
ring and that everyone would be watching her as she spoke the lines—"I'm the
young widow of Count Laurel"—but then, when her turn came, she would already be inside the "circle," and she would sing the words of that monologue by
feeling them out loud, letting them emerge from her heart the way she sang
them when she was by herself. And so, in this increasingly intimate hour, increasingly lived from within, the time of her childhood enveloped her, and she
seemed to be on one of those plazas where in late spring afternoons she would
sense the acacias' fragrance, or the garden's breathing, and the hollow of the
small square would fill with a living, rhythmic breath. The void was transformed
into a space of life, where you could not hear your own voice. This meant she
spoke without hearing herself; the air vibrated, but there was no roar; and the
applause had been increasing, becoming more and more frequent, and sounding
more and more like the sea, but fortunately there was no flooding. The turning
inward continued—they were both playing the same game, and this is why they
had understood each other the way children understand each other as they recall the beginning of the theater, the birth of tragedy, in the circle game. And
the inexplicable experience she had as she closed *Prometheus Bound* after reading
it for the first time rose from deep in her memory: she had felt that she was inside a circle and everyone was saying: "Antón, Antón Pirulero, pay attention to
the game, for the one who does not will have to pay a forfeit; Antón, Antón . . . "

Now she felt the same way, as if "Antón Pirulero" were the game they had chosen to play that afternoon: "What are we going to play?" "Antón Pirulero." And she spoke her part even though her legs were shaking; she would not have to forfeit anything. People could probably not hear her in the back, even with the microphone, but she did not feel the hollow where one's voice gets lost; she felt them close to her, and she was in the middle, inside the circle. The applause, which ended both her small speech and the event, sounded in her ears like the choruses in old operas, the one by Gluck, in which an ancient tragedy was coming to a happy ending, and a chorus was celebrating this by singing a melody almost identical to one from children's circle games. Still hearing it, she accepted the bouquets being offered to her in an endless garland. She recognized them. They were the same tight bouquets of roses still only half-open and arranged in a pyramid; carnations, which predominated because of the time of year, and even a few stray violets, along with the smell of wallflowers—all flowers people cut from their gardens as they participate in the secular ceremony customary in small towns for receiving visitors from the city or for taking bouquets to church, all of them fragrant with an earthy smell, flowers of pure, delicate colors, flowers of the earth as it opens to spring. She felt protected in the close intimacy of that ancient, intact Spain. Groups of women approached her at the exit with curiosity: "Look at her. They told us a woman was going to come, and it's a girl." "She's so young, she seems only about twenty!" Even less, less at that hour; from the depths of her childhood, drowning her, had risen the time when one lives the serious games—ancient time had risen. Why?

In the car on the way back to Madrid, still half asleep, in the sound of the motor, in the silence that was calming her soul, she heard the song from the circle game, the "Antón Pirulero" that would not go away. No doubt she had been hearing it as she read *Prometheus Bound,* translating laboriously for her Greek exam. Why? What does paying a forfeit for not paying attention to the game have to do with that venerable tragedy about freedom in bondage? And what did it have to do with this serious game, with the immense chorus that filled the plaza waiting so soberly for its freedom? Where could the secret to paying the forfeit be found, what would the forfeit be, and who would have to pay? The forfeit!

She was still not fully awake when she went into her class at the Instituto Escuela. She would continue to be that way, more or less, sleeping in a moving car, compressed between bouquets of roses opening gradually, engrossed in her game, in the seriousness of recovered childhood. She was living in an ancient time when the tragic crisis, the incessantly compressed conflict was finding resolution through the ceaseless action of those who had paid attention to the game throughout incessant centuries of patience. The archaic time of early spring. That's why she seemed, seemed to the people from those remote villages, to be just a girl. One girl, but there were others: girls whose task was to hold up the very simple yet archaically modern temple of the Spain that was awakening in a sacred instant. If awakening is not a sacred instant, it is not true awakening.

She was on the go constantly during those two weeks in Madrid, stopping only for the time it took to meet her various classes. The university had closed and most of the classes from the Philosophy Department were being held in the lecture hall of the *Revista de Occidente*. This did not mean that the spirit of university life had been stifled, but that they had taken their effort to its "natural place" of freedom and intimacy, removing that "work" of the soul's normal breathing from the place where it would have acquired a different meaning if it had remained—where it would have been something different. At that moment the spirit of university life would have become alienated if it had continued to breathe next to the familiar walls of the official building; its officials and officiality were alienating.

And now freedom! That long-repressed freedom of expression that only flowered in the last few years! How many times had they closed the Ateneo, how many times had they closed the university, how many times had they shut down the lecture series, like the last one sponsored by the Ateneo, just as the most important issues were finally being addressed? It was not in the capital that either the young people nor most of their elders were taking advantage of that freedom to speak! As if in response to unformulated instructions, they left in all directions toward the provincial cities, the towns, and the smallest villages, working their way into the most complex area of the Spanish labyrinth. Madrid was pouring out into the rest of Spain.

It was a question of inspiration. There was no reason given for it, at least none that she heard, and if someone had asked them one of those questions that demand a precise response about the basis for a person's actions—"Why are you going about it like this?"—perhaps they would have come up with some tactical, strategic reason. But the truth was different; the truth, whatever it may have been, had to do with a visceral strategy. Spain was beginning to recover its soul, and awakening is nothing other than that—the soul returns from the two hollows where it dwells while we sleep: the limbos of forgetfulness and inertia, the hell of unguided hope. We awaken when a guide descends into the limbo of inertia to lead hope and draw hope out of its hell.

Spain, beloved Spain, Spain of anonymous villages hungry with every hunger, was emerging from its hell—hope throbbing—and they, the ones from the limbo of city life, were going to meet Spain. They passed through the sacred places of Spain's history and its land, where the illustrious names, the ultimate cipher of the language, were coming alive, were on their way to welcome them. La Solana; Villanueva de la Jara; Manzanares; Córdoba; Trujillo; Medina del Campo; Huesca; Palencia; Teruel; Madrigal de las Altas Torres; Toledo; Álava: words of the first work—the first poem—ciphers of the secret mathematics. Spain!

People would go out to meet them at the entrance to the town, sometimes a double row of men in ceremonial dress, according to ancient village etiquette. They would be waiting at the entrance, on the highway; and at the front, a small group would step forward to greet them, hats in hand brushing the ground, serious and solemn. They would walk among them silently, and there would be a knot of anguish in her throat. Would they be worthy of this? She was always thinking that she would not speak in those welcoming ceremonies, that she would not be able to speak to them because, "Lord, I am not worthy!"

Sunday, April 12

They had won now; they knew it, they had won, and all they needed was verification, in other words, "they" needed to verify it. People had absolute confidence in the honesty of the elections called by the government. The government was honest; that was certain. They may not have thought things would turn out the way they did, but those thoughts were erroneous. Every security measure and every precaution were taken so the truth would be made evident. The government was driven by a single inspiration to the end; the serpent was good, perhaps even more, it was intelligent, terribly intelligent.

Since morning there had been "lines" outside the polls moving at a pace that let people follow each other unhurriedly and steadily. During the entire morning the number remained constant, as if a relief had been arranged by some invisible strategy. After so many years without elections, it was as if elections were being held for the first time, as if the right to vote, which nineteenth-century men must have found so moving, were being inaugurated. There was solemnity and happiness. Many people were voting for the first time, and no one had voted in circumstances like these.

Groups of young men and women, persistent students and young people from the political parties handed out their slates of candidates in the areas around the polling places. They had to move from one area to the other without stopping. Walking up and down the lines, they offered people flyers; almost everyone already had them, but many said: "Yes, since you're giving it to me," and throwing away the ones in their hands. With her sister and two other young women she went from door to door this way from the time the polls opened. From time to time, they ran into a male student from the university or one of their male friends who would go with them, although they would stand to the side, because, "You

155

girls are more successful." It made no difference though, because neither they—the young women—nor the young men were necessary; they were there to . . . to be there, to state boldly as they held out the ballots: "Conjunción Republicana Socialista." That was all; they just wanted to crow those words. Because people placed their votes in the boxes silently. Sometimes her group went into one of the polling places and stayed for a few minutes, to see, because it was also necessary to see, and it was good, because a person could see, could see just by looking. At one of the polling places she saw how an older, well-dressed man walked up to the box and stopped for a minute; he took the ballot out of his pocket and raised it to his forehead, then traced the sign of the cross with it over his chest, and placed it in the box, saying: "I cast my vote for the Conjunción Republicana Socialista." As he passed in front of her he added, looking her straight in the eye: "Things like this must be said out loud; it cannot be in secret."

There were also other groups of young people outside the polls, two kinds of groups. One of them was feebly shouting out the monarchist candidates and looking rather discouraged; from time to time their eyes met across the jamb of a large door, and they smiled, the others with a certain ironic resignation, as if to say: "We already know there's nothing we can do." And from her and her two companions: "There's nothing we can do either; just be patient!" That was all. The other group, which was even smaller, was the Communists, who were handing out hardly any flyers. The Communists had split off and formed their own slate. They did not say anything; they were there because they had to be; there was no other reason.

Toward noon, different candidates stopped on their rounds of the polling stations in their districts; all of the candidates would walk over and shake their hands when they saw them handing out flyers. Julián Besteiro arrived, tall, elegant, and friendly; someone with him introduced her, reminding him that she had been one of his students in his logic class. In his noble, natural presence, though, the only thing she felt was how logical it would be for him to be the president, the kind of president Spain deserved. At that moment the clock in the school struck twelve, and they smiled, looking at each other silently: it was as if those strokes were saying that it was the hour of triumph, that the election had been won.

It had. The candidates made their rounds again, this time more quickly and more jubilantly. Beginning at four in the afternoon, which is when the counting of votes began, the candidates worked their way toward the center of Madrid; it was early evening when messengers, friends, acquaintances, and many others flocked into Alcalá Street from every direction, shouting the news loudly. Telegraphs began to tap and telephones were ringing in newspaper offices, in Republican centers, in the Casa del Pueblo, in every home. In the cafes, people crowded around the tables where someone who had a pen was adding things up on a piece of paper; he raised his eyes, "Yes, yes, it's already clear." At midnight, a vast sea-like murmur poured into the street; Madrid was like a conch, an immense shell that captured a roar coming in rhythmic waves from all over Spain. As that roar crossed the Puerta del Sol, a cry from that unrepeatable republic formed within it: "Viva la República!" A group of mounted Guardias was riding up Arenal Street; they continued until they reached the Plaza de Oriente, which was empty and filled with a thick silence. In the distance, from deep in the Manzanares, a cock crowed sharply.

April 14

It was a strange morning; there was almost no one in the Paseo de la Castellana, the city's main thoroughfare, a small asphalt Seine that sometimes serves as Madrid's river, the large river the city does not have. The city was retreating in ambiguous silence. People knew negotiations were in progress between prominent figures from the worlds of both intellectual politics and intelligent politics who were trying to build a bridge over the abyss that had opened in the national life. Reality was there as a fact—the conflict that had followed such a long course had been reduced to one problem. And when that happens, solutions must come quickly; things cannot wait. This is the last instant, and inspiration must make its saving voice heard.

There was calm, absolute calm; no one had to act except the ones looking for the most honorable way out, which was to build a bridge between the past that was departing and the inescapable present. And the people, in other words, everyone, all of Spain waited, retreating into a final instant, giving the one who had to make the decision that last minute, leaving the final action to him.

History becomes manifest in drama or in tragedy, its usual form. In ancient tragedy the protagonist is a semi-god, a lineage, and finally an individual—an individual being born. History had apparently not yet gotten past this phase, this tragic phase, in which destiny supervenes, surprising consciousness unawares, a destiny that goes beyond vision, a partially blind destiny. But there are privileged hours when consciousness has surpassed destiny, as it does in one's personal life. The tragic mask is a person when it knows its entire role, when it invents that role, creates it, or directs it. Man finds it difficult, very difficult to achieve this, to be a real person. History . . . Christian history, in order for Christianity to be the common faith in the West, rose only in rare instants to this anti-tragic point.

Consciousness takes destiny upon itself, obliges destiny to enter consciousness, and guides it toward the greatest possible clarity. Then the tragic crisis is conflict, and when thought has pinned it down in events—because living reality and passions have obeyed the mandate of consciousness—conflict is problem. And one is man then, or human, if you prefer.

All in all, when something like this occurs, it is not a question of antitragedy, but of tragedy's denouement. This is the moment when the tragic conflict becomes apparent because the protagonist recognizes himself. He did not know who he was and therefore did not know what he had done; he had acted in "good faith," "he knew not what he did." There is a plague in the city, and the supplicants are right at the palace door. Since he is a man of good faith, he listens to the messenger who explains the cause of the plague—the plague the protagonist wants to cure and which emanates from his own person. And when he hears, he knows who he is, then the chorus waits. No one executes the sentence; he alone is the one, he himself. This is why he finds mercy in the chorus, whose conscience mercifully assists him. "Oh, you, the most unfortunate of men!" For what better consolation is there than hearing this said or saying it and having no one refute it at the instant the truth occurs: "You are—I am—the most unfortunate of men." Although this may not be accurate, although there may have been, may always be, someone more unfortunate, it adds stature, which sustains one in misfortune. If only all people who committed crimes because they knew not what they did would listen, at the terrible minute when they do know, to the voice of consciousness, which is no longer accusatory, which has become merciful!

There was a well-founded resemblance between the situation of that protagonist and the one of our king, who was the person forced to drain his cup and accept decisive conflict in the face of a Spain now in full agreement about its identity as it waited for him, conscious and merciful like the chorus in the exemplary tragedy. What would he do?

Everything was possible. At least that is what people thought and even more what they feared without saying it. Everything was possible. Because everything is possible at such an hour: conscience can win out, conflict will be endured fully, and a resolution is found; conflict can be refused, and things left to chance, and then the drama unfolds, and the course of history is unleashed in the abyss of blind destiny—chance unleashes fate.

There were no perceptible signs of fear; nevertheless, "everything was possible," no one knew anything, rumors, rumors. No one was afraid, because . . . because no one could have been. We were living the most lucid moment of the dream, which corresponds to the words that offer the only solution for the fact that our worst sin is having been born—Good works cannot be lost, even in dreams. Would that moment be lost? No one thought it would, because it had been even more than this, it had been the most man can do: "Dream well; wake dreaming . . . " Dream well, because even dreams dreamed in history are never lost.

How can you doubt when you're in the most lucid part of the dream, where watchfulness, consciousness, and inspiration have become identical? Only when inspired history has worked free within blind fate does such a question pierce your heart with its sword-like coldness. This is a different doubt, the anguished doubt that one has been abandoned, that fate is stronger than consciousness. Dream well, but can things really get lost, can you get lost when you've been good in your dreams, so good that the dream itself is good? Can you really get lost forever?

The certainty of the dream well dreamed is greater than the certainty provided by watchfulness, daily watchfulness, a kind of sleepwalking, sleeping with your eyes open, sleeping, sleeping without dreaming, or dragging yourself along beneath the weight of a nightmare—the nightmare in which the dream well dreamed abandons the one who dreams it, the one who has been pushed relentlessly to the point of being nothing, has just become real. When you've dreamed you've dreamed well, and you get lost, the world has fallen under a spell.

But at that instant Spain was free from the spell of the evil magicians who had stolen its soul, its will, which it had recovered pure and intact. Spain was "virgin" once again: "virgin Spain" had been rescued from the evil magicians, freed from its spell.

What would happen?

The streetcar was on its way down from the stadium, running along the asphalt river at one in the afternoon. There were only a few people on the streets, and they walked in silence the way people do when they're engrossed in carrying out some task; the streetcar stops were empty, and the cafes on Recoletos and Alcalá Street seemed deserted. Mirror-like, the asphalt reflected a clear spring sky; a shiny black car was gliding along slowly, almost like a gondola on a quiet canal, like one of those silent black gondolas pushed by an expert old gondolier, lame like them all, who come gliding by the door of a palace and stop, saying with their gestures more than their voices: "Let's go, Sir, it's time."

The atmosphere of the city remained this way from noon through early afternoon. But at three o'clock the city emerged from its seclusion; and now Alcalá Street was filling with people who gathered in small groups, coming and going, fluttering about, glancing from side to side to see if anyone was coming, or if something might be making its appearance. Instead of moving toward the Puerta del Sol, those groups, which were increasingly large and closer to forming a crowd, went down toward the Plaza de Cibeles; the goddess of Madrid, Cibele presides from her chariot, and more than ever she seemed to be bathed in a light that was growing ever more intense, more brilliant, more blue. Other groups arrived along Recoletos and some others from the Paseo del Prado and the loading platforms at the Atocha station; others came down the hill on Alcalá Street. In an instant something like an electric spark shook everything, and all the people crammed into the cafes were hurled into the street. What was happening? There was a voice running through the air. Where did it come from? Where did the news come from? Instead of going up toward the center of the city, to the Puerta del Sol, people hurried toward Cibeles. It was three o'clock in the afternoon. A man was visible in the tower of the Palacio de Communicaciones, a lone man who raised the flag of that Republic. And magically, flags began to unfurl in the street. Magically, instantaneously groups appeared at the mouths of all the streets with flags of all sizes; and they kept coming, soon surrounding Cibele the way people do in a ritual dance and singing. Repeated a thousand and one times, the cry arose uncontrollably: "Viva la República!" A strange band of fewer than a dozen instruments came from somewhere deep in the city as if by magic and began to play the Himno de Riego, as if those instruments were inventing it; there had been no rehearsals, each one came with his modest instrument, and the hymn arose, agreed on through unanimous inspiration since everyone sang it. Who knew it? Where had they learned it? Like the flags, it sprang forth magically, just because.

But what was happening? Had the king abdicated? In truth no one knew and no one came to announce it; no one asked either. It was the resolution which was now here. The street teemed with multi-colored outfits; never before had a crowd been composed of so many different get-ups; there was even a group of sailors looking exactly as if they had gotten off a boat plying Madrid's "sea." The members of the Guardia Civil were quiet and smiling, and suddenly someone had the inspiration; they picked them up, picked up the hated members of the Guardia Civil and carried them on their shoulders to the cry of "Viva la Guardia Civil." Yes, "Viva la Guardia Civil." The security guards watched without moving, and a group on horseback seemed to give their consent from the heights of destiny. The tri- colored flag rippled against the cloudless sky whose pure spring blue was like a blanket that enveloping Cibele without touching her.

But as far as things happening, there was nothing. Nothing had taken place there in the Plaza de Oriente. Someone noticed again the presence of the black car, shining like a gondola, gliding through the crowd. What would happen? What would still happen?

She returned home quickly. The crowd was different now; filling the streets, the Puerta del Sol, and even the Calle Mayor, it was now composed of groups—neighbors from different neighborhoods in Madrid, friends, people who were suddenly fraternizing, workers from some repair shop who had rushed into the streets. This was not the uniform crowd one finds at the funeral of a public figure or at demonstrations; it was made up of close-knit units, as if in every house people were celebrating their mother's saint's day, or their wedding anniversary, or a baptism, and they had all poured into the street at the same time. A single happiness was reflected differently, according to the situation, social class, character, or style of each group.

Two hours later the shape of the crowd was different. The groups were still visible, but there were hands extended between them, people were exchanging witty remarks, and the crowd was now like a garland of human circles nestled one in the other, like a gigantic circle turning round and round, breaking and closing again. There were never more people than would fit in the space—not bunched together but joined—and the men and women, stars forming constellations, formed discernible patterns, as if they were reproducing the map of the heavens here below, as if that ring were the center of the earth defined by ancient peoples, which was the first thing people did when they built their cities at the center of the universe, where the stars concentrate their light, where the souls of the dead emerge to mix with the living—the receptacle of heaven and earth, of life and death.

The streetcars had gradually come to a standstill; there was no room for another human being inside them or on their roofs or on the tiny roof of the subway station. And how people envied them; they were the privileged ones! Human bodies clustered on balconies and perched on the railings; they festooned the top-floor apartments of all the buildings and stood erect like bands of storks on the roofs, supporting themselves against the chimneys. And they kept on, more kept coming; but there was inevitably some elbowing, along with trampled toes and quarrels. People were still surging in from the Calle Mayor and Arenal Street, and the resounding wave spread, like wind in a wheatfield: "He's gone, he just left, now, this minute." And at that minute, every head turned upward, toward the government ministry; the balcony door opened, and a man appeared, a single, tall man dressed in a dark civilian suit; restrained, self-controlled, he raised the flag of the Republic he was holding in his arms and stepped forward for an instant to say a few words, a single sentence that hardly grazed the air. Lifting his arms with the same restrained gesture, his voice more resonant, like the voice one uses to sing out the truth, he shouted: "Viva la República! Viva España!" Like a single voice with a thousand registers, his shout filled the air, rose toward the round, white clouds also gathered there, and did not quite die out; then in different tones, in a hundred registers as from a gigantic organ never heard before, as in a chorale intoned by an entire people, the voice rose toward the clouds and fell again, filling the air with that shout, which would still have been present even if it had not been repeated, would have filled everything. The April sky let fall its white, blue and white light until the light touched the crowd, transfiguring it. There were a thousand reflections in that light—in a single white, the entire infinity found in white. And in that whiteness, standing out, silhouetted against the sky, the Republican flag, now completely unfurled, waved high, high in the air. Looking at it, she fixed her eyes on the clock in the tower. It was six twenty. Six twenty in the evening on a Tuesday in April of 1931.

Yes, the king had left at six sharp they said, on his way to Cartagena in a car by himself. Before that someone had arrived, drawn by the smell of a possible slaughter, offering to do whatever was necessary, absolutely anything—to call out the troops; in short the one who offered knew what to do. But the king said no; "he did not want the blood of Spaniards to be spilled for him." And that's how he went, without a drop of blood needing to flow on his behalf. He listened to the voice of his conscience or his blood. My God, why didn't he save himself? He went because he could, because he could go, because he was not tied as criminals are to their accomplices and the scenes of their crimes. It was the hour of crime, and he avoided crime. May he rest in peace!

And there in the Royal Palace, which her "faithfuls" enlarged as they paraded through it, sat the queen. It was rumored that "she's alone, she's a foreigner and she never meddled in anything." "Poor thing," some said, "given her good looks, she's bound to be crying." And the sea of that incalculable crowd surged, uncontrollably it seemed, down to the Plaza de Oriente; and when the crowd reached the edge of the plaza, it drew back. None of those processions, not a single triumphant cortege passed in front of the Palace, whose doors were guarded at the same posts as always by young men from the Federación Universitaria and the Juventudes Republicanas, on foot and unarmed. There was no need, because no one crossed the sidewalk or even confronted from a distance the solitude for which no one could provide companionship. The Count of Romanones remained at her side and accompanied her the next morning to the station near El Escorial. On the road they met up with a truck full of people singing jubilantly and flying a Republican flag; when they realized it was the queen who was passing, they lowered the flag and were silent. People say that once at the station she spoke to the small group that was with her—by order of President Alcalá Zamora a general stayed with her to the border—wiping away a tear as she told them: "On a day as beautiful as this one I entered Spain." Yes; Spain the only thing Spain could do for her was see her off with the same beautiful sun that had welcomed her.

At times people have said that the king left her all alone; but that was something else he did because he could, because he could entrust her to a people who had never been regicidal.

High tide was still rising, even as far as the most outlying neighborhoods. Those neighborhoods were not entirely empty; they were vibrating in contrast to the days during Carnival when they were sunk in an absence of death, and also in contrast to Sundays and their empty afternoons pierced by the sounds of husky boys playing ball. The light was not a Sunday light, that motionless light that tells us, even in the middle of the sea, that it's Sunday, especially Sunday afternoon. The afternoon of a holiday in the outlying neighborhoods is proof that it's truly a holiday, and we're too poor to celebrate a holiday every Sunday.

In the Puerta del Sol the makeup of the groups was changing constantly as if the entire city had to pass through there, through that magic center. A group of workers came prancing down the street toward the Puerta del Sol alongside the Ministry of the Interior. One of them broke away from the group, addressed a passerby, and shouted "Viva la República!" while the others whirled about in their improvised dance: "Viva España!" "Sure; long live Spain!" and the passerby raised his fist, about to get angry, his voice slightly hoarse: "And long die! . . . But no, death to no one, life to everyone. Yes, long live the world, long live everyone, everyone in the world," and his voice grew clearer by the moment. Raising his arms to the sky, exposing his chest, offering it as if he were facing the universe all by himself, he kept shouting: "Long live the whole world!" The beam from a spotlight bathed him from head to toe and was reflected in his white, white shirt, one so white it was whiteness itself.

Toward the New World

It was not like other times; now her house had disappeared and "that," her dreamed destiny, hung in suspense, suspended between heaven and earth or beyond. She could not have known this, since she had not yet fully grasped the defeat. She had felt defeat briefly during the first nights she spent in Salses, the little French town near Perpiñán, beneath the shadow of a castle from the time of Charles V right in the Marca Hispánica. Because of something trivial, which is how important things are usually revealed, she felt that her situation in the world, before the world, had changed. She felt afraid as she heard footsteps on the stairs of the small hotel. Thinking the police were coming to ask for her identification papers, she felt afraid even though she had her papers. The footsteps belonged to some young, cheerful travelers on their way to Paris, just as she herself had traveled along highways and through cities and villages at dawn, unaware of the anguish asleep in some closed room. And the fear and distance that separated her from those cheerful travelers showed her just how much her situation had changed, even more than crossing the border in the middle of that immense multitude. Because then it was the war, or something that was still occurring in the epic they were living. As long as she formed part of that multitude she felt neither alone nor defeated. Maybe the multitude felt encouraged because in front of her, in the row of people about to cross the border which had finally opened that morning, there was a man with a sheep slung over his shoulder; because not far away there was a woman with a cow; because she had met friends, colleagues from other times, as if everyone who was left from the first days of that fantasy, that dreamed destiny, had agreed to meet there. They had even seen each other once again right at the border; and they had even saved her, her mother, her two small cousins, the oldest servant from her house, and her dog Micky from spending their last night in Spain out in the open in the incessant rain. "Is that you? Where are you going? No, wait, there's a corner for you here," a bearded commander and two lieutenants, whom she had not recognized as colleagues from those years of the dreamed destiny, had told her three times throughout that interminable day and night. No, despite the crowd filling the meadow at the foot of the mountain in La Junquera, beneath the freezing January rain, waiting to cross the French border, she had not felt defeat, despite the warning at three o'-clock in the morning: 'Everybody out right away; you must leave too'—this time the friend was a civilian—"there's a motorized column coming." But where was she to go? Despite the constant bombardment sounding in the distance and moving closer and closer, despite . . . No; she had not felt defeat. The whole night, through the thin partition, she had heard a wounded soldier singing, "Want to marry the girl from 'round here? Guns from Madrid are what they hold dear." And then, "Listen, listen to me, the government probably has boats already waiting to take us to fight in Valencia." She had still not broken off from the community; she was nothing more than what she had been during the war, especially during the last months in Barcelona—one, one of many. As long as a person feels this way, any defeat is impossible, even if one knows defeat is certain, already decreed and drawing closer by the minute, like a dark wall, like a cloud that will be stopped by nothing.

But now, alone in her hotel room, now she did feel it. She knew she had broken away forever from the multitude of which she had formed a part, like one more, one of many; she had broken away forever, she had returned, returned to be herself, to be "here," once again, alone with herself. There was still one tie: him, her husband in the army. She never doubted that he would get out unharmed, unscathed; she knew that nothing would happen to him, and she simply waited for him. And he did come, a few days later. He had crossed with his troops, about six hours before "they" reached the border. Everything had gone well; he had handed his war material to a pair of officials from the French army who were there to collect it, he had said good-bye to his soldiers one by one, and now he was here. Someone—people were all finding each other—had told him he had seen her in Salses. "And now, I guess the government will take us to Valencia; I have to find out tomorrow." She looked at him silently. "All right; but put on these civilian clothes I brought you."

He called to her a few minutes later, he walked back to the room and handed her his folded uniform, telling her: "Put this away but don't wash it." And turning his head to the other side, "Because I know I'll never wear it again." Then much later they had heard those footsteps, which turned out to belong to some pleasant travelers looking for a few hours rest on the road to Paris, just as they themselves had done many times—walked up the stairs of a small hotel, having stopped in the middle of a trip or an excursion, walked up the stairs of a hotel without ever imagining that their steps might startle someone who was different, even though they stayed in the same hotels, took the same trains and the same boats. Now they were different. They experienced that revelation: they were not like the rest. They were no longer citizens of any country, they were exiles, outcasts, refugees . . . something different, which meant they would arouse what some of the "holy" people experienced in the Middle Ages—respect, sympathy, pity, horror, repulsion, attraction. In short, that's what they were: something different, the defeated who had not died, who had not had the good sense to die. The survivors.

And now "here," where? In the middle of the ocean, listening to the deafening roar of the waves sounding above the nauseating din of the machinery on a huge transatlantic steamer. Where were they really? Who were they really?

Her husband had gotten the vague impression from his frequent conversations with a Czechoslovakian man that things were not going to end well at all, according to the sketchy information found in the newspaper available on the ship. Across the ocean, a huge, wide motherly continent. Wasn't America a daughter of Europe's dream? And look at America. No one had needed to waken it. On the contrary, America had awakened her, them, from the nightmare that had already begun to weigh a little in Paris, where on the city's face one could see an immanent siege, a terrible siege that was bearing down, even though its exact nature was not yet known. And one morning she had received two wires—two invitations, two offers—from Mexico and from Cuba. Two days later another for him from Chile. They would answer the triple invitation of that wide, motherly America!

But now she did not feel that she was anywhere, on any part of the planet, which is what happens in the middle of the ocean when the soul does not perceive signs of land's presence, a presence that becomes pronounced before it is visible, before the flight of any bird announces it; because we experience a sort of presentiment of the earthly beings we all are, because we have a sense of our origin, of the roots of our being, which finds its fatherland, its natural place, only in the earth, despite the struggle the earth entails or because of the earth itself.

It was like feeling she was once again in the throes of being born through an altogether new agony. She had gone through so many agonies already! This is what it must mean to live: to die from diverse deaths before dying in the unique, complete way that sums up all the other deaths; and to agonize as well, to pass between life and death, to be driven from life in multiple ways without prompting death to open its doors. "To live dying."

June 13, 1940

She had been on the island for several weeks, on the small, very fragile island of Puerto Rico, which the eye can take in all at once as an island between the sea and the sky, one with no more than the tiny bit of earth it needs to support man's presence. "Puerto Rico owes much to love and little to space," she would say, paraphrasing Quevedo. Human vibration is so intense it cancels out space and the weight of the earth, as if we were all insects, dragonflies, flowers, like orchids, which grow free and hang from the trees, their roots exposed to the air with no need of earth. That's how she was too—supported by nothing but the air, the vibration of unforgettable friendship, and the tenderness that surrounded her from the first instant, as if tenderness were the air itself on that little island. And this made her terrible task bearable through lecture after lecture. More, still more, still asking for more, people followed her eagerly, all ears on those nights smelling of jasmine and night-flowering jasmine, nights filled with *cocuyos,* which made the sky fuse with the slight bit of barely existent earth. And she felt happy, if it would have been possible to feel happy at that moment, if she could have succumbed. And she could have kept talking as if she were not talking, as if before them, for them, she were dancing the dance we dance only in dreams, in certain privileged dreams, as if she had returned to a far-distant time that preceded even her own life. It seemed to her that she had lived there once. When? Or it seemed that she had experienced a presentiment of the island as a child in Segovia, where she had played many afternoons in a partly overgrown and therefore mysterious garden, where a royal poinciana blazed timidly with red, orange-red flowers. And she found herself remembering. She had heard that the tree had been brought to Puerto Rico by Señor de la Pezuela, General Conde de Cheste, the last Spanish governor of the island of Puerto Rico and a translator of the *Divine Comedy*. Now the marvelous red-flowered tree from her childhood flowered along the highways of the little island she had crossed all the way to the other tip, accompanied by the cordial vibrations of her friends, who were new and yet so old—like the tree!

And now as she watched the tree flower, the magic tree, the most magic of all the trees she had been able to see as a child, a black veil was gradually enveloping everything. Paris . . . her mother and her sister were in Paris, as well as her sister's companion, who was in great danger. Paris, Europe, her mother. There was no longer anything that could be done. She had gone to a bank to send some money to her mother. Who could tell when she would be able to do that again! And the cashier had looked deep into her eyes, from the deepest place in his own, asking her in an anguish-filled voice: "By wire, right?" And now not even by wire.

The radio broadcast the news at noon, in the sparse sentences of military reports, in the laconic language there had not been time to forget. And she would have liked to hide in some dark hole where not a drop of light could filter through—she would have liked to, but she could not. The brilliant radiance of the tropical summer day even seemed to pass through the wooden walls of the house where she was staying with some people who wept with her. She ran to a friend's *cabaña* under the trees in a dense forest. The light reached there too! She would have liked to sink into the earth which was calling her with a force she found more and more irresistible—earth, mother.

The mother! She knew her from the roads—in a truck, in a car someone probably had to leave behind in a ditch, throwing herself to the ground beneath a cloud of grapeshot, detained at a bridge now cut off, taking shelter in the attic of a *ferme*, utterly terrified, with no food, her heart broken.

And mother was also Europe—another shattered mother, one who had gone crazy. Oh Medea! Medea murdering her children, her brothers and sisters, herself—Medea in a delirium of crime that was the worst of suicides. The Mother crazed. Why? Why does the mother go crazy? Or the mother is not the one who's crazy, but whatever foreigner, enemy, "other" she surrendered to without being able to stop.

Where did civil war originate? What dreadful crime gave birth to civil war? It is the mother's craziness that drives her children crazy. Is it her children's crime that drives their mother crazy? She knew something about civil wars; her own had not died out; no, not yet! And now with Europe following the same destiny, the same fate, the question stirred in her heart: Where does civil war originate? Will this one be the last? Maybe the last one, the inevitable one, or simply the one not avoided for the sake of achieving unity. If only all Europeans could see Europe from a distance, from this continent born from Europe's dream, from the perspective of this perplexed, anguished daughter who was also forced to become the mother of her own mother—if they could see Europe from this "afar," which is not an "outside" but a dimension within history.

The consecutive march of history is an erroneous image, as is any simplified image, because historical events have several dimensions—they have an inside, a depth, as personal life does. And paradoxically, from this little island in the Caribbean Sea, one of the islands that waylaid the admiral, she felt she was inside Europe, in its innermost recesses, its innermost parts, the way children feel when they sees their mother suffer. The innermost parts of history are where the future is gestating.

And she began to feel what agony is, the agony of her mother, the only mother, who might be in her last agony at that moment. Maybe my mother is dying now! She could not stop thinking about either this or the agony of Europe, her mother in history, her country which she could not renounce.

Being in agony is not being able to die, because of hope. No; no one on the other side rejects us, no one hurls us back to life—only the hidden hope that springs up desperately in the face of every unbearable suffering; and the more unbearable something seems, the more deeply is one's hope reborn. Maybe this is why we have to suffer—so that hope will be revealed in all its depth.

This is why there is history. This is why Europe has been the most "historical" place, the one that made history most passionately. Because Europe was born one day from the revelation of the most total hope ever known, the hope man had not dared to confess to himself until Christianity gave him its story: hope pinned on history. Hence this tragedy. Upon discovering life as hope, Europe lived history as tragedy, "condemned" to agonize, to not be able to die—to be reborn from its consecutive deaths because one cannot turn back from committed hope. One must keep daring to hope!

Europe cannot die because it must continue on its path, which is agony, the cross borne by unbridled hope. And Europe will have to continue giving birth, giving birth to itself in history. "My children, I will be in labor for you until Christ has been born in each one of you," said Paul of Tarsus, a European.

From Havana to Paris

The time had passed slowly, scarcely inscribing any dates. The days had passed too, falling like drops of light on that island barely perched on the water, that island more in the light than on the sea, in a light that sometimes protected her as if she were in a blue bell jar and other times exposed her to the elements, leaving her at the mercy of the sun's fire and the moon. In "winter" the island is like a platform of earth turned toward the stars, as if it were floating on the luminous or dark ocean of interstellar space.

Friendship had protected her too, friendships that would bind her to the island, fasten her there, and make her return time after time, drawn by the cordial vibration that made her feel she was inside a human heart that was free of pathos—a simple, light heart, one still innocent of historical guilt.

And along with happiness, anguish had arrived almost simultaneously. Europe was visible again; Europe was wounded, very wounded, but you could feel that it had not died. Europe's "dark night" had been filled with lights, with lamps hidden in "the catacombs," which she had seen, felt rather, from the island within the light nature lavished so prodigiously.

Now she was waiting for her visa from France, not impatiently, the way one waits for a happiness that has been promised or for a promise that is sure to be fulfilled, but with the desperation a wait implies. Her mother was approaching the end of her agony, the agony deferred through frosty winters across deserts without food, throughout the terror that cannot be named, because there was not, nor should there have been, any base for it—for the gratuitous terror sown in waves over the European night.

She sensed that this is what her mother was experiencing, that she was postponing her agony, drawing it out as long as she could so she could see her. And she, from the island, was running toward her, fighting against time for her, trying to gain hours, instants. But the visa . . .

It came, the visa came. She also got a ticket, which was still not easy to do, on the New York–Paris flight. The friend who had managed to get it was waiting for her there in fantastic New York on a night that was nearly dawn. Friendship: she felt it beside her as more than friendship, as the personification of the motherliness she sensed about America, about Cuba, the last daughter to part from Spain.

Thanks to it, to this personification of friendship, she did not go crazy in the days she had to wait in that fantastic city. Finally the time had come, the hour had come for her to board the plane. She felt fear, an indescribable anguish—a fear of that postponed agony.

Postponed agony; in the last agony, a person is already a soul in Purgatory, and this is how she felt—like a soul in Purgatory, a captive in the large, multifarious, unfamiliar crowd. It was almost impossible not to experience this. Even her friend seemed to feel it, because deep tenderness knows and senses.

The loudspeaker called out the number of the flight, her flight. As she said a wordless goodbye to her friend, she felt that she was gradually being detached from the maternal America that had defended, welcomed, cared for her, and then that she was standing there at the foot of the plane, small, at the end of a long nightmarish corridor. Only Josefina's small, silent but real presence kept her joined to the world of her vigil. Yes, two good, beautiful words: thank you. It's good when we to have to say them.

They were soon passing over Ireland, but they did not land; and before she knew it, they were already over Paris. A huge, tall shadow appeared on her right; then it turned until it was facing her in the plane itself. She saw her sister in the distance; beside her there was a friend she recognized. But even though the friend had one arm around her sister's shoulders, she saw that a mantle of air isolated her sister from her friend and from everything, saw that her sister was alone, alone. Yes, it was true. Their mother had not been able to postpone her agony any longer; the two of them now formed a single soul in Purgatory.

And her never-ending delirium began. When hope is disappointed, hope turns into delirium. And it was as a delirium of light that she experienced the presence of the city she had carried in her heart as an image and a name, the city where she now had a little of her own earth.

The Sister

She found herself alone with her sister, since their mother had been lowered into the earth two days before the plane deposited her at Orly.

She had called her Antigone throughout the entire time destiny had separated them, removing her from the site of the tragedy, whereas her sister—Antigone—was having to face it. She began to call her sister that in her anguish, Antigone, because she was innocent but she was having to endure history; because her sister had been born for love but compassion was devouring her, because pure, compassionate deeds not based on any hope were the only action she had ever known. Yes, she herself felt regret that she had lived and was still living history in a hope devoid of ambition; her sister had lived without even hope, lived only through compassion. She had carried on infinite dialogues with her sister, she had talked to her through endless nights of insomnia when she had no idea where she was—if she was in French territory, in occupied or unoccupied territory, in a country where there was less terror even though there was war, in some concentration camp. She felt her sister weep as she held their mother, and her sister was now smaller than she and needed to be protected. And because she had talked to her so much, now she could find no words to say, only a persistent question that almost always remained unformulated. What she expected from her sister was the revelation of all the grief, her own and everyone's, an intimate revelation of Europe's dark night which her sister had been forced to live without any respite in her vigil—an innocent consciousness keeping watch, driven by compassion. Yes, Antigone.

She sensed that as a whole it was indescribable, that she would never find out about it completely, that her sister would tell her about it hurriedly, as something ordinary and natural, incidents that occasionally came to her at random as she visited a particular place, and not only then, here, here—but it's better not to continue. She would be defeated by a silence that enveloped her like a sort of veil, a sort of chasteness on the part of the soul that preserves the mystery contained in the shameful crime she had been forced to see, the debasement of the human soul she had been forced to witness—the mystery in the physical suffering of hunger, cold, and terror, and in the nobility shown by some of the people close to her as well as by the many other brothers and sisters she met in the mesh of the network that begins to form when lives are lived in fear. She did not say "I" but "we," all of us here in Paris went through this, and many times, "Paris went through this!" She formed part of a community forged in a suffering and heroism that does not call attention to itself. And she felt she could not insist; perhaps Antigone would never be able to open her soul and let the inhumanity she had seen pour out because she had lived all that history compassionately, uniting the living and the dead with love, without hate—not at all eager to create the enemy but nevertheless having to bow before the evidence of what had happened, the evidence that, inexplicably, there is an enemy. And she saw that she had drained the cup containing the depths of evil, the pure evil she wanted to understand but could not; she tried to look for reasons that would let her reduce everything she had experienced to human terms, to human life. And she was not looking for violence but for intelligent evil—the Machiavellianism of the Gestapo whose offices she had been forced to visit frequently, "the moral and physical torture" they used on her, "as they did on everyone else," she would add immediately, "because it was a method." "Maybe that's why you read *Discourse on a Method,* and don't say you haven't, because I've seen the notes in it written in your own hand; since you had to deal with a method, you had to know what it, what a method was—you, someone who always laughed at that book." But she had not realized that was what it's about. No, she had simply read it, the way she read Seneca, which she had simply devoured, and a few sections of the *Divine Comedy.* Then, as if she heard music, she felt that she was awake in the land of the living, that she had awakened from the nightmare reality had become; and she told her: "*I* do not want to believe. It may seem cowardly to you, but I have no other solution; I cannot, I refuse to believe in it. At night I dream that dreadful reality: I make myself go in terror to the Ile de la Cité and walk in front of the Palais de Justice where I saw him walk before the judges who granted his extradition, although the minister never signed it. Yes, two years of anguish, and you know the end. Yes, the reality I do not want to believe overwhelms me when I have to ride the subway, the one that during those two years took me to the Santé, the same subway I had to ride the morning they did not accept my package of clothing and food: "It's not necessary, he's left for Spain." That led me to take a detour so I would not have to walk by the Hotel Lutecia, one of the hotels occupied by the Gestapo. But this is not real; maybe some day someone will tell me that it's a lie, that it's all been my imagination or my nerves. Because if it were real, there would be an explanation for it, and I cannot find one. How am I going to explain to myself the fate of the little seven-year old boy, a Jew, whom I took in until they found him a better place? And the fate of so many others and even . . . No; no, for something to be true there has to be some reason for it. These things cannot be true; nevertheless, they have happened to me, they have happened to all of us here in this Europe that was not able to love itself enough.

Part Two

Deliriums

My children, I will be in labor for you until Christ has been born in each one of you.

From a letter by Saint Paul

The Dove's Delirium

And he went to the Spanish border to meet his brothers who would take him across clandestinely, so they could embrace, something they had not done since before the war. She remained in Paris, dreaming, accompanying him all the way to the south. Spain was so close! It was simply a question of stepping into a train . . . and she would arrive and that would be it. Why not do it? Simply step into a train and arrive there just as she had arrived in Paris, how long ago was it now, how many years? He had left around noon that sunless day; or she could walk, because a person could also get there on foot, or go by car—someone would take her. She would see the Pyrenees, a port or two, and the ocean, the bend of the Cantabrian Sea, and she would be on her way across: the white houses of the Basque Country in Bidasoa. Why had she let her husband go alone? They had gone through it together. And she would hear everyone speaking Spanish in the street—at first it would be imprinted with Basque, then truly pure, in Burgos; she would see the threshing floors, Castile golden and fragrant with wheat and . . . Madrid, empty in the summer without the civil servants, without water, dry, scorched by sun falling vertically—in Madrid everything is vertical or horizontal, spread out. Madrid is deceptively recumbent because suddenly it rises, yes, it rises, it stands up and says: NO, no more . . . And the Prado is still there—to see Zurbarán again—the still lifes—and Velázquez whom she now truly understood. And the mornings, that light at ten o'clock in the morning; and to fly to her house, to her little plaza, Conde de Barajas. Yes, number three . . . but different people would be living there now; the concierge is probably the same, and she liked her a lot, and it's *horchata* season, with its refreshment stands—there's one in front of the Department of State as you leave the main office, and of course there is probably someone sitting there now, behind a table, in his cubicle . . . If she left right now she could catch up with him in Biarritz.

She was flying toward her house beside the Seine; along the Quay d'Orsay there were no cars. Paris was deserted, and it was a sounding board for her thoughts, for her soul . . . she would fly . . . Biarritz—it's possible to go there; you don't need a visa . . . When she got home she was so wrapped up in her rambling, her sister did not even recognize her; she ate hardly any dinner and went to bed immediately so she would not have to do anything; she resumed her enumerative dream, found herself stopping in front of the Guadarrama as if she'd been magnetized, and then she was crossing the Sierra Morena and, at the foot of a grille— she could not tell whether inside or out . . . Were there flowers on the grille or not? Who was watching her from behind? A starving old woman came out to meet her from way in the back of a village cemetery: "Here I am; I've been here for eight years, and now you've come." Who was she? Those dead people, the ones who had not been buried, who were they? She knew them all, and there were so many children, so much misery. My God, I want to be dust, dust, dust of your soil, Spain, if I could be grass at the edge of an irrigation ditch growing from your meadow, a May rose, a white lily at the foot of a mound; Spain, I would be a stream of your water and one of those stones high up, the ones crying out to heaven, I would be chiseled into you so I could cry out like one of those dry elms opening their branches, or I would be a snake coiled at the foot of your cross, the cross born in you, born from your breast as that cross rises, crying out to heaven for justice and calling to earth with its open arms. At the foot of your cross, Spain. No; no more verbena or carnations or jasmine blooms, or basil, or wallflowers; no more rivers between willows: only grille and cross.

Grille and cross. My dead—your dead, Spain, always your dead. And your love, the dove that was promised, and peace, and over your soil, work, bread, sweetness and love.

Will there be forgiveness for someone who strangles a dove?

Love. The dove crucified. Haven't we humans crucified even the Holy Spirit? It is suffering from its wound, its blood is flowing, love's wounded blood, blood soiled in vain—a dove beyond all humiliation humiliated here by us. Dove, I will ask for your forgiveness until I am dust, until I disintegrate; I will ask for your forgiveness in the name of Spain.

The Madwoman

And there was that mad woman she heard screaming when they took her to mama's village. They kept the woman locked in a room, and she could hear her from the terrace on the roof of her house. Later Mariquilla la Vieja told her a little bit about her, and then she found out more. She had been good, pretty, and very pale, with black hair, very shiny black eyes, and a long nose that tapered to a point at the end. And then she had gotten that illness; she never tired of asking for water because she was so thirsty, she would be delirious from thirst, and then she could hardly moisten her lips. She had started to act like a wild woman, to do wicked things; she would escape from the house, and she no longer recognized anyone. She was always thirsty. When she escaped she would go to the river, and one day they found her already half-swallowed by the current, which was wide at that point but thank God not too strong; she had gotten tangled up in an overhanging willow branch, and she was drowning. They took her home, and after that she did not go out any more. A boyfriend? Yes, there had been one who went off one day and was never heard from again, but she never said anything; it did not seem to have upset her, since the truth is they had not been seeing each other for very long—they had talked a few times through the window grating and she never said anything . . . nothing. She began to suffer from thirst, a great thirst. And she was so good. She went to church, and she would always light a candle on the altar where Our Lord is crucified, and she gave away everything, everything—she refused to have anything of her own—she gave it all to the poor, to the sad-looking children she would see walking around, children who had nothing, and to her friends, to whom she gave her dresses and shoes: everything. All she asked for was water, and in her room she always had to have a pitcher made of fine sparkling crystal covered with a flounce of lace and some lemons too, and sometimes she wanted the water to have a bit of sugar in it. Nothing else.

And she had started to turn black. Her skin grew dark from never being in the sun, as if she were burning up from inside; her wrists burned, and they had to wet them for her with a sponge or by putting them in the blue porcelain wash-basin she always had filled with water with a geranium or hollyhock floating in it. Her temples burned, and they started to get very dry; she had to put a wet cloth on them or a cloth moistened with a few drops of María Farina cologne, since her parents denied her nothing. But she began to get worse, and there was no cure—the doctor who came from Almería found none, said it was too late or had always been too late, and went off leaving her there, the way her boyfriend had left her. She did not know about this. All she did was ask for water.

She grew thirstier and thirstier, and her voice came out hoarse, she spoke in shrieks, and her behavior disintegrated, she walked as if the floors in the house were uneven, and she went down the stairs sideways. The shrieking would start at midnight, when she would call to the neighbors, and then she would answer or call to the cock early in the morning, and she had tried to jump from the window so she could climb to the top of a tree where she had seen a nest of nightingales or thought she had.

And after the shrieking, once she was locked up, she dreamed of grapes, but they had to take her grapes with the vine shoots and all; she would roll herself up in the shoots and cover her head with clusters of fruit, and since there were plenty of grapes, they did in fact take her as many as she wanted and more, clusters of the nicest ones: muscatel grapes she would barely taste, black grapes, red grapes, and even the best grapes they usually hold back for the casks and for raisins. She had gradually thrown everything out the window, and sometimes she tore her dress and wanted to throw it out the window as well, and she sprinkled the cologne on the floor. For hour after hour she would sit very still, looking and looking at the lid of an old box from Málaga raisins that had a picture painted on it of a dancing woman wrapped in some fiery red, flame-like veils with clusters of black grapes entwined in her hair and a few vine shoots falling around her neck, and sitting beside her there was a marble head that smiled mockingly as it watched her dance. They had no idea why she took a fancy to that woman and wanted to be like her, maybe so she could decorate her head with clusters of grapes and coil herself up in the fresh, green vine shoots. Then she would start to shriek crazily, and she was getting more and more dehydrated, as if she were being toasted by the sun she never saw, since it did not even enter her room over the rather shadowy garden. After that very wild spell she began to calm down, and she no longer looked at the picture of the woman nor even at the grapes; when they took grapes to her she would look at them and smile a little as if she remembered, but she would not even touch them, and she would hardly even look at the leaves.

Gradually she grew very religious, the way she had been when she was well, and she asked for holy water, which they gave to her. And one day the priest went and confessed her, although she was without sin; she grew calm, she became quite serene and was once again sweet and saintly and smiling. They did not allow her to go down to dinner, fearing she might run away, but she did not want to go out, she only asked one day to look at the river for a little while, and since you could see it from the roof terrace, they took her up there, and she looked at the river with great fascination, seeming to feel at peace. "The water," she said, "so much beauty." And early the next morning she died very peacefully. She had a very sweet death, and she left instructions that all her belongings and everything she would have inherited from her mother were to be given to the poor and that she was to be buried in a simple coffin with no marble headstone on her grave.

People felt very sad. A dove kept circling above the coffin on the way to the cemetery and while she was being buried. And in the village they said that she had died innocent and like a saint, that if she had been sane she would have been a saint, that sanity was all she lacked, sanity would have made her a saint.

The Woman with a Sweet Name

There was not one, not a single maiden as beautiful in that village, and they had never heard of one from far away either; it seemed impossible that there could ever have been a woman like her. She was more beautiful than the women in the pictures you see in books—the one named Helen, who was the cause of a war people still talked about, or Dido who cried so much at the edge of the sea, or Dawn in her carriage with the golden horses. It seemed impossible, but that's how it was. And people did not know why, for what purpose, because there must be some reason, some mystery behind such extraordinary beauty. How did she happen to be born here on these flatlands where no one comes anymore? Before, in the old days, many knights passed through on their way to or from strange lands and even a king or two came. Now, thanks to so many flocks of sheep, the town was dusty; it reeked of wine and echoed with the cursing of muleteers. The houses were poor; people said that before, in those days, there had been very imposing houses, but what happened to them? Evidently everything had gradually collapsed and not even a trace remained; and the village was new, which made it seem even more insignificant. There were not even any ruins the way there are in some villages, and ruins command respect from anyone who might question the grandeur of a place. Only one of the houses had a tower, which was round and made from rough stones, an average-sized tower with a narrow window that let you see the countryside, the plain—everything. And the tower was where Dulce, the marvelous girl named for her sweetness, had gone, climbing up there from the time she began to grow tall and show such striking, but alarming, beauty. As a child she had been like the other girls although prettier; she did not enjoy games very much, and she was reserved—haughty, they said later, when she began to remain aloof, to make sure she was out of reach, away from people's words at first and then from their stares. She was barely thirteen when this happened, so that when she became a fully-developed woman, if her womanhood could have been the sole cause of such beauty, she was caught unawares, locked in the tower and not able to descend. She did not say a word, only that there was no use begging her to do anything against her will. As soon as they saw her, even her own parents, who were very frightened by that mystery, gave into her wishes without her having to use her hands to show them what she wanted, for this was the language she increasingly adopted—one movement of her hands explained everything and more. That's how it was at first. No men had seen her, not as a complete, incomparable young woman, not a single man, since it was inconceivable that anyone would dare climb the tower. And her parents decided that the man they had chosen for her should not see her either, although he was the one they felt would make the best husband, if she had not blossomed that way, I mean, because they now understood very clearly that a husband for her was out of the question—maybe at some other time, maybe, but even then her beauty might have brought great misfortune. Maybe this is how she understood it, since she seemed to be in control of her mystery and that was why she climbed up into the tower, because she was good and wise. Yes, she must have known a lot about something involving the most secret part of life; and even the reverend priest himself did not dare to ask her to come down to her house and live life like other girls, because there were good, timid, and pretty girls, although beside her they would have faded. She had gone to the fountain with her little jug just once along with the other girls, and when they got back she was already like that, as if she had gone instead of coming back, gone forever. Nothing had happened. They were all together, and she had put the jug beneath the stream of water, and while it was filling she stood there bent over the fountain, playing a little with the water. Someone who lived on the plaza said later that a shabby-looking man, or whatever it was, had walked by, someone who had never been seen in the village, and he had stopped to look at the girl for a moment, but he had not said anything to her, and surely she did not even see him, since she was looking at the water, and he, that . . . whatever it was, could not even see her very well, or perhaps he saw her in the water, because he stopped for a moment and stared at the cistern—the huge dilapidated fountain seemed more like a cistern—and he must have seen her face there, reflected in the tremulous water.

A singular, fleeting appearance, that of the specter-like figure, so fleeting no one noticed it except the woman who spied on everything and missed nothing; it might have been a ghost, but the matter was so insignificant the woman had forgotten it. Then one day she suddenly remembered . . . but that had nothing to do with what happened to the girl.

No; it had nothing to with her since no one had seen her.

And for a while everything went on as usual. Later, later, the girl became, how to explain it? No one knew, but she had dreams, and yet she was very awake, more awake than ever. She had started to do some miraculous things, the way maidens, as mistresses of their own mysteries always have. She seemed to see things that were happening far away, without even peering out the window, although it would not have made any difference since all she saw from her window was land and more land until it meets the sky and nothing else. She uttered unknown names and talked very softly, in her larks's voice, and she smiled and sang songs no one had taught her; no one in the town knew them either, because the only time people sang was at Mass, and not always then, or sometimes a servant while she was working, to make her work seem lighter; but this was a different music that came from a great distance. And one day they found her playing with real pearls, passing them from one hand to the other, jostling them in the hollow of her hand which was smooth as a sea shell. How did those pearls get there? Yes, her godmother had given them to her before she died, but since people around there never wore pearls, they had been kept in a drawer. Although there might have been explanations for some things, there was no explanation for her, or her visions, and none for the music, because sometimes it seemed there were instruments in the tower, and people could hear them from a distance, as they were coming back from the fields. Two or three very strange birds had found their way to her window, where they perched on the sill. One was bright gold with a fiery red head, the other one was blue, and sometimes there was an emerald green one. No one had ever seen things like that around there before.

If she had not been so good, so invisible, people would have suspected some kind of witchcraft, and some people quickly assumed that's what it was, but there was no gossip because people had guessed—and one day someone said—that she was definitely not a witch but bewitched. If she had gone out and people had seen her walking around here and there on the streets, things would have been different; maybe that's why the girl had refused to go out and climbed up there where no one could see her.

Eventually no one in the village knew whether she was living or dead. Some people believed she had died a long time before and that her parents had arranged for her to be buried in secret to keep people in the village from getting excited and wanting to see her, since they would even have come from the neighboring villages, and then who knows what might have happened, for by then her reputation had spread. But others said no, she was still alive, although they had not heard the music for a long time; they had seen the splendid birds which came and went and would spend whole days on the tower. One night a little before dawn there was a silent white bird that flew as if it were standing still, and then it was never seen again. The truth is, no one knew what had really happened, since her mother had shut herself up in the house, and her father stayed on his own lands, and when they went to church they said nothing more than a few words to the priest, who of course had to know because he buried her—"He would have been the one to bury her, but if he was in on the secret, he was not going to tell, so why would people have asked him? The truth is, no one knew the real truth."

Some people, and there were some distrustful souls, began to doubt that all this had happened, at least in the way people told it, because maybe it was not such great beauty but the pox, which had left her so ugly she refused to let anyone see her, since the idea of a girl in the bloom of her youth locking herself away like that is pure fantasy.

Little by little the rumors quieted down. Except for the woman who lived on the plaza and whose tongue would be loosened by one of the travelers to whom she had given a room or a meal or a jug of wine, as she did to make ends meet. And there was a person, a rent collector, a strange man who was lucky, or rather unlucky enough, as people learned later, to stop there, and he must have been quite good-looking—tall, although round-shouldered—and as the garrulous woman said: "A nice, reserved man, and afterwards I was sorry I hadn't gotten him to talk," because she felt so excited when she saw that someone listened the way he did, someone who knew how to be such a good listener. And she told him everything—the whole story of the girl, of Dulce, and even the part about the bogeyman that walked by and saw her in the water at the fountain. And he had sat there silently, stroking his blondish beard without saying anything; although he seemed to like the story, he might not have known how to appreciate it fully. And she suddenly rebelled, because his indifference was unjust, things like this don't happen everywhere. "And it's our misfortune, my Lord—what is your worship's name, sir Collector?—in these villages where we're so poor and isolated, that things like this happen, and afterwards we have no one, we'll never have anyone who can tell about them!"

The Queen

Isabel, my queen, what are you doing there child, thinking for such a long time? Oh, I see, you're looking at your maps; now they're talking about some brand new ones with surprising changes you'll like; we'll send a messenger to Medina for them. The things people are saying! I don't understand them very well, and they seem very strange to me, but you understand so much, my child, that you'll figure them out. She kept looking, she could not lift her gaze from those maps, and when she finally did it seemed as if all the water in that mysterious green sea had remained in her eyes. And she continued to sit there with her index finger between her lips, staring into the distance, thinking. "Yes," she said finally, "bring me those maps immediately; have them saddle the horse, something like this can't wait." And her grandmother was left, as on so many occasions, not knowing what to say, since there was no horse at their house nor any servant they could send on that errand, but she did not answer her; she went down the stairs sadly and silently because, Lord, she would have liked to possess everything, everything in this world for Isabel, her child, her queen.

Her father had died; he must have died fighting the Moors, since one day he went off too for that purpose. At first they received good news from him, and she was overjoyed because he was her son and perhaps even more because he was the father of that child, her Isabel, who deserved to be raised beneath the wing of a father who had honor, wealth, and even a title. But then the good news stopped, and they heard nothing more, and neither the wealth nor the titles came either, and she had to raise her on her own, because the mother had been a sad case. Her son had been captivated by her and brought her from another village; it was true that she was very beautiful, and one could not complain because the girl also had blond hair and her eyes. And that way of giving orders as well. But no one had obeyed the mother, even though she gave orders very spiritedly, because her orders were not relevant in such a small house where she could not have many servants, nor did she need many since most of the things she wanted them to do were figments of her imagination. Then too she did not seem to be as much in love with her husband as he was with her, or it seemed as though she missed something a great deal; she was always using the wrong threads and even the wrong patterns in her embroidery, and the most terrible thing of all was the day she called him by the wrong name, and she certainly was unaware of it, because she was definitely virtuous and there was not some man hanging around, shielded the way she was by her husband and by herself, because she looked at no one, at nothing. She was not aware of anything except the things that went on in her imagination, which was always preoccupied with the war and with parliament, especially the parliaments of Castile and Aragon but also with what was happening across the sea in the parliaments of other countries, such as England. What else could she do but gradually go crazy? And her husband hung back silently, until a month before she died he went off to fight, having virtually given up hope for that strange woman who acted as if she had real loves that he was not a part of, although he knew that she was virtuous and that she would die rather than be unfaithful to him.

The girl resembled her a lot, but no; she was serious like her father, and she was not caught up in those fantasies—the daughter was a thinker. She was almost always thinking, the way people say real queens do, because other women go around with their heads full of fantasies about dressing up in fine clothes and looking beautiful. She knew a lot, and if she did not, it was as though she did because she understood everything, and she would come out with clear, very well articulated ideas. It's such a shame that the few men of any consequence there in the village, who came to see her from time to time in memory of her father, were the way they were, so weak-willed!

Because she did not go around in a trance, one could act on the things she thought about, and when she talked about them it was obvious not only that one could, although sometimes it seemed unlikely, but that one should—this proved to be very clear.

Now she was finally going to be married; she had reached fifteen. Without showing any sign of pleasure, she had looked at all the suitors her grandmother chose from the best in the village. But this one she had noticed on her own, and she was thinking that since he was her cousin, and he knew her, although he had not seen her often, he would know how to respect her and love her the way she was, which meant it would be something like a marriage between brother and sister where she would not lose her free will, and he would always admire her, since she was the family's treasure and she deserved better fortune—not a better father—the same father but a more fortunate one. Such a delicate situation could only be understood by someone who was like a brother.

Her fiancé, who was very clearheaded, also deserved better fortune. He never rested; he slept little, although he was a young boy, and he was obviously intelligent, but he did not spend time thinking the way she did, and he did not enjoy studying as much, since he liked to be on the go constantly and to devise different projects, and he always had several in the works—if they would just turn out! He was industrious and very sharp-witted; someday he would be successful, and then his Isabel, his queen, would be the queen she was, but closer to being a real queen. If only a miracle would happen! She deserved a miracle, even one of those miracles Providence works in order to transport people to their rightful places of birth if they were born elsewhere, so that such extraordinary talents will not go to waste—for the good of everyone. What a head like that can do, a woman who can think, Lord, something so unusual and out of the ordinary!

And now so many things were happening, so much that people were talking about there in Medina and Segovia and everywhere, because even in places like that they heard rumors about seas plied here and there and far away battles waged and not waged when they should have been. Because Isabel also understood things such as those that were not happening; they were the things she understood best—the ones that should have been happening but were not.

And one day some people arrived saying that in Medina they said there was an eccentric man, who had lost his mind, wandering the highways. And what if he was only talking about the seas, about the sea that had to be plied if they were going to find an unknown route, one over the sea? No sooner had Isabel heard this than she spoke immediately, in her naturally imperial way. "Have that man come at once; it is necessary to talk with him." Because that's how her commands were, imperial but impersonal. And Fernando, her husband who was beside her, said in a slightly mocking voice: "Isabelita, dear, what does this have to do with you?" And for the first time they saw her look startled and then sink into a dark silence, as if some controlled bitterness had burst through or she had simply seen the reality of her situation, as on a map.

Because it was as if she had her head full of plans about everything. When she began to take trips with her husband, who was involved in business dealings and always deep into some venture, without realizing it she was usually the one who mapped out their journey, and without realizing it he would obey her; she was a genius at routes. If they had let her she would have put the most distant and even the most opposite points of the earth in contact with each other. What's more, she made a few simple improvements in the house, knocking down some partitions, which left corridors exposed, having a stairway built here, a door there—not much in all. That house was a labyrinth of additions and arbitrary demolitions. It was old, and once a fire had almost destroyed it; and people had made poor use of the house, because there was no sign of any order or harmony. She turned it into a spacious house that lacked nothing, putting wastelands—the scrub there at the foot of the wall beside the ravine—to good use and rebuilding the fence so that now the house was protected like a fortress and open to the horizon. It had a view of everything: all the roads approaching the village; the towers of the neighboring villages; and the distant heights, because the top floor of the house gave one a map-like panorama of the entire surrounding area, as if instead of nobility come to less it were the center of the world. And that's how Isabelita must have felt in the afternoon when at last she could sit with her sewing in the highest window. It seemed that she was there to look after everything that was happening around her, on the horizon and beyond. For behind that horizon another was repeating it, and a person could feel that the world is round and that the horizons follow one after the other like clear crystal cups; that there are no enclosed lands nor pits too deep for some communication; that the abysses also form part of the roundness and must correspond to some distant mountain, or some other fissure in the earth through which communication takes place; that everything is a road toward things in the distance and that nothing is distant in itself; and that each place is where it should be, simply, as if God had created the universe according to infallible numbers. Living alongside this, people did not understand it, because that order is not implanted in everyone. She may have been the only one who knew that some day it would have to be.

She would become very animated on their trips. And it's not that she had an adventurous spirit; on the contrary one could say that she made her home everywhere, that wherever she was became the center of the world, because she always tried to stop in places that would let her see the surrounding area, and she would sit down and look, like a little girl, with her index finger between her teeth; and nothing escaped her beautiful green eyes, which would get all sparkly when she suddenly discovered something. She would smile and take her finger from her lips, using it to point to something, some detail, in short something she had seen, saying: "Look, Fernando . . . " in a singsong voice. And her husband would look attentively; he had penetrating eyes like a bird of prey, because there was something in that boy, some ambition—he was a bold one, in other words— and when she would say to him, "Look Fernando," he always took a few steps forward, as if looking meant setting out in conquest of something or rushing off to acquire it. But since her observations could seldom be transformed into action, he would smile in disillusion and say a few ironic words she would not seem to hear and maybe she did not hear them; she might have had some kind of ear trouble or maybe that's just how she was, because she gave no sign of hearing un- less a person spoke to her in a particular way, even her husband, and he more than anyone had to stand still when he spoke to her and look her straight in the eye, or he could sit, but serenely. And since his impulse was always to move, to go so that he could return, she did not listen to one sentence he spoke when he was moving around like that. She was a natural queen.

They always got along well with each other, and they would have gotten along better if he had been able to find grounds for action in everything she saw.

But since they were not a real king and queen this was impossible. And sometimes it would drive him to distraction; seized by an irresistible impetus, he would climb on his horse and set out at a gallop without knowing where he was going. She would remain calm, certain he would have to return, even after the arrival of those rumors that he definitely did know where he was going when he went galloping off that way, because it's understandable that being constantly in front of those eyes always measuring everything would be hard for him, and he must have needed to see his image in other eyes that would send it back to him less precisely, because to stand before her was to stand before a very precise mirror, especially when there was nothing a person could do.

But she never gave any indication that she knew about her husband's excursions and she must have known, because sometimes they took him too far and sometimes not far enough. And this must have hurt her because, in spite of everything, she was very much in love with him, which was obvious when she lifted her gaze and felt nothing but joy to see him there beside her or engrossed in some task; then she would let herself look at him longer, enjoying his virile beauty, his youth, his skill—proud of that man, her husband, the only one she would not have traded for any other; there were even days when a person had the feeling that she was tamer and less severe, that she was a happy woman, nothing more, devising things to please him. Once she had music brought and a lady-in-waiting who knew how to sing, so they could listen to some songs. And when some very important foreigners came to visit she held a splendid ball, because he liked parties, and it did not make her suspicious to see him happy and outgoing; it seemed to amuse her. Because she knew so much, she was sure he would return each time he took off by himself on those adventures, which might have included something more—"like everything in life," she was quick to add. A cross had been growing inside her heart, which is the only way a person could understand how her mind could be so at rest, given all its agitation and all the vexations in her life. But she carried the cross within, and that's why it was not so heavy for her; she never stopped moving or doing things, like those people who say "everything is a cross" and then come to a standstill, as if the cross were a trap that had caught them, and they were stuck inside it. She felt it as something open; she would say that the four cardinal points encompassed the universe, and she followed the cross on all her journeys and as she went about all her tasks. These tasks were becoming very numerous, because that house was a heavy load for her, and little by little people were coming to seek her advice about all the affairs in the village. And there were moments when they found she refused to budge, to the extent that she seemed violent. She made very tough decisions that would have made some men tremble; her will recoiled from nothing, and her ability to decide in favor of such violent and even cruel things meant she wound up alone. Her husband clearly did not want those responsibilities, or he was more tender-hearted . . . what an enigma! That little girl was an enigma.

And silence fell upon that house. Everything grew quiet, and she searched for something with her eyes and grieved, although without saying anything, because she had no place to rest her gaze, as if everyone had left her with her decisions; getting rid of that old man who knew so much about accounts and medicines, complicating things now that their fortune had increased, thanks to some of her husband's dealings.

She stopped at nothing, and this worked against her interests. She wanted everyone to be one or be together as one, and she said that in other places people had already taken steps, such as introducing a terrible tribunal, in order to ensure that no one could get down from the cross that no doubt every day she saw drawn more distinctly on the entire round earth. She went too far, since she was just a woman, but in fact she was a little girl. When children want something, that's how they want it. He used to tell her: "Child, child . . . " But by then everything was useless.

It was almost sudden, the way she died and so young, although if she had continued to live she would not have aged. Her eyes were spinning constantly, and she was writing, something she'd never been much inclined to do, because she was always looking and thinking; and she would write and then she would stop, and her orders were so precise they seemed like poetry. He would go from one place to another, as if he no longer had any control over her. There had been children, and a very beautiful son who died far too young. The truth is, she was alone. She died as if she were starting off on a trip once again, with that compass she carried in her head, as if it were only a question of setting out once she had everything ready. It seemed as though she had died a queen, a real queen, with a queen's sorrows and all the other things, every one of which she recounted in detail to her confessor as if they were the tiny beads on her rosary—not to have her accounts clear when she arrived there with them, but so they would be clear here, so that everyone could read them and judge her. She submitted to the double judgement of men and heaven, because this is how she understood the cross. And this is how she died, amidst the judgments that people who knew her rained on her increasingly, even though they loved her very much; even her husband, who was always in love with her and was always her lover, despite his running around, never stopped judging her, but not the way people judge other women whom no one really judges—"how good or how pretty"—my God no, not her. She felt that increasingly they were demanding even clearer accounts, as if she were being subjected to some trial, although or because she did what no one had done: she had taken leave of the order and the horizon, which had been all pleated until she made it visible; and the house, which had been a labyrinth when she came, she was leaving spacious and round, so you could walk through it everywhere toward everywhere. The village wept for her as for a real queen; they all went to the church and carried her afterward with much weeping and lighted torches, taking the longest route to the cemetery, and they could not tear themselves away. Her husband did not seem to be the center of that sorrow, despite the way he looked and acted, because they mourned her for herself within themselves, and they grieved for her; so he was the one who had to accompany them in their suffering, and it was evident that he had ceased to be that arrogant boy, different from all the others, as if he had put aside his majesty; he had turned into a man, a man like all the rest, who felt impatient, eager to go far away. He left immediately, and the town remained—the half-blind grandmother who had not even been able to go to the burial, walking from room to room, searching, her shadow dragging behind, through the places most loved by her little girl, her little girl . . . and she did nothing but sob in the endless nights and at the anguished moments when some decision had to be made, sobbing in the garden, hugging the walls, and looking from the top of the house at the horizon she could not make out: Isabel, my queen, why did you go so soon? My little girl!

"I" Am Going to Speak about "Myself"

(Philosophical fragment from the second third of the twentieth century)

I am going to speak about myself, although in the narrow sense this amounts to a reiteration; in the narrow sense that one can only speak about oneself. Let's state the question in its most narrow terms: What is speaking and who speaks? There is only one entity that speaks: I, in other words man, but in the strict sense I, I myself, am man.

He who speaks can speak of himself only by speaking from himself. And the strict sense of his speaking is this him, discovered in the very act of speaking. The same act discovers his selfness, because only he who speaks toward himself is himself, and he who is himself can speak strictly, in a strict sense only by turning toward himself; because, rigorously speaking, to speak always and in every case means to speak of oneself and pointing toward one's own selfness.

He speaks about himself, but to put the question more precisely, precisely who is it that is speaking? The *him* or the *self*? Let's look at this as precisely as possible: if the *him* is the one that speaks, what follows? *Him* defines ultimate solitude, infinite anguish in solitude; *him* has only one syllable, so *him* cannot even argue with himself. Quite obviously, then, there is companionship only in argument. Since argument is the only type of relationship between one and other, where there is no argument—where the radical possibility of entering into an argument does not exist—solitude exists. And because solitude is where we find the concrete definition of the real, we discover that in effect the one that speaks is the *him*.

Let's look now at the other possibility that arises: the one who speaks may be *the self* instead of the *him*. The *self* comes to us without boundaries, completely

201

closed, although in reality the *self* is not enclosed; rather, without leaving anything out, the *self* includes all. In the *him* we had the essence of solitude, whereas in the *self* we find the absoluteness of this solitude, the substantivization of that essence, which as the crystallized *him* has included all.

Where has all been included, though? What place was there in the *him* to include anything? But I did not say anything; I said all. Now we discover that the *him* is the solitary essence of *the self,* with all included; the *self,* then, contains the all. And this containing is what effects the move from simple essence to substance.

But this explanation does not explain *who* is speaking. The problem persists in its original terms. And thanks to the explanation that has made us see the impossibility of explaining, we catch the subsistent nature of the problem, one that includes the absolute within its one, in other words, the *him* and the all—being. By asking about being, we have gotten caught up in the all. And now that we have emphasized the all, we grasp the fact that the all makes being indefinable.

Who speaks then? Since this is undefinable, it cannot be either the *him,* for which we have found a definition, or *the self,* because we have found the *him* whose contents envelop the self. And because these contents are simultaneously container, matter, and form, substance and its a priori condition, we realize that only it, the all, speaks, in the strict sense, but we cannot say that this all is *who,* or even "what." The all is the all, which escapes us. Since, however, we have found this all—in other words, I have found the all by speaking strictly about myself— the all seizes me up and sweeps me away. Who speaks is the all within me or I within the all—I as all.

Now let's try to discover if the radical possibility that something like I, supreme reality, exists in the all. The all would thus be the womb of whatever exists. Let's go back to our starting point. Who is the him that speaks in "himself"? But we have reached the I. Now I ask, with the same sincerity, who is this I surrounded, seized up, and swept off by the all, or by nothingness, since they are interchangeable? What happens to this "I" when nothingness assails it, and what happens to nothingness when the "I" assails it? In other words who is the agent, and who is the patient, nothingness or the I, or both—alternately or both together. Let's see . . . If the answer is both alternately, this means that they are not identical, or that they are, through an ultimate identification. Can something not identical to nothingness identify with nothingness? We recall that naive Greek philosophy only recognized identification in BEING. This type of naiveté, however, had been thoroughly critiqued by the time present-day philosophy was still barely visible on the horizon, and the same thorough critique is realized in turn by each individual as he philosophizes on his own. Because the consequence of that Greek naivety, of identification taking place in being, was that philosophers believed they philosophized together and bore each other in mind, so that each philosopher referred to the preceding one, or to the others who were thinking at the same time he was. This is not true of us, because such action lacks authenticity and amounts to an attempt on the authenticity and the identity of the himself and the "I." On the horizon of current philosophy then, each philosopher must contend alone, individually, with himself: each *I* with its *him,* and each one in *itself.*

Returning to the question, let's ask again if identification can occur in nothingness. By being neither being nor against being, isn't nothingness perhaps the negation of all being? So it is not identity that poses the worst possible threat to being by fixing being, substantivizing, and making being definable, or at least intuitable. Maybe the most intimate and radical supposition of modern philosophy is not free of the fixation and crystallization that declassifies all being as it makes being be? Because in fact, what makes something be, simultaneously gives something being and deprives being of being. In other words, being's very being, because it has received its being, is not being. For being truly to be being, identification must arise solely from the drowning virtue of nothingness.

Commentary

The text printed above was found way at the bottom of a deep well, the deepest of the wells not damaged by the destruction that preceded the beginning of the present age. It must have been written either quite some time before the atomic bomb, which could not destroy it because it was down in that well— something rather unlikely—or during the night of subsequent times by someone who survived in that well.

But this confirms nothing for us, because it could be a question of something written before and then preserved in the well of that dark atomic night. Since nearly all philosophy was destroyed, and to such an extent that today we do not know what philosophy means when we find that word in some fragment, it is hard for us to determine the date of something that apparently had a long history. We have no realization of what that philosophy was. Could philosophy as a whole have been like this fragment? The only thing we can manage to understand here is that someone, apparently the himself, affirmed the him above all and eventually destroyed that all and himself as well. But it seems very strange that this could have been accomplished without any pain and apparently without any realization of what was happening. And it's even stranger that such destruction would have been pursued tenaciously. What man could this have been? We cannot imagine him. Neither as a man nor as any of the beings with whom we have dealings. Maybe that man did not know them? There seem to have been neither animals nor plants, sun nor moon, light nor fire, nor the intelligences keener than ours whose presence we can recognize when we listen. Apparently those men did not know how to listen. Or to see, either. Perhaps they had lost their senses? Although the bodies that did manage to reach us display sensory organs identical to ours. And from what we have been able to find out up to now, those men had thought a great deal, found out many things, and been able to scrutinize numerous secrets that have become secrets for us once again. But since we are so busy returning the earth to its habitable condition as the mother of life, we have no time to find out those secrets. I myself, I, what is happening to me that now I'm talking the same way? Well, yes, I think, but no, no! I mean I do not think. Am I thinking that I do not think or that I am not I? Can a history like this one ever find a solution?

Aristotle's Sentence

When Aristotle ascended to the higher spheres, a few Pythagoreans awaited him at the perimeter. They had him at their mercy, but thanks to their gentle dispositions, they restrained themselves and merely handed him a lyre and a few sheets of rudimentary music, and then they left him by himself.

He proceeded to study immediately, quickly making progress. But his fingers were too stiff to play; he gave up and waited, with a certain sense of surprise, which turned into a demand, for someone to come to fetch him. And he began to wonder what was the reason for his strange situation.

Because the answer did not appear, and this time he could not discover it for himself, he simply had to wait, or so he thought. And he began once again to apply himself to the lyre and the music, since it was the only thing he could do, the only activity possible under such strange conditions.

And he worked with enthusiasm, until without realizing it he had grown so enthusiastic that he was engrossed. But still no one came, and from time to time he would suddenly feel frightened, and he asked himself: what's hidden in this situation? The interest he had experienced was turning to fear, which led him to ask that question, although not before he had first experienced the methodical calm that allows one to examine events. His memory was still good, and he knew how to get through this, knew the comings and goings of such a journey better than anyone, better than anyone else on earth! But that made no difference; hardly anything was the same now.

The key to it all was something one of "the so-called Pythagoreans," one of the stragglers, had said. So much time had passed! Besides time in the higher spheres revolves in a different way. The Pythagorean had said that "Music is the unconscious arithmetic of the numbers in the soul." And only when Aristotle found, but not in "theory," the numbers of his soul, when he made them sound, would he rise from where he was. No one was guarding the gates, since there were no gates, and it was not necessary that anyone come for him: he would rise by himself without meeting any resistance when he heard the numbers in his soul on the strings of his lyre—when he felt those numbers sound.

And that's what happened. Before it did, though, many things had to pass in his soul; he had to suffer, to understand as an agent but seated, to suffer life not lived and life half-lived, to drain love dry, as well as anguish and even insanity and delirium—he had become delirious in his hell. Because the musical scale prescribes it: "Dia pason." You must pass through it all: you must pass through the hells of life to hear the numbers in your own soul.

Corpus Christi in Florence

She rushed from the party impulsively, drawn by the bells of the Duomo ringing gloriously, calling people to the Corpus Christi procession. For a moment, from the terrace of the Grand Hotel where the Indian delegation was holding its party, she caught a glimpse of them pealing against a sky so blue it was purplish. A tall man, tall as an ancient king, and three tiny women, fragile as little girls grown somewhat willowy, wrapped in their saris, were granting us the favor of letting us see them, although this did not mean they had entered our world—it was as if they had emerged from their palace as far as the door so they could reach out a hand to that crowd representative of "Western culture." They were kind and wise, with a spark of irony in their black pupils. She could not help speaking a few words to the smallest woman in order to tell her that she was Spanish, and it seemed to her that the irony faded from the woman's eyes and her smile widened, softening.

She moved through the streets guided by the crowd, swept along by the multi-colored human river; everyone was dressed up for the fiesta, people from the *pueblo* with their ancient joy. Joy. What name to call the jubilation in which everything from time immemorial returns to life, in which everyone carries all their dead with them and everyone all together carries the city, from its beginnings—a thousand cities now destroyed and so many perished cultures: the entire eastern genealogy of this West?

In front of the Duomo the rivers of the crowd formed a pool and dozed in wait. She felt that she fit in perfectly with the multitude, even her sky blue, rather plain dress, as if she had not chosen it to look stylish that day but to blend with the day's splendor. People left an empty space for her and even made a sort of hollow around her, understanding that in spite of everything she was a foreigner, and she waited motionlessly next to the Battiseiro. Finally the procession appeared, following its ritual order: first the parish crosses, fantastic golden crosses, the likes of which she had never seen back in Spain. They glittered in the sun, and a polychrome painting sparkled in their midst; it was probably a painting of our Lord, but she could not see very well. The crosses were covered by brightly colored canopies made of velvet or damask—each canopy a different color, and each embroidered with gold. They stood in a row, lined up in the Vía de San Joan, shining in the ray of setting sun that wounded them obliquely. Some collided with the sky, and they were fabulous birds that had probably let themselves be caught or had come happily, pulled by a magic word. And they all shared one silhouette because of the canopies which made them round. But no, their heads and arms were poking out, and the canopy was moving in the wind; they were signs, signs of an ancient religion or of all religions, of all the great priestly religions that had surrendered their most secret symbols. Even though all the crosses were the same, they all seemed different because of their positions and the colors of their velvets, and they formed a single word she would have liked to decipher—a sacred word, the summary of all the great extinguished cultures, of all the multiple times that had disappeared forever and left their posthumous writing.

She was lost in these thoughts when suddenly she felt everything changing, even the air. Slipping down the steps of the cathedral, almost invisibly, came some thin, brown monks—a flock, Lord, of poor simple sparrows, poverty itself; their cross was made of almost unfinished wood, and it stopped still, as they did. Just the cross, nothing more. Their exit was the signal for the procession to move forward, and they themselves walked lightly, the way a flock of sparrows follows some sign that has crossed the heavens. One could barely sense them grazing the earth as they moved effortlessly up the street, and if they were walking here, among the others, it was because they had made a sort of vow not to leave yet, since they were the ones who carried the cross, which they could not forsake, because carrying that cross was the sole reason they had come from a clear, open space where day and night they had sung together beside the cross ever since "Brother Francis" taught them to see his birds, those little sparrows of the divine tree. And she felt that the cross was Paradise, Paradise itself, that here on earth only the cross was Paradise, for stark poverty and Paradise are one and the same.

Only in the starkness of the cross can one find earthly paradise! They were not alone on that stark cross. At their side, perhaps being born from their hearts almost palpably, they felt Him, the Lord, the Son of God, so poor He lacked even a body as He walked on earth in this one last way, invisible to the eyes of those who do not love Him, semi-visible to those who would like to love Him and search in whatever ways they can for the true life.

She felt the total starkness and the poverty of the earth, the planet, felt the terrible struggle humanity suffers from not knowing all this. If some day we just recognized our indigence. But a little of God's glory shines through in the magnificence of richly clad bodies, in the light reflected in the clouds, in the murky atmosphere, in the pupils that capture this light, and in the word. Because we were left with a bit of Paradise, which dazzles us in the spell of art, solaces, the crevice that lets music filter through, and the inner void where everything reverberates and from which we project images, echoes, and even more: a beam of divine light, thought. Even so, nothing can completely cover that initial misery, the beggar so poor the beggar does not know how to beg—our being.

The other religious orders followed; a wooden cross and a handful of slight, humble men. They all seemed to move in the same way, as if they did not want their bodies to shatter the air, as if they took up only the least possible room in space, or as if they brought their own "natural room" along with them, and they moved without traveling, almost free from the humiliating movement of translation, about to enter a different space where one's body will not be the weight or the clothing oppressing us now or the presence that holds us back, but a simple manifestation of the soul, which must walk this way, which must be visible, but no more than necessary, which must take up some room in space, but just the right amount, which must move, but without severing anything. And they walked nimbly, free and small, as if they had broken an evil spell.

Then little by little magnificence began to return, following a set hierarchy. When the high priests came, their dazzling costumes were dazzling beside the brilliant white of their canopy; and beneath the canopy, high in the air a fantastic bird held a gold sun that contained the white, pure, incompatible form of Love. Love: eternal birth.

After them followed the emblem of the city—white with a red lily—providing an escort, along with the mayor. People said he was a Communist but he was walking in the procession because he represented the city; or maybe it was not the mayor himself, and the city was represented by a serious man wearing a dark suit, the only man of this century in the procession, and he was also guarded by two little pages dressed as flowers—one red lily and one white.

The crowd began to break up, strangely silent, as if it were turning inward. What a strange thing—a meditative multitude! Following her own impulse now, she walked as far as the Ponte Vecchio. It was late afternoon and the sunset's phantasmagoria was reflected in the Arno; nature was following the law of its implacable beauty, and we cannot ask nature to stop, to erase its magnificence for one instant, to remain silently empty, to fold up for the night so we don't forget we are poor, poor.

The city was ablaze with festivities. In the Signoria the torches were flaming on the bell tower, which had ceased to be stone so it might catch fire against the now-black sky; below, the crowd was improvising music and songs. On the Vía Tornabuoni, people from the sophisticated international world were crisscrossing casually back and forth, on the way to or from an aperitif in bars like gold cages. Everywhere nature and human life—difference—were triumphing;

quality and quantity each was defining its abyss. Oh, the world of categories! Simply the world: substance, but then immediately quantity and quality. And there, on your cross, Lord, there is nothing in that simple ungraspable starkness— nothing of all this in pure form, incorruptible substance, where each and every quality has been totally reduced.

Is this how it will be, Lord? Will we finish being born once we are in your Paradise?

The Chalice

"What are you doing there, daughter? No, I don't mean that, you're not my daughter." "I know." "Girl." "No, not anymore." "Woman, whatever you are, what are you doing there?" "Well, you can see for yourself: this cup." "That's why I'm here, to tell you not to be stupid, because it's not necessary; or maybe you think it is?" "What? It's not necessary?" "No; it's very easy, anyone can do it, anyone so long as it's someone, well, someone important . . . Instead of asking Father, because then you'll have to drain that cup, the way it happened before, a long time ago; you just pass it on . . . " "Yes, it's easy, you only have to know it can be done and how." "But." "It's nothing, go ahead, you can do it; it's easy, you just pass it on." "That means it passes—to whom? Maybe to someone I love." "And what do you care? The important thing is it passes." "Are you sure no one passed it to you, sure you're drinking from your own? Stupid! What if it belonged to some-one else who passed it to you after it was passed on by still someone else who knows what to do. If you could at least be sure it's yours, untransferable, although even then it could be transferred." "I don't know; it had never occurred to me." "Does it make you feel ashamed? So many have done it, so many people you know, everyone knows." "But what am I supposed to do? Go from door to door saying, 'Sir or brother, would you like my cup?' What if no one wants it? Can a person just leave it, alone, forsaken?' " "But what if that's not what happened and what happens is it's not forsaken, and it gets spilled, and it spills all over every-thing? Nobody wants to drink from it, and then it spills, and confusion ensues: I don't know if it's mine; mine, my cup. But do I even have a cup, one that is mine, mine alone? What if there is just one cup, one for all of us with one lone drop that falls to me, just one drop that cannot be passed on, one drop of eternity?"

Return to the New World

They had entered the latitude of the tropics now, or more accurately the subtropics. One could feel the dense air tending toward flesh, as if the air were ceasing to exit but being replaced by a warm, humid haze, and a huge body was beginning to gestate there, a body that might become visible at any minute; the sea was not moving, as if it were made of tin; there was no sky but low, motionless clouds, and it seemed as though that cosmic animal were about to descend from them momentarily. Whether the tropical sky is cloudy or sapphire blue, there is a vitality in it that suggests a placenta, a cavity where some form is conceived. And in the presence of this imminence one's consciousness withdraws, dozes, is abolished; the body, one's own body, becomes larger, as if it were being summoned by that diffuse vitality which makes it grow heavy and foreign, as if it were returning to the time before it had received its soul. She was being overcome by drowsiness, closed up in her cabin which opened toward the bow and the side of the ship; the noise from the machinery was muffled by the time it got there, but it was denser and corporeal. "Everything tends to become corporeal," she thought, "the air, the water, the elements combine in the cavern of the sky." A desire to wake up began to stir vaguely, because the light was entering, dawn's sunless light, or maybe the sun was still on the horizon, but since there was no horizon in that celestial cavity, and sun probably acted like a focus, ready to engender forms that lacked nothing but visibility, and a person needed to struggle against the sensation of contact with something half-living and unknown; it would be better if one were able to see it. The boat was gradually coming to a standstill, and she was not moving; she could not wake up. How can a person forget that too? It's not enough to open one's eyes, to see the light entering without meeting any resistance. How one senses that light has weight! Also the way

213

light bends so it can enter here, so it can reach us, and the fact that far away, in the invisible, light has left behind its original virginity now subject to the condition of carnality this universe demands. Where are you, first light? Eternal dawn devoid of passion, virgin without history born in each instant, but still exempt from being here or there or anywhere, still giving birth to no form, free from bearing any light: where is the beginning of your work and your sorrow?

Without her perceiving it, she had come to have no feelings, no feeling of being here, she had been absorbed by an ultraheavenly clarity devoid of any design or any allusion to anything, not even to the horizon—a clarity neither coerced by the form of the "heavens," nor obliged to descend to any earth, one with no weight, number, or measure. She realized that she was only a shadow emerged from its thought, one that was struggling to wake up. Toward where? And when she became conscious of this she woke up completely. The earth was there, ruddy and humid, the color of the planet and of humanity, of the first man to bend in work, to bend over the earth, back offered to the sun. The boat was docking now, and the narrow wharf was filled with men carrying bundles, their ruddy breasts bare as they perspired lightly with fatigue. She dressed quickly in the bathroom, confronting her body which the light of Europe had left very pale; then she was beside her sister, walking down the stairs, soon stepping on the earth of the New World, in La Guayra. She realized that she was smiling as she disembarked, although no one was waiting for her; she was smiling because from the deepest part of her being a voice both hers and another's was answering a call, answering someone who had called her from very far away, imperceptibly but imperatively; and she answered, from within: "Yes, I am here, yes, I am here . . . here still."

The Context and Achievement of Delirium and Destiny

I. Genesis and Genre

Hannah Arendt characterized Walter Benjamin's method and writings in terms of a diver "who descends to the bottom of the sea, not to excavate the bottom and bring it to light but to pry loose the rich and the strange, the pearls and the coral in the depths, and to carry them to the surface. . . ."[1] Something similar could be said for María Zambrano's category-defying work. *Delirium and Destiny* is perhaps the greatest anomaly within the anomalous *oeuvre* written by Zambrano, who is known primarily as a philosopher. While her philosophical style is more literary (metaphorical and allusive) than most, *Delirium and Destiny* is the closest thing to a novel that she wrote, and it is also an autobiography or memoir. Gabriel Marcel, who sat on the jury to which it was submitted for a prize, called it a history of Europe and of Spain's place in it. Even more than a novel, a history, or a biography, *Delirium and Destiny* is a crucible for ideas that Zambrano developed more fully in her major philosophical essays of the 1950s and 1960s—*El hombre y lo divino* (Man and the divine), *Persona y democracia* (Person and Democracy), *El sueño creador* (The Creative Dream).

Delirium and Destiny's temporal dimension is likewise complex and multi-layered. The memoir focuses on 1929–1930, the eve of the Second Spanish Republic and a period of intense political involvement for Zambrano. It was written, however, in the late summer of 1952, some fourteen years after the Republican loss to Francisco Franco's Nationalist forces in the Spanish Civil War (1936–1939) had forced Zambrano into exile. *Delirium and Destiny's* chronology

215

is further complicated by its belated publication in 1989, three years before Zambrano's death in the democratic Spain to which she had returned after forty-five years in exile. Upon deciding to finally publish the book, she did some important editing of the text that obscures the stronger political overtones of the original version.

As Zambrano herself states in the forward to the published version, *Delirium and Destiny* was composed in a short period of time in Havana, Cuba to be entered in a European contest for a novel or autobiography. She was especially anxious to win the prize in order to help her sister Araceli with medical expenses. Money for the Zambrano sisters was a constant worry (as it was for many exiles). Zambrano was separated from her husband, the historian Alfonso Rodríguez Aldave, who eventually divorced her; Araceli's husband, Carlos Díez, committed suicide, and her companion of several years was extradited from Vichy, France to Francoist Spain, where he was executed. Zambrano had been a teacher in Spain, and immediately after the war she taught in several universities in Mexico, Cuba, and Puerto Rico, while writing incessantly for journals. Even with these diverse sources of income, it was difficult to cover expenses and help her mother and sister, who resided in France at the time. After the mother's death in 1946, Araceli lived with María Zambrano for the rest of her life (she died in 1972). This relationship, which is important to the development of some of Zambrano's ideas, is mentioned towards the end of the first part of *Delirium and Destiny*, where Zambrano calls her sister Antigone.

Albeit a rather maverick example, *Delirium and Destiny* forms part of a sizeable genre of autobiographies by women who participated in the Spanish Republic and/or the Republican side of the Civil War. Shirley Mangini's *Memories of Resistance* provides an account of a number of these autobiographies, some of which were written in prison or about prison experiences, and others, like *Delirium and Destiny*, from exile.[2] Many of these works are more self-consciously autobiographical than *Delirium and Destiny*, and many, especially those written in the first years after the war, have the express purpose of encouraging the Western powers engaged in combatting fascism in Europe to extend their goals to eradicating Franco in Spain. A few, like María Teresa León's *Memoria de la melancolía* (Memory of Melancholy), are narrated from the oblique third-person perspective we find in *Delirium and Destiny*. However, Zambrano's book is unique within this genre for its philosophical content, and Zambrano's use of third-person narration has a philosophical purpose, which I will discuss later.

It is unlikely that in 1952 Zambrano still held out hope that the victorious Allied powers would intervene to overthrow Franco's military dictatorship, and so her reasons for writing the book at that time are unclear (aside from the economic motive associated with the prize). It is evident, however, from correspondence she conducted with her estranged husband that she had long wanted to write about the coming of the Second Republic and what that experience meant to her personally and to the history of Spain, an exercise that she felt required some emotional distance from the events. That the book was not published soon after it was written also remains something of a mystery. She could, no doubt, have easily found a Latin American publisher for it. She had already published two major books in Mexico—*Filosofía y poesía* (Philosophy and Poetry, 1939) and *Pensamiento y poesía en la vida española* (Thought and Poetry in Spanish life, 1939)—and a book on Puerto Rico was published in Cuba. She had numerous personal and professional contacts throughout Latin America, and many Latin American intellectuals were eager to help Spanish exiles. Correspondence exists in the María Zambrano Foundation (located in her birthplace Vélez-Málaga) that indicates she had made attempts to seek publishers in the United States and in France. Perhaps she was unwilling to have her book vindicating the vanquished Republic available in the language of the regime that had suppressed democratic government in Spain and had occasioned the torture and extinction of so many intellectuals and Republican loyalists. Ironically, the book was finally published in post-Franco Spain under a constitutional monarchy of the kind the Republic had replaced.

II. The Life and Times Narrated in *Delirium and Destiny*

Zambrano's long life began with the century, and her formative years were shaped by the intellectual and cultural flowering of the first third of it, often referred to as the Spanish Silver Age. Not since the Golden Age (from approximately the mid-1500s to the mid-1600s) had Spanish literature and art enjoyed so much original talent and international recognition. Zambrano was born in 1904, the year her compatriot Andalusians Juan Ramón Jiménez (Nobel laureate poet) and Antonio Machado (a poet and educator who taught with Zambrano's father in Segovia) announced a new aesthetic sensibility in the journal *Helios*. *Helios* proclaimed the language of poetry as the supreme reality, and this philosophy inspired the most important literary movement of twentieth-century Spain—the so-called Generation of 1927, which included Pedro Salinas, Jorge Guillén, Federico García Lorca, Rafael Alberti, and Vicente Aleixandre (who in 1977 received the Nobel Prize in recognition of the efforts of the entire generation). During the 1920s Spain participated in all the major vanguard currents—cubism, futurism, surrealism, expressionism, and dada—and some Spanish writers and artists were leaders in these movements. The cultural renaissance was fomented by such institutions as the Ateneo and the Residencia de Estudiantes, where Spanish artists, writers, and intellectuals met regularly to discuss each other's work and to greet foreign thinkers like Einstein.

Zambrano's native Málaga province, trading post and home to Phoenician, Greek, Roman, and Arab cultures, points the way to two important themes in

Zambrano's thought: 1) like the Greeks, she sought a concept of the soul that captured more than just the rational properties of being human, and 2) like certain eastern aspects of Muslim thinking, mystical experience most closely approaches some of what she sought to articulate. The emotions, or passion, are the closest modern equivalent of the former, and intuition the somewhat inadequate contemporary equivalent of the latter. Both orientations are more radical attempts than those of her contemporaries (Xavier Zubiri, for example) or immediate predecessors (Miguel de Unamuno or José Ortega y Gasset) to overcome the limitations of rationalism. In critiquing her early article "Hacia un saber sobre el alma" (Towards a Knowledge of the Soul, 1934), Ortega noted that Zambrano wanted to arrive "way over there," when the rest of occidental philosophy, which Spain was desperately trying belatedly to assimilate, had only gotten "this far."

Zambrano did, however, ground her philosophical inquiry in Ortega's principal philosophical premise—"I am myself and my circumstances" (Ortega was her university professor and the director of her doctoral dissertation on Spinoza). Ortega countered Hegelian historical idealism by rooting humanity's historical situation firmly in particular, individual, biological life, and Zambrano's thought, like that of her teacher and many other Spanish thinkers, is best understood in light of the history of Spain in the nineteenth and twentieth centuries.[3] *Delirium and Destiny* weaves autobiographical, philosophical, and historical material into a seamless narration. Zambrano situates her own life and life as a philosophical category in a specific socio-political situation through numerous concrete references to historical figures and events.

Both of Zambrano's parents were educators. Her father was part of the progressive education movement inspired by Krausism (the first Spanish philosophical school in the Western tradition to take root in Spain). The movement inspired the founding of the Institución Libre de Enseñanza (Institute for Free Instruction) in 1876, Spain's first Spanish university not bound to tradition and the dictates of the Church. The Restoration of the Bourbon monarchy to the Spanish throne after the brief experiment with Republicanism in the 1870s had meant a conservative backlash that confounded intellectuals, who were increasingly aware of sociological thinking in the rest of Europe, especially Marxism, socialism, and anarchism. Zambrano's father was a member of the Socialist Party for a time, and although he eventually gave up party politics, he was ever a liberal thinker and a progressive educator.

When Zambrano was four years old her family moved from their native Andalusia to Segovia, at that time an important intellectual center. There, her father taught in a secondary school with Antonio Machado, one of the most important poets of the Spanish Silver Age; Machado was also an ardent supporter of the Republic and a martyr to it. Both men were deeply involved with a number of intellectual enterprises, including the founding of the Free University for working-class people. Zambrano's father wrote semi-philosophical works, but he is little known today. He is now vastly overshadowed by his more famous daughter, as well as by his friend Antonio Machado, with whom María Zambrano crossed into France on foot in March of 1939 as Franco's troops entered Barcelona, the last Republican outpost. Machado died in a concentration camp in southern France shortly afterward, but María Zambrano, as a woman and noncombatant (although militant with her pen in defense of the Republic), fared better and quickly found refuge and employment in Mexico and Cuba.

Clearly Blas Zambrano's politics and intellectual orientation were important to María, the elder of his two daughters. With no male children, the Zambranos (who were doubtless influenced by Krausist educational principles that promoted education for women) were free to encourage their bright elder daughter in her intellectual pursuits; the extensive family library was at her complete disposal, and there she first came in contact with the writings of Miguel de Unamuno, whose emphasis on the irrational in approaching life's dilemmas was an important source of inspiration for her own thinking. Blas Zambrano was something of a Don Juan. María, apparently disgusted with this side of her father's character, and also following her own inclinations, retreated from his more traditional (and male) kind of thinking, while her appreciation for her mother's more intuitive cognitive style grew concomitantly. *Delirium and Destiny* reveals a subtle shift from an allegiance to the male-dominated intellectual milieu in which Zambrano lived, studied, and worked in the pre-War era to a more female-centered life in the post-War period when she began to care for her sister.

In the first two decades of the century, Spain was still behind the rest of Europe in attitudes toward women and in providing opportunities for their intellectual development. The feminist movement in Spain was much less developed than in England or France, and education for girls (even at the primary level) was still rare. María Zambrano was a precocious child, and to the amazement of neighbors, at age four under the influence of a high fever she discoursed for hours on subjects such as religion and morality. She even had an out-of-body experience during this first of several serious illnesses she suffered throughout her life, one of which was the bout with tuberculosis chronicled in *Delirium and Destiny*. During her confinement for that disease, she began meditating on the nature of being and time.

Zambrano attended a grade school in Segovia where she was the only girl; her father told her she would just have to get used to it. By the time she reached the University of Madrid to study philosophy in the early 1920s, there were a few women in attendance, and some of these, including Zambrano, played a high-profile role in the anti-government movement of 1929–30. It particularly rankled the very conservative dictator José Primo de Rivera that women were among those who so very publicly advocated his overthrow.

María Zambrano reached the University of Madrid at the most propitious of moments. Intellectual and cultural life was at its zenith, and intellectuals were taken very seriously by the public and the press. José Ortega y Gasset, her major professor at the university, and Miguel de Unamuno, along with a host of other outstanding writers and thinkers, published daily articles in the press and gave numerous well-attended public lectures at venues such as the Ateneo, the Escuela Normal, and the Residencia de Estudiantes. Zambrano was already well aware of this rich cultural milieu before she took up residence in Madrid. Her cousin (and first romantic interest) Miguel Pizarro Zambrano, who went to Madrid some five years before she did, had informed her about the members of the Generation of 1927. He also brought to her attention Rosa Chacel, another precocious young woman, who became one of Spain's best novelists of this century. Later Chacel and Zambrano formed a life-long friendship that endured even when exile carried them to different parts of the globe. Correspondence between them indicates that they encouraged each other to continue to write and to keep faith with the intellectual vocations they had struggled to nurture in the male-dominated intellectual milieu of Spain in the 1920s and 1930s.

The tense political situation offered the stellar cast of intellectuals a fertile arena for speaking out on issues. A few years before María Zambrano went to Madrid, Alfonso XIII's reign (which began in 1902) incurred serious difficulties. The problems arose in various sectors, especially among the increasingly organized urban proletariat and the military. Under the Restoration, workers had been awarded the right to assemble, and their main organizations—the UGT (General Workers' Union) of socialist orientation and the CNT (National Confederation of Workers) of anarchist ideology—increased appreciably in membership (communism has never had a very large following in Spain). In the wake of the First World War and the Russian Revolution, there was a great deal of labor unrest in Spain, some of it quite violent in nature, inspired by hard-core anarchists who believed that isolated acts of violence could effect revolution.

In addition, King Alfonso had embarked on a campaign in Africa, incurring public repercussions not unlike those that plagued United States politics and public life during the Viet Nam war. As was U.S. policy during the Viet Nam conflict, Spanish public policy was strongly influenced by student protest. Spain had taken over Morocco as a protectorate to serve as a buffer from French Africa, but the ambitious native leader Abdl El Krim decided to solidify his hegemony with a military victory over the Spaniards. Low morale in the Spanish army was fomented by the difficult fighting conditions in desert terrain, and in July of 1921 the Spaniards were delivered a humiliating defeat at Annual. This event was the *coup de grace* for King Alfonso's government and paved the way in 1923 for a military dictatorship under José Primo de Rivera, who was welcomed as a kind of savior by the general populace and even by some intellectuals (among them José

Ortega y Gasset). The country remained a nominal monarchy (Alfonso was still king), but Primo de Rivera, whose notions of the state were very conservative, naive, and simplistic, made all the decisions. His dictatorship, which lasted for seven years (1923–1929), marked the end of almost fifty years of parliamentary monarchy in Spain, and though not a true fascist regime, it borrowed some ideas and strategies from Mussolini.

Even the intellectuals who had initially supported a "temporary" dictatorship as a necessary measure to curb violence and unrest soon grew disaffected with Primo de Rivera's scorn for intellectual life (for example, he closed the Ateneo and the Central University, and censored the press). Miguel de Unamuno was exiled in France for his outspoken criticism of the regime, and he became a kind of national symbol of freedom, an identity he encouraged by living as close as he could to the Spanish border and sending well-publicized open letters to the Spanish people. He would repeat this dissident behavior during the Civil War when he denounced a Nationalist general for proclaiming "Long live death." He was placed under house arrest for his defiant act and died shortly thereafter. Unamuno became a mythological figure for intellectuals in exile after the Civil War—symbol of intellectual independence and courageous defiance of repressive regimes; many exiles wrote about him and gave classes on him in universities throughout Europe, Latin America, and the United States. He is often evoked directly and indirectly in *Delirium and Destiny.*

The University of Madrid was a focal point for the campaign against Primo de Rivera's regime, and it is precisely this arena in which María Zambrano was active and on which she focuses in her novelized autobiography. The students belonging to the FUE (University Student Federation), a non-Catholic student organization, protested a Primo de Rivera decree giving private Catholic universities the right to confer degrees that were essentially licenses for coveted government positions. As student anger and restlessness escalated, students engaged in the destruction of public property, and some were jailed. At the height of the dictator's troubles, the student melées became full-scale riots. Students barricaded themselves in the Medical School building and fired gunshots at the Civil Guard sent to quell the riot. The government withdrew the police in an effort to diffuse the situation and to avoid creating martyrs.

Zambrano formed part of a group of students whose unofficial leader was Zambrano's close friend José López Rey, another of Ortega's disciples. This student group approached older intellectuals like Ramón María del Valle Inclán, Manuel Azaña, Gregorio Marañón, Ramón Pérez de Ayala, and Luis Jiménez de Asúa to encourage them to political action. At this point there was no clearly-formed support for a republic among most intellectuals or student activists. They were militating for removal of the dictator and reform in Spanish political life. There was a prescient sense that "something" was going to happen, that things could not continue as they were, and it is a horizon of possibility, a sense of expectation, that Zambrano conveys in *Delirium and Destiny*. The intuitional or prophetic quality of some of life's moments is one of the philosophical strands that she develops in later works, and that finds its definitive statement in her last published book, *Claros del bosque* (Clearings in the Forest).

After a series of individual meetings between the students and recognized intellectual leaders, a joint meeting was held at a restaurant outside Madrid; there the older intellectuals and the students agreed that a republic—democracy, freedom, and social justice for all Spaniards—was their goal. Zambrano published her first article "Nosotros creemos . . . " (We believe . . .) three days after this historical meeting. Zambrano's group formed a "League for Social Education" whose purpose was to join with the working classes in moving toward a new society. In establishing this organization, the students were fully conscious that their efforts embodied a different attitude toward the "masses" than the one that had motivated José Ortega y Gasset, Gregorio Marañón, and Ramón Pérez de Ayala to form the "League for Political Education" in 1915 to prepare Spain's underclasses for a more democratic government. The points of contention between Zambrano and her teacher-mentor Ortega were both political and philosophical. Ortega's view of the working classes was always paternalistic, whereas Zambrano's, perhaps informed by a Marxist socialism, displayed more solidarity with workers. Among the student League's activities was speaking to workers' groups in order to raise consciousness about governmental and social reform. The meeting reported in *Delirium and Destiny* at the Cigar Workers' Union is representative of these activities.

Zambrano acted as the spiritual inspiration of the League, and its key members often met at her house. Carlos Díez, one of the few Communist members of the group, actually lived for a time in the Zambrano household. He was a medical student who had come to Madrid to marry María's sister Araceli (Araceli was a great beauty and had many admirers over the years). Carlos appears at strategic points in *Delirium and Destiny*, often referred to by the narrator as "my brother." He specialized in pulmonary diseases because of Araceli's tuberculosis, and he also attended María during her own tubercular period. In fact, it was Carlos who insisted that she drop out of the frenetic political activity in which they were both engaged and leave teaching (she was substituting for a philosophy professor at the Instituto Escuela) because her health was in serious danger.

After a sequestration of many months, she emerged to find that the political situation had moved forward quickly. With the promise of several teaching positions at the Instituto Escuela and at the Central University, she devoted herself to writing her first book, *Horizonte del liberalismo* (Horizon of Liberalism, published in 1930), which outlined her theory of the philosophical foundations of the new state. The writing of the book coincided with the sudden resignation of the dictator José Primo de Rivera in January of 1930. He had managed to effect policies that alienated too many groups—the socialists and the capitalists alike. Economic woes beyond the government's control were the crowning blow. King Alfonso XIII tried to recover the powers he had lost to Primo de Rivera and return to the situation his reign had enjoyed before 1923, but his attempts failed; in April 1931 he went into exile, and the Republic was declared.

When it comes to chronicling these events in *Delirium and Destiny*, Zambrano's lyrical narrative assumes a diary-like style that organizes the material by specific dates. The pace of the narration quickens, and we feel the rush to an inevitable conclusion. Her prose imitates what Spanish historian Raymond Carr describes as the tenor of the period: "A flood of press statements and speeches to enthusiastic audiences made the politics of 1930 a suspense story."[4] In February leading writers (including Ortega) formed "The Group at the Service of the Republic." Naively unaware of the power intellectuals wielded in the public arena, King Alfonso mistakenly ignored their speeches and public pronouncements. His attitude only sharpened their resolve and their verbal and written attacks against his regime.

As is usually the case in Spain, the final blow came from the army. In April 1931, the officers, rather than rising overtly against the monarchy, simply refused to support it (in what is called a "negative pronouncement"). In August a number of Republican factions, including some army officers, met and planned a coup for December. Captain Galán, one of the conspirators, jumped the gun and began his rebellion in Jaca (Aragon) a few days too early; he and a co-conspirator were captured and summarily executed, and the rest of the revolutionary committee was imprisoned. The coup had been aborted, but it paved the way for a Republic that did not have such a military cast. Galán and his co-conspirator became martyrs to the Republic, and the revolutionary committee acquired greater prestige and leverage, operating very successfully from the Modelo Prison. King Alfonso only gained more negative publicity for his cruelty.

It was at this point that the students barricaded themselves at the university. On April 12 municipal elections revealed that a Republican-Socialist coalition had won in many large towns. The revolutionary committee demanded that the King leave Spain, and the King, with the knowledge that the army would probably not back him, complied. Like a ripe fruit, the Republic just seemed to fall from the tree, after the appropriate period of maturation. This is most of what comprises the historical portion of Zambrano's narration. She also actively participated in the Republic (1931–39) in various ways and was a fervent supporter of the Republican cause during the Civil War (1936–39), but she has elected to make almost no reference to these aspects of her life and Spanish history in *Delirium and Destiny*. Even though *Delirium and Destiny* scarcely refers to events after 1931, Zambrano's experiences between the proclamation of the Republic and the composition of the book in 1952 shaped the work she would eventually write.

III. Zambrano's Life Beyond the Narration in *Delirium and Destiny*

While writing from the perspective of 1952, Zambrano has made every effort to achieve a narratorial tone that captures the fresh, hopeful feelings that Spaniards of her age and political orientation experienced in 1929–1931, it is impossible not to detect a kind of nostalgia for what was lost or what might have been. Zambrano continued offering classes in philosophy in the early 1930s and writing articles for journals. Most notably she began to collaborate in Ortega's prestigious *Revista de Occidente* during this time, and her article "Hacia un saber sobre el alma" published there in 1934 marked a major departure from Ortega's thought. She also contributed to José Bergamín's *Cruz y Raya,* the other major intellectual journal of the Spanish 1930s. In 1935 she gave her first lecture series as an independent speaker, rather than as a member of a political activist group. She was beginning to be recognized as someone with an original voice.

She also had a government post in the Committee for Cultural Relations during the 1933– 1935 trienium. The Committee was formed in 1926 to advise the State Department on the teaching of Spanish abroad and on cultural and scientific exchanges with countries with whom Spain had diplomatic relations. During the years that the Republic was carrying out its program of reforms, Zambrano joined the group of writers, artists, and university professors who worked to educate the rural population under a program called the Pedagogical Missions. The "Missions" traveled to remote villages to instruct people in Spanish culture. Zambrano regularly hosted a *tertulia* (informal gathering) in her parents' home with many writers such as Miguel Hernández and Camilo José Cela in attendance.

In 1936 the Civil War broke out for reasons too complex to relate here, and widely known in any case. The factions that had united to oust the monarchy and proclaim the Republic were too diverse to hold against the conservative backlash evident in some of the elections held under the Republic and that erupted in the army plot of July 18, 1936 from which General Francisco Franco emerged as a powerful military and political strategist. The Republican government continued to function as normally as it could during the three-year Civil War, including sending diplomatic missions abroad. After their marriage in September of 1936, Zambrano accompanied her husband to Santiago, Chile, where he had been named secretary to the Spanish Embassy under the Republican government. On the way to their assignment in Chile, Zambrano and her husband had an eight-day stopover in Havana, Cuba, where she met a number of Cuban writers and intellectuals who would be very important to her during her exile there in the 1940s and early 1950s. While in Chile, Zambrano continued to support the Republic with her pen. There she wrote *Los intelectuales en el drama de España* (The Intellectuals in the Spanish Drama), and edited and introduced an anthology of works by the poet and dramatist Federico García Lorca, who had been executed by the Nationalists in 1936.

In 1937 Zambrano and her husband returned to Republican Spain, even though (or, as she put it, "because") the Republican cause seemed all but lost. Her husband donned the Republican uniform and went into active service, and María devoted herself to helping behind the lines as an advisor to Republican propaganda efforts and to the children's evacuation program. She also founded and wrote for journals that supported the Republic, especially *Hora de España* (Spain's Hour) which included articles by leading intellectuals such as Antonio Machado. Throughout the War, which has been called "the poets' war," intellectuals continued to believe that the pen was as mighty as the sword.

Shortly before the Nationalists entered Barcelona, María's father died, and she, her mother, sister, and four-year old cousin Rafael Tomero Alarcón crossed the border into France. There she was reunited with her husband, and they followed the course of so many Republican exiles by going to Latin America where Republican sympathies (especially in Mexico) and the common language made it possible for them to continue to teach, write, or otherwise make a living. Biographical material about most of Zambrano's life is very sketchy and exceptionally so for the period of her early exile. She was first given a professorial post at the provincial University of San Nicolás de Hidalgo in Morelia, Mexico, a situation that caused her some consternation because male philosophers of her same generation were offered positions at the University of Mexico in Mexico City. In 1940 she relocated to Havana, Cuba where she also accepted a university teaching post. In Havana she became a key figure in the poetic group that founded the journal *Orígenes* (1946–1955). In 1948 Zambrano separated from her husband, who had abandoned his profession as a historian to become a businessman. Letters from Rodríguez Aldave to Zambrano in the 1950s indicate that he found it difficult to accept her fame and her intellectual success.

In Cuba, María, who apparently had a penchant for intense relationships with men, became involved in a stormy affair with fellow Spanish exile Dr. Gustavo Pittaluga, who was helpful to her in adjusting to life abroad. *Delirium and Destiny,* while ostensibly about existential concerns and their relationship to political and historical realities, also reflects Zambrano's yearning for a fulfilling personal passion that she may never have achieved. During her years as a graduate student at the University of Madrid, she had been deeply in love with her professor, the phenomenologist Xavier Zubiri, who was an ordained priest. (The situation calls to mind the relationship between Hannah Arendt and her professor Martin Heidegger, although it is not clear that Zambrano ever had an actual affair with Zubiri.[5]) It has even been reported that Zambrano asked Zubiri to marry her, but he refused (he did later leave the church and marry Carmen Castro). Zambrano's disquisition on denial, on the "No," that we find early in the novelized autobiography could very possibly refer to her relationship with

Zubiri, and it reminds us that, if Zambrano's philosophy is particularly cogent in its reflections on the complex way human life unfolds, it is because her own personal experiences were the source of many of her meditations.

The Cuban milieu in which Zambrano had been living off and on for some ten years when she composed *Delirium and Destiny* was of central importance to her development as a writer and thinker. If the ambience created by the Generation of 1927 in Spain had been a fertile ground for the early formation of Zambrano's keen mind, the *Orígenes* group was an ideal follow-up for its further development. By all indications Zambrano was a kind of guru to the young Cuban poets. Their presence gave her the audience she needed to cultivate her ideas and receive stimulating responses to them; in one account she is called a high priestess of the Cuban intellectual scene.[6]

Zambrano was particularly close to José Lezama Lima, who became the best-known of the *Orígenes* group, and she maintained her friendship with him through abundant correspondence until his death in 1976. They had philosophical interests in common, especially Greek thought, mysticism, and the relation of language to reality. The *Orígenes* group coincided with the Spanish Generation of 1927 (and with Zambrano) in its emphasis on literary language—imagery and metaphor—as an important form of knowledge; for Lezama Lima metaphor was "a written synthesis of the known and intuitively sensed, a kernel of truth based on a secret and harmonious whole."[7] It is not surprising that Zambrano's theory of "poetic reason" found the welcome reception in the *Orígenes* circle that it had not at the *Revista de Occidente* under Ortega's more conventional philosophical guidance. Cuba was for Zambrano what she called in her article "Cuba secreta" a "pre-natal country," "carnal reality," "pure dream of unencumbered being alone with its enigma." The Cuban milieu freed her from the destiny assigned her by her native country—a woman thinker in a male intellectual world, a student of Ortega and Zubiri, who had until her exile lived in their shadow.

When Zambrano's mother died in 1946 and Zambrano took charge of caring for her sister, she reoriented her living arrangements toward Europe, where her sister apparently felt more comfortable. They lived first in Rome and then in Switzerland. Making a living became even more difficult in countries where she could not teach or publish in her native language (although she continued to publish with editorial houses and journals in Latin America). María and her sister were able to make ends meet through generous contributions from friends, some of whom sent monthly stipends at different times in her life. The Roman period was an especially fertile one for Zambrano, and there she published several books that work out in detail the ideas on dreaming and the individual in society that she had first outlined in *Delirium and Destiny*.

In 1984, nine years after the hated dictator Francisco Franco finally died, Zambrano returned to live out the remaining seven years of her life in her native Spain. She was received as a heroine and feted with some of Spain's most coveted prizes for writers. She had already received the Prince of Asturias Prize in 1981; in 1985 she was named the favorite daughter of Andalusia, and in 1988 she received the Cervantes Prize, the most prestigious of all. In 1989 she finally published *Delirium and Destiny* at the insistence of her cousin Rafael Tomero Alarcón, who had on several occasions saved the manuscript from the flames. (Over the years, Zambrano burned many of her papers, and she felt that since *Delirium and Destiny* had not served its original purpose—to help her sister with medical expenses—it should be consigned to oblivion.) Tomero Alarcón was able to convince Zambrano that the work was an invaluable testimonial that deserved a public airing. This work joined a number of Zambrano's other manuscripts that had languished in her trunks unpublished and that friends helped her to edit in the final days before she succumbed to death in 1991. Many of her works still remain in manuscript form at the María Zambrano Foundation in Vélez-Málaga, so a complete assessment of her achievement as a philosopher and writer will be slow in coming. Zambrano does, however, enjoy a growing reputation in Spain and has had significant influence on a number of post-Civil War Spanish poets, such as José Angel Valente and Amparo Amorós.

IV. *Delirium and Destiny*

An interpretation of *Delirium and Destiny* can at best be tentative. Like all of Zambrano's work, it is essentially philosophical, but it has more literary elements than most of her books—a narrator, something of a story line, real world referents couched in literary language, dialogue, and fictive, imaginative stories at the end (the "Deliriums"). It has many characteristics of the philosophical novel that was an important genre in Spain between 1900 and 1936. There are passages in which philosophical discourse predominates, and others in which the philosophical content is embodied in the autobiographical and historical material. This narrative procedure is in keeping with Zambrano's philosophical position, which could be described as an existentialism that situates the self within its historical circumstances.

By the time she wrote *Delirium and Destiny*, María Zambrano had considerably widened her philosophical background. Her early inspiration in the Greeks, Plotinus, Spanish mysticism, Spinoza, Leibniz, Scheler, Krausism, nineteenth-century social thought, Unamuno, Ortega, and Zubiri was enriched by greater familiarity with Nietzsche, Bergson's *durée*, Freudian and Jungian psychology, Heidegger on poetic language and being, and feminist ideology that had gained ground in Spain in the years before and during the Republic. To Unamuno's existentialism she added that of Sartre and de Beauvoir, and she complemented the Spanish mystics with theories of eastern mysticism interpreted by thinkers such as Louis Massignon. Echoes of all these sources can be found in

Delirium and Destiny. They serve as the underpinnings upon which she reconstructs herself and her situation in the 1920s and 1930s, a process that leads her towards her mature philosophical position. At the center of that philosophy is the notion "Adsum," the refrain that begins and ends *Delirium and Destiny,* an affirmation of "my present being" as the primary reality.

There are two main strands which emerge separately in Zambrano's early philosophical thinking: 1) the individual as a socio-political being and 2) the nature of the interior self or the soul (as she calls it). The autobiography gave her the opportunity to braid these strands together. The first strand is represented in her first book, *Horizonte del liberalismo* (Horizon of liberalism), published in 1930 in the heat of debates about republicanism in Spain. It calls for a new liberalism, in which Zambrano posits a politics that foregrounds society. She criticizes traditional liberalism that places excessive emphasis on the individual at the expense of social considerations, and calls for a "liberty . . . that does not break the cables that connect man to the world, with nature, and with the supernatural. Liberty founded, rather than on reason, on faith in love."[8] Thus Zambrano posits freedom as a social rather than an individual phenomenon. She would doubtless have agreed with Simone de Beauvoir that to "will oneself moral is to will oneself free" and that to "will oneself free is to will others free," for "every man has to do with other men."[9] Her emphasis on the social nature of being, which remains a constant in her philosophy, is a legacy from Ortega, but she diverged from Ortega as early as 1934 by making a place for emotion in life (a place that included dreaming by the time she wrote *Delirium and Destiny*).

The second strand emerges in the article "Hacia un saber sobre el alma," published in *Revista de Occidente* in 1934. In this essay, Zambrano effected what might appear to be a 180–degree turn from external political concerns to the mostly intimate and internal sphere. She sought to go beyond Spinoza, who suggested "an Ethics in which psychology is still a metaphysics."[10] According to Zambrano, the study of the soul had been left to psychology, which approached it with a scientific eye. Under those circumstances, the soul turned to literature. The soul is the key to the process of bringing external political and ethical matters into the realm of the individual subject, because it situates itself in that central and facilitating space between "the *I* and the natural exterior."[11] Literature (which embodies the soul) is the ideal intermediary between the external self and the socio-political world, because it participates equally in the public and private spheres. It is uniquely situated to unite the individual emotions with public political life in Zambrano's "poetic reason." Poetic reason both echoes and challenges Ortega's "vital reason"-cum-"historical reason."[12]

Needless to say, Ortega, who had postulated his concept of vital reason some ten years earlier, was not very receptive to Zambrano's version of reason. Vital reason—a reason centered on individual life (in very biological terms)—metamorphosed into historical reason, a useful notion that weds individual life to history through the concept of generations. Both of these concepts, however fruitful for thinking about specific life and history, eschew the realm of emotion and the transcendental that Zambrano wished to include in a philosophical account of the individual's relationship to her circumstances. Poetic reason bridges the gap between the personal and the social. If Ortega's vital reason is the personal version of historical reason, Zambrano negotiates a compromise or bridges a gap between the two.

Even before the publication of "Hacia un saber sobre el alma," Zambrano's relationship with Ortega was somewhat conflicted. For example, she wrote him letters chastising him for not taking a more aggressive role in militating for a republic. When Ortega harshly criticized her essay "Hacia un saber sobre el alma" for going too far in its critique of reason, she left his office in tears. In 1939 as she was closing up her apartment in Barcelona to go into exile, she decided at the last minute to abandon the carefully packed boxes with her notes from Ortega's courses. Ortega's mentorship was an important legacy that gave her the groundwork for thinking about the individual and society, but in working out her own version of it, she diverged significantly from "the Master." There was also tension on Zambrano's part with respect to Ortega's political position after the Civil War (as there was for many exiled intellectuals). Ortega returned to Francoist Spain in 1945, and although he was barred from the University, he lived by giving private courses and well-attended public lectures. Many intellectuals who refused to acknowledge Franco's regime felt that Ortega had sold out.

In 1943 Zambrano continued to challenge Ortega (albeit indirectly) in her essay *La confesión como género literario y método* (Confession as a literary genre and method), which flies in the face of Ortega's antipathy toward personalism in art, as expressed in books like *The Dehumanization of Art* and *Ideas on the Novel*. Ortega argued that art and life should maintain completely separate spheres. For Zambrano, confession is the kind of writing that comes closest to eliminating the gap between reason and life; it proffers the possibility of reaching those interior realms that fuel dreams. And, as Genevieve Lloyd noted about St. Augustine's *Confessions,* confession frees one from lived life to achieve a consciousness of oneself.[13] In her exile memoir Zambrano is doubly freed from temporal constraints, not only her own individual time, but that of her country. It is this atemporality that forms the centerpiece of her theory of dreams in *El sueño creador.*

In exile, deprived of the specific political milieu that had been so important to her personally and intellectually in the 1920s and 1930s, Zambrano's thought, while not completely relinquishing an interest in the political self, turned to cultivating the internal personal realm—*los ínferos* (the nether regions)—initiated in "Hacia un saber sobre el alma." *Delirium and Destiny* is the crucible where Zambrano, under the guise of memoir and autobiography, rehearsed a number of the ideas, especially the place of dreams (delirium) in life, that she developed more fully in her complex and important books *El hombre y lo divino* (Man and the

Divine, 1955) and *El sueno creador* (Creative dreaming, 1955). The autobiographical element gave her the opportunity to consider ideas on the self that had remained sketchy in earlier works dealing with the individual's relationship to the
state and the intersection of philosophy and literature. Although Zambrano
 doesn't explicitly take note of it in her book on confession, the genre also has
the positive effect of allowing the modernist woman writer to reveal the sub-
jectivity denied her in male modernist writing. It also allowed her to develop
more fully the self in time that had remained sketchy in the earlier books and
essays. The form of *Delirium and Destiny* recognizes this advantage of the autobiographical or confessional mode.

The two parts of the book—"A Dreamed Destiny" and "Deliriums"—are
theory and practicum, respectively. The first part provides a discursive, albeit lyrically discursive, representation of an individual's life as it blended with the social
entity. The narrative exemplifies a view of history in which individuals are part
of the story while being actors in it. The "Deliriums" are fanciful projections of
the ways in which human beings (usually women) can imaginatively reinvent
their lives. For example, in "The Crazy Woman," the protagonist escapes her
bourgeois surroundings, first through insanity and then by willing her inheritance to the poor.

The theory of the self that emerges in *Delirium and Destiny* has many reso-
nances of existentialism, particularly that of Unamuno and Sartre. Zambrano's
theory of the self and of the society on which it depends begins with the notion
of the image. Images or concepts are formed after primary experience and immediately become the past that accompanies us and colors our view of reality.
Lacan, no doubt drawing on Sartre's notion of the *pour soi,* likewise noted that
an individual fixes himself upon an image that alienates him from himself. The
"other" and the "gaze," which facilitate identity-formation in Sartre and Unamuno, are also important to Zambrano. In the early passages of *Delirium and Destiny,* we find an emphasis on negation and the "No," which parallel the negative
aspects of the self-image formed in the other's gaze akin to that in male existentialism (and even in Simone de Beauvoir). But in *Delirium and Destiny* these eventually take on a positive cast as the void opened up in a negative is understood
as an opportunity for creation. Unamuno's *desnacer* (unborning) becomes the lev-
eling device that is a necessary preamble to becoming, to a *renacer* (reborning; see
Delirium and Destiny 10, 69). While retaining Sartre's insistence on human freedom, Zambrano exchanges his nothingness in the self-world construction[14] for
a vacuum that allows for new self and social conceptions. For Unamuno and
Sartre the relation between "myself" and "the other" is antagonistic and conflic-
tive, while for Zambrano it is creative and constructive.

Zambrano also modifies the existential insistence on existence over essence.
Although she does not revert to a reductionist or deterministic view of humanity's relation to its history, she follows Ortega in understanding history as the so-

cial dimension of human life that we cannot and would not wish to escape. In *Delirium and Destiny* she avers that an individual does not have history; the *pueblo*, the people, has history. Likewise there is no tragedy in a people; only in individuals (155). The *pueblo* is a complex concept in Zambrano's usage. It combines elements of *volksgeist* theory she learned from Unamuno's and Azorín's "intrahistory" and "eternal tradition" with a socialist political view of the *pueblo* as the working classes. Ortega purged from his notion of history all trace of the *volksgeist*—a subterranean communal history—which he doubtless associated with thinkers such as Unamuno and Azorín from whom he was distancing himself. Zambrano reconstitutes the communal history of the people through dreaming; her version of the subconscious appears to have elements of Jung's universal unconscious, which for Zambrano is made manifest in dreams (delirium) and literature. Delirium frees us from the constraints of present historical time in order to reach back into the communal past and forward to a common future.

Zambrano distinguishes between history and tradition. The *pueblo* (the people) lives in tradition, a time when images of the past are not our own concepts but ones that are given to us. Thus the *pueblo* maintains spontaneity; its consciousness is not constantly forming images and concepts, since it lives by means of a few already-available concepts maintained at a distance: "They live in a time, which is poetically creative."[15] The traditional past in her view, however, rather than being a constraining force, opens the way for a transcendent history and a space for "creative forgetfulness." In order to forge a new future that is not burdened by the past, both individuals and nations must forget. Her phenomenology of dreams allows for this "creative forgetfulness" and for a "creative dreaming" that is essential to social and political change. Dreams for Zambrano are not the rehearsal of a past we have already lived, as they were for Freud, but an opportunity to fashion the future. According to Zambrano, dreaming is the dawn of consciousness and possibility. Likewise, her theory of the "multiplicity of time" (first introduced in *Delirium and Destiny*) frees us from an absolute chronology that locks us into determined patterns. We accumulate times that remain with us and that are a resource to us as we dream the future.

By now it should be evident why Zambrano chose to concentrate her autobiographical narrative in *Delirium and Destiny* on the several years that led up to the Spanish Republic. It was that moment in twentieth-century Spanish history when Spain seemed poised to finally enter the modern European world with a liberal form of government, when Spain could forget her past and dream a different future. It was the moment when Spain "woke up." In *El sueño creador*, Zambrano distilled the theory of dreams she rehearsed in the autobiography into a tightly written phenomenology of dreams. She applied the phenomenology normally associated with the conscious mind to the subconscious or dream state, seeking to find the form of dreams rather than their content, as did Freud. The importance of consciousness is not lost, however, as she posits dreaming as a kind of vigilance—the waking or lucid dream. This diaphanous aspect of dreaming is lyrically evoked in *Delirium and Destiny* through a pervasive use of light imagery. In *El sueño creador* Zambrano concentrates on the liberating atemporality of dreams and focuses especially on the waking moment as central to the creative process. Starting from the notion of the self developed in *Delirium and Destiny*, she notes that in dreams the person is fully present to herself. The dream frees us of our *personaje*, our mask. Likewise, in dreams, time, while not abolished, is transcended and allows for the multiple possibilities of being. Zambrano follows Freud in his notion that dreams, unlike material reality, allow for multiple possibilities (resolutions do not need to be either/or but can be open-ended). Thus dreaming is the key to freeing oneself from one's past (and the destiny prescribed by that past). There are also echoes of the pre-Socratics here, especially of Heraclitus's formulation that "in sleep the soul of the living man nourishes itself by the accretion of moisture the 'death' of which will fill the soul during the waking hours."[16] And Nietzsche's exaltation of the Dionysian should not be overlooked as a source of the concept of delirium, just as destiny bears traces of Greek tragedy.

Perhaps Zambrano's thought comes closest to that of some members of the Frankfurt school, who likewise combined such diverse sources as psychoanalysis and political theory to a kind of apocalyptic end; Walter Benjamin's mystical, cabalistic vision and his orientation towards literary texts as philosophical inspiration have much in common with Zambrano's method. In her exile she could enter what Walter Benjamin has famously called "homogenous empty time,"[17] and dream a Spain that was going to be, but perhaps never was. As Homi Bhabba has written, "Nations, like narrations, lose their origins in the myths of time and only fully realize their horizons in the mind's eye."[18] This dream, this delirium, which is both individual and communal, unites people in a sense of commonality that is reinforced in the final "Deliriums" of *Delirium and Destiny*, especially "Corpus in Florence" and "The Chalice."

V. Zambrano on Women's Issues

I have deliberately left a discussion of women's issues in Zambrano's life and work till the end, even though her status as a woman is evident throughout her life and work (in her schooling, relationships to her mentors, and her teaching assignments, and perhaps in her philosophical interests and style). Taken as a whole, María Zambrano's *oeuvre* does not appear to participate in a feminist project (especially if compared to that of declared feminist philosophers such as Luce Irigaray, with whom Zambrano's thought has much in common—the literary allusive/elusive style and the self-conscious working out of and against the male philosophical tradition). Zambrano was, however, constantly aware of the position of women during her long career; although her major books focus on issues that concern "humanity" rather than women alone, she wrote both published and unpublished articles from her earliest period onward that center on women's struggle for equality.[19] Her republicanism itself is a testament to her interest in progress for women. Under the republic women gained a more public role and made legal gains, such as the right to divorce. There were women ministers in the Republican government, and numerous women like María Martínez Sierra, who worked in less official ways during the Republic for the betterment of women's lives. Women were crucial to the Republican Civil War effort; they fought as militia alongside the men, and were the mainstay behind the lines. All these gains were erased when Francisco Franco assumed absolute power in 1939.

Delirium and Destiny is the major book-length work in which her awareness of a woman's special place in philosophy and history is somewhat more identifiable because the central character or "consciousness" in the book is "she." The studiously employed female pronoun that replaces the traditional autobiographical "I" serves several purposes. It abjures the male "logo-centric" subject of traditional philosophy, which is parodied in the "Delirium" entitled "I Am Going to Speak of Myself." In this "Delirium" extreme individualism ends up destroying the world. In addition, the third person "she" is a social mask that shields the central consciousness of the work from a radical individualism and moves it towards the communal, social self that is increasingly implied as the narrative progresses. In *Persona y democracia* (Person/Persona and democracy, 1965) Zambrano developed a theory of the mask (starting with the masks of Greek tragedy) in which she interprets the persona as the agent of articulation between the personal and the social. She says that, while the word "individual" indicates an opposition or antagonism toward society, "persona" includes the individual and insinuates something positive, something "more," the means by which we enter into the social world.

The focus of *Delirium and Destiny* shifts subtly over the course of the narration from a male-centered world—Zambrano's early tutelage under her father, the university environment in which she studied with Ortega and Zubiri, and the Republican political movement in which most of the major intellectual figures were men—to the new world in which, bereft of father, husband, male mentors, and fatherland, she reorients herself toward her mother and sister. She has gradually shed the trappings of patriarchy to find, if not a matriarchy, at least a secure place where her kind of thinking can flourish. Her sister Araceli assumes the guise of Antigone, who though not responsible for the disasters of recent history, has suffered from their consequences. If Araceli is Antigone, María is positioned as Antigone's sister Ismene, the observer who witnesses events from afar and who is able to theorize about them thanks to her emotional and geographical distance. The position of the passionate but uninvolved onlooker, the "judicious spectator," in Adam Smith's words, is also the one in which literary works—especially narratives—place the reader.[20] By combining the emotions and reason in a felicitous balance, the literary work can mobilize the community to imagine new social forms that allow greater and more universal freedom. This is the ultimate message imbedded in *Delirium and Destiny*, a literary work that encompasses a specific life in a specific history that dared to transcend its immediate parameters through lucid dreaming.

Notes

[1]"Introduction," to Walter Benjamin, *Illuminations*, tr. Harry Zohn (New York: Schocken Books, 1968), 50.

[2]Shirley Mangini, *Memories of Resistance* (New Haven:Yale UP, 1995).

[3]It is a peculiarity of twentieth-century Spanish philosophy that many major works, while meditating on the perennial philosophical themes—the nature of being human, the definition of a moral life, and how we acquire knowledge—incorporate meditations about Spain and the Spaniards, often comparing them to Europe and the Europeans. I am thinking especially of Miguel de Unamuno's *En torno al casticismo* (1895 On purism) and *Del sentimiento trágico de la vida en los hombres y en los pueblos* (*The Tragic Sense of Life in Men and Peoples* 1934), José Ortega y Gasset's *Meditaciones del Quijote* (*Meditations on the Quijote* 1984), *La España Invertebrada* (1920 *Invertebrate Spain*), and *La rebelion de las masas* (*The Revolt of the Masses* 1932).This geographical (and often temporal) specificity is unique within continental philosophy and is one of the strengths and contributions of Spanish philosophy, if also perhaps one feature that has contributed to its marginalization. María Zambrano works very much in this tradition, especially in her early career preceding the Civil War and during the first years of her exile in Mexico and Cuba (1939–1953).

[4]Raymond Carr, *Modern Spain 1875–1980* (Oxford: Oxford UP, 1980), 111.

[5]And like Heidegger and Arendt, Zubiri's reputation has always overshadowed that of his pupil. There is now ample evidence that the intellectual exchanges between Heidegger and Arendt were enormously fruitful to him, and it is entirely possible that Zubiri also gained important insights from his precocious pupil.There are numerous literary and philosophical relationships in the pre-war period in which a female writer or intellectual was overshadowed by a male partner-mentor. Simone de Beauvoir and Jean Paul Sartre provide another parallel to the Ortega-Zambrano or Zubiri-Zambrano relations. It was difficult for the intellectual establishment to think of a female intellectual except as an appendage of a well-known male.When María Zambrano was introduced to Simone Weil, the person who presented them could think of nothing better than to say that Zambrano was the disciple of Ortega and Weil the disciple of Alain.

[6]Zambrano seems to have had a magnetic presence.Testimonials abound as to her ability to create an almost magical ambience wherever she was. Many found her discourse spellbinding.

[7]Raymond D. Souza, *The Poetic Fiction of José Lezama Lima* (Columbia: U of Missouri P, 1983), 8.

[8]Maria Zambrano, *Horizonte del liberalismo* (Madrid: Morata, 1930), 139.

[9]*The Ethics of Ambiguity*, tr. Bernard Frechtman (New York: Citadel Press, 1994), 24, 73, 74.

[10]*Hacia un saber sobre el alma* (Madrid: Alianza, 1987), 22.

[11]Ibid. Zambrano continued to work out her ideas on poetic reason in her two books published in Mexico in 1939: *Filosofía y poesía* (Philosophy and poetry) and *Pensamiento y poesía en la vida española* (Thought and poetry in Spanish life).

[12]Poetic reason doubtless was partly inspired by Xavier Zubiri's "inteligencia sentiente" (feeling intelligence), and it can be usefully compared to Theodor Adorno's "subjective reason" or the "reasoning madness" that Lacan found in Salvador Dalí.

[13]Genevieve Lloyd, *Being in Time: Selves and narrators in philosophy and literature* (London: Routledge, 1993), 40–41.

[14]"The being by which nothingness comes into the world is a being in which, in its own being, there is question of the nothingness of its being: *the being by which nothingness comes into the world must be its own nothingness*" (Jean Paul Sartre. *Being and Nothingness*. Tr. Hazel E. Barnes. New York: Washington Square Press, 1956).

[15]*Delirium and Destiny*, 163.

[16]Quoted in David B. Claus, *Toward the Soul. An Inquiry into the Meaning of $\psi v \chi \acute{\eta}$ before Plato* (New Haven: Yale UP, 1981), 132.

[17]*Illuminations*, 261.

[18]Homi K. Bhabha, "Introduction: Narrating and the Nation," *Nation and Narration* (London: Routledge, 1990), 1.

[19]Her principal published pieces on women focus on female literary characters—"Delirio de Antígone" (Antígone's Delirium), "La tumba de Antígone" (Antígone's Tomb), "Eloísa o la existencia de la mujer" (Heloise or the existence of women), "Diótima de Mantinea" (Diotima of Mantinea), and a series of articles on female characters in the novels of Benito Pérez Galdós. What she finds exemplary in these female figures is that their primary means of relating to the world is through the emotions, which allows them to find a transcendent reality.

[20]Martha Nussbaum (*Poetic Justice* [Boston: Beacon Press, 1995]) argues for a literature with the potential to make a contribution to "law in particular, public reasoning generally" (xv), because "[l]iterature focuses on the possible" (5). Both Nussbaum and Zambrano understand that the emotions are most effective in influencing public policy if they are tempered by distance (or reason), which gives literature a unique role as mediator between raw passion and abstract aloofness.

From Delirio y destino to
Delirium and Destiny

An urge analogous to the one that leads me to sight-read an unfamiliar piece of music prompted me to translate *Delirio y destino*. As I read María Zambrano's book in Spanish, I wanted to sound out the words into English, even if haltingly, to participate actively in the distilled energy I sensed in them. At first I considered my rough versions exercises and felt satisfied with them. Before long, however, I realized that I wanted to work with *Delirio y destino* in a more accomplished way, to perform a translation of it. I thought of this performance as a recovering because of two associations. First, the "dream of the dead/acted out in me" that "dances" and awakens the speaker in "Recovering";[1] one of my favorite poems by Muriel Rukeyser; and second, the scarcity of information about Zambrano available even in Spanish. Danced by *Delirio y destino* and

237

Zambrano's raw, affecting recovery of her dreams for Spain during the 1920s and 30s, I felt convinced that her words could be recovered affectingly in English.

As I began to think of publishing my translation, I decided that *Delirium and Destiny* could be located most appropriately in a series devoted to work by women writers. Zambrano herself notes and regrets the near absence of women from both the discipline of philosophy and the group of young people with whom she was involved in the late 1920s and early 1930s. Throughout her life, she wrote about female figures in literature, art, and philosophy, in an effort both to explain the polarization that has divided the sexes throughout history and to envision a more unified relation between them. In addition, a list of Zambrano's mentors (Miguel de Unamuno, Xavier Zubiri, and José Ortega y Gasset, for example) and the Spanish writers of her generation who have received sustained critical recognition (Federico García Lorca and Rafael Alberti, for example) suggests that the lack and the quality of information available about writers such as Zambrano and novelist Rosa Chacel, her contemporary, owe a great deal to their being women. Furthermore, my readings of pertinent material in European and American literature and history and the responses I received from readers and prospective publishers suggested that what an English-language audience would find most engaging in *Delirio y destino* was Zambrano's struggle to define herself simultaneously as a woman and a philosopher. In the context of 20th-century philosophy and literature, this struggle as well as Zambrano's expression of it— despite the innovation *Delirio y destino* represented at the time—can easily strike an English-language reader as familiar, even outdated. Within the context of women writers and philosophers, however, and in the context of current scholarship on women's autobiography and on Hispanic women, the book may well seem new and unfamiliar. The candor and urgency with which Zambrano chronicles the development of her thinking—not to mention the structure and language of *Delirio y destino*—is far from ordinary, and few women have probed and documented such development with comparable candor and immediacy.

After working with *Delirio y destino* for several years, I continue to believe that any commentary about the book and its composition that may accompany the translation will necessarily address gender-related issues. My understanding, however, of gender with respect to Zambrano has changed considerably since I prepared my first translation samples. The change was a gradual one, because I never believed it appropriate, or even possible to discuss Zambrano with respect to "feminism" as the word is now used in the United States. On the contrary, I felt from the beginning of my work that Zambrano should not be presented as *either* a feminist *or* a "woman" writer and philosopher. Not only do both definitions limit Zambrano's identity severely, they also contradict her rejection of conventional definitions of identity. She even went so far, in certain instances, to refer to herself in the masculine. Far from paradoxical or inconsistent with Zambrano's thinking, this verbal gesture was entirely consistent with her expressed desire to be "man" as well as "woman" and with her determination to force not only "man" but also "humanity" to include her, a woman. As she asserts in *Delirium and Destiny*, making a deliberate use of *hombre* (man) rather than *humano* (human), when "tragic crisis is conflict . . . one is man then, or human, if you prefer" (156). What is more, letters Zambrano received from relatives and friends during the many years she lived outside of Spain suggest that she made such concessions to "humanity" grudgingly, resenting the restrictions imposed by her gender and preferring instead a definition of being that presented "self" and "circumstances" as inseparable. Perhaps she states this most clearly in her prologue to a volume that includes six of her books when she explains "author" as "something that seems neutral, not masculine, to me. Neutral because it is beyond, not closer to the current differentiation between man and woman, since it refers to thought. When one thinks, such differences—and others—are forgotten."[2] The same inclusive definition, is also present in *Delirio y destino*, where "woman" does not predominate over "colleague," "philosopher," "republican," "sister," "Spaniard," or "twentieth-century," to cite just a few examples, in alphabetical order. Rather, all of Zambrano's "circumstances" interact simultaneously, and if any of them could be considered predominant, I believe it would not be "woman" but "Spaniard" and "twentieth-century." For it is as a Spaniard, at a particular moment in history, that Zambrano developed *razón poética*, "poetic reason"—an interaction between delirium and destiny, between self-assertion and surrender, as she saw individual doubts and uncertainties give way to the hope for the Second Spanish Republic she shared with so many others.

Zambrano's expression of that hope in *Delirio y destino* had impressed me from my first reading. However, not until I re-read her book and her letters in the context of several other writers with parallel lives or works did I begin to develop a translation practice that would be consistent with her many circumstances. In particular, I was reminded of commentary I had read about "misrepresentation" in translation of work by the philosophers Simone de Beauvoir and Luce Irigaray. Some of Luce Irigaray's remarks seemed especially pertinent to a translation of *Delirio y destino*. When asked to comment on the translations of her work that have been published in English, Luce Irigaray pointed not so much to deletions or inaccuracies (as was the case in the English version of Beauvoir's *Le deuxième sexe*), as to the failure of translators to "read me as a philosopher."[3] She expressed regret that in the United States her books have been read principally as "literature," when the "heart of my argument is philosophical."[4] This misreading, she believes, led readers and translators to approach her writing with expectations that have made it difficult if not impossible for them to engage her thinking in the terms necessary for an understanding of what she proposes philosophically.

Thinking about Luce Irigaray's remarks, I realized that my own decisions as a translator, especially those concerning Zambrano's words and concepts related to gender and philosophy, would have to be made in the context of the most comprehensive "identity" possible. To cite an epitomizing example: despite Zambrano's lifelong resistance to the historical idealization of woman that she considered arbitrary and crippling, "Los veinte años de una española" would not best be translated, as I had once intended, as "Twenty Years in the life of a Spanish Woman," which separates gender and nationality in a potentially misleading way. Rather, I would use "A Spaniard in Her Twenties," in which "Spaniard" includes both "man" and "woman," "her" specifies gender, and, together, the two words indicate the inseparability, for Zambrano, of "Spanish" and "woman."[5] Although it is valid, and useful to discuss Zambrano's protagonist as a woman, I do not believe one can fairly say that the protagonist of *Delirium and Destiny* is presented more as a (Spanish) woman than as a (female) Spaniard.

The belief expressed in that last sentence would of course be difficult to substantiate. I can, however, explain it more thoroughly, because my work at the Fundación María Zambrano prompted me to consider still further the issues related to the translation of "una española."

About midway through my first draft of *Delirium and Destiny*, I went to the Fundación María Zambrano in Vélez-Málaga, Spain, because the numerous inconsistencies in punctuation and syntax I found in the book prompted an examination of the carbon copy held in the Zambrano archives. In particular, I wanted to investigate typographical errors and instances of irregular punctuation in order to understand their meaningfulness for Zambrano's writing. Such an understanding, crucial for any translation, is especially necessary for Zambrano's writing, which is highly heterogeneous and cannot be considered either conventional autobiography, novel, or philosophical exposition. In addition, sentences often move, at times abruptly, from the informal, conversational—even *oral*—recounting of an incident to a dense philosophical reflection, one marked by both philosophical terminology and allusions as well as raw thoughts that the sentence is registering as a discovery in progress rather than as one previously made. How to interpret, for example, the relationship between a clause about Unamuno and the long, irregularly-punctuated sentence preceding it in which the Spanish philosopher is compared to Angel Ganivet?[6] Did Zambrano really intend for Horatio not Polonius to tell Hamlet that the actors had arrived?[7] Is sound or sense more determinate in Zambrano's continual use of alliteration in "una razón poética" en "vías de realizarse?"[8] I wanted to be able to answer such questions knowledgeably and to render the affected passages appropriately in English. To do so, I needed to read the carbon copy of *Delirio y destino* and examine its syntax and punctuation.

A careful reading of the carbon copy showed that it too contains many errors, as one would expect, since the book was written quickly and under the pressure of the fast-approaching deadline for the competition Zambrano describes in her introduction. Many of those errors were corrected at the time of publication in 1989, but not a few errors and misunderstandings were also created. Because Zambrano was in poor health, several people assisted her with the revision of the manuscript, and the inaccurate transcription from which they worked apparently occasioned some inaccuracies and inadvertent omissions. In addition, several much longer passages, as well as individual sentences or phrases, were removed from the carbon copy, although they have not been removed from the files related to *Delirio y destino* in the Fundación María Zambrano. All those passages bear some negative comment on Alfonso XIII or on the monarchical system, especially as it existed in Spain during the decades immediately preceding the Civil War. My guess was that they had been removed deliberately, probably for two reasons. First, Zambrano had never been opposed in principal either to monarchism or to a republican system that included a monarchy; what she opposed was an ineffective, irresponsible monarchy.[9] And second, at the time *Delirio y destino* was published, Zambrano was living in Spain and enjoyed a most cordial relation with King Juan Carlos and his wife Sofía. She would not have wanted to offend them. I could imagine a possible concern that the passages might have proved offensive if read out of context, although I did not believe that the material omitted would have contradicted, or even altered, Zambrano's account of the Republic.

Consultation with members of the board of directors of the Fundación María Zambrano, in particular Juan Fernando Ortega Muñoz, the director of the Fundación, and with Rafael Tomero Alarcón, a cousin of Zambrano who worked with her in 1989 on the revisions of *Delirio y destino*, confirmed my thoughts about the omissions. Zambrano had indeed decided to make the excisions in 1989, when the book was prepared for publication and she had stipulated that the excised passages not be published in future editions. In this sense *Delirio y destino* remains definitive as it was first published. I also discussed with Mr. Ortega Muñoz the revised edition of *Delirio y destino* that the Fundación expected would be undertaken in the near future. In the absence of that edition, Mr. Tomero Alarcón generously allowed me to see the revisions he would suggest for such an edition. Consequently, I feel confident that the English translation is based on the most accurate version of the Spanish available. At the same time, however, my work at the Fundación María Zambrano and my contact with the Fundación's board of directors showed me that a totally accurate version of *Delirio y destino* may not be possible in either language. Not only is it impossible to determine with certainty which of the apparent irregularities in the carbon copy reflect haste on Zambrano's part when she wrote the book, it is impossible to know which of her seeming inaccuracies resulted from deliberate decisions either then or in 1989. What is more, I learned from Mr. Tomero Alarcón that a substantial part of *Delirio y destino* may well have been dictated to an amanuensis, whose identity is now unknown.[10] In other words, my developing hunch about Zambrano's sentences had been correct: not only was the book written quickly and its narrative "mixed" with both philosophical thinking and poetic association, parts of it may also have been spoken and simultaneously recorded.[11]

Clearly, I needed to establish principles for translating such an unstable text, unstable perhaps even to the point of what Jenaro Talens has referred to as a "missing [author's] original".[12] I have inserted "author's" to indicate the distinction between (a) a written text whose inscription one can assign to a specific human being and (b) a written text whose inscription is realized by what Talens refers to as the "authorial voice" that "we construct through reading and interpreting a text in order to allow it to make sense."[13] In many ways, the true "original," at least to some extent, may not have been a written document at all but a spoken occurrence, even a performance. Where could I find some guidance about creating, in English, from such a text, the dynamic, oxymoronic tension affirmed in *Delirio y destino*? I have deliberately referred to that goal in terms of an occurrence rather than a product, because what results when delirium (with its precarious and potentially rewarding consequences) and destiny (with its precarious and potentially rewarding possibility) interact is the occurrence I most wanted my translation to convey. In other words, I wanted to translate, above all, Zambrano's *razón poética*, which is present in *Delirio y destino* more as an event, a manifestation of what Giles Deleuze has discussed, also in terms of writing, as "a possibility of life" that "invokes the oppressed bastard race that ceaselessly stirs beneath dominations, resisting everything that crushes and oppresses."[14] I wanted (to use Luce Irigaray's word) to achieve the most "literal" translation possible of *razón poética*,[15] and I realized that such a translation could conform only partially to Luce Irigaray's definition of "literal." A rather singular approach was required.

I looked first to material about translating the work of women writers as well as about translating and editing their punctuation. (Although I was not preparing an edition of *Delirio y destino* per se, with respect to punctuation, I was confronting many of the same decisions editors of texts must make). Reading and thinking about punctuation led me to discussions of scoring such as Alfred Brendel's comments about his struggles with Schoenberg's musical notation,[16] Peter Kivy's work on authentic performance in music,[17] and to recent work in feminist editing. Each of those sets of readings was helpful and provocative but ultimately limited and limiting. Schoenberg's scores are not verbal; any extended comparison between the musician's performance and the translator's work must grapple with the question of whether the translator is best considered a performer, an arranger, or even a composer—a question that would have required a not unrelated, but at that point excessive, digression—; and feminist editing often involves a prescriptiveness I prefer to avoid. As Rosemary Arrojo indicates, it is on the basis of a translator's own "bias" (in this case a feminist one) that translation theories and the work of other translators is contested.[18] One feminist editor, for example, speaks of omitting from the interviews she publishes comments she finds misguided or offensive;[19] one feminist translator refers to "highjacking" an author's work and either emphasizing its feminism, even if that feminism is only implicit, or bringing an explicitly feminist approach to translation practice.[20]

I did find, however, in Susan Kirkpatrick's article about editing work by two nineteenth-century woman writers comments that were both provocative and appropriate.[21] Kirkpatrick's assertion that "if a feminist edition can register the complex interaction between the idea of a work and its multiple material realizations, it will have done more than enough" led me to relinquish what was at first a fear that my translation or any other translation of *Delirio y destino* might be less than definitive. Above all, I was encouraged by Kirkpatrick's use of acceptance of "textual fluidity over textual fixity"[22] and by the related suggestion that it might be necessary for editors to "give up the idea of a perfect text as an essentialist one."[23] These words prompted me to realize that the task I had articulated for myself involved precisely the type of refusal-affirmation that occurs in *Delirio y destino*. I would have to refuse the conventional definitiveness implied in "literal" and affirm a different "literal."

Kirkpatrick's article also led me to Jerome J. McGann's work abut textual criticism, and I have found many aspects of that work pertinent, in particular his request that editors understand, "assess," and ultimately convey the circumstances under which a work has evolved.[24] That request was crucial to my thinking about translating *Delirio y destino* literally in a way akin to McGann's "continuous production text".[25] I began to envision a translation that would register the "complex interaction" for which Kirkpatrick calls and McGann argues when he describes "a textual condition in which we all participate, and which we shall not master."[26] Rather than shy away from the changes that Zambrano's manuscript has undergone over the years, in the hands of many people, I began to think of a translation that would convey them, thereby conveying at the same time the immediacy of Zambrano's *razón poética* as an activity as well as a contribution to philosophical thought.

In conjunction with my readings, I developed three general principles, each of which is related to one of the three elements that I considered the principal challenges of translating *Delirio y destino:*

(1) The English punctuation would be determined by reading all the available versions of a particular passage and by reading the Spanish aloud in order to sound out at least one version of it as spoken language. I would then try to imagine the passage without punctuation before I punctuated it in English, much as one would score a continuous, unmarked piece of music, paying special attention to tempo, rhythm, and valence. I found this practice particularly helpful in the case of stops, and I relied on it at times when deciphering individual words that did not clarify the relationship between them. In such instances, as in the passage about Unamuno and Ganivet referred to above, I worked both with my oral reading and with the connotations suggested by the words, since Zambrano

often assumes the reader's familiarity with the thinkers and thoughts she mentions. I also relied on oral reading in my use of suspension points, which occur frequently in *Delirio y destino* when the narrator experiences doubt or fear; and in no instance do they seem to indicate omission in *Delirium and Destiny*. Thus they may be considered marks of ellipsis only in the way that ellipsis is used at times in English, as in Virginia Wolf's *Three Guineas*, to indicate similarly discontinuous thought or speech.[27] Although Zambrano's frequent use of ellipsis may seem excessive to an English-language reader, I risk this reaction because I believe that ellipsis is integral to her use of language and thus best conveyed by the ambivalent stop that suspension points provide.[28]

(2) For philosophical terms I would be as precise, or "literal," as possible, finding and using English equivalencies if they existed, even in instances when those equivalencies did not provide "literary" or "fluent" translations but drew on relatively unfamiliar or secondary connotations of an English word, as in "phenomenon" or "intelligence," both of which Zambrano employs frequently in *Delirio y destino*. A similar "precision" would guide my decisions about Zambrano's references to specific works or individuals. I would locate those references and, if possible, cite a published English translation that readers might consult if they wished. For the not infrequent times when Zambrano's references are more restatements—even glaringly inaccurate ones—than precise quotations, I would translate her words as recorded, with the exception of obvious misspellings and the capitalization of some nouns. The probability is remote that such inaccuracies were in fact deliberate, but I had in mind not so much Zambrano's intention as her circumstances when she wrote *Delirio y destino*. Like Erich Auerbach as he wrote *Mimesis: The Representation of Reality in Western Literature* "during the war and in Istanbul, where the libraries are not well equipped for European studies,"[29] Zambrano wrote in exile, "from memory," as she told Chacel in 1941, having fled Spain without her books and papers.[30] I believe, as Auerbach did about *Mimesis*, that in some way the book's very existence may have resulted from "just this lack of a rich and specialized library."[31] Consequently, in *Delirium and Destiny*, Horatio tells Hamlet that the actors have arrived, repeating an inaccuracy but possibly prompting the reader's return to Shakespeare's play and a reflection on Zambrano's replacement of Polonius.

(3) Translation of *razón poética*, when it occurs in *Delirio y destino* as an activity rather than a definition, would call for a continuous interaction between "poetry" and "reason." Although the relation between many words, images, and passages in *Delirio y destino* is highly associative, Zambrano's narratives never cease to be reasoned; there is a balance, albeit at times a tenuous one, with both poetry and reason continuously present. This balance means that the translation would continuously need to retain both, following Zambrano's associations, propelled by the rhythm of the narrative and the sound of its constant alliteration, but always alert to the "reason" within those associations and, more specifically, more

challengingly, alert to the continual repetitions their reason altered each time by new circumstances, although never beyond recognition.

Work with specific passages would involve equal attention to repetition and alliteration—to the "what" of Zambrano's thinking (its "reason") but also to the "how," the way in which she reasoned poetically. For her, such reasoning was not a question of poeticizing reason but experiencing reason and poetry as inseparable activities in which thought is propelled by both. What does this mean, for example, to the translator of "una razón vital en vías de realizarse"? How might one convey in English the sense of the phrase and also its alliteration? In order to answer, I tried to determine in which words I discerned the "springboard" that drove them forward. It seemed to me that the greatest force was in "razón" and "realizarse." "Vital en vías" seemed secondary, adjectival. The principal alliteration, then, needed to occur in the translation of "razón" and "realizarse," or in another verb related to "razón." There also needed to be additional, even if less evident, alliteration in the adjectives closely related to the phrase.

I followed these principles singly or in combination, although always in relation to the other principle or principles, when they seemed appropriate to "circumstances" in the text. In doing so, my overall goal was to convey an occurrence not unlike the "raw electrons jumping from orbit to orbit across the gap between expression and intent" of Rosmarie Waldrop's *Lawn of Excluded Middle*.[32] As Waldrop says, it is best to "cultivate" rather than to fear that gap, "with its high grass for privacy and references gone astray. Never mind that it is not philosophy. . . ." No, philosophy it is not. Neither is *Delirio y destino*. Not philosophy as one commonly thinks of it or as Zambrano studied it through Ortega's lectures. At the same time, however, it is not "not philosophy" in the context of what I would call a new "key." And "key" here seems more than apt. Not only are there two passages in the book in which the most appropriate rendition of *tono* is "key" (rather than ""tone" or "pitch" or "intensity") although encompassing all three of them),[33] there is also a striking resemblance between that passage and the "new key" Suzanne Langer proposed at about the same time Zambrano was writing *Delirio y destino*.[34] I believe that a literal translation, in the sense I have defined it, of the "key" as described and exemplified in *Delirio y destino* makes available the sense of electrons jumping that I find in the dynamic interaction of sound and sense in Zambrano's *razón poética*.

I have also been guided by the belief, which I might more appropriately call a fourth principle, that such a translation, as an entire project or volume, will provide the reader with information both about the circumstances of *Delirio y destino*, as it has developed since Zambrano first composed it and about the translation's own circumstances. This principle Roberta Johnson and I have followed jointly by including her essay about Zambrano and *Delirio y destino*, my translator's afterword, and the glossary. As a whole, we intended the translation to refuse any absolute definition, including an absolute definition of "woman," and to suggest redefinitions, in particular a redefinition of "woman" that would reflect the continuous tension between "man" and "woman" and within "human" that is present throughout Zambrano's book. This "man," rather than the "humanity" or "humankind" current in English usage, appears in some passages of *Delirium and Destiny*. May his appearance be disquieting and awaken further redefinitions of Zambrano's *hombre* and her *razón poética* in yet other circumstances.

Notes

1. Muriel Rukeyser, "Recovering," *Out of Silence: Selected Poems*, ed. Kate Daniel (Evanston, IL: TriQuarterly Books, 1992), p.154.

2. María Zambrano, "A modo de prólogo," *Obras reunidas: Primera entrega* (Madrid: Aguilar, 1971), p. 10. Translation mine.

3. Luce Irigaray, "Je-Luce Irigaray: A Meeting With Irigaray," *Women Writing Culture*, ed. Gary A. Olson and Elizabeth Hirsh (Albany: SUNY Press, 1995), p. 146.

4. "Je-Luce Irigaray," p. 145.

5. For a discussion of an earlier version of the subtitle, see "Issues in the Practice of Translating Women's Fiction," *BHS (Bulletin of Hispanic Studies)* 75: 95–108 (1998). Many thanks to Kathleen Ross, her students at NYU, and the other members of the audience with whom I discussed that article and my translation of *Delirium and Desitny*. Their questions led me to focus my attention with respect to the subtitle not only on gender and "una española" but also on the imprecision of "los veinte años" (literally, "the [unspecified] twenty years." Not all the events that Zambrano recounts in *Delirium and Desitny* occurred when she was in her twenties (1924-1934), but the principal ones, particularly her training in philosophy and the adherent of the Republic, did take place during those years.

6. *Delirio y destino*, 85–86.

7. *Delirio y destino*, 93.

8. *Delirio y destino*, 183.

9. As Zambrano explained in a letter written in 1953 to Spanish novelist Rosa Chacel, who left Spain in 1939 to live for many years in Argentina and Brazil, *Delirio y destino* was a "history" or a "story"—an account—of the "origins of the Republic" *(Cartas a Rosa Chacel*, ed. Ana Rodríguez-Fischer (Madrid: Versal, 1992). pp. 45–46.

10. Telephone conversation, April 20, 1996.

11. For all the reasons explained in the two preceding paragraphs, I decided to publish *Delirium and Destiny* without taking into account the revised edition of *Delirio y destino* that appeared while my translation was in production (ed. Rogelio Blanco Martínez

and Jesús Moreno Sanz, Madrid: Areces, 1998). I believe that a future translation would have to be based not only on the new edition, which its editors describe as "complete" and "revised," but not "definitive," but also on extensive research that would include, for example, critical response to the revised edition and further study at the Fundacíon María Zambrano.

12. Jenaro Talens, "Making Sense After Babel," *Critical Practices in Post-Franco Spain,* ed. Silvia L. López, Jenaro Talens, and Darío Villanueva (Minneapolis: U Minnesota P, 1994), p. 22.

13. "Making Sense After Babel," p. 24.

14. Giles Deleuze, "Literature and Life," trans. Daniel W. Smith and Michael A. Greco, *Critical Inquiry* 23 (Winter 1997): 229.

15. "Je-Luce Irigaray," p. 151.

16. See, for example, Alfred Brendel, "On Playing Schoenberg's Piano Concerto," *The New York Review of Books* (16 February 1995): 27–29.

17. In particular, Peter Kivy, *Authenticities: Philosophical Reflections on Musical Performance* (Ithaca, NY: Cornell UP, 1995).

18. Rosemary Arrojo, "Fidelity and the Gendered Translation," *TTR (Traduction, Terminologie, Rédaction)* 7.2 (1994): 154.

19. Andrea Juno, "Talking on Minna Street," Dodie Bellamy/Andrea Juno, Special Issue on "Gender and Editing," *Chain/*1 (Spring/Summer 1994): 12.

20. See Luise von Flotow, "Feminist Translation: Contexts, Practices, and Theories," *TTR: Traduction, Terminologie, Rédaction* 4.2 (1991): 78. In her use of this term, von Flotow is affirming a translation strategy named by David Homel, who wrote in opposition to its use.

21. Susan Kirkpatrick, "Toward a Feminist Textual Criticism," *The Politics of Editing,* ed. Nicholas Spadaccini and Jenaro Talens (Minneapolis: U Minnesota P, 1992): 137.

22. "Toward a Feminist Textual Criticism," p. 136.

23. "Toward a Feminist Textual Criticism," p. 137.

24. Jerome J. McGann, *A Critique of Modern Textual Criticism* (Chicago: U Chicago P, 1983), p. 94.

25. Jerome J. McGann, *The Textual Condition* (Princeton: Princeton UP, 1991), p. 30.

26. Jerome McGann, "The Case of *The Ambassadors* and the Textual Condition," in George Bornstein, *Palimpsest: Editorial Theory in the Humanities* (Ann Arbor: U Michigan P 1993), p. 165.

27. See Shari Benstock's discussion in "Ellipses: Figuring Feminisms in *Three Guineas,*" *Textualizng the Feminine: On the Limits of Genre* (Norman: Oklahoma UP, 1991), pp. 123–162.

28. I have used suspension points that would have reproduced the three closely spaced periods used in Spanish since, as Ronald Christ pointed out to me, the use of these periods are found "by the book and not in the practice of the books, not books in English. There is a meanness, a stinginess to their look . . . at odds with our typography" (personal correspondence, early June 1997).

29. Erich Auerbach, *Mimesis: The Representation of Reality in Western Literature,* trans. Willard R. Trask (Princeton, N.J.: Princeton UP, 1953), p. 557.

30. *Cartas a Rosa Chacel,* p. 42.

31. *Mimesis,* p. 557.

32. Rosmarie Waldrop, *Lawn of Excluded Middle* (Providence, RI: Tender Buttons, 1993), p. 22.

33. *Delirio y destino,* pp. 187 and 191.

34. Suzanne K. Langer, *Philosophy in a New Key: A Study in the Symbolism of Reason, Rite, and Art,* 3rd ed. (Cambridge, MA: Harvard UP, 1957). See, in particular, chapter one ("The New Key"), in which Langer explains the primarily interrogative (as opposed to theorizing or systematizing) thinking she has in mind. My thanks to Bill Kenney for helping me think through the translation of "tono."

Glossary

"¡Adentro!" (Get inside things!): essay by Miguel de Unamuno published in 1900. The essay marked a change in Unamuno's interests from a rather scientific, secular approach to a less rational, passionate internal exploration of life that is directly related to a religious crisis in 1897 and to his readings in Kierkegaard, which began in about 1901. It initiates the phase of his career that lasted until his death in 1936, the phase in which he extolled agony and suffering as the principal markers of existence.

Alberti, Rafael (1902–): poet, playwright and painter. One of the central figures of the Spanish Generation of '27, he is its only living member. His writings follow the vanguardist aesthetic of combining traditional (and/or popular) and innovative forms, and, like his good friend Federico García Lorca, he incorporated elements of his native Andalusia into his poetry. His major books of poetry include *Marinero en tierra* (Landlocked Sailor 1925), *Cal y canto* (Passion and Form 1929), and *Sobre los ángeles* (*Concerning Angels* 1929). As a militant Republican, he, like Zambrano, spent many years in exile. He and Zambrano coincided in Rome in the 1960s where they formed a Spanish exile community that included Alberti's wife María Teresa León and others.

Alcalá Street: major Madrid artery running between the Alcalá Gate and the Puerto del Sol (Sun Gate) in the heart of the city. A number of historical buildings are situated along this street.

Alcalá Zamora, Niceto: See Romanones, Count of.

Aldonza Lorenzo: name of the coarse peasant girl whom Don Quijote imaginatively transformed into the unequalled beauty and "lady of his thoughts," Dulcinea del Toboso.

Aleixandre, Vicente (1898–1984): Spanish poet associated with the Generation of 1927; perhaps the one most influenced by surrealism in the early part of his career. Winner of the Nobel Prize for Literature in 1977.

Alfar: one of a number of ephemeral literary journals that sprung up in the fecund 1920s. *Alfar* was begun in 1924 in La Coruña, the capital of Galicia.

"Angel of Forgetfulness, The": poem by Rafael Alberti.

"Antón Pirulero": children's game in which the boys and girls move in a circle while singing: "Antón, Antón, Antón Pirulero, pay attention to the game, for the one who does not will pay a forfeit."

Arenal Street: street near the Puerta del Sol in the old part of Madrid. It is named for the sandy (*arena* = sand) nature of the soil in the nearby parishes of San Ginés and San Martín.

Ateneo, The: building in Madrid where there is an extensive library and where intellectual events, such as lectures and discussions take place. It was founded in 1820, but has survived continuously since 1835. It has been one place where intellectuals could meet to exchange ideas in a Spain that was frequently inhospitable to new ideas. Only members have access to its facilities.

Azaña, Manuel (1880–1940): politician and writer who was president of the Second Republic in 1936. He wrote novels, plays, and literary criticism and was very active in the Madrid Ateneo. After he became associated with the pro-Republican movement in the late 1920s, his writing career declined in favor of political involvement.

Azorín (pseudonym of José Martínez Ruiz 1873–1967): essayist, novelist, and playwright usually associated with the Generation of '98. He was primarily a journalist, but one of a decidedly literary bent. His prose style is deceptively simple in his lucid descriptions of his native Alicante and his adopted Castile. He is best known for his prose sketches in such works as *The Little Philosopher* (1904) and *Castile* (1912). His writing often has a decidedly philosophical content, and he was particularly interested in the problem of historical versus eternal time.

Besteiro, Julián (1870–1940): socialist politician and writer of philosophical works. He entered the Socialist Party in 1912, and his presence along with that of Francisco Largo Caballero increased the influence of socialist ideology among Spanish intellectuals. In 1931 he was president of the Cortes (Parliament) under the Republic. After the Civil War he was imprisoned in Carmona and died shortly thereafter.

Baroja, Pío (1872–1955): novelist generally associated with the Generation of '98. Baroja created an innovative form which he called the "porous novel;" these works (such as *Camino de perfección* [*Road to Perfection* 1902], and *El árbol de la ciencia* [*The Tree of Science* 1911]) have no real plot and depict a will-less character who is frequently engaged in philosophical conversations.

Calderón de la Barca (1600–1681): one of Spain's leading dramatists of the Counter-reformation period. His complex plays deal with theological issues, such as free will, couched in effective dramatic vehicles. His best-known play is *Life is a Dream* in which a prince, who has been sequestered by his parents because of bad omens at his birth, returns to civilization.

Canalejas, José (1854–1912): politician belonging to the Liberal Party, who as president of the Parliament was charged with forming a new government in 1910. He initiated a series of reforms, abolished sales tax and established compulsory military service. He took swift measures to quell violent social unrest and was killed by an anarchist for his efforts.

Cárcel Modelo: prison in Barcelona which was originally called Cárcel Modular. It was used during the Franco regime to incarcerate political prisoners.

Casa de Campo: large park on the right bank of the Manzanares River on the outskirts of old Madrid. It was acquired by Philip II for his personal pleasure. Today, in addition to extensive woods, it has a lake for boating and is open to the public.

Casa del Pueblo: series of socialist institutions in a number of Spanish towns and cities in the early twentieth century where workers could meet for cultural events and to plan political action. They contained rudimentary libraries and sponsored lecture courses. The Casas del Pueblo were closed by the Franco regime, but recently the Madrid Casa has reopened under the auspices of the UGT (General Worker's Union).

castizo: untranslatable Spanish concept that refers to national purity. *Casticismo,* which assumes that there is something called a Spanish national character, has a long history in Spain. After the Middle Ages in which Christians, Moors, and Jews tolerated one another in many parts of Spain for long periods of time, the Inquisition was established to attain Christian purity in the peninsula. During the Counterreformation, which began in the second half the sixteenth century, religious purity took on an anti-Protestant cast. From the latter part of the nineteenth century *castizo* referred to a desire to keep Spanish traditions (Catholicism, a spiritual rather than a materialistic approach to life) free from the secular trends of the rest of Europe.

Cernuda, Luis (1902–1963): Spanish poet associated with the Generation of 1927. María Zambrano corresponded with him when they were both in exile in the Americas after the Civil War.

Chisperos: men in the Maravillas district of Madrid whose residents named their neighborhood for the many blacksmiths (*chispero*=blacksmith) who lived there.

Cibeles: central traffic circle in Madrid where the massive and ornate building housing the central post office is located. The intersection is named after the large statue of the goddess of nature and mother of Saturn, Juno, Pluto, and Neptune found at its center. The statue of the goddess in a chariot drawn by two fierce lions forms part of a monumental fountain. The monument, which has become one of the most important landmarks in Madrid, was completed in 1781.

Cigarette workers's union: union of cigarette makers. Cigarette manufacturing (as Bizet's opera *Carmen* reflects) was an area of Spanish industry staffed almost entirely by women after the mid-nineteenth century. Of the organized professions occupied by women, it was unusual, because women tended to continue to work in the industry after they married, and so female cigarette makers had more in common with male workers. In 1898 the cigarette workers asserted themselves as a politically active unit by joining well-publicized riots over a food tax. They continued to be politically active throughout the socially tense period of Alfonso XIII's reign.

circumstances: concept developed by María Zambrano's teacher José Ortega y Gasset in his first book-length work *Meditaciones del Quijote* (1914; *Meditations on Quijote* 1984), where he said "I am I and my circumstances," countering pure rationalism, which privileges the mind over the world. This often quoted notion, derived from German phenomenology, appears in a variety of ways in María Zambrano's work.

cocuyo: large firefly.

Concerning Angels: collection of poems by Rafael Alberti in which the influence of Surrealism is evident.

Corpus [Corpus Christi]: religious holiday that falls on Thursday, the sixtieth day after Easter Sunday. There are numerous processions in Spain and other Catholic countries on this day; religious statuary is carried from churches and paraded through the streets.

Cossío, Manuel Bartolomé (1865–1935): important reformist educator, who attended the Institución Libre de Enseñanza and became an associate of its founder, Francisco Giner de los Ríos. Cossío was a professor of art history at the University of Barcelona and later a chaired professor of pedagogy at the University of Madrid. He was an advisor to the Pedagogical Missions in which Zambrano worked during the Republic. His most important publication was a study of El Greco published in 1908; this decisive work rescued the sixteenth-century Spanish painter from oblivion.

CNT-FAI: initials of the Confederación Nacional de Trabajo-Federación Anarquista Ibérica (National Work Confederation-Iberian Anarchist Federation). The CNT, an anarchist workers' organization founded in 1911, combined anarchist ideology with worker's concerns; it was especially influential in rural agricultural areas and grew rapidly. The FAI was a secret association established in 1927 to keep the CNT under anarchist control and free from Communist influence. The FAI was the group most devoted to revolution in Spain.

Dato, Eduardo (1856–1921): Conservative member of Parliament for many years and later a government minister. He was president of the Council of Ministers in 1921 when he was assassinated by anarchists looking for a significant political target.

Dictatorship (1923–1930): Primo de Rivera, a military general, through a palace coup, assumed dictatorial powers under the reign of Alfonso XIII. Alfonso XIII had become increasingly ineffective and had lost credibility over a series of colonial wars in northern Africa. Under Primo de Rivera, Alfonso continued as titular head of the government, which nominally remained a monarchy. Primo de Rivera returned power to the king in 1930, but the latter abdicated shortly afterward when local elections showed clearly that Republican sentiment had become predominant.

Diego, Gerardo (1896–1987): poet, critic, secondary school teacher, and prolific member of the Generation of '27. He founded the journals *Carmen* and *Lola*. After the Civil War he produced the first anthology of the group's poetry thus keeping the legacy of the rich cultural flowering of Spain's Silver Age (1900–1936) alive in the dismal postwar years.

Dulcinea: See Aldonza Lorenzo.

Dwelling Places, The: See Saint Teresa of Ávila.

Escorial, The: monastery-palace built by Philip II to commemorate his victory in the Battle of San Quintín. Situated in the Sierra Guadarrama to the northwest of Madrid, it was begun in 1563 and designed according to classical Renaissance principles of symmetry and equilibrium. The shape of the edifice recalls the grate on which Saint Lawrence was martyred by being burned, and the building suggests the religious intensity of Philip's campaign against the protestants and other infidels.

Fortunata: character in Benito Pérez Galdós's *Fortunata y Jacinta* (1886–1887; *Fortunata and Jacinta* 1987) about whom Zambrano wrote several essays. She is a lower-class woman, seduced by the son of a wealthy merchant family. Fortunata has several children by her lover while his wife Jacinta remains barren.

Free Sheets of Paper: clandestine anti-government political pamphlets circulated during Primo de Rivera's dictatorship to which Miguel de Unamuno contributed during his exile in Hendaye, France.

FUE: acronym of the Federación Universitaria Escolar (Federation of University Students), the non-Catholic student group at the University of Madrid and other Spanish universities that played a significant role in the activity leading to Primo de Rivera's and the monarchy's loss of political power.

Fuenteovejuna: sixteenth-century play by Lope de Vega in which the residents of the town Fuenteovejuna murder a nobleman who has been raping women of the locality. The authorities torture a number of the townspeople in an attempt to learn the murderer's name, but the town insists that it was a collective act. Finally, the local authorities and the townspeople request that King Ferdinand and Queen Isabel intercede, which they do in favor of the people of Fuenteovejuna.

Galdós, Benito Pérez (1843–1920): Spain's best-known nineteenth-century realist writer, who can be favorably compared to Balzac and Dickens. He painted a wide canvas of Madrid life and cast an ironic eye on the values of Spain's emerging bourgeoisie in major novels such as *Fortunata y Jacinta* (1886–1887; Fortunata and Jacinta 1987) and *Misericordia* (1897; *Compassion* 1966). María Zambrano wrote a number of essays on Galdós in which she analyzes his ability to create individual characters that also are representative of Spanish life; she was especially interested in Galdós's female characters, whom she interprets as representations of the soul of Spain.

Gallo Crisis, El: one of the ephemeral Generation of 1927 journals.

Ganivet, Angel (1865–1898): novelist and essayist frequently cited as a precursor of the Generation of '98. His writings, like those of that group, focus on the problem of Spain.

García Lorca, Federico (1898–1936): the best-known poet and dramatist of the Generation of 1927. Native of Andalusia, he moved to Madrid in 1919, but Andalusian references are central to his work—gypsies, the flamenco song, horses, and orange trees. While in Madrid, he resided for a time in the Residencia de Estudiantes where he associated with such surrealist artists as Salvador Dalí and Luis Buñuel. He achieved international recognition with his *Romancero gitano* (*Gypsy Ballads* 1953), first published in 1928. He spent time in New York in 1929, an experience that provided the material for his *Poeta en Nueva York* (*Poet in New York* 1968), published posthumously in 1940. His lyrical plays, which draw on elements of Greek tragedy, include *Bodas de Sangre* (1933; *Blood Wedding* 1953) and *La casa de Bernarda Alba* 1936; *The House of Bernarda Alba* 1953). In 1936 shortly after the beginning of the Civil War he was arrested and executed by the Nationalist forces.

Generation of '98: designation traditionally given in literary histories to the group of writers who were born in the mid-1860s to mid-1870s and who began to write in the late nineteenth century. These writers, known for their concern with the decline of Spain as a nation and their desire to find the root of the "Spanish problem," formed the dominant group in Spanish literary circles in the first decade of the century. They were greatly influenced by nineteenth-century ideas about national character as well as by positivistic science and theories of the influence of external factors on the development of individuals and nations. Those most often cited as members of this generation are Miguel de Unamuno, Pío Baroja, Azorín (who is credited with naming the generation in 1913), Ramón del Valle-Inclán, and Ramiro de Maeztu.

Guadarrama Mountain Range: mountain range of moderate height a few miles to the west and north of Madrid.

Giner de los Ríos, Francisco (1839–1915): philosopher and educator. He was greatly influenced by Krausism during his studies at the University of Madrid; after winning a chair in philosophy at that university in 1865, he resigned the following year in solidarity with the leading Spanish Krausist, Julián Sanz del Río, who had been removed from his university professorship. From 1875 to 1881 Giner himself was deprived of his university chair. At this point he founded the Institución Libre de Enseñanza, whose purpose was to reform Spanish education by instituting more interactive teaching methods, fomenting education for women, working for greater cultural dissemination and religious freedom.

Gómez de la Serna, Ramón (1888–1974): one of the major promoters of vanguardism in Spain and a prolific writer of essays and novels. In 1908 he founded the journal *Prometeo*, which published a translation of Marinetti's "Futurist Manifesto" that same year; his *tertulia* at the café Pombo was also important to disseminating new European artistic currents in Spain. He is best known as a writer for his invention of the *greguería*, a humorous saying that is a cross between a metaphor, a visual image, and a joke.

Guardia Civil: national police corps founded in the eighteenth century to keep country roads safe from bandits. It became more paramilitary before and during the Spanish Civil War and was an important means of repression during the Franco regime (1939–1975).

Guillén, Jorge (1893–1986): senior poet of the Generation of 1927. He strove for a "pure poetry" in which expression is tightly condensed. His most important collections of poetry are *Cántico* (Canticle 1936, 1945, 1950), *Clamor: Tiempo de historia* (Clamor: Time of History 1957, 1960, 1963). He taught Spanish literature in a number of foreign universities, including Oxford University and Wellesley College in the United States, and published works of literary theory and criticism such as *Language and Poetry: Some Poets of Spain* (Harvard University Press, 1961).

Historical Reason: José Ortega y Gasset's concept, which takes his notion of vital reason to the socio-historical realm; he postulated that man has no nature, only history, and that true history is the incorporation of the past into the lives of people living in the present. His theory of a social history organized by generations was his means of bridging the gap between the individual and the social. To arrive at this mature philosophical position he drew on Husserl's phenomenological reduction and Dilthey's notion of the shifting structure of human beliefs. See especially *Historia como sistema* (1935; *Toward a Philosophy of History* 1961) and *El hombre y la gente* (1949–50; *Man and People* 1957), and *Sobre la razón histórica* (1979; *Historical Reason* 1984).

horchata: drink made of almonds or *chufas* (groundnuts).

House of Austria: dynasty of the Hapsburgs that included Charles I (V of the Holy Roman Empire) (1517–1556), Philip II (1556–1598), Philip III (1598–1621), Philip IV (1621–1665), and Charles II (1665–1700). Charles I was the son of Isabel and Ferdinand's daughter Juana la loca (Jane the Mad) and her German husband Felipe el hermoso (Philip the Handsome). Through both his parents he inherited the largest kingdom in the sixteenth-century world, with possessions in America, Flanders, France, and Italy. Charles initiated the policy continued by later Hapsburgs of attempting to keep the empire intact through a series of economically disastrous wars. Philip II gave the imperial campaign a religious tone, making it an attack on Islam and Protestantism. The last three kings of the dynasty were rather weak, and they delegated their duties to subordinates. Pieces of the empire slipped away, and the decline of the House of Austria was complete when Charles II, who was probably mentally deficient, failed to produce an heir.

Idearium español (1896; *Spain, an Interpretation* 1946): essay by Angel Ganivet in which this precursor to the Generation of '98 pondered the decline of Spain. He believed Spain's principal problem was a lack of guiding ideas, which produced abulia in its citizens.

Iglesias, Pablo (1850–1950): founder of Spanish Socialist Worker's Party (PSOE) in 1879. In 1910 he was the first socialist to be elected to the Spanish Parliament.

Institución Libre de Enseñanza: see Francisco Giner de los Ríos.

Instituto Escuela: educational institution that, along with the Centro de Estudios Históricos (Center for Historical Studies) and the Instituto Nacional de Ciencias Físico-Naturales (National Institute for Natural Physical Sciences), was an arm of the Junta de Ampliación de Estudios (Committee for the Enhancement of Study). The people who carried out its labors were pedagogical specialists who had been trained at the Institución Libre de Enseñanza.

Irún Highway: one of the principal roads that lead radially out of Madrid and connect the capital to other major Spanish cities. The Irún Highway runs northward to San Sebastián on the northern coast and thence to Irún on the French border. It is now a major freeway.

Isabel I, the Catholic (1451–1504): queen of Castile and Aragon (1474–1504). She and her husband Ferdinand, who brought Aragon to the joint throne, completed the unification of Spain by expelling the Jews from Spain and conquering Granada, the last Arab stronghold in the peninsula, both in 1492. Reference is made in the "Delirium" entitled "The Queen" to the fact that her male heir Juan died young.

Isabel II (1830–1904): queen of Spain from 1833 to 1868, when she was dethroned. She was a controversial monarch on several counts. Her reign got off to a difficult start because conservatives did not want a woman on the throne, and they began a movement known as *carlismo* to place her uncle on the throne instead. Throughout her reign, there was a series of wars over the succession. Isabel II was also noted for having numerous affairs (in a climate in which bourgeois values of female virtue were gaining hegemony); her morality and some disastrous economic policies led to her being deposed in 1868.

Jiménez, Juan Ramón (1881–1958): Spain's first modernist poet, awarded the Nobel Prize for Literature in 1956. He began his career with poetry that showed the influence of Latin American *modernismo* (in its turn influenced by French Symbolism and Parnassianism), but he soon began to pare down his poetic expression to its bare essentials, paving the way for the poetics of the Generation of 1927. He lived for a time at the Residencia de Estudiantes early in its existence and thus helped to set the intellectual tenor of that important cultural institution. Juan Ramón (as he is generally known) was a prolific poet, and the list of titles of his poetry collections is very long. Some of the most representative are *La soledad sonora* (1908 The Sonorous Silence), *Laberinto* (1913 Labyrinth), *Diario de un poeta recién casado* (1917 Diary of a Newly-Married Poet), and *Animal de fondo* (1949 Animal of Depth). He is perhaps best known outside the Hispanic world for his lyrical prose narrative *Platero y yo* (1916; *Platero and I* 1967). During the Spanish Civil War Juan Ramón was a cultural attaché for the Republic in Washington, D.C., and after the war he lived in Cuba, the East Coast of the United States, and finally Puerto Rico.

Krausism: a neo-Kantian philosophy introduced in Spain by Julián Sanz del Río in the 1850s and 1860s and the first major secular philosophy to take root in Spain. Karl Christian Friedreich Krause was a minor German philosopher who appealed to Sanz del Río and to Spaniards in general because he did not eliminate the concept of God from his explanation of man's position in the world. Krause viewed all things human as moving towards a perfect (or divine) harmony. Krausism as a philosophy was rather short-lived, but it had a practical side that emphasized the importance of education and profoundly influenced Spanish social institutions. Krausism was the motivating force behind the founding of the Institución Libre de Enseñanza and education for women. María Zambrano's father, an educator, had extensive contact with Krausist thinkers.

La Ciudad Lineal: a town that occupies a narrow strip of land several kilometers long. It typically has a single long street with lateral streets that lead out into the countryside.

La Guayra (also spelled La Guaira): important Venezuelan port city.

Largo Caballero, Francisco (1869–1946): important socialist politician after 1912, when he joined the Socialist Party. As the head of the UGT (General Workers' Union) he sometimes caused dissensions within the party. He and the UGT, for example, adhered to the Second International, which the Socialist Party did not. His wing of the Socialist Party was sympathetic to the revolutionary goals and strategies of the CNT (Anarchist syndicate) that gained momentum at the outbreak of the Civil War in 1936, and he became the president of the government in that year. He was incapable of juggling the various factions that supported the Republic and finally resigned the presidency in 1937. After the War he died in exile in Paris.

Larra, Mariano José de (1809–1837): essayist, dramatist and novelist of the Spanish Romantic period. Larra is best-known for his acerbic and highly literary articles on Spanish life and letters in which the tone hovers between irony and satire. He was greatly admired by the writers of the Generation of '98 for his unflinching criticism of Spanish customs and institutions. Larra's personal life had a Romantic cast as well; he committed suicide at age 28 when his married mistress left him.

La Mancha: large area in the province of New Castile, which extends from around Albacete to Ciudad Real. For climatic and historical reasons (such as royal donations to religious orders and noble families) its towns are situated fairly far apart, often by some 20 to 30 kilometers. La Mancha is perhaps best known as the home and site of many of the adventures of the fictitious Don Quijote.

Life of Don Quijote and Sancho, The (1905): work by Miguel de Unamuno to commemorate the quincentenary of Cervantes's famous novel. Unamuno's reworking of the seventeenth-century novel emphasizes Unamuno's concern with uniting life and the mind. He understands that the two central characters in Cervantes's novel achieve this symbiosis.

Litoral: one of the most important of the Generation of 1927's literary journals. It was founded by Manuel Altolaguirre and Emilio Prados in 1926 in Málaga, and issues appeared sporadically until 1929.

Machado, Antonio (1875–1939): poet often associated with the Generation of '98 because, even though he was Andalusian by birth, he adopted Castile as the subject of many of his best-known poems, such as those of *Campos de Castilla* (1912 Castilian Countrysides). He was a close friend of María Zambrano's father, Blas Zambrano, when they both taught in secondary school in Segovia in the second decade of the century. María Zambrano left the car in which she was being driven across the border into France when Barcelona fell to Franco in March of 1939 in order to walk at Machado's side. He perished in a concentration camp in France shortly after his exile.

Madariaga, Salvador de (1886–1978): historian, essayist, literary critic, and novelist. When World War I broke out, he began to work for *The Times* in London and from 1921 was the secretariat of the League of Nations. Madariaga returned to Geneva in 1935–36 as the Spanish delegate under the Second Republic. He taught Spanish literature at Oxford University (1928–1931) and was Spanish ambassador to Washington in 1931 and to Paris from 1932–1934. His published works include *Guía del lector del Quijote* (1926 Reader's Guide to the *Quijote*) and *Englishmen, Frenchmen, Spaniards* (1928; Spanish version 1929).

Maeztu, Ramiro de (1874–1936): essayist associated with the Generation of '98. He traveled widely and wrote extensively on the need for Spain to reform and Europeanize in such books as *Hacia otra España* (1899 Toward another Spain). He supported Primo de Rivera's dictatorship and was awarded an ambassadorship to Argentina in 1927. Maeztu was a member of Parliament in 1934 under the Republic and was executed by Republican militia during the Civil War.

Maimonides, Moses (1135–1204): Spanish-Hebrew writer born in Cordoba. His father was a scholar who taught him mathematics and astronomy. Maimonides wrote on philosophy and law. (*The Mishnah Torah* [1168] is an exposition of Jewish law.) His family left Spain in 1160 because of the religious persecutions under a fanatical Arab regime. Zambrano would have been particularly interested in the medieval Jewish and Arab philosophers who had ties to her native Andalusia.

manolas: a term that arose in the late eighteenth and early nineteenth centuries to designate young women of the working-class districts of Madrid who wore distinctive dress and had a free manner.

Manzanares: river that runs through Madrid. Its headwaters are in Navacerrada, and it runs into the Jarama. The Manzanares is often referred to as the most joked about river in the world (it frequently has very little water).

marca hispánica: the name Charlemagne gave to the territories he conquered south of the Pyrenees.

Marcel, Gabriel (1889–1964): philosopher, dramatist, and critic. He is considered a Christian Existentialist thinker, whose thought has been characterized as an "itinerant philosophy" because it eschews traditional philosophical abstract systemization in favor of a permanent contact with the concrete world. One of his best-known works is *Être et avoir* (1934; *Being and Having* 1949).

Master: name frequently given to José Ortega y Gasset by his disciples; it bespeaks the great influence he had over the intellectual life of his generation.

Mediodía: literary magazine following in the tradition of *Alfar* and *Litoral;* it was founded in the 1930s in Seville.

Meditations on the Quijote: see José Ortega y Gasset.

Menéndez y Pelayo, Marcelino (1861–1921): prolific scholar and writer of a conservative orientation. It was his mission to prove that Spanish culture has a "pure" strain uncontaminated by the many races and peoples (especially of Jewish and Arab heritage) that had lived within Spain's borders over the centuries.

Meseta: minor literary magazine published in Valladolid in 1928–1929.

Monarchs, The: King Alfonso XIII and his wife who succeeded Alfonso XII to the throne in 1902 (see Restoration).

"Moncloa Executions" (*Tres de mayo*): painting by Francisco Goya, possibly done in 1814. It measures 2.66 meters by 3.45 meters and is currently exhibited in the Prado Museum. The title of the picture "May Third Executions" recalls the night of May 2, 1808, when French soldiers who were occupying Madrid under Napoleonic edict shot Spanish patriots after an uprising.

Ominous Decade: Fernando VII's reign (1814–1823). Fernando was the son of Carlos IV, who was deposed by Napoleon in 1808. The Spanish people looked to Fernando when they won their independence from the French in 1814, but rather than uphold the liberal constitution drafted by the patriots, Fernando dissolved parliament and reverted to an absolute monarchy. Many reprisals ensued against liberal Spaniards, a number of whom fled the country.

Ortega y Gasset, José (1883–1955): philosopher, educator, and statesman. Ortega undertook post-doctoral studies in Germany under Georg Simmel and neo-Kantians such as Hermann Cohen and Paul Natorp. Later he fell under the influence of German phenomenology which underpins his first book *Meditaciones del Quijote* (1914; *Meditations on Quijote* 1984). He was the leading intellectual in Spain in the second and third decades of this century, and his philosophy continues to echo in current Spanish and Latin

American philosophical production. Like Heidegger and other twentieth-century philosophers he sought ways to overcome the dichotomy between reason and life (the mind and the body) initiated by Descartes and continued by nineteenth-century idealism.The philosophical concepts that underpin most of his work are "vital reason" and "historical reason" (see separate entries) that emphasize humanity's situatedness within specific circumstances and a historical continuity.These ideas are developed in his major books: *El tema de nuestro tiempo* (1923; *The Modern Theme* 1961), *La rebelión de las masas* (1925; *The Revolt of the Masses* 1932), *El hombre y la gente* (1957; *Man and People* 1963), and *Historia como sistema* (1935; *Toward a Philosophy of History* 1961). Ortega was also very involved in Spanish political life from at least 1914, when he gave a landmark public lecture entitled "Vieja y nueva política" (Old and new politics). In the same year he initiated a short-lived group—La Liga de Educación Política (The League for Political Education)—in order to prepare the masses for a more democratic form of government. He was also one of a group of intellectuals that founded the Agrupación a Servicio de la República (Group at the service of the Republic) in 1931. From his earliest writings he argued for Europeanizing Spain, and his prestigious journal *Revista de Occidente* (Occidental Review, founded in 1923) had the express purpose of introducing the main currents of European thought into Spain. Zambrano took courses from Ortega during her years at the University of Madrid, and Ortega directed her doctoral thesis on Spinoza. Ortega, as a Republican sympathizer, was exiled for a few years after the Civil War, but he returned to Spain in 1945, where he supported himself by writing, lecturing, and teaching private courses.

"Our time": José Ortega y Gasset's principal concern. Ortega's philosophy is rooted in a sense that we are our circumstances. He wrote that his own circumstance was Spain and that he had to save the country if he was to save himself. In *El tema de nuestro tiempo* (1923; *The Theme of Our Time* 1961) he identified the major problem of his age to be that of overcoming the split between reason and life that had dominated Western thinking since the seventeenth century.

Parábola: minor literary magazine published in Burgos in 1927 and 1928.

Plaza de Oriente: large and historically important plaza in Madrid across from the Royal Palace. Isabel II's tutor, Augstín de Argüelles, planned the arrangement of the gardens, balustrades, and statues in the early nineteenth century.

Plus ultra: from the phrase *Non plus ultra,* which in ancient times referred to the columns of Hercules flanking the Straight of Gibraltar, the limit of the known world. *Plus ultra* refers to the "beyond" and thus the columns are incorporated into the heraldic symbolism of the Catholic Kings and Charles V. The Spanish Falange and the dictator Francisco Franco adopted this and other symbols of empire into their ichnography.

Prados, Emilio (1899–1962): poet from Andalusia who was associated with the Generation of '27. He collaborated with María Zambrano in the founding of the journal *Hora de*

España, the organ through which a number of Spanish writers attempted to aid the failing Spanish Republic during the Civil War.

Prieto, Indalecio (1883–1962): socialist politician who actively conspired against Alfonso XIII's monarchy; he served as a government minister under the Republic.

Primo de Rivera, Miguel (1870–1930): see Dictatorship.

PSOE: Spanish Socialist Workers' Party founded by Pablo Iglesias in 1879. Its numbers increased significantly after 1917 when it was joined by a number of intellectuals.

pueblo: term that has no exact equivalent in English, especially as Zambrano employs it. She takes the word, which often means the common people or the masses (not in a pejorative sense), and adds echoes of the notion of *volksgeist* (spirit of the people or a collective unconscious) that was important to the Generation of '98. Her use of the term also takes on shades of the socialists' positive view the working classes.

Puerta del Sol: the official geographical center of Spain and the heart of the older part of Madrid. It is lined with typical shops and is the site of much street vending. Many Spanish patriots were shot here during the War of Independence on May 2, 1808.

Quevedo, Francisco (1580–1645): major satirical writer of the Spanish Golden Age. Quevedo's razor-sharp wit found outlets in poetry, the picaresque novel, and other prose vehicles like his *Sueños* (Dreams). He used complex wordplay to criticize myriad aspects of the Spain of his day (an imperial power whose local infrastructure was in full decline).

Restoration: reinstatement of the Bourbon monarchy after the revolutionary period (1868–1874) following the dethroning of Isabel II. Isabel's son, Alfonso XII, was recalled to the throne in 1874 and reigned until his death in 1885. The architect of the Restoration was the politician Cánovas de Castillo, who installed a political system known as "peaceful alternation." It was a corrupt system in which the liberals and conservatives ruled by turns; the elections were insured by local political bosses known as *caciques.*

Residencia de Estudiantes: residence for outstanding students founded in 1910 to provide a place where cultural events and dialogue could take place. In some ways a continuation of the Institución Libre de Enseñanza, it became the seat of Spanish vanguardism when authors such as Juan Ramón Jiménez and Federico García Lorca lived there and other artists such as Salvador Dalí and Luis Buñuel frequented it. Today it continues this tradition by serving as a residence for scholars who are in Madrid for limited periods of time.

Revista de Occidente: journal founded by José Ortega y Gasset in 1923 to disseminate European intellectual currents in Spain. It published translations of essays by writers such as Georg Simmel and essays by all the major Spanish writers. María Zambrano published her first philosophical essay "Hacia un saber sobre el alma" ("Toward a knowledge of the soul") in the journal in 1934, as well as other essays and book reviews in later issues. The journal had a very important impact on Spanish intellectual life in the 1920s and 1930s; it has continued publication until the present day (with a brief interruption during the Spanish Civil War).

Romanones, Count of: Álvaro de Figueroa y Torres, twice mayor of Madrid, who in 1901 became Minister of Public Instruction, a post he occupied for a number of years. He also held other ministerial posts in the second decade of the century, but he fell out of favor under Primo de Rivera's military dictatorship in 1923. As a friend and counselor to King Alfonso XIII, Romanones advised the king to recognize that Republican sympathies had made a strong showing in the elections of April 12, 1931. The count, along with Gregorio Marañón, the king's personal physician, negotiated a transfer of power with Niceto Alcalá Zamora, the prime minister of the new provisional government. Romanones authored a book about these events titled *Las últimas horas de una monarquía* (1931 The Last Hours of a Monarchy).

Saint John of the Cross (1542–1591): Carmelite monk, mystic poet, and reformer. He is best known for his extraordinary poetry, which employs images of secular love to convey intense religious experience. Among his best-known poems are "La subida del monte Carmelo" (1578–85; "Ascent of Mt. Carmel" 1979), "Noche oscura del alma" (1582–85; "Dark Night of the Soul" 1979), and "Llama de amor viva" (1585–87; "The Living Flame of Love" 1979). He was canonized in 1726.

Saint Teresa of Ávila (or Jesús) (1515–1582): nun, founder of the reformed Carmelite order, writer who interpreted mystic experience. Santa Teresa was born in Ávila to a noble family. Inspired by reading the lives of the saints, she ran away from home at seven years of age. After spending some time in the Augustinian convent at Ávila, at age 19 she became a Carmelite. With the help of Saint John of the Cross, she set out to reform the Carmelite order; she founded the Carmelitas Descalzas (Barefoot Carmelites). She was denounced to the Spanish Inquisition by conservative Carmelites for her autobiography *Libro de la vida* (1562; *The Life of Santa Teresa* 1960), which describes her mystical experiences. She traveled and wrote tirelessly; her books include *Las moradas* (1577; *Interior Castle* 1961), and *Camino de perfección* (1562; *Way of Perfection* 1964). She was canonized in 1622.

Salinas, Pedro (1891–1951): eldest of the Generation of 1927 poets, also a scholar, playwright, and fiction writer. He held teaching posts at several Spanish universities as well as at the Sorbonne, Cambridge University, Wellesley College, and Johns Hopkins. His poetry explores the relation between inner and outer reality and the problem of human time. His best-known poetry collections include *Presagios* (1923 Presages); *Seguro azar* (1929 Steadfast Chance), *La voz a ti debida* (1933; *My Voice Because of You* 1976), and *Todo más claro* (1949 All Things Made Clearer). One of his few forays into fiction—*Víspera del gozo* (1926; *Prelude to Pleasure* 1993)—is a classic of vanguard prose.

Sbert, Antonio María (1901–1980): politician and founder of student movements during the Primo de Rivera dictatorship. He was expelled from the School of Agronomy at the University of Madrid. Along with other intellectuals he founded the Asociación Universitaria Escolar (University School Association) in 1927. In 1931 he founded the Esquerra Republicana de Cataluña (Catalan Republican Left), and in 1936 he signed a manifesto in favor of the Republic and served in several Catalan government posts. At the end of the war he was exiled in France, where he founded the Fundación Llull to help exiled Catalan writers. When the Nazis invaded France, he relocated to Mexico, where he published the *Revista de Cataluña* (Catalonian Review).

Sanz del Río, Julián (1814–1869): Spanish philosopher who introduced Krausism into Spain. His books include *Ideal de la humanidad para la vida* (Ideal of Humanity for Life), *Sistema de la filosofía* (System of Philosophy), and *Filosofía de la muerte* (Philosophy of Death). See Krausism.

Second Republic: name given to the Spanish government from 1931–1936. Spain has adopted republican forms of government twice in its history. The First Republic, installed in 1873 several years after Isabel II was dethroned and Spain could not find a dynastic successor who could rule, lasted only a year. The Second Republic was declared in 1931. It went through an initial liberal phase with the promise of many social and economic reforms, which occasioned a two-year period of conservative backlash. The conservative period further polarized the radical left, which gained power in 1936 under the Popular Front. This political polarization led to the Civil War, which erupted in that year.

señorito: somewhat scornful term for the son of wealthy parents; generally indicates a dandy who does little of a productive nature.

Three Civil Wars: the Carlist Wars of the nineteenth century that had their origins in resistance to the accession of Isabel II to the throne in 1833. Arch-conservatives who preferred a male heir (Carlos, brother to the dead king) initiated the first war. Later wars, while continuing to support the Carlist line, were defined by a polarization of conservative and liberal ideology (the latter associated with Isabel's long reign). The last Carlist War ended in 1874 with the Restoration.

UGT: Initials of the Unión General de Trabajadores (General Worker's Union) founded in 1882 under the guidance of the socialist, Pablo Iglesias. It staged the first successful strike that same year. It was primarily the union of industrialized and mining areas; the CNT of anarchist persuasion had more power in rural, agricultural areas. These two powerful unions often clashed (especially over the importance of hierarchy and the nature of revolution) during the political turmoil that led up to the formation of the Republic, and during the Republic and the Civil War these tensions continued to frustrate the leftist cause.

Unamuno, Miguel de (1864–1936): philologist, university professor, chancellor of the University of Salamanca, existential philosopher, essayist, novelist, poet, and playwright. Arguably the most versatile Spanish intellectual of the twentieth century. Educated in Catholicism and Positivism, he suffered a religious crisis in 1897 and began to militate for a "turn inward" in essays such as "¡Adentro!" (Get inside things!) early in the century. Kierkegaard, whose work he read in the original Danish, further strengthened his resolve to extol an irrational or emotional approach to life. He struggled to recover the innocent religious faith of his childhood but finally settled on the idea that it was enough to wish to believe. The major themes of his essays, novels, and plays center on the need to forge a personal identity and to assure its continuity after death. His first major essay *En torno al casticismo* (1895 Concerning Purism) explores the nature of the Spanish soul and earned him a place in the Generation of '98. *Del sentimiento trágico de la vida* (1913; *The Tragic Sense of Life* 1954), perhaps his best-known essay, is his most complete philosophical discussion of the problem of reason and faith. He dubbed his highly original novels *nivolas* because they shun nineteenth-century realist descriptions of exterior detail in favor of dialogue and interior monologue. Representative of his novelistic art are *Niebla* (1914; *Mist* 1928), *Abel Sánchez* (1917), and *San Manuel Bueno, mártir* (1933; *St. Manuel Bueno, Martyr* 1979). Unamuno was exiled during the Primo de Rivera dictatorship and was placed under house arrest during the Civil War, in both instances for his open criticism of the government's policies. He died while sequestered in his house in 1936 and became an almost mythological figure for Spanish Civil War refugees.

Uncle Fernando: Fernando de los Ríos (1879–1949), a Socialist thinker, essayist, professor, and minister of education for the Second Republic. He was a mentor of Federico García Lorca and sponsored the poet-dramatist's traveling theater, La Barraca. He wrote *Mi viaje a la Rusia soviética* (1922 My Trip to Soviet Russia), and *Estado e Iglesia en la España del siglo XVI* (1928 Church and State in Sixteenth-Century Spain), republished in 1957 under the title *Religión y estado* (Religion and State). Fernando de los Ríos was Republican ambassador to Washington during the Spanish Civil War.

Valle-Inclán, Ramón del (1863–1936): one of the foremost dramatists, novelists, and essayists of the early twentieth century in Spain. He is often associated with various turn-of-the-century movements, such as decadentism and Latin American *modernismo*, but his work goes beyond any movement, as he masterfully combined elements from his predecessors in a highly original style that in his mature work he called *esperpento* (a stylized parody of society's ills). Valle-Inclán was a kind of guru to the younger generation of writers who flourished in the 20s and 30s; one of the writers influenced by him was María Zambrano's contemporary Rosa Chacel, who studied with Valle in Madrid's Escuela de Bellas Artes.

"Velázquez's Christ": Miguel de Unamuno's best-known poem in which he extols Velázquez's very human portrayal of Christ on the Cross.

Villa: name given to Madrid when it was pronounced a township probably during the late Middle Ages. The title Villa de Madrid continued to be a popular way of referring to Madrid even after it became the capital, when Philip II moved his court there in 1561.

"Virgen de la Paloma, La": very popular *zarzuela* (comic light opera) that is considered representative of typical life in Madrid in the nineteenth century.

Vital Reason: José Ortega y Gasset's solution to the long-standing dichotomy in philosophical thinking between a rational approach to life and a more positivistic approach, often summarized in the phrase "I am I and my circumstance." Ortega's first formulation of this central notion occurs in *Meditaciones del Quijote* (1914; *Meditations on Quijote* 1984), and he later merged it with his concept of Historical Reason.

Zubiri, Xavier (1898–1983): Spanish philosopher and professor of philosophy at the University of Madrid. In some ways he was a disciple of José Ortega y Gasset but, like Zambrano, moved beyond Ortega's vital reason to forge what he called *razón sentiente* (feeling reason). Zambrano studied with Zubiri at the University of Madrid and substituted for him during a year while he was in Germany.

www.ingramcontent.com/pod-product-compliance
Ingram Content Group UK Ltd.
Pitfield, Milton Keynes, MK11 3LW, UK
UKHW011401080625
2138IPUK00008B/24